Bryce Pierponte had ~~been left~~ left alone for the summer to mind the farm, or at least the mission-style ranch house. He had enough money to live on, but entertainment pretty much consisted of TV, internet and the odd garage sale.

And odd definitely applied to this one.

The contents of the old Seidel place were displayed on the driveway: dingy portraits, jewelry, crystal jars, piles of books, and a taxidermy project that looked like someone had crossed a kitten with a spider monkey then added spare parts from a bat and a scorpion. "What's that?" Bryce asked.

The young woman tending to the sale smiled and pointed to the brass tag on the base. *Manticore Cub.*

"How much you want for it?"

"Oh, the usual: your soul, your shadow, the light in your eyes, the voice in your throat, or the answer to a great mystery."

The woman was telling him that everything here was out of his price range.

"I thought Mr. Seidel died years ago."

"Master Seidel did. We're simply executing the last of his will. How did you know of the sale?"

"I saw the gate open and I'd always been curious." He looked up. "Would that be the answer to a mystery?"

Still the smile. "I said 'great mystery.'"

"Okay," said Bryce, "it wasn't a ghost, it was a big dog painted with phosphorous."

"What?"

"The answer to a great mystery, the end of *The Hound of the Baskervilles.*" Bryce grinned.

The woman's smile became pained. "Well and fairly bargained, young master."

—from "Tacos for Tezcatlipoca"
by Kevin Andrew Murphy

Witch Way to the Mall

Edited by
Esther M. Friesner

BAEN

A Baen Books Original

Baen Publishing Enterprises
P.O. Box 1403
Riverdale, NY 10471
www.baen.com

ISBN: 978-1-4391-3274-6

Cover art by Tom Kidd

First paperback printing, June 2009

Distributed by Simon & Schuster
1230 Avenue of the Americas
New York, NY 10020

Pages by Joy Freeman (www.pagesbyjoy.com)
Printed in the United States of America

Contents

Introduction

Esther M. Friesner

Ah, Suburbia! Proof positive that people aren't the only entities out there subject to prejudice and profiling. In a world full of knee-jerk reactions from some of the biggest jerks in the business, if you mention Suburbia you're fairly well guaranteed to get a condescending chuckle or a haughty sneer out of your audience as visions of Levittown dance through their heads.

Or perhaps Levittown's a bit dated (and is still the undisputed turf of ever-so-hipper-than-thou-so-don't-even-*try*-outhipping-me folksingers, as well as Bill Griffith, the gent who continues to entertain me and other *cognoscenti* with his comic strip, *Zippy*). Suburbia with or without Levittown is still something to mock, though now more for being the realm of the McMansions instead of the tacky tract houses. The white picket fences are an anachronism, along with the DonnaReedShowLeaveItToBeaverFatherKnowsBest housewife, wearing pearls, a crinolined dress, a lace-trimmed apron and high heels while dealing with

1

domestic crises ("Oh my gosh, Madge, all the fruit in my Jell-O Brand Gelatin salad keeps falling to the bottom and we're out of gin!").

Good thing people are continually inventive about finding new things to patronize about the suburbs. (I mean, weren't the Stepford Wives just *awful*? Well, isn't that Suburbia for you? It's not bad enough that all the houses look alike, the people there think nothing's acceptable unless everyone acts and dresses alike too! I'd complain about the suburbs more, but I've got to go to a gallery opening in ten minutes, all of my black clothes are still in the dryer, I haven't had the chance to read the reviews so I know what to say about the pieces, and we're out of absinthe!)

Though Suburbia is far from perfect, I'd like someone to show me one major category of human habitation that isn't in the same boat, with or without benefit of yacht club membership. Or better yet, don't try. It's easier to fudge over the shortcomings of your own environs and bolster your self-image by scorning the place where someone else lives. Bring on the cheap shots at Soccer Moms for starters. (It's okay, you'll be safe from retaliation. They're usually too tired doing silly things like taking care of their kids to fight back.) Take a potshot at SUVs while you're at it, because now you've got the added Moral High Ground of how much high-priced gas they're guzzling. (What if some families actually *need* all that passenger and cargo space? Tchah! How dare their necessity not bow before the only acceptable automotive choice, namely your own? 53 miles to the gallon of self-righteousness, baby!) And don't forget the mall.

Yes indeed, the mall: What could shriek *"Suburbia!"*

louder than that fine example of commercial kudzu, strangling the life out of all other retail venues? Forget the fact that many of the most innovative, unique, creative small businesses die the death daily in our great metropolitan centers. Ignore the fact that malls exist in urban settings, too. Urban malls are hip, stylish, cutting-edge, so you can browse through their utterly glam stores without losing a pinch of your coolness street cred.

Oops. Wait a minute. I just noticed: Most of those are exactly the *same* stores you find in the suburban malls. Oh dear. How did that happen? *Ciao*, coolness cred. *Ciao*.

Well, at least there's one ultracool and super-chic thing that cities have which Suburbia can never hope to get its *macchiato*-stained paws on: The denizens of our darker fantasies. Just because we call it fantasy doesn't mean we're not keeping it *real*, man. What self-respecting witch, vampire, or werewolf would be caught dead—or undead—anywhere but the Big City? Never mind that these are the same beings whose original stomping grounds were the deep forests, the mountain passes, the blasted heaths, and the rest of the non-urban landscape.

Look, let's give the uncanny crew a little credit for intelligence: If they had the smarts to see the advantage in packing up and moving *into* the cities, why wouldn't they have the smarts to move *out* of said cities if it looked like they could get a better quality-of-life/death elsewhere? (Tough enough going about your otherworldly business and evading the occasional mob wielding halogen torches and designer pitchforks, but have you ever *seen* city real estate prices?)

So join me now in welcoming our first group of supernatural suburbanites, the witches. Their powers are awesome, their methods of coping with the lumps, bumps, and idiosyncrasies of Suburbia are ingenious, and they always bring the loveliest gingerbread to the PTA bake sale.

But whatever you do, don't try telling them that life in a non-city setting is bland, banal and boring, or else . . .

ribbit!

Harry Turtledove writes science fiction and fantasy, much of it alternate history and historical fantasy. Recent books include *The Man with the Iron Heart*, *The Valley-Weside War*, and *The United States of Atlantis*. While he is not as obsessive a birder as the characters in "Birdwitching," he has taken birding trips to Nome, Alaska and Quoddy Head, Maine. He spends time combing the wilds of Chatsworth, California, tracking down reports of vagrant Siberian Dreeble-Finches, but with little success.

Birdwitching

Harry Turtledove

Lucy Parker was a birder. So was her son, Jesse. Lucy was a witch. It wasn't obvious whether Jesse had the Talent; he was only nineteen, and it didn't manifest itself till people got into their mid-twenties. John Parker, Lucy's husband and Jesse's father, was terminally mundane and had no interest in birds except dark meat. These character flaws notwithstanding, he did have other talents, and the three of them lived happily enough in Sunset Grove.

Fred O'Neill was also a birder. So was his daughter, Kathleen. Fred was also a witch, as well. Kathleen was only eighteen, so nobody knew whether she had the Talent, either. Her mother—Fred's wife—Samantha was every bit as mundane and at least as uninterested in birds as John Parker (though she liked white meat). So you can pretty much forget about her and John.

You do need to remember that the O'Neills lived in Fernwood, just over the barony line from Sunset Grove. You also need to remember that Lucy Parker couldn't stand Fred O'Neill, and that it was mutual. Who done what to whom? It all started a long time ago, and they tell different stories. They both sound sincere when they do, too. By now, that hardly matters. They ain't friends, and they ain't ever gonna be.

Jesse Parker, on the other hand, thought Kathleen O'Neill was pretty cute. She had red hair and freckles and everything else an eighteen-year-old girl ought to have—and Svarovski binoculars besides. She didn't think Jesse was half bad, either. This horrified and amazed his mother and her father. Not Montague-Capulet country, maybe, but you could see it from there. Also not your basic California Dreamin'.

And you need to remember that the annual Yule Bird Count was coming up. Sunset Grove and Fernwood birders would have been rivals even if Lucy Parker and Fred O'Neill were thick as thieves (which each thought the other was). They lived next door to one another, for cryin' out loud. If you can't brag on yourselves and woof on your neighbors, well, what's a heaven for?

So every year there was a mad scramble to spot as many different sparrows and raptors and waterfowl and other feathered critters that happened to lurk anywhere close by, and to publish same, and to laugh at the neighboring birders whose count happened to come up short. About every other year, there were charges that Sunset Grove's birders—or Fernwood's, depending—counted birds they didn't really see, just to make their numbers bigger.

Everybody denied everything, of course. Of course. Nobody would stoop to such evil, underhanded tactics, of course. Of course.

"We'll get 'em this year," Jesse told Lucy as the

big day approached. Fernwood had outcounted Sunset Grove the year before. Suspicions of cheating were more than usually rampant—among Sunset Grove's birders, anyhow. Jesse was a competitive kid. It all added up.

"You'd best believe we will, kiddo," Lucy answered. She was even more competitive than her son. It wasn't easy, but she managed. "We'll whip 'em good. You can count on it."

"Cool." Jesse grinned. Then, perhaps incautiously, he added, "Kathleen says—"

"What does Kathleen say?" Was that frost in Lucy's voice? As a matter of fact, it was ice. A competition with Kathleen was a competition she'd lose. Come to that, a competition with Kathleen was a competition where she couldn't even compete. She knew it, too. She hated it, but she knew it.

For his part, Jesse knew something wasn't quite right there, but his hormones made sure he didn't know what. "She says some of Mr. O'Neill's birding buddies were talking with him the other day. They were asking him what he could do about, like, finding some extra birds for the Yule Count."

"Oh, they were, were they?" Lucy's ice turned into a glacier and started overrunning a continent. "Magicking birds into place for the count is immoral and unethical." She paused. If you listened near the edge of the glacier, you could hear woolly mammoths trumpeting. "And I wouldn't put it past Fred O'Neill for a minute."

"Kathleen says that they said that some of them thought that maybe you'd done some birdwitching before," Jesse said.

It was a good thing he needed three dependent clauses to get where he was going with that, or the whole glacier—and probably the poor woolly mammoths, too—would have flashed to superheated steam. As things were, what Lucy said made Jesse's jaw drop. Moms weren't supposed to talk like that.

"I haven't," Lucy continued, biting syllables off between her teeth. "I didn't. But if Fred O'Neill is crooked enough to think he can get away with pulling that kind of stunt, he'd better think twice. Those nearsighted yahoos in Fernwood won't cheat their way past us again. Not a chance."

"Cool," Jesse said again. Then, even more incautiously than before, he started another sentence with, "Kathleen says—"

"What?" Lucy barked.

Her son flinched. When he got his nerve back, he finished, "She says her dad says he won't let us win by cheating, either."

"Oh, he does? Oh, he won't?" Lucy echoed ominously. "Well, we'll just have to see about that, won't we?"

Yule dawned clear and cool. It would get up into the high sixties later on, maybe even to seventy. Winter in Southern California. Lucy, who'd been born in Cleveland, loved it. Jesse, a native, took it for granted, the way he did his upper-middle-class lifestyle. Lucy and John (maybe you can't *quite* forget him) had busted their humps for years so he could do exactly that.

The Parkers had a big back yard, full of trees and flowers. Flowers at Yule? Sure. Why don't *you* pack up and move here? Everybody else has. It was also full of hummingbird feeders full of sugar water, of seed feeders on poles with big iron baffles to keep squirrels away (there were even bigger ones to keep raccoons away, but the coons didn't come around very often), of suet left out for woodpeckers and other birds that found it tasty, and little fountains so the feathered beasties could sing in the shower.

Behind the Parkers' yard were fields and scrubby chaparral. Plenty of birds that wouldn't come into a yard on a bet liked it fine out there. Some of them were even willing to be spotted.

Even though it wasn't *very* cold, John (yeah, there he is again) had set the Yule log burning in the fireplace at midnight. Tradition? Tradition! It was down to coals when Lucy and Jesse got up a little before sunrise. She smiled as she lurched into the kitchen to make coffee. The embers and the smell reminded her this was a holiday.

Holiday or not, it would also be a small war. She needed no witchy Talent to figure that out.

Jesse hated coffee. He bounced around anyhow. Nineteen did that for you, or to you. He peered out the kitchen window. An early-rising Anna's hummingbird that was about to tank up at the feeder hanging outside buzzed away instead.

"One Anna's," he sang out.

"Well, we're started." Lucy poured sugar into her cup. Her mix had less sweetness and more caffeine than hummer water. Hummingbirds were speedy enough—they didn't need caffeine. She darn well did.

"You ought to note it down," Jesse said, reproof in his voice.

"I will—once I get to the bottom of my mug here. I don't think I'll forget till then. If you can't stand to wait that long, do it yourself, Charlie," Lucy said. He sighed. He was no good at waiting. Along with being able to function in the morning without coffee, that went a long way toward tagging him by age.

Something moved in the magnolia not far from the window. Jesse stared intently. "Yellow-rumped warbler," he said after a couple of seconds.

"Okay. An Anna's and a butterbutt," Lucy said. Even half a cup of coffee started to clear the cobwebs.

"Butterbutt," Jesse echoed. "That's a silly name."

"I know. So what?" his mother answered. "Birders have their own secret lingo, same as witches, same as any other bunch of people interested in the same thing." There were differences, of course. Misusing birders' jargon wouldn't get you toasted by a salamander or drowned by an undine. But it would show the people you were trying to impress that you didn't really belong with them. As often as not, that was the main function of jargon.

Lucy thought about a second mug of coffee, at least as much to annoy Jesse as to get herself up to speed. It could wait, she decided, not without regret. She went over to the kitchen crystal and attuned it to the Cosmos-Spanning Consortium. Mystically linking all the crystals in the world was the greatest sorcerous achievement since the megamagics that had swept two Nipponese cities off the map at the end of the Second Great Slaughter. And CSPANC had a lot more peaceful possibilities than sorceries of mass destruction any day.

She quickly steered to the CSPANC scroll that

recorded birds seen in the Sunset Grove Yule Count. Other local birders had already identified house finches, house sparrows, white-crowned sparrows, and a California towhee. All of those, like her Anna's and yellow-rump, were completely unsurprising, which didn't mean they didn't count.

"Oh!" she said, spotting another check on the list.

"What's up?" Jesse came over to see for himself. "A barn owl! That's pretty neat."

"It is," Lucy agreed. Barn owls lived over most of the world—they had one of the widest ranges of any bird—but weren't common anywhere. You sure couldn't rely on conveniently spotting one for Yule. Somebody'd done it, though: somebody who'd crawled out of bed too bloody early, odds were.

"What have they seen in Fernwood?" Jesse asked.

Murmuring a charm, Lucy shifted to the rival town's CSPANC scroll. They must have had somebody out at the lagoon early in the morning, because they were reporting double-crested cormorants and a pied-billed grebe and a northern shoveler, which was a duck with a bill shaped like a serving spoon. And they'd spotted a California scrub jay and some American robins.

"Nothing they shouldn't have," Lucy said grudgingly. "Not yet, anyhow." She trusted Fred O'Neill as far as she could punt him. Since she was no football player, and since *dear* Fred weighed about 250 pounds . . .

A flock of tiny, twittering birds flew into the leafless apricot tree from the yard next door. Then, one by one and two by two and several by several, they fluttered into the magnolia. They hopped around the branches, looking for bugs. A moment later, they were gone, as abruptly as they'd appeared.

"Bush tits," Lucy said.

Her son nodded. "Tree fleas," he said scornfully—the birders' nickname for the bouncy little birds.

"Hey, I like 'em," Lucy said. Jesse looked at her as if she were dribbling marbles out her ears. Most birders thought bush tits were nothing but nuisances that disturbed less common, more interesting birds. They reminded her of a pack of first-graders turned loose on the playground for recess. They were fun. If you couldn't have fun with your birds, why watch them?

To keep track of how many different kinds you've seen. Plenty of birders, Jesse among them, would have given the answer without even pausing to think. He was a good kid, so good she almost forgave him for liking Kathleen O'Neill. No denying he could be too serious for his own good, though.

Another quick spell brought Lucy back to the Sunset Grove Yule list. "How many bush tits would you say there were?" she asked. "Maybe twenty-five?"

After careful consideration—he was Jesse, after all—her son nodded. "Sounds right."

"Okay." The bush tits they counted would get added in with all the others Sunset Grove birders spotted today. Somewhere behind the scenes at CSPANC, a sprite with an abacus would draw overtime.

Lucy did pour herself another cup of coffee then. She split a bagel and put honey on one side and jam on the other. Then she slapped them together and started eating breakfast. Jesse scrambled eggs. He was young enough so he didn't have a healer clucking reproachfully whenever he did something like that.

His pocket crystal made a noise like a rhythmic

kangaroo as he was sitting down at the kitchen table. Till he started using that particular ringspell, Lucy hadn't imagined there was any such thing as a noise like a rhythmic kangaroo. But there was, and Jesse was far from the only kid with that ringspell. Hip-hop music was all the rage these days. You could either put up with it or wear earplugs, one.

"Hello?" Jesse said, and then, on an altogether different note, "Oh. Hi!"

Kathleen, Lucy thought unhappily. She knew that note, all right. *He's talking with fat Fred O'Neill's daughter. Talking with the enemy's daughter. With the enemy.* Was Jesse sleeping with the enemy? Lucy didn't know. She couldn't very well ask. Parents who snooped on their pretty-much-grown children's love lives deserved the trouble they landed in. Lucy did know one thing: if Jesse wasn't sleeping with Kathleen, he sure wanted to. He was male. He was nineteen. He had a pulse. 'Nuff said.

"Nothing real exciting here so far," he was saying. "Tree fleas, a butterbutt, an Anna's . . . Oh, wait. A couple of stoogebirds just landed on the platform feeder."

"A couple of *what*?" Lucy could hear Kathleen's voice coming out of the pocket crystal.

Stoogebirds was family slang, not regular birders' slang. Jesse had to explain it: "You know. Mourning doves, on account of their wings go *woob-woob-woob-woob* whenever they take off. Just like Curly, right?" He paused, listening, then answered with more than a little pride in his voice: "Sure I'm weird. Like you didn't already know." He listened one more time, then said "'Bye" and stuck the crystal back in his pocket.

Lucy checked the Fernwood scroll on CSPANC again. As soon as she did, something way more strident than a hip-hop kangaroo went off inside her head. "They can't get away with that!" she yipped.

"With what?" Jesse ambled over to see what she was talking about.

"With *that*." Quivering with indignation, Lucy pointed out the offending entry. "Yellow-billed magpie? Here? Or in Fernwood, I mean? No way, Jessay." She pronounced his name so the phrase rhymed, which made him wince. She went on, "No way unless Fat Freddy magicked it in, I mean. Well, if he's gonna play that way, we can play that way, too. *Oh*, yeah!" So much for immoral and unethical. What were rules, in war?

"What'll you do, Mom?" Anticipation and alarm jangled in Jesse's voice.

"I'll make sure those no-good, lousy cheaters in Fernwood don't steal this year's count, that's what." Lucy stormed out of the kitchen and into her study. She came back with several grimoires and an armload of *materia magica*—oh, and a few birders' guides, too. She paged through one of them, then smiled carnivorously and nodded. "We'll have people down by the old slough, right?"

"We always do," Jesse answered.

"Right," Lucy said again. "Now we find out whether they're awake." You could conjure in a bird—sure. But if you did and nobody spotted it, you might as well not have bothered.

Lucy's *materia magica*, unlike those of a lot of witches, included feathers of all different colors . . . just in case. She pulled out a dark green one, and a little bronze crown that might have graced a doll's head once upon a time. She knew where her target birds lived. She knew where she wanted to put one. The charm and the passes that got the bird from A to B were second nature to her. After umpty-ump years of training and practice they were, anyhow.

"What exactly did you do?" Jesse asked. "I mean, I can guess, but—"

"Go ahead and guess," Lucy said. "We'll find out if it worked pretty soon." If it didn't, if the loafers at the slough were standing around yawning or just not paying attention . . . Well, she'd find some other way to make sure they weren't asleep over there next year, by God!

She made herself sit there for fifteen minutes before she checked the Sunset Grove scroll on CSPANC again. That was at least fourteen minutes longer than Jesse wanted to wait. By the time they finally looked, he had a bad case of the wiggles.

His grin almost made the top of his head fall off. "Green kingfisher!" he whooped. "I thought that's what you were up to!" Belted kingfishers, larger and blue-gray, were common over water. Green kingfishers barely came north of the Rio Grande, and never visited California—not unless a friendly witch lent a hand.

Not two minutes later, his pocket crystal made hip-hop noises again. "If that's Kathleen bitching—" Lucy began.

Her son waved her to silence. A call on the pocket crystal was *important*. A parent standing right there? Fuhgeddaboutit. "Hello?" he said, and then, "Hi!" His face got all goofy. It was Kathleen, all right. He listened, then looked at Lucy. "She says her dad's not real happy about the kingfisher."

"T.S., Eliot," Lucy answered. "What about the yellow-billed magpie?"

Jesse asked the question. He listened some more, then reported: "She says her dad says it just happened to be there. He didn't have anything to do with it."

"Yeah, right," Lucy sneered. "And the check is in the mail."

"Uh, my mom's not so sure of that." Talking to a girl he was sweet on, Jesse was more polite than Lucy had been. He listened to Kathleen. To Lucy, he said, "She says her dad says the magpie was legit. But if you want to play that way, he can play that way, too."

"Tell Kathleen to tell him to bring it on," Lucy answered. Only later did she realize there were ways to say things like that, and then again there were ways. One particular fellow who'd used almost her exact phrase was still trying to shovel his way out of Mesopotamia.

But the Great Yule Bird Count in Sunset Grove and Fernwood was never the same again.

WATCH THE SKIES! the old posters shouted—as if there could be life on other planets, when magic had proved that planets were nothing but lights attached to moving crystal spheres. But weird-looking invaders from Mars were fun to tell stories about, even if they couldn't be real.

Fernwood and Sunset Grove got invaders, too, but they didn't come from Mars. And if you weren't watching the skies, you'd miss them. Birds that hadn't been seen there in a long time—birds that had *never* been seen there—showed up one after another. It was a life lister's heaven on earth (appropriate enough for Yuletide, after all). And it was one of the worst cases of Anything You Can Do, I Can Do More Of in the history of American witchcraft.

Lucy couldn't watch the skies, or even the back yard, as much as she would've liked. She was too busy checking the Fernwood scroll on CSPANC to find out what Fred O'Neill was up to and the Sunset Grove scroll to make sure the birds she magicked in got properly counted. She could picture Fat Freddy doing the same thing, only back-asswards.

Four black vultures spiraled above Fernwood. They had no business being there, not when the nearest sighting of a black vulture was an accidental bird right by the California-Arizona border. Did Fred O'Neill give a rat's patoot? Not when he had a chance to win the bird count, he didn't.

When Lucy saw the report of the black vultures, she called Fred a son of a witch, or something like that. Then she pulled a big black feather and a little yellow one out of her *materia magica*. She incanted like nobody's business.

Some Sunset Grove birders at a park were surprised and delighted to spot black-backed woodpeckers drilling on pines. Black-backed woodpeckers didn't live within hundreds of miles of Sunset Grove. Well, hey, if you were going to fuss about every little thing . . .

Lucy waited to see what Fred O'Neill would come up with next. It was like a prizefight, with all the punches in extremely slow motion. *Sure*, Lucy thought. *A featherweight prizefight*. She poured herself more coffee. By all the signs, she was pretty punchy herself.

Fernwood birders declared they'd seen a smew at a pond. "What's a smew?" Jesse asked, reading CSPANC over her shoulder.

"I don't know. What's smew with you?" Lucy returned. Yeah, she was punchy. Her son sent her a reproachful look. She tried again: "A kind of merganser—a diving duck. It lives in Europe. Once in a blue moon, one gets over here by itself."

"You don't think this is a blue moon?"

"Now that you mention it, no."

"What'll you do about it?"

Lucy was already thumbing through guides, deciding exactly what she'd do about it. She plucked a black feather, and then a shiny blue one, from her *materia magica*. The charm she chanted had a Latin rhythm.

Something started squawking raucously in the magnolia tree. Crows and ravens and jays aren't very musical, but the noises they make show they all come from the same family. This raucous squawking was corvid racket, too, but it wasn't the kind of corvid racket Lucy'd ever heard before.

Jesse grabbed his binoculars. "Whoa!" he said, nothing but admiration in his voice. "What *is* that thing?"

"Black-throated magpie-jay," Lucy answered, not without pride. It was a jay the size of a crow or bigger, with a fancy crest and a long, droopy tail. It flew away, skrawking as it went.

"Whoa!" Jesse said again. "Where's it from?"

"Middle of Mexico," Lucy answered, recording it on the Sunset Grove SCPANC scroll.

Jesse got another call from Kathleen as soon as her father saw the claim for the new bird. "She says her dad says you aren't gonna beat him," Jesse reported.

"He started it. I'll finish it," Lucy said grimly.

The next exotic bird reported from Fernwood was a condor. That left Lucy unimpressed for a moment.

Thanks to captive-breeding programs, California condors weren't impossible to spot these days, but a lot of birders didn't count them because they weren't truly wild. *Even a lamebrain like Fred ought to do better*, she though.

And Fred had. It was an Andean condor. It was even bigger than a California condor, and even uglier. Lucy showed Jesse a picture in a book about Chilean birds. The head was large and naked and pink, with wattles and a comb. You were in no danger of mistaking it for any other bird ever hatched.

"What are you gonna do now, Mom?" Jesse was caught up in the competition, too.

"You'll see. I'll bring in several of these, 'cause I've always liked them," Lucy answered. "Maybe they'll hang around once the count is over." That intrigued her son, as she'd hoped it would. She got busy spellcasting.

Bringing in a bunch of birds was a lot harder than bringing in just one. She was good, though. One of the birds appeared in the backyard apricot tree. Crest, brown belly and back, black-and-white striped wings. "*Poo! Poo! Poo!*" it called.

"A hoopoe!" Jesse exclaimed in delight. "Awesome!"

Maybe it heard him. It flew off, skipping through the air like a butterfly. "The Bible says it's not kosher," Lucy said. "Twice, in fact. I bet I know why, too."

"Why?" Jesse asked when she didn't come out with it right away.

Lucy wrinkled her nose. "Because it smells like *poo-poo-poo*, that's why."

She didn't post the hoopoe on the Sunset Grove Yuletide scroll. Before long, some other local birder did. The mundanes in the birding crowd had to be talking to themselves about all the weird stuff going on. They wouldn't be complaining, though. Oh, no. She knew birders well enough to be sure of that.

She didn't know Fred O'Neill well enough to guess how he'd retaliate. She only knew he would. And he did. Not fifteen minutes after Sunset Grove reported hoopoes, Fernwood reported Carolina parakeets.

"Wait. I've heard of those." Jesse flipped through the Sibley guide. "Why doesn't this book have a picture?"

"I'll tell you why—they're extinct." For the first time in the contest, Lucy felt shaken. Reaching across space was one thing. Reaching across time was something else again, something much harder. She hadn't believed Fred could. She wasn't sure she could herself. Trying not to think about that, she went on, "They've been extinct for almost a hundred years. There's a wonderful Audubon painting, if you want to know what they looked like."

Jesse nodded eagerly. "I've seen it. But now they're back, huh? How cool is that? What are *you* gonna do now, Mom?"

Lucy wasn't sure how cool it was. Didn't it cross a line somewhere? But, assuming it didn't, what *was* she gonna do? Whatever it was, it was liable to take just about all the witchcraft she had in her.

Then she started to laugh. If she was gonna do it, she'd go all-out. She gathered herself. She chose her feathers. She chose her spell. She took one moment to wonder if she'd gone off her rocker. Well, if she had, it was a grand madness. After a deep breath, she started.

It took everything she had, all right. The lights flickered. The CSPANC crystal went black. She'd have to rebless it later.

John came in (see?—you couldn't quite forget him). "What's going on?" he said. "How much crowleyage are you using, babe? What'll our magictrixity bill look like next month?"

Lucy waited till she'd finished the Summoning to answer. Then she gave him three words: "I don't care." They'd been married a long time. He looked at her, nodded, turned around, and walked away.

Jesse was peering out into the back yard. "What did you call up, Mom? All I see are a bunch more stoogebirds."

"Take another look," Lucy said wearily. If she'd just turned herself inside out for the sake of more dirt-common mourning doves . . . In that case, Fred O'Neill and Fernwood would win the Yule Count, that was all.

"They're funny-looking stoogebirds," Jesse said. "Kinda salmony breasts, red eyes . . . No. They can't be."

There were lots of them. That was part of what had worn Lucy out—and made the lights flicker. The other part was reaching back through the years. She eyed them through binoculars. No, they sure weren't stoogebirds. "Passenger pigeons," she said proudly. They all flew off together.

By the time Lucy had CSPANC up again, someone else had already spotted them (and recognized them, which also impressed her). And Jesse had got another call from Kathleen. "She says her dad won't quit, no matter what," he said.

"Big deal," Lucy declared. Later, she wondered if she should have sounded so arrogant. That was later.

In the middle of a war, you only cared about winning. You'd figure out what it all meant later.

They didn't hear about the newest Fernwood bird on the CSPANC scroll. John (here he is again!) called them in to look at the news crystal. "Some kind of monster's loose," he said.

That rated a look, all right. And he wasn't wrong. People were sending pictures from a flying carpet. The thing stalked through a park labeled FERNWOOD in the bottom left of the news crystal. It was taller than a man. It had chickeny feet, about the size of the ones that would have walked around under Baba Yaga's house. Its wings were useless, except for flapping to show it was ticked off. It had a big feathery crest on top of its head and a hooked beak that looked as if it could bite through steel bars. The only people in sight wore Tilly hats and carried binoculars, which made them birders. Even they had the sense to keep their distance.

One of the flying carpets swooped low. The monster bird snapped at it and let out a loud, furious screech. "Wow!" Jesse said. "Oh, wow! What *is* that thing?"

As if on cue, an announcer said, "A paleo-ornitholologist has identified this creature as a *Titanis*, a flightless predatory bird previously believed extinct for almost two million years. Witchcraft is suspected in its strange resurrection."

"Right on, Sherlock!" Lucy laughed, but shakily. She hadn't dreamt Fred O'Neill could do *that*. He was just lucky it hadn't taken a bite out of one of the Fernwood birders. Yet.

Her son's thoughts ran in a different direction. "How can you top him this time, Mom? A *Pteranodon*?"

"NFF," John said. Lucy stared at him. All these years together, and she hadn't imagined he knew *that* bit of birders' slang. He was right, too. A *Pteranodon* didn't have any feathers. If she was going to top Fred, she had to come up with something that did.

She laughed again. This time, hysteria—or maybe just plain lunacy—lay under the mirth. If you were gonna go for it, you should *go* for it. "One thing," she said. "If I bring this off, Fred's whupped." If she didn't, chances were the spell would toast her. She tried not to think about that. The crowleyage? The magictrixity bill? Count the cost later. That kind of thinking was probably why people did so many really stupid things during wartime—one more point Lucy did her best not to think about.

Back to her *materia magica*. Which feathers to choose? She had no idea. But Fred wouldn't have known what color the *Titanis* was, either. He'd managed. If he had, so could she. She hoped.

The form the spell would take would resemble the ones she'd used before, especially the charm that brought the passenger pigeons up to be counted. But reaching back over a hundred years was one thing. Reaching back a million times that far . . .

"It's the same principle," she said, and hoped she was right. Discovering she was wrong in the middle of the incantation wouldn't be much fun.

Do I really want to try this? she wondered. She'd already started by then, though. It was either this or admit Fred O'Neill had won. She was damned if she'd do that. . . . A moment later, she wished she'd phrased that differently. One more thing it was too late to worry about.

Lights didn't just flicker—they went out. So did the CSPANC crystal. John's yelp from the family room said he couldn't watch *Titanis* any more, either. Lucy noticed all that as if from a hundred million miles—or a hundred million years—away. She was deep in the spell by then. Backing out would be worse than going forward.

"Come forth! Come forth! Come forth!" she commanded. Then she slumped to the floor. She'd never fainted before. Outside of women with the vapors in Victorian novels, who did? When she woke up—it couldn't have been more than a few seconds later—she felt silly. Her head spun as she stood up, but she made it.

Jesse hadn't even noticed. He was scanning the yard with binoculars. "See anything?" Lucy asked. Her voice seemed shaky—to her, anyway.

Again, Jesse didn't notice. "Nooo," he said slowly. Lucy's heart sank. Had she half-fried her brains for nothing? Would Fred O'Neill and Fernwood spend the next year gloating? But then her son stiffened like a bird dog pointing. "Holy crap! There! In the magnolia." Darned if he didn't point, though not with his nose.

Lucy went over to the window and stared. For a second, she didn't see it. She was looking for purple and white or something else gaudy, the way artists always showed it. The real critter, though, was brown and green. Which made sense, when you thought about it. Even way back then, protective coloration mattered.

It was about the size of a crow. It didn't look like one, though, and wouldn't have if it were all black. It looked like a lizard that had decided to play bird. Trouble was, the poor lizard might've heard of birds, but it had never seen one, so it got stuff wrong. It didn't have a beak—it had a mouthful of teeth. It had a long, lizardy tail. But feathers sprouted from the tail, and from the wings, too, even if those also had claws to remind everybody they weren't done being arms yet.

"I did it. I really did it." Lucy sounded amazed, even to herself. "*Archaeopteryx*."

"*Archaeopteryx*," Jesse agreed, awe in his voice. "There's one for the life list! Can it really fly?"

"Don't know," Lucy replied. She got her answer a moment later. An Anna's hummingbird dive-bombed the funny-looking stranger. The *Archaeopteryx* snapped at it, but missed. It had a long, lizardy tongue. Another dive-bomb persuaded it not to hang around. Off it flew. Not gracefully, maybe, but it flew.

Jesse was talking on his pocket crystal. Lucy's spell hadn't blasted that, anyhow. "No way!" she heard Kathleen exclaim when Jesse told her what they'd just observed.

"Way," he assured her, and then said to Lucy, "She's telling her dad."

"An *Archaeopteryx*?" That was Fred O'Neill's bull-in-a-china-shop bellow. "Well . . . fudge. I'm not gonna top that this year."

You'll never top it, Lucy thought. *You can't, not till they find an older bird. If they ever do.* Even so, he'd come up with *something* next year, sure as sure. He always did. This time around, though, the Yule Bird count belonged to Sunset Grove. And, as far as Lucy was concerned, that was just how things were supposed to be.

Steven Piziks teaches English in Michigan. His students think he's hysterical, which isn't the same as thinking he's hilarious. When not writing books and grading papers, he plays harp, wrestles with his three sons, and spends more time on-line than is probably good for him. Although he adopted two of his children from Ukraine, his story in this anthology bears no resemblance to his life whatsoever. Really. Writing as Steven Harper, he has produced the critically-acclaimed Silent Empire series. Visit his web page at http://www. sff.net/people/spiziks

Witch Warrior

Steven Piziks

The knock exploded through the house. I bolted out of my chair and rushed for the front door. What kind of *idiot?* Eva had just gone down for her afternoon nap, and waking her at this point would change her from a darling, dark-haired toddler into a howling hurricane of death. Not only that, we have a sign out front that clearly says SOLICITORS WILL BE HEXED. THIS MEANS *YOU*.

I reached for the knob, expecting to see Witnesses with *Watchtowers* or Latter-Day Saints with leaflets, and working myself up into a royal snit over the situation. I'm a tall guy, and rangy, with red hair, green eyes, and a fair Irish complexion. My wife Collette calls me her suburban Celtic warrior. Not quite the fearsome nickname most men want to hear from their wives. Still, I can get as ticked as the next guy when some overly-religious dickwad pounds on my door, wakes my daughter, and expects an on-the-spot conversion.

I yanked the door open and found myself staring at a big, saggy bosom.

I blinked. The bosom filled the doorway and threatened to spill over me like an avalanche of bread dough. This was a bosom that had never known the touch of elastic, and it was only a few inches from my nose. The expanse moved slowly up and down as the owner inhaled and exhaled. It slowly dawned on me that I was looking at a woman who was at least two heads taller than me. I slowly raised my eyes to her face. Old. Ancient. Paleolithic. You could have lost an SUV in the wrinkles. Moles sprouted hairs long enough to braid. Iron-gray hair scraggled in a hundred different directions, though a bejeweled golden comb was stuck in the mess as an apparent afterthought. Her lower lip hung down like a toboggan run. Two dark eyes gleamed like sharp shards of night sky. She wore a frankenstein dress made of a thousand patches, and I think her boots were soled with iron. An apron covered her waist, and a blue dish towel embroidered with little yellow fishies was tucked into the string. This wasn't the grandmother from hell. This was the grandmother from hell's second sub-basement.

"William McCrae?" she rasped in the voice of a professional cigar smoker.

I had to clear my throat twice before I could answer. "Yeah?"

"Hand over the children." She thrust out a horny hand tipped with blackened nails. I had taken down our screen door to fix it, meaning there was nothing between her and me, and she was practically thrusting her hand into the house.

"No!" Reflexively I shoved her arm aside. It was

like pressing a steel bar, but she dropped it. "Who the hell do you think you are?"

"I think you know the answer to that," she croaked, then shifted her gaze to a point over my shoulder. "Ah! Here comes one of them now."

Involuntarily, I flicked a glance behind me. My twelve-year-old son Danilo was coming into the living room. In one hand he held a remote-control airplane. In the other, he held the remote. Like his sister Eva, Danilo has the dark hair, dark eyes, and stocky build typical of many Eastern Europeans. We adopted him and Eva last year from Ukraine. Eva was just entering toddlerhood at the time, but Danilo was eleven and retains clear memories of his homeland and birth family.

"Tato?" he said, using a Ukrainian word for *Dad*. "Who that?"

"Danny!" I said. "Get back!"

Then he caught sight of the woman at the door. The color fled his face and I swear he almost fainted. "Baba Yaga!" he squeaked. And he rushed out of the room.

A cold chill swept over me and I forced myself to turn back to the door. Of course I had known who the woman was. I had known the moment I had opened the door. But denial isn't just for alcoholics. Baba Yaga, the great Witch of Ukraine, grinned down at me with iron teeth. Her breath was warm and sour as whisky mash. The Celtic warrior and Wiccan Witch inside me nearly wet themselves, but I made myself stand in the doorway like a stack of bricks, though that was probably because I was dropping them from my rectum and they were propping me up.

"You can't have Eva or Danilo," I said, surprised at how steady my voice remained. "They're mine."

"They belong to Ukraine, Billy-boy. You and your wife took them away from their homeland without permission."

Now I was getting angry, which made the whole situation a lot easier to handle. I drew myself up. "The hell we did! Collette and I jumped through every legal hoop, sometimes twice. We got halfway through the adoption process with one agency before they found out both of us were Wiccan and freaked out, so we started over with a second agency. When we finally got Ukraine's *permission* to come over there, we went to the National Adoption Center in Kyiv. They told us no infants were available—so sorry, those are the breaks—but there *was* a toddler with an eleven-year-old brother no one wanted. They gave my wife and me *permission* to meet the kids. When we did, we instantly realized Danilo and Eva were meant to be our children. A week later, a judge signed the papers and gave us *permission* to bring them home. All. Perfectly. Legal." I sketched a Celtic rune for *power* in the air and whispered a small word. My knuckles glowed blue. "They're *my* children now, old woman."

"I didn't ask about the law," Baba Yaga said. "And your puny charm only proves my point. You didn't ask *my* permission, one Witch to another, to take my children out of my country."

Ah. It was just another hoop to jump through. But my pride rankled. And the old bitch had scared Danny. Still, I made myself bow and forced my tone into one of smooth respect.

"I beg your pardon," I said. "As one Witch to

another, may my wife Collette and I have your kind permission to take Eva and Danilo from your country and raise them as our own?"

She adopted a thoughtful pose, running one thorny finger down her drooping lower lip. Saliva followed the tip in a snail trail.

"No," she said at last. "I'm taking them back tonight at sunset. Maybe I'll eat one on the way home as a snack, hey?"

The suburban Celtic warrior and the Wiccan Witch roared to life together. "You just try it, old woman. You'll have to cross the wards we set. And then you'll have to get past me."

She cocked her head at me. "Are you a Witch or a warrior, boy?" And she deliberately thrust one long, bony arm through the doorway into the house. Violet light flared along her forearm, and I felt the wards the entire coven had set for us pop like stale bubble gum. An instant migraine rammed my eyes three feet into my head. I cried out and clapped my hands over my face until the pain subsided.

"Can't decide, eh?" Baba Yaga rasped. "Sucks to be you. Say your good-byes, Billy-boy. At sunset, those children are mine."

With that, she stomped down the porch steps to the front lawn, where sat the biggest mortar I had ever seen. You could have ground a healthy oak into mulch with it. She clambered aboard, picked up a pestle the size of a bull walrus, and shoved herself down the street. The mortar glided like a hovercraft, but the thudding pestle left a series of potholes in the concrete. Dully I wondered if she was visible to the neighbors and what they might think if she were.

I shut the door and allowed myself a few moments of internal drama. Let's see. We had anger, fear, shakiness, a general what-the-hell-brought-this-on sensation. No denial, though. The image of that horrifying bosom was burned too deeply into my retinas for that. I gulped and panted. But thirty seconds of internal freak-out time was all I could give myself—I had to see if Danny and Eva were all right.

Eva was still asleep in her crib. I reached out to smooth her dark curls, then noticed my hand was shaking and stopped myself. I didn't want to accidentally poke her cheek and wake her up. She was two years old, and a little behind in her development—a common situation among orphanage babies. According to the court records, her father had died (causes unspecified) two months before she'd been born. Her mother never quite recovered from the birth and died the winter before Eva's first birthday. She and Danilo had lived with an aunt for a while, but the aunt had been barely able to support her own three children, let alone two more, and she had eventually sent Eva and Danilo to the state-run orphanage.

Eva shifted in her sleep. I wanted to snatch her up and hold her close. She was my daughter, no matter what Baba Bitchka said. But how the hell was I going to fight the most powerful figure in Ukrainian folklore? My mouth went dry at the thought. I was a mortal Wiccan who'd been practicing magic for over twenty years. I had exorcised ghosts and faced down the fae. Once I'd even tracked down a vampire. With help. But Baba Yaga was on another plane. Hell, she owned the airline.

I ran through options in my head. It was August, the worst possible time for something like this to happen.

All women in the coven, including Collette, were on a women-only camping trip near Lake Michigan this week. All the men except me had taken advantage of the wife-free time to go on trips of their own. I could call Collette on her cell, but she and the women would never get home before sunset. Fear and worry gnawed at me, and I dealt with it by moving forward.

I found Danilo hiding under his bed.

"No," I said, halfway underneath the frame. "She is *not* going to take you away. I won't let her. Mama and I are Witches. Remember how we scared away the pixies in the basement? And when we got rid of the ghost in the Patterson's pantry?"

"Baba Yaga not pixie," Danny said from the corner. "She eat children."

"I have magic. I am strong." Though I wondered how strong I looked with my rear end sticking out from under a bed and clumps of dust in my hair. "I will stop her. You will be safe."

Danny gave me a "who are you fooling?" look, and that hurt more than anything. My son didn't believe that I could defend him. Whether I really could or not didn't matter—the fact that he didn't *think* I could stabbed like a glass knife. I backed out from under the bed.

Keep moving, I told myself. *If you stop, it'll all come crashing down on you.*

I went into the living room. The carpet needed vacuuming, and a pile of bills sat on the coffee table. Several were unopened because I didn't want to know what they said, though the words glared at me through the envelopes. SECOND NOTICE. FINAL NOTICE. WE PULL FINGERNAILS. Our finances still hadn't recovered from the adoption. It hadn't helped that the bank had decided it couldn't afford to give us employees a raise this year, though I noticed the president still got his annual Lexus.

A Saturday summer breeze blew through the sliding door at the back of the house. Suddenly the house felt stifling, and I followed the air out to the back deck.

I like our backyard. Past the wooden deck I had laid with my own hands stretches half an acre of perfect emerald lawn. An oak tree and an ash are spaced perfectly between high privacy fences that separate us from the neighbors. In the right back corner stands the double-sized garden shed that doubles as my workshop. In the other corner sits the outdoor altar. It's a half-moon of shale roughly stacked to knee height, done in such a way as to create dozens of little shelves and alcoves. We tuck candles and charms and statues and anything else we deem appropriate there. The rear boundary of the back yard is a simple chain link fence. Beyond it, our world opens up into a nice meadow filled with creeks, hills, and abundant wildlife.

I strode across the perfect lawn. Yeah, yeah, yeah—I spend hours every weekend mowing, mulching, trimming, and weeding. No, I don't plant wildflowers or grow herbs. Sorry, I have no desire to dip my own candles, milk organic goats, or harvest my own granola. I want air conditioning, cable, and a hardware superstore less than fifteen minutes away. I use a weedwhacker to trim around my altar, and when my ritual candles go out, I relight them with a barbecue lighter. And I'm still a Wiccan Witch—or a Celtic warrior.

Nothing in the Wiccan Rede or the *Mabinogion* says I have to live in the sixteenth century.

I knelt in the center of the stone crescent. Grass brushed my bare knees—I was wearing shorts with tennis shoes—and I felt my gaze drawn toward a small figure of Mother Berchte. She's a little-known German goddess of fire and chaos. When she shows up at the winter Solstice and opens up her sack, you never know if she's going to dump the gifts out or stuff the kids in. Not many Witches invoke her, but I've always liked her. Besides, talking out loud to her statue might help me figure out what to do. I started to cast a circle, then decided the hell with it and just waved my lighter in front of Berchte's face and sketched the rune for *goddess*. "What the hell is going on?" I snarled. "Why can't you guys leave us alone?"

"Wimp," Berchte said.

I dropped the lighter, scrabbled for it, then gave it up. I leaned in for a closer look. The Berchte statue stared back at me, her tiny eyes glittering in the late afternoon sunlight. She looked a little like Baba Yaga, though half her body was in shadow and half was in sunlight, and she wore a headcloth over her hair.

"What do you mean wimp?" I didn't know what else to say. I hadn't actually expected Berchte to talk to me. It had never happened before. On the other hand, Baba Yaga had never knocked on my front door before, either.

"I meant what I said, dearie." Her voice was small and raspy, like a rat-tail file. "Baba Yaga challenges you to fight, so you come out and whine at me? Wimp."

"It's not fair!" I snapped. "Collette and I worked and sacrificed and put ourselves into debt so we could adopt two children no one else wanted. Eva has developmental delays, Danny *still* doesn't trust me, creditors are knocking our door down, and now Baba Yaga wants to . . . to . . ." I thought of the stories about the cannibal Witch and my throat closed with fear. "We did something *good*, but our lives have only gotten harder as a result."

"What do you want?" Berchte said. "A bye?"

"Yeah!" I said, half laughing. "For one round of bad shit, I want a bye."

"Sorry, dearie. The universe doesn't work that way. No good deed goes unpunished, yada yada. You want to keep the kids, you'll have to fight."

"How, dammit?" I almost screamed. "I've read the stories about her. What am I supposed to do? Go to her house and tie her trees with ribbon? Feed bacon to her cat and put oil on her gate? That was a thousand years ago. She's the bitch queen of Ukraine. I'm a forty-year-old American Witch."

"I thought you were Collette's suburban Celtic warrior." Berchte smirked.

"Whichever. I can't beat her."

"That's why you're going to lose," Berchte said. "You've split your power in half and let Baba Yaga dictate the terms of the battle. Fight her with *your* weapons and you might have a chance." The figure went still.

An airplane screamed down from the sky and crashed into the grass beside me. I jumped, then plucked the toy from the ground. One of the wings was bent. I turned. Danilo was running toward me, remote in hand.

"Danny!" I called on Dad autopilot. "Be careful!"

Danilo held out his hand for the plane without looking at me. Remote control toys are his obsession, have been since we stepped off the plane in Detroit. Planes, cars, boats—if you can stick a radio in the engine, Danilo can operate it. The amateur psychologist who set up shop in my head the day we adopted him says the operant word is *control*. The toys do whatever Danilo wants, unlike his life.

"It's bent," I said, getting to my feet. "Come on—let's see if we can fix it."

I was heading into denial again, knew it, and didn't care. I'd earned five minutes in Egypt. Danilo followed me silently into the workshop-shed, and I jerked the string to turn on the overhead light. The familiar, calming smells of gasoline and sawdust hung on the air. Assorted gardening tools hung from the walls, each in its place. One half of the shed was taken up by my lawn tractor, a Deforester 3000. It's a behemoth you can harvest corn with, complete with a small trunk, attached Wet-Vac (handy for cleaning gutters), and an engine outfitted with explosive turbo-boost. The thing is way bigger than anything I need to maintain our little lawn, but it satisfies my inner urge to have an enormously powerful machine that obeys my every command, which is why I bought it. This was before the adoption took over our lives and finances, of course. I'd recently placed ads to sell it, though the thought of saying good-bye to old faithful and getting a push mower gave me a twinge. It would be like trading a war stallion for a moo-cow.

The other half of the shed was taken up by my workbench. My hand tools hung from hooks on the wall above it, and I had a decently clear space to work in. I set the model airplane on the bench. Danilo came in and leaned against it to watch while I selected a pair of rubber-coated pliers from the rack on the wall.

"These will straighten the wing without hurting it," I said.

Danny said nothing as I carefully used the pliers to right the wing. Once it was fixed, I gave it back to him and he gave me a small smile. I smiled back. A pure father-son moment. It was exactly the kind of thing I'd fantasized about while we were grinding through the endless forms and meetings that made up the adoption process.

"What you do about Baba Yaga?" Danny asked, and the moment crumbled to dust.

I sighed. "I don't know yet. But you don't have to worry. I'll take care of it. That's what dads do."

"Right." For a moment, Danny sounded exactly like an American teenager. "You not my real dad, and you can't stop Baba Yaga."

For a long, cold moment, I felt completely alone. Collette was gone. The coven was gone. It was just me against the most powerful fairy tale in the world. Behind a privacy fence, no one can hear you scream. But for Danny's sake, I kept my expression neutral as I knelt in front of him. Danilo is short for his age—a lifetime of bad nutrition at work. "No matter what you might think, you're a part of this family forever. And Baba Yaga never fought a Wiccan Witch or a Celtic warrior before."

"What is Celtic warrior?"

A loud crash stopped my answer. Both of us lunged

for the shed door. Across the lawn I saw Baba Yaga
stepping through the remains of our sliding glass
door. In her arms she held Eva. Baba Yaga's wild
hair writhed like gray snakes around the bejeweled
golden comb. Eva was awake, her dark eyes wide,
though she remained silent. Fear stabbed my heart
with a frozen blade.

"No!" I whispered.

"*Це моя сестра!*" Danny shouted, and ran toward
her before I could react. A small part of my mind caught
the Ukrainian words for *my sister*. Baba Yaga laughed a
harsh, grating laugh and snatched Danny up with her
free arm. He screamed, the airplane and remote still
clutched in his hands. My body came to life then and
I lunged for the witch. She blew a small puff of breath
at me, and it knocked me backward like a cement fist.
The buttons on my shirt popped off, laying my chest
open to the afternoon air. I landed on my back and
skidded across the grass. Hot pain thudded against my
breastbone. The back of my shirt tore.

"Mine," Baba Yaga said.

"You said I had until sunset," I found myself shouting.

"And you're too obsessed with rules, Billy McCrae,"
she snorted.

I caught a glimpse of Danny's face. His expression
mingled fear and resignation. He knew I wouldn't be
able to save him, had known it all along. Baba Yaga
stomped across the yard and I found myself wondering where her mortar was. Maybe it couldn't handle
passengers. She kicked the chain link fence flat and
strode out into the meadow beyond the subdivision.

I sat there on the grass, unable to comprehend
what was going on. My heart pounded, my stomach

felt like stone. It wasn't fair, it wasn't *right*. Baba Yaga was already receding into the distance, Danny and Eva looking over her shoulders at me with heartbreak in their eyes. I glanced at the altar. The Berchte figurine, normally facing outward, was facing to my right, toward the shed.

"You've split your power in half and let her dictate the terms. Fight her with your weapons and you might have a chance."

My terms. My weapons.

My shed.

I shucked the ruined shirt, bolted into the shed clad only in shorts and tennis shoes, and grabbed a few things from shelves and hooks—gas-powered hedge clippers, gas can, spare tools. I leaped onto the seat of my Deforester 3000 and twisted the key. It sprang to life with a lion's roar. I summoned all the magic twenty years of Wicca had taught me and started to sketch the Celtic rune for *power* on the mower's casing. Then I stopped. The Witch and warrior warred for dominance. The Witch wanted to fight magic with magic. The warrior called for blood. And neither one felt particularly strong.

I glanced around the shed. Perfect tools, powerful machinery, sharp blades. I was pretty good at magic, though not great. My inner Celtic warrior cried out for weapons, but suburban men—sensitive modern men—aren't allowed to have them. Hungry, I had turned to witchcraft for power and tried to placate the inner warrior with toys. The split had divided my strength in half. I had a chance against Baba Yaga, but only with full strength. I had to decide—Witch or warrior?

I looked around the shed again. The answer was clear. The rune died with a flick of my fingers. I slammed the mower into gear and hit the turbo boost. The mower leaped forward, and the back of the shed exploded in a billion shards. Without slowing, the Deforester 3000 bolted across the flattened fence into the meadow beyond. The speed almost unseated me, and I gripped the steering wheel like the reins of a war chariot.

The mower rushed up a rise nearly as fast as a galloping horse, leaving a strip of perfectly-mown meadow behind. I crested and saw Baba Yaga ahead of me, making for a clump of trees. She heard' the mower's thunderous engine and turned in surprise. Danilo and Eva stared as well.

"Dada!" Eva screamed.

Baba Yaga's surprise didn't last long. From her apron she snatched the blue dishtowel with embroidered fishies and flung it between us. The towel hit the ground and rippled, shifted, widened. A full-blown river flowed across the rise in its place. I swore and hit the brakes. The Deforester 3000 roared in protest. The sound and smell of rushing water washed past me as the two of us came to a halt. Baba Yaga waved and continued on her way.

I didn't hesitate. I grabbed the mower's attached Wet-Vac, shoved the business end of the hose into river, and switched it on. The motor bellowed and water exploded out the rear of the vacuum like a firehose. The water level dropped, the river drained, and in seconds, the bed was dry.

Fear the suburban Celtic warrior and his weapons.

I blasted across the riverbed on my lawn tractor and

in less than a minute was catching up to Baba Yaga
again. This time Danilo looked amazed and a little
relieved. Eva reached for me. Baba Yaga slapped my
daughter's hands down and in that moment I burned
to use the bitch's blood to smear war emblems on my
bare chest. But before I could get close, Baba Yaga
snatched the golden comb from her hair and threw
it down between us.

The earth rumbled. I felt it even through the vibra-
tions of the Deforester 3000. Green leaves poked up
through the ground and burst into full-blown bushes
and hedges so thick I couldn't see through them. I
cut power to the mower, leaped off, and yanked the
starter cord on my hedge trimmer. It purred to life.
I swung the trimmer like a sword, and the blades I
kept razor sharp sliced through twigs and leaves like
green butter. Sticks scratched my bare chest and legs
and tore my shorts, so I dashed back to the mower
and grabbed the plastic lid off the Wet-Vac to hold
in front of me. That helped. In less than a minute,
I carved a rough path through and stepped out the
other side, bleeding and nearly naked, but through.

Only then did I realize the opening was too narrow
to bring the Deforester 3000 through. No time for self-
recrimination. I ran. Two hills later, I caught up to Baba
Yaga and the kids. She was waiting for me, Danilo on
her left, Eva on her right. I stood less than an arm's
length in front of her, hedge trimmer in one hand, Wet-
Vac lid in the other. I couldn't read Eva's expression.
Danilo looked scared. He was still clutching his airplane
remote, but the airplane was nowhere in sight.

"No negotiation, no talk," I said. "Let them go, or
I will kill you."

Baba Yaga laughed and held out an arm. I could see the thin violet light surrounding it and the rest of her body, the same light that had broken my wards. The light also surrounded the kids. "Try."

I swung the trimmer at her neck. She didn't even try to dodge. The humming blades bounced off the light, and I felt the shock all the way up my arm. Baba Yaga flicked a fist at me. I flung up the Wet-Vac lid. It shattered, and my arm went numb.

"You see?" she said. "You can't touch me. You never had a—"

And Eva bit her on the leg. She always gets cranky when someone wakes her early. Baba Yaga screeched in pain and surprise and the violet light went out. Just at that moment, Danny's airplane buzzed down from the sky and crashed straight into her left eye. Baba Yaga screeched again. I swung the trimmers with my good arm. The blades opened up a long gash across her chest. Dark red blood spilled out. It hissed where it touched the ground, and the grass withered and died. Baba Yaga staggered back. Some feeling had returned to my other arm. I scooped both kids behind me, then brandished the humming trimmers again.

"These children are mine," I said. "By water and wood and blood, I have proven they are mine. Leave now or you will die."

Baba Yaga, huge hands clutching at her wound, gave me a long, hard look. Then, to my surprise, she looked at Danilo. He glared back at her and clutched my arm.

"*Мій отець,*" Danny said fiercely.

Baba Yaga nodded once and turned to me. "You have earned the right. Warrior." And she vanished, blood and all.

All the strength left me. I sagged and used the hedge trimmers as a cane to prop myself up.

"Dada!" Eva said, and I picked her up. She buried her face in my bare neck, and I inhaled the safe scent of her dark hair.

Danilo tapped me on the arm. I looked down at him. He put his arms up like a child a third his age. "Dad?"

And I picked him up, too.

Then I had to put them down. Even suburban Celtic warriors caught in emotional dad moments have their limits.

On our way back, we discovered that all traces of the hedge had disappeared. The Deforester 3000 sat patiently in the middle of an empty meadow. It was scratched and dented, and one of the mower blades was broken. No way anyone would buy it now. Great. At least we could ride it home. Already I was wondering how we were going to pay to replace the damaged shed, rear fence, and sliding glass door. I also realized my shoulders were starting to sunburn. Berchte was right—the universe never gives you a bye. I boarded the mower with Eva and held out an arm to help Danny climb on.

"Dad, what this?"

Danilo was holding an object out to me. I took it and stared. It was Baba Yaga's golden comb, the one encrusted with glittering jewels. Sunlight sparkled off a diamond, a ruby, an emerald, a large black pearl, and other stones I couldn't name.

"Well?" Danny said. "What this?"

"I think" I said weakly, "it's a bye."

And the Deforester 3000 roared to life.

Lee Martindale is a short story slinger whose work has appeared in such anthologies as *Turn The Other Chick*, *Catopolis*, *A Time To . . .* , *Outside The Box*, *Arcane Whispers*, *Lowport*, three volumes of the *Sword & Sorceress* series, three of the *Bubbas Of The Apocalypse* anthologies, and three chapbook collections from Yard Dog Press. She also edited the ground-breaking *Such A Pretty Face*. When not slinging fiction, Lee is a Named Bard, Lifetime Active Member of SFWA, a fencing member of the SFWA Musketeers, and a member of the SCA. She and her husband George live in Plano, TX, where she keeps friends and fans in the loop at http://www. HarpHaven.net.

Nimue and the
Mall Nymphs

Lee Martindale

All Nimue Reynolds wanted to do was wash her hands.

The pamphlet shoved into them by a total stranger sporting an arrogant, "you obviously need this" smirk had felt— She wanted to say "slimy," but that was probably a psychological reaction to the subject matter: yet another new weight loss clinic. Psychological or not, she wanted to wash her hands.

Finding the requisite facilities was not the easiest of feats in Stonebend Mall. For starters, the place had been designed by a trendy wunderkind with an unhealthy admiration of Escher and a tendency to channel Sarah Winchester. Getting from any Point A to any Point B required a switchback to Point F and the good fortune not to get turned around along the way. Or temporarily blinded by shafts of late-spring North Texas sunlight focused to near-laser quality by artfully-faceted glass. Acres of the stuff, soaring multiple stories above the corridors. So far, in what Nimue considered a miracle, all of that glass had managed to avoid being introduced to another late-spring North Texas staple, softball-sized hail.

Further complication lay in the apparent notion that the sensibilities of genteel shoppers should be spared reminders of mundane things like bodily functions. Signs pointing the way to public restrooms were tiny, tastefully well-hidden, and rendered in a font that was probably and appropriately called *Obscura Elegante*. A good thing, she thought as she entered a camouflaged corridor supposedly leading to her destination, that she wasn't seeking the restrooms on more urgent business.

It didn't take long for Nimue to begin thinking she'd taken an unmarked entrance into Faerie, the direct result of another example of architectural whimsy. The grand concept called for the mall to "emerge ethereally" from the side of a hill, ignoring completely the reality that the building site had, not all that long ago, been flat-as-a-pool-table prairie. But a hill was demanded, and a hill was built—or rather piled—on a supporting structure of pre-fab concrete boxes that provided stability and, just incidentally, cut down on the amount of fill dirt needed.

Then someone got the idea to turn the boxes into utility space. The narrow concrete tunnels were painted a uniform, depressing blue-grey and designated as maintenance and access corridors.

The result was a subterranean maze that would have delighted the heart of King Minos and prompted Nimue to wish she'd brought breadcrumbs to drop behind her. Six times, at each of six intersections, she stopped and tried to decipher letters and numbers stenciled in black on the corners—coordinates, apparently, with no discernable pattern or logic. Next she listened for any sound that might give her some clue as to what might lay beyond the pre-fab and, more importantly, in which direction. But there was no hint of din from the food court, no echo of commerce from a shop, no telltale sound of passersby from a concourse. There was, oddly enough, no sound at all.

Arriving at the seventh intersection on her accidental journey, she repeated the process. This time, blessed be, there was a tenuous reward. From somewhere along the tunnel to the left came the faintest wisp of vibration, the barest suggestion of sound. That it resembled girlish giggles . . . well, Nimue didn't care. It was a direction, an indication that she hadn't slipped through a portal into an otherwise-uninhabited limbo. In the absence of something more substantive, she made for it.

She'd gone only a few steps when she noticed a tingling at the back of her neck. A tingling that spread slowly across her scalp, then danced down her arms, growing stronger with each step toward a partially open door on the left wall of the tunnel. She'd encountered several such doors, all securely locked. Not only was this one open, from it came the sound of chanting.

Take Texas upscale suburban schoolgirl slang and type it into a language translation program set to output Texas high school first-year Latin. Hand the resulting text to three adolescent females with voices that could peel paint, and instruct them to read it in unison. Ragged delivery, abysmal syntax, truly horrible pronunciation, and yet it was working. All known arcane logic aside, there was power being raised. Nimue could feel it: raw magick scraping against her senses in waves.

What she *didn't* feel was the slightest hint of protective circle or the barest glimmer of shielding. For a moment, Nimue lightly mourned the passing of "survival of the fittest" as a teaching tool for the young. Then she did what she knew she couldn't avoid. She slipped through the door and into the space beyond.

For the most part, it was dark, the result of electricity to the space being shut off and a temporary plywood partition being thrown up to hide the evidence of commercial failure from shoppers walking by. It was also overly-warm, the air-conditioning having been likewise disconnected. The air itself was stale, dusty, and becoming increasingly smoky; apparently the smoke detectors had been disconnected, as well.

What little light there was came from—oh please— black candles stuck on top of plaster pedestals and pillars that had been spray-painted a tacky gold and arranged in rough approximation of a circle. In the center was a plated metal—Nimue hoped it was metal and not spray-painted plastic—champagne bucket "cauldron," from which smoke, oily and reeking of various noxious and potent herbs burning on charcoal briquets, rose. Walls and floor had been generously decorated with symbols from no identifiable source other than syndicated reruns of *Charmed*.

Whatever shop had once occupied the space had apparently gone out of business quickly and quite some time ago. Nimue suspected it had been a clothing store for trendy teenaged girls, not unlike the three she spied standing together facing the "cauldron" and a flimsy folding metal music stand. Long blond hair, rail-thin bodies, varied-in-only-minor-details clothing. The woman marveled at the amount of effort it must have taken to give them the appearance of having all come out of the same cookie cutter.

Oh, joy. I'm dealing with the Brittany Brigade.

Yet another round of quasi-Latin chant dissolved into yet another bout of giggling. "This isn't working," remarked Brittany #1 when the twittering had died down. "It's just too hard. We need to try something else."

"Like what?" the two others asked in unison.

"I don't know," the first replied, frustration pushing her already high-pitched voice into an even higher, more grating range. "Maybe there's something else in here we can use. I downloaded a bunch of stuff from that website I found last night: WomanPowerRevenge.com." She started leafing through pages of computer print-outs while her companions, looking bored, glanced at each other and rolled their eyes. "Here's one that doesn't look as hard. I say a line, and you guys say it after me like a—what did Ms. Batterson call it?—Greek chorus." She seemed a little surprised, and very pleased, that she'd actually remembered something from World Literature class. "Just repeat everything I say, okay?"

"Fine," Brittany #2 snapped. "Only let's get this over with, okay? I've got a ton of homework, and I haven't updated my FaceSpace page in *days*."

"Me, too," Brittany #3 chimed in.

"I've got homework, too," Brittany #1 shot back, a touch of petulance in her voice, "but this is about something bigger than homework. This is about sister-hood, and goddess power, and . . . and . . ."

"And being really ticked off about losing to a no-style nerd like Marsha Castlebury. So read, already!"

Brittany #1 opened her mouth as if to continue the argument, then turned back toward the music stand. She took a deep breath and drew herself up into a posture someone had once told her conveyed "dignified authority." Another deep breath, and then she closed her eyes and intoned solemnly, "Goddess Hecate, hear our plea." She waited expectantly, and when she heard nothing, repeated the phrase more forcefully. A few, silent beats later, she opened her eyes and glared. "Come *on!* It's not like I'm speaking French or something. Get with it, willya?"

She closed her eyes and tried it again. This time, her efforts were rewarded with a feeble echo in two halting voices. "Better, but this time at least *try* to put some will behind it, okay?" The fourth attempt and the response to it were far more to her liking.

There was, apparently, a target for the day's work, if the number of times the name "Brad" came up was any indication. And he had, apparently, fallen significantly out of favor with the teen trio, if the frequency and vehemence with which the word "vengeance," and variations on the theme, were assayed.

"Goddess Hecate, heed your servants."

"Goddess Hecate, heed your servants."

"Mighty Hecate, work our revenge."

"Mighty Hecate, work our revenge."

"Terrible Hecate, accept this sacrifice and do our bidding!"

This, thought Nimue, *would be a fairly easy fix.* Short-circuit whatever the girls were trying to do, and slip away without them knowing she'd been there.

Let them go home thinking they'd failed or—even better—that their attempts were all just so much nonsense. She was preparing a psychic wrench to lob into the middle of the adolescent works when the yowl of a very young, very put-upon feline changed her plans.

Drat! Just . . . drat! Oh, well . . . on to Plan B. Nimue stepped out of the shadows. "Good day, ladies."

Had Nimue materialized out of thin air to a fanfare of thunder, sparklers and red smoke, it could hardly have caused more of a shock to the three. Brittany #3 squealed. Brittany #2 gaped, then whispered, "Ohmygod, we've summoned Hecate." It took Brittany #1 three tries to stammer out, "Who—who are you?"

"The adult supervision you so obviously need," Nimue replied, doing a leisurely scan of the surroundings, the set-up, and the girls, and letting exaggerated-for-the-level-of-the-audience amused disdain play on her face. "Didn't anyone ever tell you not to burn charcoal in a room without sufficient ventilation? It's a wonder you haven't keeled over from carbon monoxide poisoning."

"Is that why I have a headache? I've got this really bad hea—"

"Amber, shut up," Brittany #1 snapped.

Brittany #3 now had a name.

"Why don't we start with who this Brad person is, and what crime he committed that was so unspeakable you three would risk getting permanently banned from the mall to bring down all this righteous wrath on him?"

Amber glanced sideway before replying. "Brad is Carol's boyfriend."

"He *was* Carol's boyfriend," Brittany #2 corrected.

"Except that he broke up with her today, right after school. Right before the junior prom. We're making him sorry he did that."

"*Really* sorry."

"I see. Hell having no fury, etc," Nimue chuckled. "And what did you have in mind as a suitable punishment?"

"We're putting a curse on him."

"A really bad .curse."

"Yeah. We're *witches*."

"Witches," Nimue echoed as she crossed her arms. "A curse," she continued, pointedly looking around again. "Interesting. And you," she paused and leveled her gaze on the girl in the center, "must be Carol."

"Yeah . . . ah . . . how did you know that?"

Nimue cocked her head to one side. "You're the one holding a letter-opener in one hand and a kitten in the other. Cute kitten, by the way. This . . . curse . . . calls for the blood of a black cat, does it?"

"Well . . . no," stammered the sole unnamed Brittany. "But Carol said it would make it more powerful and . . ."

She was interrupted by Carol hissing "Shut up, Shelley!"

That drew not a chuckle, but a full-blown laugh from the older woman.

Carol might not know what to make of the unexpected turn of events, but she knew she didn't like being laughed at. She drew herself up and did her best to look menacing. "Look, lady, this isn't any of your business, so why don't you just waddle your fat ass back to wherever you came from and leave us alone."

Nimue raised one eyebrow and smiled. "You're going to have to better than that, kid. Derogatory references to the size of my backside haven't gotten a rise out of me since I was about your age."

The girls exchanged another round of confused looks. Not having a target dissolve into tears over being called "fat" was a new experience for them. It took them a couple of beats to find another weapon. "Okay, then," Carol continued, doing a rough—very rough—attempt at being threatening. "You're as stupid as you are fat. I already told you we're witches. We're *powerful!* Go away or we'll do something really bad to you."

Nimue chuckled again. "Something bad?" She raised her right hand and her fingers began to move, weaving intricate signs in the air. The foul-smelling smoke billowing out of the champagne bucket reversed direction and was sucked rapidly back whence it came. To the accompaniment of dropping teenaged jaws, the bucket rose slowly until it hovered several feet in the air. Then it upended itself and slammed to the floor. Silence followed, finally broken by a young voice reverently murmuring, "Wow."

"So," Nimue continued conversationally. "What exactly did you have planned for Brad?"

Still staring at the upended "cauldron," Shelley mumbled, "We're going to make his thing fall off."

"Ambitious. And you, Carol, are willing to offer sacrifice for this piece of work?"

Carol, looking a trifle dazed, pulled her eyes up and blinked. "Well, yeah. It's my kitten."

"Hecate's favors come a little pricier than one scrawny—what is it, eight-weeks-old?—kitten. Let's see . . ." Nimue regarded the trio for a moment. "As the price for unmanning Brad, The Dark Lady would undoubtedly demand the un*womaning* of you. And given Her traditional personality . . . the messier and more painful, the better." She began to chant, softly and steadily, Gaelic phrases that layered one upon the other and shimmered around the three girls like ice crystals.

The kitten, still hanging by its scruff from Carol's hand, began to glow and change, becoming larger and heavier until Carol, staring at it in shock, let it go. It landed lightly on the floor, where it continued to grow—lengthening, stretching—until what crouched on the floor was a black panther in all its fully-mature, sleek and lethal glory. It rose, its shoulders nearly waist-high to the girls. One by one, it regarded each one of them as if trying to decide which would make the tastier first course.

The cat leveled glowing yellow eyes on Carol before opening its mouth and giving her an unobstructed view of flesh-rending fangs. A low growl vibrated the air. One front paw sketched a languid arch toward the girl, unsheathing claws that looked even more wicked than the fangs, before the creature melted into a boneless stretch. The end of the stretch brought it one long step closer to its prey.

Nimue's voice slid gently through the terror. "Did you really believe what it said on those *Become A Witch For Fun And Profit* websites? That you could do what you want, have what you want, at no cost to you beyond a ton of spam in your email?"

Carol took a step back. The big cat answered it with one of its own, eyes narrowing.

"Magick *always* has a price, youngling."

Another step backward by the girl, another step forward by the cat.

"Pay it willingly, pay it unwillingly, it matters not which. You *will* pay it."

Halfway through the next step backwards, Carol's back bumped into the wall behind her. Eyes and mouth both wider with fright, she whimpered.

"Say you now, child," said Nimue in a voice that suddenly rang off the concrete and swirled around the girls like ritual robes, "if the price for the magick thou seekest to wield shall be paid and the deed it buys shall be done. Say you now!"

"Please!" Amber all but screamed. "We didn't know. We didn't mean it. Make it go away! Please make it stop!"

Nimue deliberately ignored everything but Carol. "Your spell, Carol. Your call. Yes or no?"

As if to prompt an answer, the panther again rumbled low in its throat. It crouched, settling back legs beneath it in preparation to spring. Carol threw her arms in front of her face, sobbing and babbling incoherently. As rubbery legs gave way and she slid down the wall, one word made it through intelligibly. "No."

Nimue smiled to herself and uttered a short gutteral phrase. From one eyeblink to the next, the panther was gone and the kitten was back. Crossing to it, Nimue bent down and picked it up, cuddling it for a moment before tucking it safely into the deep pocket of her jacket. Amber and Shelley both rushed to where Carol slumped, her back still to the wall.

Nimue gave them some time to recover before saying, "You three know I should call the cops, don't you? Or at least mall security?"

"Yes, ma'am," they replied in perfect unison.

"I'm going to do neither, if . . ." she let it hang for

the space of three heartbeats, "you agree to the following conditions. First, that you clean up this mess."

"Clean up. Yes, ma'am."

No one moved until Nimue raised one eyebrow. "I meant now."

"Oh!"

The older woman watched as they scrambled to comply like a trio of hyperactive Merry Maids. When blowing out the last candle plunged the room into total darkness, Nimue conjured pale blue light among the exposed conduits and pipes in the ceiling. So intent were the three on completing the first condition that none of them commented on it. They hardly seemed to notice. Eventually, every piece of paper, every pedestal and pillar, and every candle had been piled in the center of the room with the champagne bucket.

The spray-painted symbols on walls and floor were another matter, vigorous effort with various potions from their purses—nail polish remover, styling gel, pre-moistened toner towlettes, age-defying moisturizers—notwithstanding. Shelley turned frightened eyes toward Nimue. "They won't come off," she whispered.

"I'll take care of it." Raising her arms to shoulder-height, she began turning slowly around in place. Pseudo-arcane graffiti evaporated from every surface, as did the pile of props on the floor.

Once more, three young voices uttered, reverently and in perfect unison, "Wow."

"Well done, ladies. Now, the second condition for my not turning you over to the authorities is this: that you each, individually, swear that you will never, ever, try to do anything like this again. Who wants to go first?"

Amber, by virtue of being shoved forward by her

companions, volunteered. The glare she shot at the two changed to a look of apprehension as she found Nimue looking at her intently. "Will . . . will this involve blood?" she asked, voice shaking.

"No blood. Just your word. Now, what's your full name?"

The girl looked puzzled. "Amber Aimes."

"Your *full* name."

The girl looked even more puzzled. "Oh! Amber Katherine Aimes."

"Very good. Hold out your right hand, palm up, and listen very, very carefully." Nimue placed her own right hand over Amber's until the two palms almost touched. "Do you, Amber Katherine Aimes, before this company seen and unseen, pledge solemn oath by name and word, life and power, that you will not, from this hour to the ending of your days, seek the use of magick in bringing to harm any living being, regardless of provocation?"

"I . . . yeah . . . I . . . do?"

Nimue leaned forward and whispered, "As is my will, so mote it be."

Amber nodded and squared her thin shoulders. "As is my will, so mote it be."

As the last syllable sounded, brilliant silver light flashed from between the palms of the outstretched hands. "Awesome," breathed Amber.

Shelley found herself pushed into being next, and the process played out again, up to and including the flash of light. Then it was Carol's turn. "How will you know if we break our promise?"

Nimue said nothing for a long moment as her eyes caught those of the girls, each in turn. "Not 'promise.' Oath. And I'll know."

They all swallowed hard. They believed her . . . oh, indeed, they believed her.

"Now for the third condition. You will show me how you got in here."

Nimue followed as the girls went out the back door of the defunct shop, turned left into the tunnel, went less than twenty-five feet to the end, and exited the building through an unmarked service door. And, blessed be, she wouldn't have to hike to the other side of the mall to get to her car; they'd come out near the same entrance she'd come in originally. She could almost read her "Something Wiccan This Way Comes" bumper sticker from where she stood.

She turned and found the girls waiting for her to speak. "Thank you, ladies. There's one last condition. You will each go straight home, and spend the next few days thinking about how close you came to making a very big mistake."

"Yes, ma'am," they all replied before starting to leave.

They'd gone a few steps when Carol turned. "What about my kitten?"

Nimue gently patted her pocket. "He's found a new home. But I do have one more question for you. Why Hecate?"

The three girls looked at each other. "We learned it from a really powerful witch who called on Hecate all the time to do really amazing stuff. You know . . . Willow. On *Buffy*."

I should have known, Nimue thought. Then she remembered one of her favorite lines: "*Any girl with a period and a spice rack . . .*"

Like a familiar, **Kevin Andrew Murphy**'s short fiction keeps appearing various places, including Esther Friesner's *Chicks in Chainmail III: Chicks & Chained Males*, several anthologies for White Wolf's *World of Darkness*, and George R.R. Martin's Wild Cards series, including the latest volume, *Busted Flush*. Kevin's short story "Clove Smoke" is currently being turned into a film in San Francisco, the city of its birth. Kevin himself lives a bit further south in Silicon Valley with three whippets. He is a member and regular contributor to the group blog Deep Genre (www.deepgenre.com) and also has a personal website at http://www.sff.net/people/Kevin.A.Murphy

Tacos for Tezcatlipoca

Kevin Andrew Murphy

It had gone from one of those summers to *that* summer. The last summer before college or finding some sort of job more meaningful and lucrative than fast food. Dad and Mom, now divorced, were off with girlfriends and business trips, and Bryce Pierponte had been left to mind the farm, or at least the mission-style ranch house. He had enough money for food, a little gas, maybe a movie, but entertainment pretty much consisted of tv, internet and the odd garage sale.

And odd definitely applied to this one.

The contents of the old Seidel place, the farm from before the surrounding acreage had been transformed into subdivisions, had been turned out onto the actual carriage drive. There were dingy portraits that would probably be worth a mint on *Antiques Roadshow*, trays of gothy Victorian silver jewelry, crystal jars and pickle castors, piles of books, and this wacky taxidermy project that looked like someone had crossed a kitten with a spider monkey then added spare parts from a bat and a scorpion. "What's that?" Bryce asked.

The overdressed young woman tending to the sale smiled and pointed to the brass tag on the base. *Manticore Cub.*

This didn't tell Bryce much, but was entertaining anyway. "How much you want for it?"

She smiled brightly. "Oh, any of the usual: your soul, your shadow, the light in your eyes, the voice in your throat, the answer to a great mystery, or anything similar. Make me an offer."

Bryce nodded. Bargaining was fun, and this woman had a cute way of telling him that pretty much everything here was out of his price range. The rest of the people browsing the books and curios had the feel of old money, impeccably and eccentrically dressed in their overly fussy Sunday best, except for the ancient guy in the bathrobe and house slippers. He was probably the richest one there.

"I thought Mr. Seidel died years ago."

"Master Seidel did. Since he has not as yet returned, we're simply executing the last of his will." She continued to smile. "I do not recognize you. How did you know of the sale?"

Bryce shrugged, still looking at the 'manticore cub.' "I saw the gate open and I'd always been curious." He looked up. "Would that be the answer to a mystery?"

Still the smile. "I said 'great mystery.'"

"Okay," said Bryce, "it wasn't a ghost, it was a big dog painted with phosphorous."

"What?"

"The answer to a great mystery, the end of *The*

Hound of the Baskervilles." Bryce grinned. "Seems a bit Scooby Doo, but I guess standards were lower a hundred years ago."

The woman paused for a moment, considering, and then her smile became pained. "Well and fairly bargained, young master." She placed the stuffed monstrosity in his hands. "May your purchase bring you wonderment."

She went off to attend to the old guy in the bathrobe who was looking at a grandfather clock that could have belonged to Washington. Bryce left before she changed her mind.

Bryce had read about these critters. They were called Jenny Hanivers or Fiji mermaids, things whipped up by mad taxidermists a couple centuries back to fool clueless rubes at carnival peep-shows. It would probably go for a fortune on Ebay.

Of course, he kind of liked it himself. He regarded it, sitting in the middle of Mom's dining room table, grinning at him like a Cheshire cat. Actually, more like a Cheshire shark—it had three rows of teeth, and was stitched together so seamlessly it looked like a real creature. A real creature assuming God had got even more stoned than the day he made the platypus.

"Need to give you a name." Bryce thought a bit. "I know: Matabor." It was a name he used for online games, a serendipitous typo of 'matador,' but sounded just perfect for a manticore. Or manticore cub, according to the plaque.

He giggled slightly and patted it on the head. "Matabor, I choose you!"

Bryce snatched his hand back. The shark teeth were

shark sharp and a bright red drop welled up on the tip of his left ring finger.

The manticore cub's lips closed, then a long pink tongue licked them. "Matabor," the creature repeated squeakily like a Pokemon summoned for the first time. Then the little monstrosity yawned, stretched, and finally sat down on its base. It grinned at him. "Ancient charms." Its voice jingled like clockwork or digital cell phone bells. "A drop of heart's blood and one of the magician's names for my own. You've not only awakened me, young master, but bound me to your service." It grinned wider and more toothily. "Well done."

Bryce sucked on his ring finger, uncertain what to say. Several obscenities sprang to mind, but speaking blasphemy didn't seem a particularly good idea at a time like this.

The manticore—Matabor—swished its—his?—tail, a tail banded like a tabby cat's but tipped with a scorpion's sting. Blinking eyes bright as a monkey's, Matabor surveyed the dining room, at last looking askance at the evidence of Bryce's mother's questionable talent with watercolors.

Bryce was used to that look and the answer was automatic: "My mom took an art class."

"Then you get your training in the arts from your father?" Matabor surmised.

"Uh . . . no."

Matabor regarded him, tail swishing like a poisonous metronome. "Natural talent," the manticore cub mused. "Rare in a magician, but useful. Instinctive? You know the right words to say, the gestures spring to hand unbidden?"

"Um, I guess so. . . ." Bryce refrained from mentioning Pokemon cartoons and online gaming. "But, um, nothing like this has ever happened before. . . ."

"Unsurprising," Matabor said. "Most magic is jealously guarded. My old master wove spells and glamours to hide his treasures, then secreted his finest prize among gaudy baubles and lesser wonders, awaiting one canny enough to not only find it but charm its guardian beast. . . ."

Something shimmered distractingly in the corner of Bryce's eye, and while he wanted to keep all his attention on the walking talking hodgepodge of animal bits sitting in the middle of his mother's dining room table, he looked down further and saw that what he'd taken for the stained wooden base of a taxidermy project was in fact a very old leatherbound journal.

Matabor leapt aside on little cat feet. "Behold," said the manticore cub, pointing with his tail's sting, "my former master's formulary. . . ."

The formulary was mostly in English, thankfully, with little swatches of Greek, Latin, Arabic and Old Norse just to keep things interesting, 'interesting' in the same sense that Matabor brought 'wonderment.' The content, however, was a mix of dry theory and esoteric gobbledegook. But Bryce had the luck to be a natural magician, or at least he could cut through the waffle and figure out what Master Seidel had been trying to say.

Glamours were pretty simple. They worked like subliminal advertising, a pinch of truth supporting a false assumption. Bryce pointed his wand, actually the tapered handle of one of his mother's old watercolor brushes, and concentrated. "Appear as a cat."

With wink and a shimmer, Matabor's image changed. A ginger-striped tom sat on the table, looking at him.

Bryce squinted past the glamour, seeing where the kitty fur matched up in both lie and truth, but also perceiving the barest flicker of bat wings. "Appear as a bat."

This illusion was a bit less believable, mostly because it was kind of weird to see a fruitbat sprawled on the dining room table.

"Appear as a monkey," Bryce said, tracing the curl of Matabor's tail he saw beyond the bat glamour. Immediately a round-eyed monkey sat in the bat's place.

"Appear as a scorpion." The tip of the wand described the shape of a giant African scorpion he'd once seen in the bug house at the zoo, and the next moment one menaced the dining room. "Go back to the monkey," Bryce said quickly, dismissing his last illusion.

Matabor the monkey regarded him. "Does this Seeming please you, Master Bryce?"

"More than the scorpion." Bryce shuddered. "And if anyone spots you doing something weird, a monkey will explain it better than a cat. Anyway, wizards with cats are overdone."

"Wizards are dull creatures," the monkey remarked, clambering to his shoulder. "Magicians are far more interesting."

Bryce raised an eyebrow, but wasn't going to ask for extra clarification just yet. Seidel's formulary wasn't particularly clear on distinctions, and Matabor often less so.

He turned back to the open workbook. "Are you sure this spell is necessary right now?"

"You have no guardian save me," Matabor explained, "and most skilled in the arts have been about for centuries. It is best to start in the present if you wish to have a future."

The book was open to the section on IMMORTALITY, and like everything else, it was badly organized. But amid references to everything from spells for stealing bodies to ways to become undead—the former dismissed by Master Seidel as *Potentially amusing, but an unnecessary complication*, the later as *A problem, not a solution*—there were two long passages in Greek, attributed to the sorceress Medea: The Greater and Lesser Baths of Hebe, Goddess of Youth.

Her Greater Bath was pretty extreme, requiring not just owl heads and a sacrificial ram, but slashing the throat of the subject then boiling them into a skeleton before rolling them in an elaborate rib rub. This would supposedly cause their flesh to spring back onto their bones, miraculously restoring the aged to youth and vigor. There was obviously a huge chance for screw-up and an even bigger need for a competent assistant if one wanted to use the spell oneself.

In comparison, the Lesser Bath looked like something out of Martha Stewart, basically herbal Oil of Olay plus a simple lunar ritual to keep the subject from aging for the span of one moon. Daily flossing as opposed to oral surgery. As an added bonus, Hebe's blessing would work as misdirection: Most ancient practitioners, on spotting Her astral signature, would assume Bryce had been using Medea's beauty secret for centuries, as opposed to just starting this month—a false assumption supported by an ounce of truth, the same as any glamour.

Or at least that's what his new familiar advised.

Matabor clung to Bryce's shoulder. "Can we acquire the necessary herbs at the bazaar?"

"Most of them. But these days it's called the Farmers' Market."

One corner of the mall parking lot had been taken over by booths and tables selling organic fruits and vegetables, artisanal bread, artisanal cheeses, kettle corn, cheesy corn, cheesy music and face painting. "*Get some of the ceremonial pigments,*" Matabor whispered, and Bryce spent some of the meager supply of bills that were supposed to last him the summer on a set of 'Be A Clown!' fun-and-safe non-toxic face paints. Of course the alternative was being seen at the drugstore trying out shades of lipstick and eyeshadow. The face paints were a bargain at half the price.

"Hey Pierponte, where'd ya get the monkey?"

Bryce turned. It was Gwen Heffernan, second-string cheerleader and class sleaze, trying for the sexy farmgirl look with a strategically knotted plaid shirt but only succeeding in the sunburnt cleavage look. The same Gwen who, junior year, had asked him to the Sadie Hawkins dance and even got him to show up with a corsage before blowing him off for Zack Schmidt.

"Begone, slattern!" hissed Matabor.

Gwen looked at him. "What did your monkey just call me?"

The strength of glamours lay in suggestion, offering a prettier lie than the bald truth. "It's a monkey," said Bryce, glancing to Matabor. "*Monkeys say 'Ook.'* What do you think it said?"

Unfortunately, Gwen was just stupid enough to

believe in talking monkeys. "It kind of sounded like it called me a slut. . . ."

" 'Ook,' " Matabor repeated pointedly.

Gwen looked at both of them. "You're a serious geek, Pierponte," she pronounced at last. "Monkeys *and* ventriloquism? Wait till I tell everyone. . . ." She flounced off into the crowd.

"Highschool's over, Gwen!" Bryce called after her lamely, a minute too late, then looked at Matabor. "Everyone's going to think I'm nuts."

The monkey grinned. "Wizards are mad. Magicians are eccentric."

Bryce checked the formulary. He had procured a virgin brazier. He'd first read it as 'virgin's brassiere' and wondered what sort of kinky magician old man Seidel had been, but after rereading and consulting Matabor, he figured out it meant a charcoal grill that had never been used. A new Weber seemed fine, and dad had one from pre-divorce Father's Day that had never been out of the box. And charcoal was thankfully still charcoal. Now for the fragrant woods . . .

"Are the gods more pleased with hickory or mesquite?"

Matabor, again in manticore cub form, switched his poisonous tail. "The bazaar had no sandalwood and gum tragacanth?"

"Unfortunately no. Maybe the candleshop at the mall?"

Matabor glanced to the sky. "Nightfall is nigh upon us. The moon will not favor us so for a month."

Meaning it was time to make a guess and hope Hebe liked hickory and mesquite as much as Bryce's parents. They were wood, they were fragrant, and they were both on the coals. The olive branch, obtained from the trees planted outside The Olive Garden, was used to stir the brew as Bryce added the Martha Stewart-esque *bouquet garni* of herbs to his mother's stock pot, then set forth the ritual offering of flat breads, spiced meat and cheeses. He worked part time at the Taco Bell-Pizza Hut-KFC combo, so the last was easily done, plus they had free hot sauce. Bryce squirted the charcoal starter and watched the flames leap as the bag caught fire.

It didn't seem right to burn perfectly good tacos and skip dinner, but that had to be the definition of 'sacrifice' and 'fasting.' Plus the reward looked reasonably worth it: immortality at the price of monthly taco incineration. And since Bryce's dad had gone bald by twenty, eternal youth sounded like a better plan than Rogaine too.

Making older magicians overestimate his age would also be nice.

Bryce broke out the 'ceremonial pigments' and his mom's auto-defogging battery-operated magnifying mirror, another household item that doubled as magical focus. He did his best to mark his brow with the symbol of Hebe, a golden cup filled with ambrosia, food of the gods. The gold cup was easy, but Seidel had left no notes as to what color ambrosia actually was. Bryce suspected the gods' favorite dish was not in fact coconut mandarin marshmallow salad. On inspiration, he used the brown facepaint, filling the cup with the other food of the gods: chocolate.

The hot tub worked for the sacred bath, and the herbal infusion Bryce added to the water smelled like one of his mother's bath bombs. Now to just take the plunge . . .

"Enter the water skyclad," Matabor reminded him.

Bryce remembered looking up the term. "Well duh." He shucked off his shirt and shorts and got into the hot tub.

He was a teenager alone in his own backyard. Who didn't use a hot tub in the buff?

The steam cleared and Bryce realized he'd fallen asleep in the tub. He turned off the jets, feeling boiled and no younger. It was already daylight as he stepped out and toweled off.

"Make haste, master. Make haste," Matabor stressed, but instead of a small kind-of-creepy-cute manticore cub, Bryce was looking at a full-size manticore, full size meaning the size of a Buick with teeth like a great white. "Don the garb of a supplicant and climb atop my back."

Bryce balked, then realized Matabor had said "atop my back" and not "in my belly." He quickly complied, straddling the great beast. He noticed that he'd somehow gotten on his Taco Bell-KFC-Pizza Hut uniform and now had the take-out bag in his hands, no longer incinerated.

They flew through the air, flying on winds scented with mesquite and hickory, until they landed atop a high plateau. There stood a temple with a great mirror, remarkably similar to Mom's make-up mirror but on a grand scale, smoking and shining like the sun.

Guards appeared, men in spotted loincloths with skull-faced masks and obsidian spears.

Lots of obsidian spears.

Bryce bowed his head and presented the take-out bag. One guard took it, opening it suspiciously, then they conferred. Whatever they said was Greek to Bryce, but one left with the bag, coming back a few minutes later with a goblet made from a gilded skull. There was something thick and reddish-brown inside. There was also a very clear implication that Bryce was expected to drink and refusing would not be good for his health, physical or spiritual.

Bryce drank, and the taste was bittersweet. But it burned. . . .

Bryce awoke to the taste of chocolate and taco sauce. This wasn't surprising, considering the empty Taco Bell packets, the open can of cocoa powder, and half the contents of the spice rack littering the counters. There was a recipe scribbled in his own handwriting on a sheet of paper affixed to the front of the refrigerator, and he was standing nude in the kitchen, holding a gold plastic skull mug his parents had got in Vegas at Treasure Island.

"What the hell happened?"

"You are a natural magician." Matabor lounged on the counter and grinned. "I have never visited that god before."

Bryce recalled more of his dream—vision—whatever, then looked at the name scribbled atop the insane recipe on the refrigerator: The Immortal Draught of Tezcatlipoca.

He took a sip of the mixture in the skull mug, then set it down. The burning in his mouth and throat had not been a dream.

Bryce consulted old man Seidel's formulary, trying

to make better sense of what had happened, finally finding a note that certain incenses and smokes were sacred to certain gods, but sacred didn't mean pleasing, it meant specific. It wasn't just a matter of making things smell nice, it was more like using the right zip code, and offerings were similar. So instead of using a spell to deliver gyros to Hebe, he'd taken tacos to Tezcatlipoca, and in exchange apparently been given Tezcatlipoca's recipe for Ding Dongs and taco sauce.

Then came the sound of bells, and it wasn't Matabor purring. It was his cell phone. Bryce missed the call, but the message was clear: He was late for work.

Combining a KFC with a Pizza Hut and a Taco Bell made sense like a manticore did: It looked better once you actually saw it together.

Matabor, on the other hand, currently looked like a monkey. Which might be cute for the Farmers' Market, but wouldn't cut it with Jim the shift supervisor. Bryce had his familiar hide in his backpack, along with the formulary, and stowed them both in the supply closet.

Bryce was also not feeling well. He'd spent the night in the hot tub, eaten nothing the night before, and now had a belly full of chocolate and taco sauce. Five minutes into his shift, he excused himself to the restroom. He was sweating profusely and starting to get hives, or at least spots. Black spots, all over his body. Bryce shut himself in the bathroom stall, watching as his fingernails lengthened into claws, then felt the pain as his canine teeth became more feline and he hunched over the toilet, puking up the chocolate and taco sauce mixture as he convulsed and transformed, his ears moving up on his head, his hands shrinking into clawed paws, and a tail emerging and getting painfully cramped and tangled in his underwear.

At last the convulsions stopped, and Bryce reached out with a paw and batted the toilet handle, flushing it. Once it cleared, he looked down and took in his reflection. He was a jaguar. A jaguar in a KFC-Taco Bell-Pizza Hut uniform.

The door of the bathroom opened. "Bryce, you fall in?" It was Jim.

"Uh, no." Bryce said. "Just, uh, a little sick."

"Damn, well, get over it soon. We're going to get slammed with the commute crowd."

Bryce was left alone, a jaguar in a restroom stall. Okay, a talking jaguar in a restroom stall. Bryce looked into the toilet. *"Yo quiero Taco Bell."* He giggled slightly. They'd fired the Taco Bell chihuahua. Would they want a Taco Bell jaguar?

He had to find some way to change back, but Matabor and the formulary were in the supplies closet, and even the paintbrush he used for a wand in case he wanted to cast a glamour. If he could hold a paintbrush in this form, which didn't seem too likely.

He had to think. He'd drunk a potion, a magical brew invented by an Aztec god, and while it was neat to have discovered something not in Seidel's formulary, writing it down in Pierponte's formulary required changing back.

Bryce thought. The common wisdom when dealing with a poison was to throw up, and if that didn't work, drink lots of milk or water. A potion shouldn't be very different.

Bryce looked at the toilet. There was no way he was operating the soda machine in his current state, and it's not like dogs didn't do it. . . .

Jim checked in three times before Bryce was done. He was still spotty, and he'd had to piss like a racehorse, or at least an anthropomorphic jaguar man, but at least he was able to able to stand up on two legs. "Appear as usual. . . ." Bryce said into the mirror, watching as a glamour of his normal Seeming overlaid the hybrid form he was in now. He had realized that while a wand was a focus, an extended conductor to cast magic at another creature, a mirror worked too.

Jim was grumbling but didn't stop Bryce from opening the dairy case and downing three single-serving cartons of milk before starting in on his shift. Bryce had a bit of trouble, since Nachos Bel Grande and Personal Pan Pizzas weren't intended to be made with claws, but his shift supervisor didn't care. He was there and it was the commute slam.

"Taco Pizza KFC, may I take your order?"

"Yeah, Pierponte." Gwen Heffernan's whiny voice came over the intercom, and when he looked at the video monitor, he saw her and her friends in her dad's convertible. "You can."

Bryce took her order. "I'll make it personally."

"There better not be any monkey fur in it. If I find any monkey fur, I'll have my brother punch your face in."

"No, no monkey fur," Bryce promised.

The formula sprang to mind unbidden, Tezcatlipoca's sacred brew for his jaguar priests, mostly chocolate and spices and certain herbs. A jaguar had a sensitive nose and all it took was a pinch of the Colonel's secret blend, a squirt of taco sauce, and a few splashes of chocolate milk.

"Enjoy your order," Bryce said, handing the bag to Gwen.

"Are these *diet* Pepsis?"

"Of course. Enjoy."

"We will. Later, loser."

By the time Bryce finished up his shift, his actual form had pretty much synched up with his illusory Seeming, the last of the draught of Tezcatlipoca leaving his system. The police were in, hanging out at their usual table, and talking the night's business.

A convertible had been found abandoned on the side of the road, the keys still in it. And someone had been reporting leopards escaped from the zoo.

Jaguars, Bryce corrected mentally, then stifled a chuckle. Let Gwen and her friends discover their own toilets.

Just before closing, an old man came up to the counter. "May I take your order?" asked Bryce.

"You bought Seidel's formulary," the old man said, his eyes twinkling. "The one with Medea's spells."

Bryce recognized the old man from the estate sale. He'd swapped his bathrobe for a rumpled sportcoat, but it was the same man. "Excuse me?"

"No need to play coy," the old man said. "I just saw your work. Jaguars? Very nice. I hadn't realized that was in the formulary."

"Um, that's my own," Bryce said. "Actually, Tezcatlipoca's."

"Oh? Where did you find it?"

"In a dream."

The old man looked favorably impressed. "Pleased

to meet you. You may call me, oh, Roger Bacon." He squinted at Bryce's nametag. "And I suppose I should call you Bryce, given your current Seeming."

"You're a wizard."

The old man looked insulted. "Please, forgive my youthful follies. I'm a fellow magician. We magicians don't concern ourselves with petty nonsense like good and evil. Leave that to wizards and the sillier witches."

"And magicians?"

"Range from the entertaining to the wicked. Usually both." He smiled. "I can tell you're new to the area, but I'd really like to get that jaguar spell, and the others would love to hear about it. We meet on Fridays over on Frisby Street in the back room at Denny's."

Bryce nodded and the old man chuckled again. "Tezcatlipoca's jaguar spell. Oh, wait till the boys hear about this. There's so much more to vengeance spells than frivolous death curses, don't you agree?"

"Yes," said Bryce, "couldn't agree more. Fridays at Denny's?"

"Fridays," the old man agreed. "Bring, oh, five or ten new spells. Show the others what tricks you've been up to the past century."

"Past century?"

"Just the past century. Leave some surprises for later meetings. After all, we have all the time in the world." He looked up at the board and mused. "But for right now, I think I'll have a Nachos Bel Grande." He leaned forward conspiratorially. "Magic makes life interesting, and it's always interesting to reinvent oneself, isn't it?"

"Yes," Bryce agreed. "Yes, it is."

Hildy Silverman is the publisher of *Space and Time*, a 42-year-old magazine featuring fantasy, horror, and science fiction. She is also the author of several works of short fiction, including "The Soul Cloister" (2003, *Wild Child*), "Play Misty for Me" (2004, *The Adventures of Mist and Vale*, Ordover, ed.), "Picky" (2008, *Dark Territories*, Frank and SanGiovanni, eds.), and "Damned Inspiration" (forthcoming, *Siren Songs*, Ackley-McPhail, ed). She is a member of the Philadelphia Science Fiction Society and the Garden State Horror Writers. In the "real" world, she is a freelance consultant who develops corporate training and marketing communications materials for high-tech corporations.

The Darren

Hildy Silverman

When Mariah Gottkind was a five-year-old, she found out that she was allergic to cats. Every time she got within a foot of a cat, her eyes watered and swelled. Within inches, she'd wheeze like a discarded accordion. None of it kept Mariah from yearning for one of the furry familiars.

"Cats are bad for you!" Her mother, at the end of her rope, once yelled. "Just stay away from them and you won't suffer. How hard is that to figure out?"

Little Mariah considered her words and stated, "But I *want* one." In response, her mother turned beet red and caused a row of knickknacks to fling themselves to their deaths on the parquet floor.

That was a good twelve years ago. Mariah knew she'd outgrown such stubbornness.

She set Miss Thang down on the sofa, where the tabby licked her paws and regarded Mariah with serene golden eyes.

"It's just a dance." Mariah reached for a tissue and dabbed her nose.

Miss Thang switched her tail to the left.

"I'm not having a *litter* with anyone at the Fall Ball, thank you very much." Mariah rolled her eyes.

Miss Thang reminded her of Prudie Barrows. Prudie'd eloped with a Darren *ubermensch* the summer after she graduated from high school and returned to find that she was no longer welcome in Coventry. The little *uberbaby* growing in her womb failed to soften the hearts of her parents or the town Elders.

Prudie wound up slinking out of town and moving to Poughkeepsie with her Darren and little Halfling, leaving behind only a cautionary tale and a curse— something about perpetually rebellious children.

"If I don't go with Sarah, she's the one who's going to wind up banished to Poughkeepsie," said Mariah. "My chaperoning her is a selfless act."

Miss Thang turned and proffered her hindquarters.

Mariah sighed and scratched the base of the cat's tail. "You always expect the worst from me." She glanced at her watch. "Oh, damn, I've got to get dressed." She hurried upstairs to her room, ignoring Miss Thang's final *meow* on the subject.

Mariah popped an allergy pill and put drops in her itchy eyes. She pulled on a simple, fitted black dress and slid into a pair of low-heeled black ankle boots. She eyed the silver pentacle necklace her grandmother had given her for her Ascension but decided against it. Not because she was ashamed or afraid of advertising her beliefs. It wasn't that at all.

When she returned downstairs, her parents were

waiting. "Well, I'm going." She meant to sound upbeat, but it came out defensive.

Her mother, a woman comprised of equal parts bitterness and resentment, turned to her father and said, "This is your doing. I wanted her to go to a nice, private school with her own kind, but *noooooo*." She crossed her arms and glared. "You had to go all *egalitarian*!"

Her father shrugged. "It's important that she know how to live with all kinds of people. It's the reality of the world we live in, Poopsie."

"Don't you 'Poopsie' me," her mother grumbled.

"I've got to go." Mariah scooted around her parents and grabbed the car keys. "I won't be back late, I promise."

Mother followed her to the door. "Midnight, or your father sends a whirlwind to level that so-called school!"

"Whatever." Mariah opened the door and waved absently behind her. "Have a good night."

"Stay away from those *other* boys. There'll be at least a few of your own kind to dance with." Her parents followed her out onto the porch.

Mariah resisted the urge to sprint to her car. "I won't dance with anyone," she said, "I'll just stand in front of the punch bowl and look menacing."

"Do you hear how she talks to me?" Mother turned to Dad and waved her arms.

"Poopsie, please." Dad put trembling hands on her shoulders. "If you keep gesturing like that you're going to zap a hole through the house. Again."

"I'm just hanging out with Sarah, that's all," Mariah said. She edged halfway into her car; escape was nigh. "Don't worry."

"Don't worry, she says. You forget what they've

done to our kind. Salem, England—not that long ago in the grand scheme of things!"

This was an old rant and Mariah could replay it in her head without hearing another word. She slammed the door to her car and revved the engine.

In the rearview mirror, Mariah saw her mother gesticulating on the porch while her father kept intercepting her hands and pulling them down to her sides. Mariah sighed and drove off to Sergeant York High.

Sarah greeted her at the door to the gym with her arm looped through Danny Taverse's. Any hope Mariah had held of the two of them hanging out and snarking on their classmates' dance abilities was dashed.

"Hey, Sarah. Danny." Mariah barely glanced at him, though she did manage to keep her smile plastered on her face.

"Ry! You did come!" Sarah let go of Danny and gave her a hug. She quickly whispered in Mariah's ear, *"OhmygawdessDanny'sbeenallovermesinceIgothere!"* She pulled away and relocked arms with Danny.

"Hey," said Danny. He couldn't have sounded less interested if he were comatose.

Mariah's cheeks ached. She wasn't used to keeping a smile glued on for so long and this one was taking more effort than usual. "Hey, Dan. How's . . . stuff?"

He shrugged.

"Glad to hear it." Mariah locked eyes with Sarah. *What do you think you're doing?* she sent.

Sarah cocked her head to one side. *Are you kidding? Look at him!*

Mariah looked. She saw what she always saw when she looked at Danny: a passably attractive guy who spent a lot of time in the gym compensating for the extra inches denied to him by Nature. *You're not going to go Bewitched on me, are you?* Mariah sent.

Sarah's eyes narrowed. *Don't be such a bigot.* She turned to Danny and batted her heavily mascara-coated lashes. "Oo, I love this song. Let's go back in!"

Danny's face lit up as though a switch had been flipped. "Yeah, sure babe. Let's tear it up!" As they walked away, his hand slid down and cupped Sarah's right butt cheek.

"Yeah, okay, I guess I'll see you in there. Don't worry about me." Mariah's smile melted away. So much for Sarah wanting a chaperone. Not to say she didn't *need* one.

Once inside, Mariah quickly located a long table set with all the unhealthy necessities for a school dance. After ladling some suspiciously-green punch into a plastic cup, she positioned herself against the wall and tried to look comfortable.

How could she call me a bigot? Mariah frowned into her drink. How was it bigoted to be concerned about the potential, very-real consequences of her best friend's actions? She knew Sarah had been nursing a crush on Danny for awhile. The surprise was that he reciprocated.

Mariah watched Sarah and Danny dance amidst a sea of students. The majority were plain humans whose parents fancied themselves open minded enough to let their kids go to school alongside witches.

"Separate but equal," Mariah mused. More like "separate but separate." Sure, there were friendships that crossed party lines, but for the most part cliques were based on common interests—and abilities.

Mariah had never seen Danny so into anything other than his between-class weed breaks behind the school. He was a simple sort, even by Darren standards. Yet here he was, busting out what she assumed were his best moves—poor *shlub*—and looking at Sarah like she was wrapped in EZ Wider. It wasn't natural.

A fishy feeling stirred in Mariah's stomach. She eyed the punch, but decided it wasn't entirely at fault. Did Sarah do something to get Danny's attention beyond slapping on three coats of Sephora's finest and shimmying into a skin-tight red dress?

Sarah looked over Danny's shoulder at her and winked. Mariah tried to hold her gaze and sent, *Sar, did you do anything to Danny?* But Sarah either didn't receive her or chose not to answer. She simply twirled in for a quick dip that revealed her lacy panties to anyone who cared to see. A couple of Danny's buddies glanced over, snickered, and jabbed one another in the ribs.

Classy. Still, Mariah was worried that the real problem was Sarah. Love spells were pretty strict no-no's, as were any emotion-manipulating castings. Using magic to ensnare a Darren could necessitate discipline by the Elders.

Mariah swallowed the rest of her punch in a single gulp and crushed the plastic cup in her hand. She had to step in, convince Sarah to dispel whatever she'd cast, before anyone in authority noticed.

She plowed a path through gyrating couples. She was almost to Sarah and Danny's side when someone caught her arm and pulled her around.

"Hey, Ry! I didn't know you were gonna be here." Sam Rivera beamed at her with more enthusiasm than Mariah thought was actually called for. She'd known Sam since freshman year and he was in three of her classes this year. He was a good guy for one of them.

My Goddess. She grimaced. *I really am kind of a bigot.*

Sam was an interesting hybrid, by human standards. He once told her that his mother was half African-American, half Navajo and his father was a Brazilian Jew. From what Mariah could see, it was a good genetic result. She wasn't sure why he'd confided so much about himself, but he was pleasant enough that she didn't mind.

"Oh, hi, Sam," she said. Her eyes were still on Danny and Sarah shimmying nearby. "I didn't know you were, uh, here."

"Paris Hilton stood me up, so. . . ." He shrugged. "I'm glad you made it. I didn't think this was your scene."

"I was conned into coming." She pointed over his shoulder.

He looked, then turned back and nodded knowingly. "Sarah suckered you into coming, huh?"

"Said she didn't want to risk being the lone wall-flower." Mariah snorted. "Not much danger of that."

"Somehow I can't picture you—either of you—pinned against the wall alone." He looked her up and down and his eyebrows twitched. "You clean up nicely."

Mariah looked at him for the first time and thought, *So do you*. She liked his tie; a black background with a hand-painted red dragon blowing flames. "Where'd you get that?" she asked, giving it a flip.

"Oh, this?" He chuckled, cheeks reddening. "Picked it up at a con last year."

"I can't believe you go to those things." She laughed.

"I'm surprised you don't."

She tilted her head to one side. "Why?" Her good humor withered. "We're not all Goths, you know. Just because we practice magic doesn't mean. . . ."

"Whoa, whoa!" He raised his hands. "I meant because you seemed to really like that Bradbury book we read in Lit class last year. Geeze, over-sensitive, much?"

"Yes, very much." Embarrassment warmed her face. *Get out of my psyche, Mother!* She offered an apologetic grin. "Sorry, Sam. I'm just feeling a little bit . . . vulnerable tonight." She gestured around them. "My kind's not exactly in the majority."

"I wouldn't know from majorities." He poked her stomach playfully.

She felt herself relax for the first time that night. Sam was so easy to hang out with. Except she shouldn't be hanging. She had a mission to accomplish.

"Say," said Sam, "since we're here with friends who've decided to totally ignore us, would you like to take a spin 'round the floor? With, um, me?"

Mariah glanced over at where Danny and Sarah had been boogying moments before. She blinked at their absence and her heart sank to her boots. "Did you see where they went?"

"Who?"

"Sarah and . . . oh, damn it." She'd blown it. She'd let herself get distracted and now they were probably off conceiving a next-gen Halfling. "I've got to go."

She caught the disappointed look in Sam's eyes and added, "I'm really sorry, but I've got to stop—er, find—Sarah. It's kind of major."

Sam brightened. "Then I'll assist you in your mission. Lead on!"

Grateful for the company, Mariah led Sam through the crowd toward the spot she'd last seen Sarah and Danny. She hesitated when she saw the plastic cup knocked over on the floor where they'd been. Had one or both of them drunk out of it? If so, that would give her somewhere to start.

She scooped up the cup and cradled it in her left palm. As casually as possible, she closed her eyes and pressed her forehead to the rim. She murmured a couple of seeking Words.

"What are you doing?" Sam asked. She ignored him, focusing instead on the image forming in her mind.

It was dark, but soon she was able to make out two figures. They were snuggled together in a confined space. Every so often, the heads came together and she felt an empathic rush of heat.

Mariah hastily broke from the vision and blinked at Sam. He looked at her with expectation and just a trace of fear. "Wh . . . what's up?"

She didn't have time to explain the mechanics. "I think they're in a car. Come on!" She turned and scampered for the door, not checking to see if Sam was following her. It was probably for the best if he didn't.

Out in the parking lot she found Sam was right behind her. "You want to tell me what the problem is?" He struggled to catch his breath.

"The problem?" How could she explain it so that he understood? She considered her words carefully, even as she dashed from car to car, peering into back seats. "Sam, you know how you told me your great-grandfather said that prayer for the dead when your grandfather married your grandmother?"

"*Kaddish*. What about it?" He paused and answered his own question. "Oh. Oh! Danny's a Darren and Sarah's a—not."

Mariah turned and looked at him, surprised. "Where'd you hear that term?"

"What, Darren? Please." He snorted. "You think no one hears you guys talking about us like that?"

"Oh, we don't mean anything by it. It's just a silly way to describe you." As soon as she said it, she wanted to crawl under the chassis of the Ford she'd just inspected.

"Yeah, well, us *guys* really appreciate being equated with some Sixties sitcom bozo. Thanks for that." Sam glared. "I guess that we should just call you Endoras or . . . what was the kid's name?"

"Tabitha." This conversation made her feel like shoe scrapings. "Yeah, well, your kind's called us a lot worse, right before they squashed us under rocks or strung us up!"

"And shit's never happened to another people on Earth, just yours."

Stop it, he didn't do anything! Yet her mouth kept going, as if possessed. "Fine, you're right. The difference is that we're *still* the oddballs, the ones to watch out for lest we rise up and exert our great powers!"

She waggled her fingers at him. "Oogy-boogy! Fear me! Never mind that there's hardly any of us left and we've got zero interest in seizing control of anything beyond our own destiny, which, by the way, is still at the mercy of your sort. The day someone comes into power again who thinks we're too much of a risk, you'll see us rounded up and marched into bonfires like it was 1599!"

Sam stared at her, open-mouthed. All the fury leaked out of her at once. "Sam, I'm . . . I don't know where that came from." That was a lie of course; she knew exactly where—no, *whom* it had come from.

"I'll see you in class," said Sam. He started back to the gym, but then hesitated and looked back at her. "You know, there are such things as individuals. 'I' does not equate to 'all of humanity.'" He nearly added something else, but then just walked away.

"Sam." She couldn't summon the energy to chase him. Besides, Sarah and her unauthorized love spelling were still her foremost concerns.

She continued her search through the parking lot, pondering the effects of maternal brainwashing. She caught one couple half-undressed in the back of a well-aged LeBaron, but it wasn't Sarah and Danny. She waved a halfhearted apology and considered giving up.

"Hey!"

Mariah turned, surprised to see Sam. She was even more startled by the surge of relief she felt at his return. "What's up?"

Sam jogged over to her, looking deeply worried. "Ry, there's something I've got to tell you."

"Go on." Her pulse thudded in her ears.

"I went back into the gym to cool off." He cleared his throat. "You know, 'cause we were running . . . it's warm out."

"Sure." She bit her lower lip and looked away.

"Yeah, well, I overheard Rich and Oliver. Danny's buds?" He put his fingertips to his lips and mock-inhaled. "They were talking about how Danny came here tonight with an agenda."

"Which was?"

Sam stuck his hands in his pants pockets and stared at his feet. "Apparently, Danny's been onto Sarah's interest in him and decided she'd be a heck of a notch on his bedpost—so to speak."

"Oh, Hecate." Mariah closed her eyes and tilted her face heavenward. Here she'd pinned the blame on Sarah, when all the time it was a simple boy-plays-girl, boy-lays-girl scenario.

She opened her eyes and fixed them on Sam. "Do you know where Danny is?"

Sam nodded. "Where's the most clichéd place to take a girl for her first time?"

Together, they said, "The bleachers."

"Exactly." Sam held out his hand. "Shall we go save the fair maiden's honor?"

"If she has any left," said Mariah.

They sprinted across the lot to the football field. Mariah could see two shadows wriggling in the narrow space between the first and second row of bleachers. She was close enough to shout when Sam snagged her wrist.

"Hold up," he said, "are we actually going to yell at them like angry parents? 'Cause I don't see that resulting in a positive outcome."

He had a point. Sarah'd be mortified and she wouldn't believe a word that came out of Mariah's mouth. She and Sam might prevent immediate con-summation of Danny's plan, but they couldn't police Sarah 24/7 thereafter.

No, if anyone was going to stop Danny for good, it would have to be Sarah herself.

Mariah waved Sam behind a clump of trees at

the edge of the football field. "I've got an idea but it involves me doing something that might make you, uh, nervous."

Sam shrugged. "What've you got in mind?"

"A little hocus to stop the pocus." She nodded toward the rocking Trans Am. "You know it's pretty much illegal and definitely unethical for me to use magic on a Dar . . . dude."

Sam placed his right hand over his heart and held up the left. "They'd have to pry my testimony out of my cold, dead mouth."

She grinned and nodded. "Okay, then."

She searched her memory for the words to an enchantment she'd learned as a kid from *My First Book of Spells*. It was simple but, hopefully, efficient enough to accomplish what she needed.

She sketched a pentacle into the ground with a twig and rested her fingertips on the uppermost point. Drawing power from the Earth, she chanted:

> "*I am rubber;*
> *You are glue;*
> *Whatever Danny says;*
> *Must be true.*"

Sam snorted.

"I know it ain't Shakespeare," Mariah sighed, "but it should 'git 'er done.'"

"So, how will we know it worked?"

Danny flew off the bleacher and landed with a puff of dirt on his rear.

Mariah jumped and Sam grabbed her by both arms. They huddled close enough that she could smell Sam's nice, spicy aftershave.

"You son of a toad!" Sarah stood over Danny. Her

face was redder than her disheveled dress. Her hair looked like it'd been combed by bats.

"I'm sorry!" Danny crab-scuttled away from Sarah, eyes wide from confusion and terror. "I don't know why I said that . . . *you easy, sleazy, broom hugger.*"

Danny slapped both hands over his mouth. Sarah balled up her fists and screamed.

"Awesome." Sam squeezed her arms. "This is better than *Passions!*"

Mariah couldn't help but grin. He enjoyed soaps *and* dark vengeance? The more she learned about Sam, the more she liked.

Sarah raised her hands and began weaving a pattern in the air. Wherever her fingers passed, sparks flashed and remained; a weave of magic that grew brighter and larger.

Uh, oh, thought Mariah.

Danny flipped onto his knees and clasped his hands. "Please, oh, please, don't!" he gibbered. "I can't. Stop my. Mouth. I . . . *bet you levitate when you come.* Oh, God!" He clawed at the ground, came up with a handful of leaves, and shoved them into his mouth.

"You'll never find out," said Sarah. She took a deep breath.

Mariah leapt out from behind the trees. She cleared the space between her and Sarah in mere moments.

Not fast enough.

Sarah completed her command just as Mariah tackled her. They both wound up on the turf with stray gravel in their knees. Mariah yelped, but quickly forgot her pain when a sizeable demon popped into their reality.

"Holy shit!" understated Danny. He turned a shade of white usually reserved for vampires.

"Whoa." Sam hugged the tree closest to him and looked down at Mariah. She didn't need to be able to read his mind to know exactly what he was thinking, *I didn't know you guys could do* that!

Well, they could. It wasn't easy and it sure as hell wasn't permitted, barring very extreme conditions such as advancing, torch-wielding villagers. Sarah had obviously achieved a level of furious emotion that boosted her normal abilities from *teen witch* to *dark lord*. Even Sarah looked stunned to see what she'd wrought.

The demon stood about eight-odd feet tall, with green-gray scaled skin and eyes the shade of bile. It stank of excreted gym socks and looked pissed enough to eat them all, which, if Mariah remembered her Sunday school class on the habits of Dark creatures correctly, it might just.

"What were you *thinking?*" she hissed.

Sarah pushed her aside and sat up, rubbing her scraped knees. "Do you have any idea what he said to me?" She jabbed a finger at Danny, who curled into a ball and wept. "There we were, making out, when he all of a sudden tells me that his new nickname's Danny the Witch Layer. That mother . . . !"

"Yeah, well, don't you think this is a little extreme?" Mariah stood up with a groan and nodded at the demon.

Sarah sulked. "Maybe."

"MEAT," said the demon. Twin, pointed tongues darted out of the corners of its too-wide mouth and licked its thick, black lips. It bared triple-rows of fangs and reiterated, *"MMMMMMMMMMEEEEEEEE-AAAAAAAAAAATTTTTTTTTTTTTT!"*

"I'm peeing!" Danny declared in all honesty.

"Um, Ry? Suggestions?" Sam had released his tree and made his way to her side. His eyes never left the monstrosity looming nearby. Mariah had to give him props; most boys would've already sprinted off like a cartoon avian with an Acme-armed coyote on his tail.

"Send it back, Sar! Dismiss it before it's too . . . !"

The demon plucked Danny off the ground, unhinged its jaw, and stuck Danny's entire head in its mouth.

Mariah grabbed Sarah's hand. Sarah clutched hers in return. Together they shouted, *"Freeze!"*

The demon, Danny's thrashing legs, and even the wind in their immediate vicinity stopped.

Mariah let out her breath in a whoosh. Raw instinct, fueled by stark terror, could work wonders.

"Well," said Sam. He shook his head in amazement. "I guess that takes care of that." He hustled over to Danny, grabbed his dangling legs, and yanked him out of the demon's lolling maw. He dropped to the turf under the bulkier boy's frozen weight.

"It's only temporary," said Mariah. A quick exam revealed that Danny's head was still firmly attached, although a triple ring of red droplets on his neck attested to just how close of a call he'd had.

"Huh?" said Sam. His eyes widened, even as the wind began to blow around them again.

"We don't have the power to hold back time very long, even in a contained area," said Mariah.

Sam's Adam's apple bobbed in his throat. "Then what happens?"

The demon's mouth clamped shut on nothing.

Sam looked up at the perturbed demon, who'd expected flesh, but slowly bit down on air. *"Oy, gevalt,* we're dead."

"M-E-E-EAT?" drawled the demon.

"Sarah, you summoned it," Mariah said quickly. "Tell it it's released!"

Sarah shook her head. "That isn't the way it works. My grandmother was a Summoner. She passed along some stuff about . . . anyway," Sarah's lower lip quivered, "the gist is it can't go back until its purpose here has been fulfilled."

Sam's expression was downcast. "Still dead?" Mariah nodded. "That sucks." He drummed his fingers against his chin. "Sarah, what exactly was the purpose you had in mind when you called this thing?"

"ME-EAT." The demon took a deliberate step toward them, its eyes locked on Danny's soiled, prostrate form. Danny's mouth slowly dilated into an O of terror.

Sarah spoke quickly. "I wanted to make Danny-boy here shut the hell up."

"Uh, huh." Sam looked down at Danny, whose chest was expanding in preparation of letting out an enormous scream. He was nearly back to real time, as was the demon reaching down to snag him again.

Danny got out the syllable, "N," but then Sam grabbed him around the ribcage and squeezed with all his strength.

"Pass out!" cried Sam with inappropriate delight.

Mariah wondered if he'd lost his mind from fear. Goddess knew she couldn't blame him. He maintained his bear hug around Danny and shut his eyes tightly. The demon's hot, stinking breath washed over them as it shifted fully into normal time and darted forward with its mouth wide.

Danny abruptly went limp in Sam's arms.

The demon's teeth clanged together on nothingness.

Its outsized features twisted into a frown of confusion, then disappointment. "Awwwww, meat."

Mariah waved frantically at Sarah. "Dismiss it now!"

Fortunately, Sarah caught on fast. She redrew her sparking symbol in the air and cried, "I dismiss you, I dismiss you, I dismiss you!"

The demon gave her a baleful look, then *pop*! It was gone.

Mariah sank to the ground next to Danny's motionless body. Sam landed with a plop right next to her. She looked at him. "How did you know?"

"I hoped that spells were literal," he said. "So if Sarah wanted Danny shut up, I figured . . ."

"It didn't matter who did the shutting up," she finished with a knowing nod. "Just so long as he was silent, the demon's purpose was fulfilled."

Sam nodded. "I knew all those games of Pass Out I played in sixth grade would come in handy one day." He chuckled. "Well, okay, I didn't know that, but I'm glad they were good for something other than drain bramage." He stuck out his tongue and wobbled his head.

"I think I love you," said Mariah. She was joking when the words started, but as soon as they made it all the way out of her mouth, she regretted them.

Sam sat up, rigid. "You what now?"

She swallowed. "I . . . only meant. . . ."

"Well this changes everything." Sam frowned. "I'll have to quit school now."

Mariah's stomach knotted. "Sam, no! I was just . . . !"

"How else will I have time for that full time job I'm going to need to pay for the ring?" He took her hand and gazed into her eyes. "It's all settled then.

I'll go down to Starbucks tomorrow and apply for the assistant manager's job. You'll have to quit school too, of course. I expect my woman to be home, barefoot and pregnant."

Mariah sagged with relief. She smacked Sam's shoulder. "You goofus, you had me going there!"

"Bet you thought Darrens had no sense of humor," Sam hopped to his feet and extended a hand to help her up. She took it, enjoying his firm yet gentle grip.

"I thought a lot of things before tonight," she said. "Most of them wrong." She looked, really looked, at Sam's open, smiling face. Here he was, an ordinary guy, who'd just saved the bacon of two *mighty* witches plus one dipshit and he could still crack jokes. Human, *shmuman*, here was a guy worth risking a little exile for.

Sarah glared at Mariah. "So, I guess you're the real reason for Danny's sudden diarrhea of the mouth?"

Mariah couldn't meet her eyes. "I'm sorry, Sarah. I didn't want you to get hurt. I knew you wouldn't believe me if I just told you."

"Forget it. He had to be thinking it for you to make him say it." Sarah sighed and kicked Danny's limp foot. "Just help me implant a false memory of him getting piss-pants drunk and we'll call it a night."

"Sounds like a plan." Mariah turned to Sam. "Meet me inside? That is, if you don't mind being seen with a somewhat rumpled date for the dance."

It was Sam's turn to look flustered. Good, she was glad to see it was possible. "Uh, date?" he said. "Sorry if I wasn't paying attention this entire whacked-out night, but isn't that *verboten*?"

Mariah leaned over and kissed him. His lips were as warm and soft as she'd imagined for the past half hour.

When they parted, Sam nodded as though he'd been hypnotized. "Okay, then, I'll see you in the gym. Bye now." He turned and wobbled off.

Sarah jabbed her in the side. "Did you learn nothing from my stupidity tonight?"

"I learned that you owe me at least a semester of shut-the-hell-up," said Mariah.

Sarah heaved a put-upon sigh. "Fine, do what you will."

Mariah grinned. Not since her mother had caved in and bought her Miss Thang had she felt such a rush of satisfaction. "Make sure you visit us in Poughkeepsie."

Sarah A. Hoyt was born in Portugal, a mishap she hastened to correct as soon as she came of age. She lives in Colorado with her husband, her two sons and a varying horde of cats. She has published a Shakespearean fantasy trilogy with Berkley/Ace, Three Musketeers mystery novels, as well as any number of short stories in magazines ranging from *Isaac Asimov's Science Fiction Magazine* to *Dreams of Decadence*. Forthcoming novels include *Darkship Thieves* and more Three Musketeers mystery novels.

The Incident of
the Inferno Grill

Sarah A. Hoyt

"What do you mean the grill is possessed?" I asked
my new boss.

He shrugged. "Sometimes, things just are," he said.

Now, while I had often had my suspicions about
my computer, and wasn't about to put hands in the
fire about my tv either, I'd never gone so far as to say
they were possessed. Self-willed maybe. And perhaps
agents working for down-below. But *possessed?*

It didn't make me feel better about driving into
Oak Leaf Subdivision in the passenger side of Ken's
tenth-hand vintage early eighties Volvo, our backfires
making gentlemen in chinos and white t-shirts look
up from tending their already immaculate lawns and
the car's appearance making the tots playing on the
sidewalks abandon their bicycles and plastic pedal cars
and run screaming inside for mommy's protection.

What the sign painted on the side of the car,

Nephilim Psychic Investigations might make the moms do was anybody's guess. I certainly didn't want to think about it.

The job wasn't exactly something I'd set out to get, either. It's just when you've gone through all the ads that relate to your training—and of course, the thing about being a classical historian is that there are hundreds of people out there just waiting to shove the big bucks at you for your knowledge of the impact of Augustus' monopolies on Roman economy—and the ads for secretary and receptionist; when you've gone to more retail stores than you can count and filled out all their applications, only to be told you're overqualified; when you have tried the Work At Home Carding Wool jobs, what is left is not the merely improbable, but the impossible.

For me the impossible had arrived in the form of a brightly colored flier stuffed into my mailbox with all the bills. *Local Business Looking For Reliable Employee* it said. *Creativity and Love Of Adventure a Plus. Industry Standard Wages.*

My first thought was that anyone who needed to put out a flyer asking for an employee during one of the tightest job markets ever to hit our city—in a college neighborhood, yet—could not be on the level.

However I took the flier inside, and looked over the pile of bills that had also been in the mailbox. Then I drank the last bit of the milk in the fridge. There was no money to buy a new gallon—or quart. Or pint, for that matter. I looked at the flier again. Perhaps the person looking for an employee just wasn't very good at public relations. And perhaps he needed a guiding hand. Not to mention a firm but friendly employee to cure him of his sad addiction to capital LETTERs.

All of which had got me to Ken's dingy office over the corner deli. I'd balked a little at the sign on the door. Nephilim Psychic Investigations didn't exactly inspire confidence. Neither did his explanation that his given name was Nephilim Kentucky Jones III. Regardless of his explanation that his great grand-mother had been into biblical prophecy and missed Kentucky, any family capable of perpetrating that name not once but three times probably had other genetic issues. Madness, for one.

And yet, Ken looked like a perfectly reasonable man. Black, in that indeterminate age range between thirty and fifty, with a lean physique, slightly receding hair and the oddest tone of skin I'd ever seen. He looked exactly like he'd been born to be very dark skinned but went around with a permanent pallor. He smiled, keeping his teeth hidden, and told me that he went by Ken. Ken Jones. He just thought given the nature of the job, Nephilim was a good name for the business.

Which it was. Just not for any business I would be involved with. But he gave me a hundred dollar advance, which kept me from bolting when, after he had hired me, he asked me, "So . . . do you think you might have any psychic abilities?"

"I don't think I have any more psychic abilities than your average cat," I said, calculating the distance between me and the door, which wasn't very large considering the whole office could be crossed in a dozen steps in each direction.

"Ah well," he said, picking up a pen and making

some random notation on a notebook on his desk—I swear he wrote cat—"Cats are actually very psychic." After which he seemed to lose interest in me, as he looked through his desk for something.

When I cleared my throat, he said, "Oh. You're hired. Otherwise I wouldn't have given you a cash advance."

Which he had, for which I was grateful. But all the same, I thought I needed to know some minor things. Like, "Uh . . . when do I start? What do I do?"

"Oh. I'll call you," he said. "When we have a case." He looked over my resume. "I do have your cell number so just keep that on."

And I had. But I hadn't expected to be called in less than two hours. Nor had I expected to be picked up in a Volvo that backfired constantly. Much less did I expect to be driving through the burbs with that ridiculous business name on the car door.

Which was just as well, because Ken pulled into a cul-de-sac, and up the driveway of the last house. This house could have fit my two bedroom apartment in it at least ten times, not that it would, since it was much better kept than any place I'd ever lived. In fact, it looked like painters had just finished touching up the exterior, and making sure the picket fence going around the spacious yard was as immaculate as possible.

Ken opened the car door with an audible shriek, and got out. I got out on my side, cringing at the sound of unoiled metal. As we approached the broad porch with its unsat-upon-by-human-behinds wicker chairs, I swear I saw a hand twitch the lace curtains in the window next to the door. So I fully expected no answer to the doorbell. She had seen that car. What sane suburban matron would answer the door to someone who arrived in that car?

Only, of course, there was an answer. A woman in a white dress opened the door and smiled at us. "Yes?"

She didn't at all look like an inmate from a lunatic asylum, so I had to assume that whoever had called Ken and complained of a possessed grill had been playing a prank on her. Or on us.

But when Ken said, "Good afternoon, Ma'am. We're here about the—"

She blushed slightly and said, "Of course." And stepped back, opening the door wide.

We crossed a hallway and a kitchen, and though she said "Forgive the mess" I didn't see anything even out of place other than a Barbie doll on the counter.

Out back, there was a little brick patio and a neat lawn strewn with kids' toys. And just as I thought the woman was about to say that she wanted an estimate for aerating the lawn or the like, she gestured helplessly towards the grill.

The grill took up the entire side of the brick patio, perpendicular to the house and it looked more complex than some upper model cars. It was one of those deals which could accommodate five full racks of ribs side by side, and cook the sauce on the side, on a little gas burner. Grills like that always made me feel inadequate since I couldn't even imagine having the sort of social life that required that sort of cooking implement. This one was all polished black and chrome and gave me a strange feeling that I should fall on my knees and worship.

For some reason, Ken reached over and grabbed

my elbow. "Steady now," he said, in an undertone, before turning to the homeowner.

"So, Ma'am," he said, as he pulled a notebook from his back pocket. "What were the first signs of trouble?"

She hesitated, then sighed. "Well . . ." she said, and stepped aside reaching for a plant stake that was leaning against the house, beside the patio door. She used the stake to raise the grill cover from a distance.

A column of flame shot up, to the second floor window level.

I jumped back and attempted to take cover behind a child's bike. The homeowner lifted the stake, clearly with the idea of closing the grill again, but Ken held her wrist. "No, no," he said. "Leave it open." He looked up and down the blue and red flames, which gave off a distinct smell of sulphur. "I imagine that must have been disturbing."

The woman wrung her hands. "It ruined the brisket," she said, with a sort of sob in her voice. "It was the best brisket, too, and we were going to have a cookout. We had invited all our friends."

Ken nodded sagely. The blue and red flame acquired purple highlights.

"And when did you realize that you were in true trouble?"

"That . . ." She looked thoughtful. "That would be when it demanded human sacrifice."

"I see," Ken said. Behind him, the purple flames were forming faces, with huge, gaping mouths. "And did you give it that?"

The woman's mouth dropped open and her eyes opened wide. "What? No!"

"Good," Ken said, flipping a page in his notebook, and making some cryptic note. "Human sacrifice always complicates things."

The woman's mouth opened and closed, like that of a fish recently removed from water. I was probably doing the same. I was also still cowering behind the little kids' bike. It had pink streamers on the handlebars and a plastic basket with plastic flowers glued on in the front. The flames had now grown and shaped into beckoning fingers. I hoped the plastic flowers were sturdier than they looked.

"So, do you have any idea what might have brought this about?" Ken asked, calmly.

From the grill, a voice was hissing, in what would be enticing tones, if there were not the stench of evil in every syllable. "We know you. Come to us. Come to us . . ."

The homeowner was looking at the grill. "Perhaps if we could cover . . ."

"Nah, don't worry. It always says that sort of thing," Ken said, waving his hand as if to say that the grill could wait. "Just tell me if you have any idea what caused this."

"I . . ." She wrung her hands together. "I don't know."

"Well, you know, grills don't normally become possessed," he said. He sounded very much like a plumber talking about some foreign object found in the drains. "So there must be something special about this one." He looked over his shoulder, at the obscene mass of images that the flames had formed—arms, hands, lips, tongues, and some very lascivious faces leering straight at him—and narrowed his eyes in professional

THE INCIDENT OF THE INFERNO GRILL 111

appreciation. "Remarkable," he said. "Would you tell me where you bought it?"

"House Despot," she said, with a quiver in her voice.

"I see. And . . . well, forgive me, it is of course, none of my business, but you and your family don't happen to be Satanists?"

"No!" It was a wail.

"Any practitioners of the black arts hereabouts?" he said, as he scribbled furiously. "Suspicious teenagers, shape shifters, wizards, vampires?"

"Vampires?" she said with a sort of a gurgle.

"Well, not every vampire, you know, but some are true bad lots, and—"

And I could see if I let Ken go on with this, the woman would have a nervous breakdown and give the grill the human sacrifice it demanded, probably in the shape of Ken. I got up from behind the bike, with the reflection that, at any rate, it wouldn't save me from the worst. I mean, if the hellish forces dragged me off to, well, hell, at best I could make sure to take a bike and a handbasket with me. And at worst, I'd have bike-shaped scorch marks on my body.

Instead, I decided to save my job, such as it was, and possibly my life, not to mention my immortal soul. I advanced on the two of them with what I'm sure seemed like a semblance of bravery, though I was careful to keep them between me and the grill, where a thousand flame tongues were lolling out at me, while the hissing flames called out obscene suggestions.

"Ken," I said. "I'm sure you have other diagnostic tools. I'm sure Mrs—"

"Smith," she said, looking away from Ken and the flames towards me.

"I'm sure Mrs. Smith doesn't know anymore about the origins of the trouble, or she would have told you already, isn't that right?"

"Of course," Mrs. Smith said, with such a tone of relief, that it cut at my heart. "We're going to go inside, and she can have a cup of tea, while you do your thing, all right?" I said.

Ken looked somewhat put out. He put his notebook in his back pocket, turned around to face the grill and said, "Right. It's time to roast."

I didn't want to see what he was going to do next, so I just led Mrs. Smith into the kitchen, where I nuked a cup of water and, following her directions, found her her favorite herbal tea.

"We moved here two years ago," she said. "Such a nice place we thought. I mean, our children go to the school just down the street."

I handed her the cup of tea, which smelled strongly of mint, and she took a sip. "And never a hint of anything strange, you know? I mean, the children play outside, and my husband has a lot of friends that he golfs with and—"

I found a tissue box and handed her one just in time. She blew her nose. "We were so happy here. Every month or so, we had a barbecue and everyone in the neighborhood came. Best ribs in the state. My grandmother's recipe. Everyone loved them." She took another sip of the tea. "But now it's all ruined. No one will ever come to our parties again. We're the crazy people with the special effects grill."

"Have you tried getting rid of it?" I asked. "Just putting it out with the trash?"

"Yes. Oh, yes. But, you know, it popped open,

and the garbage collectors came and knocked at the door and said that if we did that again they would report us." She wailed again. "For trying to dispose of dangerous materials." She took another sip of tea, like a woman drowning. "We even . . . we even tried putting it at the corner, with a sign saying free. We thought some . . . some college student might take it, or something." She put her hands to her face, as if to cover the raging blush on her cheeks. "But all that happened is that by the time we came home it was back there, with the flames shooting up to the second floor.

"And it's so bad," she said. "I mean, the lid will open in the middle of the night, with the wind, or some vibration, or something. And the flames will wake our daughter in her room. It's just . . . just facing the grill. And our son thinks it's cool. He's thirteen, you know."

I provided another tissue. She sniffled, daintily. "And he's learned all sorts of bad language from that grill. The flames hiss it, you know. He called his teacher a den of iniquity last week. Let me tell you that was a fun conference. And then he said the principal was a beast of concupiscence." She finished her mint tea at a go, as though trying to fortify herself. "I don't know what to do anymore. We'd move, but I'm afraid the grill will get there ahead of me." She put a hand up and grabbed my wrist, and motioned with her other hand towards Ken, who was out there, making wild gestures and seemingly negotiating with the demon in the flames. "Is he any good?"

For one crazy moment, I toyed with telling her the truth: That all I knew about him was his pamphlet design skills and his name, and that neither of those inspired me with confidence. But I looked at her woebegone face, her tear-filled eyes, and I decided the lie was the best part of valor. "Oh yes," I said. "He is . . . uncanny. Such power and psychic, er, perception. He's almost as good as a cat."

"Oh, that's good then," she said. And I must have sounded convincing, because she didn't even bat an eye at the cat thing.

I thought I'd better get out of that kitchen, though, before I were tempted into a sin of telling the truth. I mumbled something about helping Ken and stepped out.

He was facing the grill, which was singing in a thin, reedy voice. It sounded like "staying alive, staying alive."

"Well?" I said.

"It's very bad," he said, turning around and frowning at me. "Those flames are straight from the pits of hell themselves, and judging from the sound of it, that's Disco. That means it's from the lower pits. The only worse ones are the accordion players' pits."

"What can we do?" I asked.

He shook his head. "Damned if I know," and glared at the faces that were now chortling at him. He ran a hand backward through his very short hair. "Or at least, the grill is."

"So what can we do?" I asked. "She's terrified in there."

"It has to be the work of someone around here," Ken said. "A neighbor or something. I mean, if they're not Satanists, then someone has invoked this and wished it on them."

"Okay. So, how do we go about finding who it is?"

"I don't know," Ken said, exasperated. "Look for familiars or brooms or something."

"Brooms? Are you seriously suggesting I go to every house, knock at the door and ask to see their broom?"

He chewed on his lower lip, as though deep in thought. "No," he said. "Too time consuming. Besides, if it's a new broom, or if they fly relatively slow, the scorch marks aren't really obvious."

"Nephilim Kentucky Jones, are you telling me that people really fly on brooms?"

He looked confused. "Uh . . . yes?"

It was clearly hopeless to bring him in touch with reality. And besides, looking at that grill with its outright sentient flames, I was having trouble telling him that flying brooms were impossible. So I cast a look around the immaculate lawn, the carefully tended bushes and flowers surrounding it, and the white picket fence encircling the whole. Just in time to see a cat looking over the fence.

Okay, it was just a black cat. Maybe. It had intent, curious eyes and the strongest claws I've ever seen, holding on to the edge of the fence.

"You'll never figure it out," the grill was hissing at Ken. "You should give up and let us cook you." It turned around 180 degrees, in a way that was probably more repulsive for a human head.

And the cat was looking over the fence. Another cat head appeared right next to his. I noticed that Mrs. Smith was in the patio door, looking distraught.

"Whose cats are those?" I asked.

"Oh, that's Black Cat and Black Cat Two."

"They're yours?" I asked.

She shook her head. "Sort of the neighborhood cats," she said. "Their mother dropped them in our yard. Mama cat has moved on, but they stay here. We . . . we feed them. No one else would, you know? Poor things."

And the two of them were looking over the fence, their yellow eyes shining and intent. The bigger one seemed to be muttering cat curses under his breath. Right. As psychic as a cat. Black cats as agents of the devil. And then there was the whole familiar thing. I looked down, happy that not only did I have jeans on, but I had my grubbiest jeans on. That meant I could climb that fence.

I approached the cats slowly, passing Ken, who muttered as he looked at the grill, "Oh, pea soup, now. Really bad."

I didn't look, but the air was filled with the smell of burnt split pea soup.

I headed for the fence and the two cats. I expected them to run when they saw me coming. And they did. Sort of. Only it was a slow-mo run, with looks back to make sure I was following. And I did: Over the fence, onto another immaculate lawn and all the way to the garden shed.

Where I looked through the side window, to see a woman—at least I hoped it was a woman—tracing figures in chalk on the floor, and lighting candles and muttering, "That will fix them."

I loped all the way back, jumped over the fence. Mrs. Smith was still standing in her doorway. I said, "How do you get along with the neighbor next door?"

She looked puzzled a second then shook her head. "Well, not at all. You see, she tried to steal my ribs recipe. Her family is not . . . very popular here. She resents my husband and I. Her parties used to be the best attended before we moved here."

Bingo, I thought, even as part of my mind told me I was over the edge and far away. "Ken," I said, as I approached him and pulled him by the arm, away from the grill which was now vomiting wave upon wave of pea soup onto the brick patio. "Come with me."

He looked as if he was going to protest. He had a book in his hand, which he'd clearly been reading from. I confiscated it, and dragged him behind me. It wasn't till I was near the fence that I read the title on the leather. "War and Peace?" I said.

"I thought it might put it to sleep," he said, defensively. "It often does for me."

"Never mind that. Come."

I led him, on tip toes all the way to the shed, where I showed him—through the same grimy window—the woman who was now engaged in a hopping, skipping backward dance around some mystic symbol on the floor.

"Right," he said. "Wait here. This isn't going to be pretty."

"War and Peace?" I asked.

"Worse. Much worse," he said. "I think we're into the territory of Collected Anthology of Romantic Poetry." I thought he was joking, but as he went he took a small black-bound volume from what appeared to be a bottomless back pocket.

He went in and I heard a woman's voice say, "What are you doing here?"

Ken's voice answered, deep and resonant, "She found me roots of relish sweet . . ."

The woman screamed, loudly, drowning out Ken's voice. There was a series of thumps. Then Ken's voice rising again, "So are you to my thoughts like food to life."

Another couple of screams, followed by an explosion and a sudden smell like burning lavender. And then Ken's voice, resolute and confident, "How do I love thee? Let me count the ways. I love thee to the depth and breadth and height . . . Is that enough? Yeah. That's what I'm talking about," he said, in the tone of someone who has finished some difficult work.

He emerged from the shed bedraggled, his shirt rumpled and burned in three spots, as if someone had applied a cigarette to it. His short hair managed to be on end, and it looked like there were a couple silver threads mingled in. He held something in his hand. It looked like a sachet woven out of straw with a couple bones and things tied to it. "I tell you," he said, shaking his head. "Whenever these suburban women get some book on dark magic out of the library, they always go for the nastiest stuff."

He seemed to be walking back to the grill, so I walked with him, and helped him over the fence. He looked like he was barely able to remain standing. At the moment we came into sight, the flames froze in the classic cartoon uh-oh faces and I swear I heard, "Well, if that will be all," coming in the hiss of the flames, as the lid started to swing shut.

"Not so fast," Ken said, and flung the sachet of workings overhand into the flames.

There was a sound like the scream of a thousand pierced accordions, and the flames died suddenly. The pea soup that had been pouring over the edge of the grill disappeared too, leaving a scene of sub-urban calm.

"Wow," Mrs. Smith said. "That was good work!" She seemed all polite eagerness and I detected just the faintest wish to see us leave. Not that I blamed her. I mean, if a possessed grill was bad, the sort of oddballs we were would be bad too.

"It was just your next door neighbor," Ken said, slowly, as he wiped his sweaty forehead to his sleeve. "You don't have to worry about her anymore. She'll be going very far away."

"How far away are we talking about?" I asked him, as we were back in the car and headed for our safe downtown neighborhood.

"What?" he said, looking over at me. "Oh, I suggested Bermuda. In that state of mind, it's likely to become a fixation. I just stripped all her psychic defenses and removed her witchcraft. If she can convince her husband—and maybe even if she can't—I'd guess it's Bermuda or bust."

"Oh," I said, feeling terribly relieved. "I thought you'd killed her or something."

He looked startled, and the car wavered on the lane. "I don't kill people," he said.

I gave him a sideways look. He could be a madman. Except . . . what he'd done had worked. And we had a thousand dollar check to prove it. "How did you find out how to do psychic investigations, anyway?"

"Online course," he said.

I gurgled with laughter despite myself, and said "What? How did you find such a course?"

"It was that or computer programming, and psychic

investigations was cheaper," he said. "And less competition."

"But . . . most people don't think there's anything to investigate," I said, trying to sound reasonable. "I mean, psychic stuff . . ." I couldn't say it didn't exist, after what I'd just seen, so I just opened my hands, helplessly.

"Young lady, when your parents named you Nephilim Kentucky, you know there is far more to the world than is dreamed of in anyone's philosophy. And evil is always a possibility."

"Okay," I said. And smiled to myself. "I wonder what our next case will be."

"A sense of adventure," he said. "I knew that about you first time I saw you." He turned off the interstate towards downtown. "I just hope our next case is not in the burbs. Thing about the burbs is, if anyone has any beef at all, it all ends up in a big cookout."

Dave Freer is a former Ichthyologist/Fisheries Scientist turned sf/fantasy writer. He now has ten books in print, a number of which are co-authored with Mercedes Lackey and/or Eric Flint. He is also the author of about twenty other short stories, and a teens novel. He lives in Zululand, South Africa, where he is permitted to serve four cats. They say he wastes entirely too much time on other things like the writing, cooking, cuddling his fellow cat-slave Barbara, and of course we will not even mention the dogs. Yes, they do talk.

Soot

Dave Freer

My name is Sothbubastis. I am an almost black cat, with green eyes. I live in a little gingerbread house with a witch. It is on the corner of Apogee Crescent and Diana Avenue, and is quite unlike any of the other houses around here. Suburbia has sprawled out of London and engulfed us. We even have a shopping mall just down the road.

Cassandra, my witch, calls me Soot when we are alone. It is a little lacking in dignity, but for fish, warm milk and catnip mice I will put up with it, and with having my white paw dyed black. She has assured me that the dye is not toxic, unlike some of the jangling charms which she insists on wearing, and the incense that she keeps on burning. I sometimes think she tries too hard. Few if any of the clients will know the ancient meaning and purpose of frankincense.

Our house is proof that people will believe almost anything. It is, supposedly, a Queen Anne relic with Victorian additions. Ha ha. The house is actually much, much older, but little remains of the original building. Still, humans believe what they want to believe, and therefore it has a preservation order. It cannot be demolished, altered, or otherwise interfered with, without approval from the Historical Structures, Monuments and Buildings Commission, the Department of County and Urban planning, and the local authority, none of whom will co-operate with any of the others, on principle. Cassandra says it has been very awkward for plumbing. However, this a human problem and not one of mine.

I would like a preservation order too. It would be very useful in my aspect of our work, especially if dogs and motor vehicles were informed.

We watch the way. It sounds easy, doesn't it?

It is mostly done in darkness.

"I'm worried about Leanne. My daughter," said the client.

I would worry about her daughter too. But then, I am out at night. I can see very well in what you humans call darkness. I reclined on the mantel behind Cassandra, next to the stuffed owl. Curse Harry Potter. The taxidermy left something to be desired and the bouquet—uneasily mingling with the incense—made me want to sneeze. That would disturb the unblinking stare that was my task with clients. It unnerved them. An unnerved client was more likely to part with cash, and some of that was needed to pay the taxes, the electricity bill, the Internet connection, as well as for human food, and, more relevantly, catnip mice.

Cassandra fanned the cards onto the baize table.

"What is troubling you, Mrs Syrus?" she said in her best mystical medium voice.

The plump client fondled the protective crystal around her neck. She was wearing an embroidered blouse of Egyptian cotton, complete with a hieroglyphic inscription. It was part of a funerary prayer to Osiris, unless I was much mistaken. She leaned forward, her generous breasts nearly sending Cassandra's planchette tumbling, and said, in a hushed whisper. "I think she's messing about with the Oh-cult."

Huh. Not unless young Ralph Rachen had changed his name to "Oh-cult." But no, the boy had kept a part of an old name, which was why we were watching him. So far the two kids hadn't done anything that involved more than lip and tongue gymnastics. Humans are strange like that. We cats have a far more sensible attitude to sex.

"Take a card, Mrs Syrus," said Cassandra, and, as the client's beringed hand reached out she asked: "So, what makes you think that she's toying with the forces of darkness?"

The woman turned over the card. The devil looked up at her. It was an original Dürer. The artist had captured the sardonic expression on the face perfectly, and of course the chained boy and girl at his feet. "Oh, it was Clint, I mean . . . Father Pillman, who told me," she said coyly.

I stood up and arched my back, but kept up the stare. I'd get a blink when she looked down at the next card. I'd have to forgo hissing and spitting.

"I see," said Cassandra, with remarkable control. Cassandra really was very, very good. "Take another card, Mrs Syrus. And what did Father Pillman say?"

Mrs Syrus would remember exactly what he said. Our new, very modern and radical priest had all the suburban housewives clinging to his words . . . and anything else they could get their hands on.

"Oh it was something Leanne said to him during the counselling session. He likes to hold one-on-one counselling sessions with the younger members of his flock."

"I bet he does," I muttered.

Mrs Syrus stared at me. I stared back. "Your cat. It . . . it spoke."

Cassandra looked reproachfully at me. "He does it all the time. Never knows when to hold his tongue."

What a foolish expression that is! If cats had the equipment for holding things, short of sticking a claw into them, we would not need to keep humans. As usual, Cassandra's magic worked perfectly. Mrs Syrus tittered. "Oh, you are a silly, Madame Cassandra." It was a good thing that one of the job requirements for godhood had not been intelligence, or Cassandra might have had a harder time of the curse placed on her.

Cassandra smiled. "Take another card, Mrs Syrus. You were saying, before my cat so rudely interrupted?"

"Well," said the woman, drawing the Sorceress, "He wouldn't tell me exactly what she said . . . but he said I would have to keep a strict watch on her. Lock her room door at night. And keep her away from Bad Influences. That boy." She sniffed. "She's not my child, you know. She's adopted."

"That would explain it," said Cassandra. "Take another card."

"Father Pillman has given me some blessed silver

crosses to keep her safe from Oh-cult forces," confided Mrs Syrus happily.

The reading went on. Cassandra unsettled her client, and found out more than Mrs Syrus had meant to tell. She gave her a reading that impressed her . . . and that Mrs Syrus would naturally disbelieve.

"Did you have to talk?"

I licked my paw, ignoring her.

"You'll wash the black off. It could have been very awkward, you know."

I twitched my whiskers. "Oh yes. She might have called the Inquisition down on us. They might suspect that you are a witch. It's just as well that you don't have a sign above the door which reads 'Madame Cassandra, White Witch, Charms, Tarot Readings and Crystal Therapy', or they might possibly suspect you."

She sighed. "Sarcasm doesn't suit you, Sothbubastis. Pillman is planning something."

"Sarcasm is natural to a cat. The new emissary is up to something, I agree. We suspected that when he arrived. We now know that it will probably be soon. It will involve a young girl. What he plans seems self-evident," I said dryly.

She nodded. "It's how and where that are a little more obscure."

"I suppose a pre-emptive strike is out, as usual."

"You know the rules."

Cats believe rules are for other people, with the emphasis on the people part. But in this case she was right. These rules are not petty constructs put in place to soothe the ego of some panjandrum or hierophant. They are based on experience: if one crossed those lines, one died. Of course, any self-respecting cat will tell you, you have to keep testing the boundaries, and searching for ways around them. "I'll go and scout. There's a chance I'll see something."

"Better wait for nightfall."

"They'll expect me then."

I slipped out of my window, up onto the fence, down onto a wheelie-bin and off into the shadows towards the church. And then I took sharp left. Some force was repelling me. Now, cats are more resistant to compulsions than most creatures, but I did not want to alarm it. So I sheered away. I went to consult an associate of mine instead. Cassandra disapproves of him. The previous watcher and he clashed. But he gives me fish.

On the way I met a lanky teen in a hoodie slouching along the sidewalk. He even had the obligatory can of lager. "You're not fooling me, Wolfie," I said.

"Shut up, cat. It's not you I am trying to fool."

"Won't fool her mother either. The priest ratted you out, wolf-boy. She's got the girl protected."

"Curse him."

"If you'll tell me why you want her then I might help you."

"I'm in love with her."

I sniffed, disbelievingly. And then hastily slipped through the gap in the fence, dodging the hurled can and the spray of frothy horse-urine-substitute that splattered from it. There was a vague possibility that he spoke the truth. But cats are not trusting. Down Styx Street (humans and street names—I ask you) I wove and darted across hidden weedy backyards, slow-rotting Wendy houses and past sagging wash-lines on the secret side of suburbia.

The Peaceful Rest Funeral Parlour was tucked away at the back of a dead end. Very appropriate. "What took you so long, cat?" asked Cassandra, crossly.

I forget just how accurately she foresees things. It's patchy of course. She tends to see those she cares about. "I stopped to talk to Wolfie. He threw beer at me." I wound my way between her legs.

Cassandra bent down and stroked me. Gave me the benefit of her famous crooked smile. "Wasted your time. He'll be along later."

"You could have told me."

"You could have told me you weren't going to the church."

"It's warded. I didn't want to trigger any alarms. Shall we go in?"

"He gives me the creeps."

I stretched. "That's what he does, witch. His kind can't help it."

"Ugh," she said, as we skirted around the funeral parlour to his back-room.

"I prefer Oogh," said the squat, shaggy headed fellow, peering out at us from under his low, heavy brow. He whiffled his big stick-out wobbly nose at us. Trolls are more scent-orientated than humans. This doesn't mean they smell any nicer, because trolls don't. They stink nearly as much as humans, but differently. It's at the root of the ancient distrust between the species. "What can I do for you, woman-who-foresees-the-future?"

"I am not too sure. I foresaw that the cat and the wolf-boy were coming here, and that it would be important."

He nodded. "Well, you'd better come in. I am having tea, which is also important."

"How come you believe me?" asked Cassandra, accepting a chipped mug of tea from him (and thereby proving she was not infallible. Her foretelling skills are typical Greek God shoddy, not a patch on decent Egyptian workmanship), and finding a rickety chair to sit on.

He rubbed his too-broad, too-low forehead. "Your curse only affects humans, I suppose," said Oogh. His speech is a little odd. He told me he battles with consonants. There was a tentative knock on the door. "That'll be Wolfie. You'd better let him in. They tend to run away from me," said the troll.

Sure enough, it was. He looked doubtfully at Cassandra. "I thought you lived in that cutesy house up on Apogee?"

"You're lucky my house isn't here to hear you," said Cassandra. "Come in. We've been waiting for you."

"How did you know I was coming?" he said warily. "I just decided to follow the cat." I should have thought of that. Wolves track well by scent. He sniffed. "Something smells very odd about this."

"It's the troll," said Cassandra. "He stinks, but he is mostly harmless."

"It is you modern humans that stink," said Oogh. "You want tea, wolf-boy?"

Wolfie's eyes narrowed. "There is something very weird going on here. And," he said, looking hard at Oogh, "something that looks human, but isn't."

"And you, wolf-boy. What are you doing here?" said Oogh. "I've been here since prehistory. But we get very suspicious when one of your kind turns up suddenly."

"I . . . I am not too sure," he said, walking in to Oogh's pseudo-cave. "What are you doing here?"

"I clean the crematorium. And I do odd jobs around the place."

"Very odd jobs, sometimes," I said, my tail weaving an S. "He's in pest control. Good with mandragoras and vampires."

The wolf-boy blinked. "I meant . . . magical creatures. Here in suburbia?"

Oogh shrugged. "We were here before suburbia. What did you expect us to do? Go off and look for a rickety-rackety bridge? Operating a troll booth, when you're not allowed to eat anyone without the right change, is so yesterday."

"And we want to know why a werewolf has come to town," said Cassandra, sternly. I knew that tone of voice. I tensed my muscles and readied myself to spring.

"There is something special about this place, isn't there?" said Wolfie. "It . . . attracted me."

I relaxed slightly. He sounded genuinely puzzled.

Cassandra raised her eyebrows. "Von Rachen. You would have us believe your parents didn't tell you?"

"I never met my parents. Well, not that I remember. I'm an orphan. And it's Rachen. Not Von Rachen."

Cassandra stared hard at him. I knew that stare. The reading trance. "I think," she said, "that it is time that you told us about yourself. Sit down."

He did, warily. "This is something to do with my being able to turn into a wolf, isn't it?"

"You might say so. Tell us about this orphaning?"

He shrugged. "My parents were killed in a car crash. I wasn't hurt, apparently. The cops found their ID, but failed to find any next of kin. So I ended up in an orphanage. I got adopted twice . . . but it never worked out. Odd things happened and I got sent back. And when I was eighteen I had to leave."

I didn't say anything. But weres didn't die that easily.

"Ah," said Cassandra silkily. "And then you did what? You've been hanging around here with no visible means of support for nearly a month now. Yet you have clean clothes, and you only chase rabbits in the park at night occasionally, and very ineffectually. You don't appear to work."

He shrugged. "I was a Ward of the Crown. They looked after things . . . I get an allowance every month. See, when I left St Stephens . . . I found out that I actually had inherited quite a lot of money. I was eighteen. The trustees pay me an allowance until I'm twenty-one. I didn't have a family or any real friends. I didn't know what to do with myself. I kept turning into a wolf at awkward moments. It . . . unsettles you a bit. So I thought I'd travel. I was just passing through this place . . ."

"And you stayed here?"

"Well, there was the girl. She just . . ."

"Attracted you," said Cassandra, sardonically.

"Smelled different, if you must know," said wolf-boy, looking sulky. "I've always seemed to be able smell so much more than other people."

"Leanne Syrus. She does," said the troll. "She's a half-breed. Fey. What you would call a fairy. Damn colonists."

"She's a fairy princess?" said Wolfie-boy, impressed . . . but rather doubtful.

"Nah. Probably just a common-or-garden fairy," said the Troll. "They're quite indiscriminate. Shag anything. Have the morals of a cat."

I like that! Cats are exceptionally moral. We just have a different set of values. Most of them concern ourselves.

"So . . . why does she attract me? And why is she here? Why are you all here?"

"Is this a real question or a philosophical one?" asked Cassandra, dryly. "And just how do you know who we're talking about, troll?"

"Couldn't be anyone else, could it?" said the troll.

But wolf-boy was persistent. "So why are you all here, in this town?"

I arched my back and stretched. "To stop the likes of you coming here. And her. Or rather, her real Daddy," I said, staring at him.

"The cat talks too much," said Cassandra, coldly.

Because wolf-boy was not human either, he had no trouble believing her. I could see his neck muscles tense. Next thing there'd be fur sprouting. "What are you going to do about it? Is this why you lured me in here? To . . ."

"Don't be any more foolish than you have to be. It's not you we're interested in, unless you try to open the way."

"It's millions more of your kind that we don't want."

"Millions?"

"Are you a half-wolf or a half-parrot? There is a way from here to otherwhere. It's closed. We keep it that way. There are other portals, but few as easy as this one. Periodically they attempt to open it again. It can only be opened from this side, so they send emissaries to try. If you're one, I'll kill you," said Cassandra, raising her power, her bound hair flying loose and forming a nimbus around her head.

"Personally I'm in favor of letting them in again. They're good eating," said the troll. "What do you think, cat?"

"No. Even transformed into a mouse, the last one had a fey taint to it."

Wolfie-boy was nothing if not determined. "But you are also magical creatures. Why do you want to keep magic out?"

"Oh Boy! Fantasy writers have something to answer for. Listen, Wolf-boy: For starters they're not all sweetness-and-light and just misunderstood. Back when the way was open, humans found out that the fey regard them as lower lifeforms. A few of them are nice to the lower lifeforms. And some of them are like the troll. They think of us as sport or dinner. Anyway, none of us are fey."

"I'm the indigenous inhabitant," said Oogh. "You and this witch's kind—modern humans—calling them *Homo sapiens* is undue flattery, invaded later. Her kind from Africa, you lot from the ways." I stared unblinkingly at him. "Cats have also been around for a while," he admitted.

I jumped up onto Cassandra's lap. "And we find Homo sapiens make better staff than Neanderthals like him did. The fey and us reached a misunderstanding quite quickly."

"So, Wolf-boy, back off and find another place to be. The troll and I have some business to discuss," said Cassandra, stroking me.

He went. Looking appropriately chastened. She can be scary at times.

"It didn't work," said Cassandra. "I feel that he is still going to be involved."

The Neander-troll grunted. "You could have told him that he was a half-thing too. Or what they plan to use her for."

"I could have," said Cassandra, evenly. When she speaks in that tone I go and find shelter behind her fragile, precious glassware. She doesn't like to be told her business, even by those who know better, like me. "But I wanted to keep him away from the priest. We don't need any were-killings, if we can help it. So what are you going to do about it, troll?"

"Nothing," said Oogh. He was lying, but there was no point in arguing with him.

So we too went on our way.

Mine was not the same as Cassandra's. Cats do not walk with people. We just sometimes happen to be going the same way. My way this time happened to be to where Wolfie-boy was hanging out behind the oleanders. I had an idea Cassandra wouldn't approve of. "You might try skulking up to Leanne's window tonight," I said quietly, as I walked past.

Days and nights of watching had paid off. We knew who Pillman's assistants were and a little eavesdropping had given us the night it was planned for.

The Neander-troll was watching too, although he pretended that he wasn't. I had spotted him popping out of a manhole in the church parking lot. He was better at the subterranean stuff than me. He knew the Victorian era sewers well . . . and therein lay our clue. We should have spotted it earlier. He wasn't only using them to spy. He was following the conspirators. I'd seen the thirteen of them arrive in dribs and drabs. Saw the girl dropped off, protesting that she didn't want to be there. Heard Mrs Syrus's assurance that it would do her good. Saw her walk sulkily to the door, and turn to sneak off the moment that her mother's Volvo had pulled away . . . but a hand came out and dragged her inside.

Then I waited. They would surely leave soon for wherever they planned to hold the rite. It couldn't be here: it was too far from the way. I waited. Cats wait well, which is odd because we're also very impatient. We also hear small sounds, sounds that humans, dogs—and even mice—don't realise that they are making. That's how we can do that patient-appearing wait by a rat-hole.

And right now the human rats weren't making any sounds. I decided to risk triggering the alarms. I swayed down the catwalk-branch of an old oak, under the spotlight of a full moon, and leapt onto the scabby old roof-tiles next to the steeple. Then I balanced along the rotting stonework gable, and up through a narrow window. I slipped, silently as a shadow, into the darkness of the belfry, and then along cobwebbed, dusty beams to where I could look down into the church hall.

It was empty.

The long bar of moonlight from the tall leaded windows spilled across the pews and onto the aisle. There it was broken by a square of blackness.

A hole.

I growled to myself. Damned troll might have told me, even if he didn't trust Cassandra. I'd better get back to her, fast. It must be the house itself they planned to attack, from underneath.

Their timing was just perfect. I had to cross the High

street. The snarl of traffic as the tired and impatient commuters heading back from the city on a winter evening was in full cry. Not easy for a cat, and I'd swear they had been bespelled to be extra vicious. Oh, for that preservation order. But with a Jaguar spearing me on its headlights and missing my tail by a whisker, I made the security of the gutter. Only to almost jump back into the road again, because of the hell-hound. Well. Doberman. I dived under an illegally parked Lancia, too low for a Doberman. But there was no chain of cars. I was trapped. Time was running out. The dog snarled and barked. And a little yipping noise said the Doberman had called in the Daschhund sappers. Hiss!

"Get lost, dog." There was a yelp.

I emerged. Cassandra's prescient powers may be spotty, but when they work they're great. She scooped me up. Very undignified, but under the circumstances I was glad of it. "I was coming to fetch you, Soot. They're coming at us from underneath."

"Why do I bother spending cold nights spying when you can see all this?" I asked grumpily. "You'd better hurry. They're on their way already. I was coming to tell you."

"I didn't foresee it. I got a note. Addressed to you."

"Oh. Who from?" Maybe I had misjudged Oogh.

"It didn't say. Just 'watch out for moles'."

"They must be in the old Victorian sewer-system. They have an entry in the church. I spotted Oogh popping out of a manhole."

"He must be right at home," she said sardonically. "And love the bouquet. Well. I have my Wellies on. We'd better get down there." She opened a manhole. Don't be fooled. Cassandra might be slight, but she's

able to call on exceptional strength. We climbed down
the iron staples. It was dark. Even for me.

I really don't like sewers. Besides the dark and the
smell, there are few places to climb, and running is
quite limited.

"Can you see, Soot?"

"No. You'll have to make us a light."

She made a ball of Hekate's glow in her left hand.
The sewer was red-brick lined and, lucky us, had a
channel and a walkway above it. It was obviously a main
line, intended for storm-water too. I sniffed . . . not
something that a cat wanted to do down here, but
needs must when the Unseelie court drives. Cats too
have keen noses. Oogh . . . and something more worrying were down that passage. "Left," I said.

We followed the main line for a distance, and then
a branch, and then there was . . . new construction. A
roughly hewed tunnel, with some inadequate pit-props.
We could hear the chanting, and there was no other
way to approach it. The moles must have got very
close to the house. The watchtower.

Most people don't know that inverse square law
affects magic as much as it does radiation or magne-
tism. Whoever had raised this little pack of nasties
had positioned them carefully. I could feel the force
of the ley-lines from here. They'd break a window
right into that power and open the way, if they could
channel enough magic out of their ritual. Cassandra
dowsed the glow in her hand. Put me down. We
walked forward into the baleful, flickering red light.
Cassandra began to raise her will. She didn't look
like a funny fake witch any more. There is a time
for disguise. This was not that time.

It was also not the time for two slatted garage roller doors—one before and one behind us—to suddenly clatter down. The slats were wooden. I didn't need second sight to know that they'd be rowan, toxic to magic users and impervious to their spells. The walls were panelled with it too. The doors were clever carpentry, with a gap of an inch or so between planks, and no way out. Yet we could see the priest, complete with his strap-on horns, his hooded hench-idiots, and the victim tied to the altar. Well, to a slab of slate on a mound of earth.

"Ah. We have the witch. If the first plan does not work we'll use her," said Father Clint.

"Why not use her first?" asked one of the acolytes. Humans might be fooled by a mask. But I recognised the voice. I thought I'd smelled wolf-boy.

"She may resist. The spilling of virgin fey blood is still the best method."

If I had not been so angry I would have sniggered. I had removed some of the guardian silver from Leanne's window. Cats are not worried by silver and are far less affected by curses and cantrips than werewolves, half-fey or even humans. Wolfie-boy had paid his girlfriend a visit and, with her eager co-operation had made sure that she was no longer their ideal sacrifice. I wondered—seeing as the were-wolf was, after all, one of the renegade priest's followers, how he was going to explain that. But right now I was too busy yowling. Besides letting them know that the first one to try and touch my witch was going to need stitches, I was telling the troll that I was here. He just might help. I was also scratching a few hieroglyphs on the floor. I'm a temple cat from Bubastis in Lower Egypt. I've been around a long time, and learned a few things. I wasn't affected by rowan like Cassandra was. To me, it was just a cage. Bast still owed me some favors. Her original aspect had been the sweet warmth of the sun. She could strip the heat out of their brands. And in her hand was the sistrum—the rattle . . . I asked her for some shake, rattle and roll.

I have to reluctantly admit that cats, especially angry ones, can be rather stupid. The flames shrank, and we all fell down. So did a few pieces of the roof. Causing an earthquake while you are underground is not clever. Everything rattled. Us too. Screaming and chaos reigned. But Father Clint was not going to be stopped. It was almost dark, but I saw him raise the long knife to plunge into Leanne . . . and Wolfie-boy was frantically wrestling with him over the white body of the fey-girl. He was still a young wolf—and his opponent was fighting with manic strength.

Then, as the flames flared briefly, the altar stone lifted, and the drugged girl, the wolf and Father Clint rolled off . . . as a dark shape with long reaching fingers lurched free of the earth mound, to more screams of horror from Father Clint's coven. The wolf wasn't as strong as he would be, but Oogh, hidden under that sheet of stone, disguised with earth, was ancient and very strong indeed. Even the hysterical strength of the priest was no match for those throttling hands.

In the meantime I had wriggled my way through a broken slat, into their makeshift temple, and had at last managed to scratch someone. Wolfie-boy was struggling under the weight of his girlfriend, when someone started shooting.

Ricochets could kill all of us except Wolfie-boy, unless they were using silver bullets.

There is a time for courage. And a time to yowl: "Oogh. Get us out of here."

Oogh flung the stone slab at the rowan trap. Some of the wood had broken anyway. He half dragged wolf-boy and his burden along and through. And then attacked the other side, breaking rowan slats . . . Cassandra was weak, but we got her out too, as one of the coven behind us found a flashlight. Another shot. Wolfie grunted, but we staggered on.

They came behind us, frantic and eager to shoot. They had flashlights and guns. We dared not show any light.

But Cassandra was rapidly recovering. She turned, made a glow.

"Enough," she said to the advancing minions. "Stop or you will die!"

They were close, armed and ready to kill. Because they were human, and she was Cassandra, they did not believe her foretelling.

People are stupid like that.

But never twice.

The troll gave the wounded wolf-boy a hand with the girl. It was only lead, so he'd live. "It may cause some ructions, twelve of the respected local citizens disappearing," said Cassandra regretfully, holding up the Hekate glow.

"Thirteen," said Wolf-boy. "They came down here in single file. I killed the last one in the line and stole his mask."

"I was unsure about you, Von Rachen."

He hung his head. "You were right. I had come to open the way. There was a letter about it with the will . . . But I changed my mind when I found out what was involved. See, I went back to the troll. He explained and recruited me. I think he really is a Neanderthal, you know."

Oogh grinned, big blunt meat-eating teeth gleaming. "Of course. That's what trolls were. We stopped the first Fey invasion. But it left us too weak to deal with Cro-Magnon man."

Cassandra's no better than a cat at admitting she was wrong. But she swallowed her pride this time. "I owe you," she said to Oogh.

He shrugged. "The cat and I get on. And humans are still better than Fey, for what is left of my kind. Although some of them are not too bad." He gestured at Leanne, who was beginning to stir in the Were's arms. "You'd better see she's not a suitable sacrifice, soon-ish."

The wolf-boy blushed. Looked at me. "Too late," he said.

Cassandra and Oogh looked at each other. Shook their heads in unison.

"Cats," they said together.

We immortals still watch the way. And still no-one believes Cassandra's foretelling. Oogh visits sometimes. Cassandra's coffee is nearly as bad as his tea.

Storm Christopher is a tech writer and editor in the advertising and marketing industry. He lives in the midwest with his cat, Renfield, and is hard at work completing his first mystery novel. This is his first fiction sale.

The House of Lost Dreams

Storm Christopher

It was a nondescript little shop off to itself at the farthest end of a dilapidated and otherwise abandoned strip mall on the edge of that strange twilight zone that separates the city from the vacuous wastelands of suburbia. The highway by which it set seemed old and forgotten, too, an aging two-lane concrete ribbon that paralleled the newer bypass a hundred yards away.

Howie Davis didn't know why he circled back five miles out of his way or why the shop had even caught his attention. But his eyes had misted over as he passed it, and he thought he'd heard the merry strains of a calliope as if from far away. A flood of half-forgotten memories rushed over him, evoked merely by the name of the shop—*The House of Lost Dreams*.

Reaching the lunar landscape that once had been a parking lot, he steered his old Dodge off the road and carefully navigated the crater-sized potholes. He still hit a particularly deep one. The impact jarred his teeth, and the front end of his car made a loud metallic protest. "Thank God for warranties," he grumbled aloud. "On the car, if not my dentistry."

He was grateful when he finally reached the curb. He shut off the engine, leaned back in the seat and let go the breath he'd been holding. When he opened the door and slowly stood up to stretch, his knees creaked, protesting almost as loudly as the car's front end.

His back ached from long hours of driving, and he rubbed it with both hands as he looked up at the shop's name again. The neon letters were stained and covered with grime. There was something both sad and comical in the way the *H* and the *D* flickered sporadically, as if on the verge of shorting out.

The storefront window had been blacked out. So had the glass door. Howie frowned, feeling a wave of disappointment, even betrayal. He'd seen similar storefronts before along the highway—roadside porno palaces for truckers and traveling salesmen. He'd even stopped in a few, and the name could fit that kind of business.

Yet, there wasn't a truck or big-rig in the parking lot.

Still, he hesitated. Turning his back to the shop, he studied the gray sky, which promised rain, and felt a moist wind on his face. With the wind came the whisper of the calliope again, and something else—the smell of cotton candy, the pink kind that came on a paper stick, that dissolved on your tongue and left sticky sugar crystals on your fingers. It made Howie remember a carnival and a time when he was a kid. . . .

A car whizzed by on the old highway, its wheels humming on the broken pavement. The sudden sound snapped Howie out of his reverie, and he jerked his head up to watch the car and its driver go by. In a too-brief moment, it was gone. So was the memory and the cotton candy smell.

Inexplicably, his eyes misted up as they had before. He turned yet again to read the shop's name. Maybe it was just a porno palace, or maybe it was some kind of souvenir shop hawking cheap tee shirts and kitschy coffee mugs for travelers. Yet, the *H* and the *D* winked at him with a crazy seductive rhythm. At him . . .

Howie. Davis. Howie. Then, *Davis.*

Howie slipped his suit jacket off and tossed it into the car. Despite the gray sky and the threat of rain, the air was warm and humid. He locked his car. Not knowing what to expect, he stepped up onto the cracked sidewalk and put his hand against the shop's door. A small, but startling shock of static electricity flashed over the tips of his fingers, and he gasped in surprise.

The door swung inward.

Just inside, the stoop-shouldered proprietor sat on a high stool behind a counter. His face looked like a withered morel, pasty and pocky, and his scant hair stuck out on both sides of his head and around the largest ears Howie had ever seen. He looked up from an open magazine on his lap and flashed a gap-toothed smile.

"Been tryin' ta get that fixed," he announced in a high voice. "Dang door's supposed ta open automatically. Always liked automatic doors, myself. They're so welcomin'. But danged hard ta get anythin' fixed around here lately. It works jus' fine from this side, though." He ran his gaze up and down Howie, and then fell silent and gave his attention back to his magazine.

Still on the threshold with the door automatically open behind him, Howie looked around. The shop made him strangely anxious. The long fluorescent lights that hung overhead seemed a little too dim. Even the illumination they gave off had an odd quality. He felt mildly dizzy, but told himself it was just the natural adjustment from the bright sunlight outside. Despite his anxiety, he took another step inside, and the door closed behind.

Rows and rows of shelves filled the store. Upon the shelves were boxes of all sizes—big boxes and small, plain boxes and ornate, paper boxes and wooden boxes and tiny chests, boxes of every conceivable color. Still more boxes rested on pedestals or wooden stands around the edges of the shop. A few of them even seemed to glow.

Howie could discern no apparent order or organization to any of the boxes. "I was just driving by and thought I'd stretch my legs," he lied to the proprietor. "Any chance you might have a coke machine?"

The proprietor closed his magazine and placed it on the counter. "Now, Mister, ya didn't stop for no coca-cola." He stared at Howie for a long minute, his mushroom face and mushroom eyes inscrutable. Then he lifted his hand and wagged one thin, bony finger. "You got a smell all over ya, like snow-cones an' popcorn an' cotton candy. An' ya got music clingin' to ya that I know, too, like merry-go-rounds."

The finger continued to wag like a steady metronome. "But ya got somethin' else that kinda stinks up, an' that's a lot of sadness. The sadness of regret." He wrinkled his nose and reached for his magazine again.

Howie reddened and clenched his fists at his sides. Turning angrily on his heel, he prepared to exit. True to the proprietor's word, the automatic door opened automatically from the inside, as if showing him the way out.

Then, Howie calmed. A smile turned up the corners of his lips as he turned back again. The door closed indifferently. "Man, I've been a salesman for twenty-five years, but that's just about the cleverest pitch I've ever heard." He waved a hand at the shelves of boxes. "What the hell kind of place is this?"

The proprietor looked up again and leaned on the counter. "Well, I suppose ya could call it sort of an antique shop. For some, it's a second-hand store. For still others, I guess ya could say it's a Lost-and-Found."

Howie scratched his head and approached the nearest pedestal. A pentagonal, pearl-colored wax box caught his attention, and he bent closer. The swirls and knot designs pressed into the lid held a mesmeric quality that confused his senses. Straightening, he backed away and rubbed his eyes.

"I've never seen so many boxes," he said after a moment, aware that the proprietor was watching his every move. "Are they just decorative, or is there anything in them?"

"Dreams," the proprietor said simply. "Lost dreams. Just like the name of the shop says."

"Yeah, right," Howie muttered. He was beginning to wonder why he'd stopped. After all, it was just another roadside gyp-joint full of kitsch and crap.

"Isn't that why you stopped, Mr. Davis?" The mush-room eyes behind the counter suddenly shone with a deep, diamond light as the proprietor rose from his stool, and his strange, backwoods accent vanished. "You've lost something. A dream you once had. You wonder if you can possibly find it again."

"Now that would make me something of a fool, wouldn't it?" Howie shot back. He reddened again, feeling his blood pressure rise. "You can't go chasing lost dreams, not at my age. I've got a good career and a good life! And even if you could, what kind of a dream would you find in a box?" He grabbed the pearl-colored box and angrily ripped the lid off.

The heady smell of the rose garden filled his nostrils, and camera flashes filled the air. He faced a sea of microphones and tape recorders and stared past them at all the adoring, upturned faces. Never had he felt so good, so proud, so confident! The day he'd hoped and prayed for—the day he'd dreamed about—had finally come! Vindication!

With the White House for his backdrop, and all of Congress on their knees before him, he raised his hands. "Today," he proclaimed, "I can finally declare—and this time it's for real—Mission Accomplished! Yes, I mean it! Victory in . . . !"

Howie lurched sideways and caught himself by grabbing for one of the shelves. The proprietor caught him, instead, with one hand and put him back on his feet. Howie shook his head, surprised and a little bit embarrassed as the proprietor put the lid back on the pentagonal box.

"What the hell?" Howie exclaimed. "For a moment, I thought I was . . . I was the president of . . . !"

The proprietor replaced the box in its position on the pedestal. "Everybody has lost dreams," he muttered. "But trust me, this one's unique, not to mention dangerous and demented. Even if it was for sale, you couldn't afford it."

With vestiges of the experience still swimming in his head, Howie stuttered. "But, but . . . ! I don't understand! That wasn't my dream!"

Crooking a finger, the proprietor beckoned for him to follow. Down a long row of shelves they walked and into another, darker room entirely. Howie sensed there was still another room beyond that. The shop was large and deep. Impossibly large and deep. Everywhere he looked, he saw shelves and stacks of boxes.

"Yours are here," the proprietor said. "Somewhere. You'll just have to search. Take your time."

Howie raised an eyebrow. "But don't a lot of these dreams belong to other people?"

The proprietor pointed to a curtained area. "There's a fitting room over there. Feel free to try anything on. But if you open a box, just be sure to replace the lid when you're finished."

A frown of doubt creased Howie's lips. Boxes and boxes everywhere, and the strange proprietor was offering him the chance to peek as he would? "It seems kind of prurient," Howie said.

"Suit yourself," the proprietor answered with a shrug, donning his accent again as he turned away to leave Howie. "If ya find your own dream, it's yours ta keep." Then, he turned back toward Howie and wagged that bony finger once more. "Just be careful," he warned. "Don't get too caught up in someone else's dream."

"Hey, wait," Howie called as the proprietor walked away. "How did you know my name? You called me Mister Davis"

The proprietor didn't answer, but just kept on walking until he disappeared in the gloom among the seeming miles of shelves, and only his footsteps echoed in the weird air. Finally, even those faded.

Alone, Howie pursed his lips and wondered what to do, where to start. He ran his finger over what looked like a satin hatbox. Beside that was a shoebox. A small, porcelain ring box glimmered on the shelf beside the shoebox. Howie reached for that with utmost care. It seemed wrong somehow. An intrusive thing to do. Yet, he lifted the delicately hinged lid just a crack.

"Oh, Robert!" Howie exclaimed as he stared at the incredible diamond Robert had just placed on his finger. "You've made me the happiest woman in the world!"

Howie slammed the lid down on the porcelain box and drew a sharp breath. Instinctively, he pressed a hand to his chest, then to his crotch, to reassure himself of his masculinity. "This could seriously warp somebody's mind!" he muttered as he returned the box to its place. Yet, his fingers lingered on the box as he pushed it back on the shelf. He could feel sadness along its edges, an emptiness, and he wondered what had become of the woman to whom the dream belonged.

He took down another box. This one was an old cigar box with a faded picture of a pretty señorita and the word Havana stamped on the worn lid. Howie lifted it close to his nose. The box still exuded the crisp, distinctive aroma of fine tobacco.

Yet he hesitated. Howie looked nervously over his shoulder to see if anyone was watching. Hadn't the proprietor said something about a fitting room? He glanced around, turning almost in a circle before he spied the curtained area. He chewed his lip, and his eyes narrowed.

Then Howie Davis loaded up his arms with boxes and scuttled behind the draperies. The fitting room contained an overstuffed armchair and a table. Arranging the boxes in haphazard fashion, Howie sat down and balanced the cigar box on his knees.

He grinned with anticipation, licking his lips, and slowly lifted the lid.

The scents of ocean breezes and perfume filled his nostrils. The surf boomed on the sandy shore, and behind him, the strains of a Cole Porter song, adapted to a heady mambo beat, wafted out from the beachside Cuban nightclub. The tropical night glittered with stars.

But he held the brightest star in his arms. He pressed his mouth to hers, and her lips tasted like cotton candy.

"Stephen!" she breathed in his ear. "Please don't go! I'm so afraid!" She gripped the lapels of his flight jacket and pressed her head against his chest.

Stephen/Howie thought he'd never seen a woman more beautiful, more desirable. He wanted her with a passion that matched hers, and he meant to have her right here on the beach.

"The squadron leaves at dawn," he answered, drawing her down. "You'll join me in England in a few weeks,

and we'll be married. This damned war won't come between us, Maria, I swear it!"

"You American pilots!" she whispered as she yielded to him. "Tell me again the three most important words in the world!"

Stephen/Howie grinned. It was their private joke. "Pitch, yaw and roll."

Howie closed the cigar box lid and sagged back into the armchair. Tears ran down his cheeks. He could still taste Maria's mouth, still feel her heat, and still feel her hands upon him. So much joy!

Yet, so much pain.

Stephen's dream had gone down in flame and bullets, and though Stephen had survived, Maria hadn't wanted a man with no legs.

Howie leaned forward and cradled his head in his hands and wept. It was Stephen's dream, but he had shared it, and he couldn't shake it off.

His heart hammered. His tears turned to beads of sweat. Howie leaned back again and thrust his hand into his pocket for a bottle of tablets. He swallowed one and set the bottle aside to stare at the pile of boxes still on the table. "No more," he murmured.

Yet, as he set the cigar box among the others, his hand brushed a small chest. It teetered on the edge and started to fall. Howie made a lunge to catch it.

The lid flipped open.

Howie flopped back in the chair and cried. His right hand made a fist around the bottle of tablets. His heart was racing. Or maybe it was breaking. His head reeled with dreams that were never his. Except, now they were. They were in his memories, as much a part of him now as his hands or his name.

He floated in a world of blackness. The walls of the room, even the curtain, had long since disappeared. It was just him and his armchair and boxes dotting the timeless dark like stars. He'd opened them all, one by one, like an addict unable to resist. They teased him with hope and laughter and joy, but in the end, every time, hope shattered, laughter turned to grief, joy to regret.

Lost dreams.

Howie tightened his grip on the bottle of tablets. A bad heart and high blood pressure. A dangerous combination, especially for a salesman on the road alone.

All alone. No family, no friends. No dreams.

One tablet kept him alive. The bottle contained thirty. And maybe none of it mattered anyway, he thought, as he unscrewed the bottle cap. Maybe he was already dead, and this was some kind of hell.

From out of the bottle came the faint sound of a calliope playing a jolly little march that conjured images of merry-go-rounds with painted horses and bouncing rabbits and long-necked ostriches going up and down and around and around.

Howie was beyond surprise, but still he opened his eyes. First, he looked at the bottle. It looked like an ordinary medicine bottle, but there was something different about it. Something unusual about the prescription.

He opened the lid for a closer look.

It was night, but no longer dark. The sky swirled with bright neon carnival lights. They made Howie dizzy with their colors. The ferris wheel loomed on his right, and the tilt-a-whirl spun crazily on his left. Right in front of him, the octopus tossed riders up and down with senses-stealing abandon. He turned in a circle, observing the roller-coaster and the mile-high parachute ride, the flying Dutchman, all the booths and games of chance with their kewpie dolls and stuffed toys, and he drank in the wonder of it all, the magic, wide-eyed as only a nine year old child could be.

In his right hand, he held a cotton candy, the pink kind on a stick, the kind that made sticky sugar crystals on your fingers and lips. In his left hand, he held a cherry snow cone.

Power cables stretched across the ground like black snakes, but he was careful not to trip and drop his treats. With no one to guide him, he wandered alone among the laughing crowds of thrill-seekers from one wild, incredible ride to the next, past the haunted house and the tunnel of love, past the tent with Hitler's body and the amazing transforming ape-woman from the deepest heart of Africa.

Howie was lost. But at nine years old, he didn't care. He had no money for the rides, but he had his cotton candy and his snow cone, and he was having the most astonishing night of his life!

When a clown appeared suddenly at his side, Howie didn't jump. The crazy wig and the huge red nose were just two more wonders. He smiled, and offered his left hand to the clown. But then, he realized he couldn't shake hands without dropping the snow cone, so Howie just smiled.

"Hi, Mister Clown!"

The clown bent low and placed his immense, white,

rubbery hands on the knees of his red-and-yellow checkered pants. It was hard to hear over all the loud music and the screams and the laughter, but the clown spoke his name.

"I'll bet you're Howie Davis," he said through red-painted lips that stretched all the way up to his ears. "Your parents are worried. Half the carnival is looking for you!"

"I'm right here!" Howie shouted back. Then he took a bite of cotton candy and turned his attention to the merry-go-round. He particularly loved the big black stallion with the white mane and golden saddle.

As if by magic, the clown produced a token and held it up between his gloved fingers. "Would you like to ride that?" he asked.

Howie's eyes grew even wider. "Wow! Would I!"

The clown's eyes twinkled. "Finish your treats," he said, "then take this to the man at the gate. Tell him your name and that Chuckles said to put you at the head of the line and to give you the best ride he ever gave anybody."

Howie couldn't believe his luck. A free ride! He tore into his cotton candy. The sticky strands stuck to his face, even to his hair. In his eagerness to finish the pink mass of fluff, he dropped his snow cone. But it was only flavored ice and didn't matter as much.

With the last bite gone, he cast aside the paper stick, dashed to the roustabout at the gate and thrust out the token. The roustabout grinned as he repeated word for word everything Chuckles had said, and sure enough, he got the best horse—the big black stallion with the white mane and golden saddle.

That ride seemed to go on forever. Clinging to the

pole upon which the painted stallion was mounted, Howie flung back his head and laughed as the world churned into one buttery mass of candy color. His heart beat faster and faster. The music of the calliope poured from loud speakers as he and his horse went up and down.

When the ride finally ended, Howie leaned breathlessly on the pole and waited for the world to settle down again. When all the other riders had dismounted, the roustabout came to get him, pried his small hands from around the pole, and helped him down.

Chuckles waited by the exit gate with his parents. His mom held out her arms to embrace him, her face tear-stained with worry. But Howie flung his arms, instead, around the clown. "Thank you," he said, barely audible over the carnival din. "I want to be a clown just like you when I grow up."

Howie gave a quiet sigh before he gently screwed the cap back on the bottle. He closed his fist around it again, but not out of anger this time or out of pain. That bottle had just become the most precious thing in the world to him. What was a bottle, really, but another kind of box?

The fitting room curtains parted, and the proprietor looked down at him for a long moment before taking the bottle from Howie's hand. He studied it, read the label, then inclined his head as he returned it. "Dreams are the best medicine, wouldn't you agree, Mister Davis? You thought you'd lost yours, and you've been carrying it all along."

Howie looked up with a puzzled expression. There was still so much he didn't understand. He made an encompassing gesture with his hand. "But you said it was back here somewhere."

The proprietor looked mildly indignant, but also amused. He pointed to the bottle with his bony finger. "Well, it is back here! Isn't this where you found it?"

Howie couldn't argue with that. He leaned back in the armchair, uncertain whether to laugh or to cry again. "I wanted so much to be a clown," he blurted. "I even went to clown college. But when my parents got sick, I needed a real job, something with money and security so I could take care of them, so I became a pharmacy systems salesman." He glanced at the medicine bottle. "I hated it. I still hate it. I travel from city to city, but I think now that I've just been running from that fact."

Howie leaned forward and set the bottle on the table among all the other boxes. "I'd completely forgotten that carnival. How could I have forgotten Chuckles?" He threw his head back suddenly and laughed as he hadn't laughed in years. "Oh, God! I flunked out of clown college! I couldn't juggle worth a damn!"

The proprietor pushed open the curtains with a swish and began to collect the many boxes scattered about. Howie rose to help him, and together, they returned the boxes to their shelves. When the last box was back in place, the proprietor fixed him with his mushroom eyes.

"You have a rare opportunity, Mister Davis," he said. "An opportunity these others never had. Their dreams are still lost dreams. Many of them can never be retrieved." He turned away and started toward the front of the shop. "You, on the other hand, have found your dream. It's in your front pocket right where it's always been. The question now is, what will you do with it?"

Reassuring himself that the bottle was indeed in his pocket, Howie fell into step behind the proprietor. "I don't know," he said doubtfully. "I'm a bit old to be a clown now. I've got a lot of seniority and job security, too, and a sizable 401K plan."

The proprietor said nothing. They had reached the front of the store, and he took his place behind the counter where his magazine still lay open.

Howie chewed his lip. He looked at the proprietor for some hint or guidance, but the strange man just climbed back on his stool. Howie took a step toward the door, which opened automatically. But then, he stepped back, and the door closed.

"Maybe I could be a clown part-time," he blurted. "Do hospitals and things like that for sick little kids! They'd like that, wouldn't they? Or maybe birthday parties!"

The proprietor turned a page of his magazine. "It's your dream," he answered. "Follow it the way you will."

Howie beamed, suddenly excited at the prospect of finally living his dream, if only in a small way. "Thank you," he said in a quietly earnest voice.

The proprietor didn't look up. "Don't mention it," he answered.

Howie grinned and gave the proprietor a look. "I was thanking Chuckles. I have a feeling he heard me, too. But thank you, also."

He stepped again toward the door, and again the door opened. This time, it didn't seem to be showing him the way out. Rather, it showed him a beginning.

Still, he turned toward the proprietor once more, almost reluctant to leave.

"You know, I still can't juggle worth a damn."

The proprietor looked up. "Are you sure?" He made a gesture, and from the pages of the magazine, three red rubber balls sailed across the room straight at Howie.

Without thinking, Howie caught them. His hands became a blur, and the rubber balls went around and around in the air. Howie laughed. He felt younger than he'd felt in years.

He felt like a nine-year-old boy, and the world smelled of pink cotton candy, and the music of merry-go-rounds filled his ears.

Selina Rosen's stories have appeared in several magazines and anthologies including *Marion Zimmer Bradley's Fantasy Magazine*, the two new *Thieves' World* anthologies, and HelixOnLine. Some of her fourteen published novels include *Queen of Denial*, *Chains of Freedom*, *Strange Robby*, *Fire & Ice*, *Bad Lands* (with Laura J. Underwood), and *Sword Masters*. She owns Yard Dog Press and created their *Bubbas of the Apocalypse* universe.

Queen of Suburbia

Selina Rosen

Selantra sat poised on the seat of power—her ergonomic chair in her home office in Matawan, New Jersey.

"Curses," she hissed as she saw the E-mail. "How stupid can you get! The message specifically says send it to ten friends but not the person who sent it to you." It was the second one she'd gotten back since she'd sent it out yesterday afternoon. This meant she had to find yet ten more people to send it to and hope that none of those idiots sent it back. "They're ruining my spell. I'm running out of friends to send it to," she grumbled.

Selantra looked at the clock and scowled. She couldn't put it off any longer; she had to get ready. "But soon all will bow to my will." She laughed manically, pressed the Send button, stood up and went to get dressed for work.

Tamara just wanted to get through her E-mail so she could get back to work on her book. She deleted all the unwanted spam, answered a couple of fan letters, and then started answering the E-mail from friends and relatives which she had let stack up over the last few days. Why? Because all she wanted to do was work on her book.

She opened the E-mail from her mother-in-law Sara—to whom she had given the Native American name Woman Who Fills World With Spam. Tamara cringed: A chain letter! There was a picture of a woman playing a lute in a field of flowers and there was some weird written language coming from the strings. Under that was a poem all about self-empowerment, mostly just like all the other chain crap that idiots insisted on sending her.

Of course Robert would have a fit if she told him his mother was a moron, and the truth was that she liked her mother-in-law. In fact, right then better than she liked her husband. But anyone who sent one of these things to a friend was in Tamara's opinion a total idiot.

A poem filled with love and self-empowerment or some sappy-assed story of human kindness was always followed with: "Send this message to ten friends in ten minutes and something amazing will happen today. Send it to twenty friends in ten minutes and have good luck for a year. Send it to fifty friends in ten minutes and have good luck for life. If you let the message end with you doom and despair will fall upon you and you will have bad luck for two years."

This one was no different.

"Just what I need," Tamara said with a sigh. 2007 had sucked. Her main publisher went under and she'd had to rush to sign with someone else at half

what she was used to getting just to stay in the game.
Her adult son got a divorce. Her best friend died of
cancer. Bush was still president. She had high hopes
that 2008 would be the start of a long cycle of good
luck. She normally wasn't superstitious, or at least she
liked to believe she had outgrown all that. Over the
last eight years she hadn't had much of anything but
bad luck—and maybe, just maybe, it was because she
just kept deleting these stupid-assed things.

She sure as hell couldn't make herself send it on
to ten friends. She didn't understand the people who
felt compelled to forward this crap. The fact that
they did it meant that they believed it was true. If
they believed it was true then they were either A)
demanding that you bend to their will and send it on
or B) sending you a damned curse—and what sort of
friend sends their "loved ones" a curse?

What sort of mother-in-law sent her suddenly under-
employed daughter-in-law a two-year curse on the
second day of the new year?

She deleted the damn thing, inwardly seething, and
wishing that the person who started the damn chain
letter in the first place would grow a giant boil on
their ass. Then she felt better.

Just five days after starting the chain letter Selantra
started to feel the power growing within her. When
she got up that morning she felt younger and the air
smelled sweeter.

When she pulled into the parking lot at the office
her favorite parking spot was empty. When she walked
into the employee lounge Tom handed her a cup of
coffee just the way she liked it and told her to take

it easy that she was working too hard and making them all look bad.

When she sat down at her cubicle to work she had a new chair. The old one that hurt her back and had been repaired with duct tape was gone and in its place was sitting a brand new ergonomic chair like the one she had at home only in her favorite shade of purple. It broke about fifteen office codes.

"Surprise," her boss said at her shoulder.

"Thanks," Selantra said.

"No problem, Sally, you deserve it. I've overlooked how important you are to this office for too long." He walked away and she smiled. It was working. She wasn't important to the company. All she did was type up reports and she certainly didn't work as hard as most of the other employees did. The spell was working; it was changing people's perception of her.

Selantra—for that was the name she'd given herself, Sally was just the drone who worked for the advertising firm in cubicle seventeen—had figured out that the true route to absolute power was not to actually change, but to make people change their perceptions of you. And she'd found the perfect tool. She sat down in her new chair with her perfect cup of coffee and patted her monitor.

A few minutes later, as she was typing up the first report of the day, she felt it: a sudden loss of power that made her cringe. Someone had deleted without sending, but more than that they had deleted with animosity, even hatred. There had been power behind their keystroke and a will to destroy whoever had started the chain mail. It took her till noon to fully recover. Most people didn't seem to mind the possibility of cursing their friends as long as they thought they might actually get some good luck, and they sure didn't want any bad luck. So they just kept pressing that Send key and every time they did, Selantra's power grew. Most people rationalized sending the curse on by saying that all their friends had to do was send it on to ten people and then they'd have good luck, too.

The sheep didn't know that there was no luck for them, good or bad. They couldn't read those words coming out of the lute, didn't know their magic meaning, and probably wouldn't have cared if they did. They'd still send it on and every person who believed in it enough to send it on made Selantra stronger. The few who deleted it could not possibly contend with the thousands who would send it on and soon, very soon, Selantra would be queen of all she surveyed.

She didn't give another thought to the person who had deleted with such malice. The bad feeling passed and her day just got progressively better.

In the weeks that passed her power grew in leaps and bounds. She was given a promotion at work to be an advertising executive even though she knew not one damn thing about it. And even when she screwed everything up they praised her. When she went to the mall someone always let her have a parking place close to the door. When she shopped, if she grabbed something on sale at the same time someone else did, the other person apologized and let her have it. When she went to Starbucks they made her mocha latte with foam perfectly and she never had to repeat her order. Not once.

Hell, the kid that mowed her lawn even did it just

when it needed it, not because she called to tell him the city was going to fine her if he didn't. Though she doubted at this point the city would have bitched at her anyway.

Her mother called and spent thirty minutes apologizing for all the horrible things she'd said and done to Selantra over the course of her life.

Then there was that fateful day when, without being told to do so, everyone stopped calling her Sally and started to call her Selantra. If this kept up she had no doubt that soon she would be Queen of the World. It was amazing how nice people treated you when they perceived that you were important.

She saw no end in sight. The E-mail would keep circulating, going round and round and round again and making her constantly stronger.

Selantra'd had a hard day getting everything she wanted, so she lay back on her bed. As she started to drift off to sleep she started to think about how she would rule the world, what she would change, whom she might choose to be her boy toy. She chuckled. Why stop at just one? She could have anyone she wanted, as many as she wanted. Nothing could stop her.

Tamara had been working on the book all day, about fifteen hours, interrupted only by her husband coming home to bitch that she hadn't done a damn thing all day. She had mostly ignored him, told him to heat up the chicken casserole from the night before and kept writing. Now she wasn't really tired but she knew she had to quit writing because when she looked up to see what she had just typed it said: "Jamie caught gerferkle in his galingle and slide down the janket."

She decided to check her E-mail to wind down from the day. Her friend Katy wanted to know if she could meet her for lunch. "Sorry, Katy, it's 11:45 at night so a little late for lunch. How about tomorrow?" She added a little laughing emoticon at the end.

She checked the rest of her E-mail. There was a lot of spam but not one fan letter, which was distressing. She wasn't a big star, far from it, but she had a small, loyal fan club and she usually got mail from at least one of them a day. She needed that encouragement because she had never gotten any from her family. They thought her writing was a hobby. In fact, her kids made a point of telling her they didn't like to read. Her husband considered her writing to be nothing more than a manifestation of her obsessive compulsive disorder. Oh he had more than supported her writing when it had been bringing in good money. Now that it wasn't bringing in what he considered to be even decent money he constantly told her it was a huge waste of time.

Their marriage was in trouble. She knew it, he knew it; hell, she was sure everyone did. Things had been mostly bad for them for seven years. Going through bad things together didn't necessarily bring a couple close together, not when they both handled stress and loss in different ways. When her publisher had gone under last year, taking her career with it, things had deteriorated between them to the point that they hardly spoke at all these days except to argue.

This was probably why she was in no hurry to go to bed. She could either sleep with him, just the thought of which sent a cold shiver down her spine. Or she could curl up on the couch and then have to explain why she had done so in the morning.

She pressed Send and then Receive and was almost relieved to see she had a new message until she opened it and saw what it was. Her friend Amy, who she hadn't seen or heard from in weeks, had sent her that same damn chain letter her mother-in-law had. Tamara was livid. While she didn't dare tell her mother-in-law what she thought of these things, she was more than capable of telling Amy. She hit Reply sending the chain mail back to Amy with this message:

Amy,

Sending some stupid-assed chain letter is not the same as writing, calling or coming by.

Never, ever, ever, send me any of this crap again!

Did you ever have good luck after sending one of these things?

I've had lots of bad luck for years now. I don't think it's because idiots keep sending me this crap, but who knows? Maybe it is.

I think the morons who start this crap deserve to die a slow and painful death, death by crabs or some such thing. I don't know what they get from wasting their time this way but I hope whatever it is it's worth all the grief they cause.

Yes, I am this mad. It's late, I've had a hell of a day, and this was the last thing I needed. You're sending this thing all over and you don't even know what it says.

Tamara

Tamara didn't care if Amy never talked to her again. If she sent her another one of these things she was going to have to hunt her down and kill her, so it was just as well. Feeling better than she had in a while she shut her computer down for the night and crawled off to sleep on the couch.

Selantra woke with a scream and a strange crawling sensation on her skin. She ran to the bathroom and threw up, then she just lay on the floor trying to get the world to quit spinning. She felt her power being drained and she was so weak she couldn't get up.

Someone powerful was deleting without sending. No! This was worse than before. They'd done something else, but Selantra couldn't be sure what. All she could be sure of was that whatever it was, it was causing her physical pain and draining away the power that had been building up. She started to panic, but then as she lay there, the power started to come back. About an hour later she was able to get up and stumble to her bed where she slept and woke up so filled with power she almost forgot what had happened.

Almost.

"Selantra Dupree, what a joke." Tamara laughed without joy as she changed the channel.

"Are you kidding, Tamara? She's a genius," Katy said, grabbing the remote away and turning the channel back so that she could watch the idiot girl from Matawan speak.

"There will be more parking at the malls," Selantra was saying. "No more handicapped spots means more and better parking for everyone. Let's face it, the handicapped mostly don't work so they can afford to waste their time parking further away and hey, they're on wheels so it's not like they have to walk like the rest of us."

"She's brilliant," Katy said.

"She's a freakin' moron," Tamara said in disbelief. "Don't tell me you voted for that thing?"

"Sure I did," Katy said excitedly. "She's going to be the greatest congresswoman ever."

"Whatever." Tamara got up from the couch. She couldn't afford to argue with Katy because she had nowhere else to go. She'd moved in with her friend three months ago when she'd finally gotten fed up and decided it was time for her and Robert to split the sheets.

Last week the divorce was final but she wouldn't have enough money to get her own place till the house sold. She didn't think that would be happening any time soon; the housing market was in the toilet. The advance she'd received on the book she'd just turned in was half of what she was used to getting. If she didn't watch every penny she spent she wasn't even going to be able to pay Katy what she owed her for her part of the rent.

She felt defeated and displaced. Tamara couldn't even afford to have an opinion. Watching the idiot girl talking on the idiot box was more than she could take, so she walked to her room and shut the door.

A forty-seven year old woman with everything she owned stuffed into a ten by twelve room. It was pathetic. She was sharing an apartment and subsequently a bathroom with a thirty-five year old woman who hadn't dated in twelve years and who obviously used the shower massage as a surrogate man. Katy was often in there for hours at a time, forcing Tamara to take a trip to the Quik Pik a half-mile away just to use the toilet. It was pathetic *and* embarrassing.

She was angry and bitter and at the very end of her rope. Her kids didn't even offer to help. She had an ex-husband she was glad to be rid of and who was glad to be rid of her, but who really felt he deserved to have everything they'd worked together to acquire since she was the one who wanted out. Truth was—and she knew it—Robert was in no hurry to sell the house he was living in and it would have been a chore even if the housing market were good.

She couldn't get a decent advance and there were no more royalty checks because her old publishing house had gone under and declared bankruptcy. She was going to have to get a "real" job. A frightening prospect since at her age and having been out of the job market for close to twenty years she'd be lucky to get a job flipping burgers or as a door greeter.

She'd sold a couple of short stories and knew she'd sell more but that was never steady income and at best it might pay a couple of bills.

Some pretty twenty-something moron who cared about nothing as much as making things easier for people who already had it easy had just been elected to congress, and Tamara would have had trouble getting arrested in this screwed-up country.

She switched on her computer and called up her E-mail. There was lots of it, mostly spam which she just deleted. She'd tried spam filters, but they had wound up keeping out stuff she wanted and still let spam in, so what was the point?

Her agent had sent her a copy of a review of her new book. It was half-assed, though he of course thought it was a good review because he was a moron.

In fact, lately Tamara was more and more sure that

everyone she knew or ever came into contact with was a complete and utter idiot.

She was sure it was mostly her point of view. She just needed something good to happen to counterbalance all the utter crap she'd been put through. She needed the equivalent of a circus coming to town in her brain to wipe out all the bile of the last few years.

If she could just totally lash out at any of the people who were responsible for how she felt that would help. She couldn't of course because she was pretty sure that everyone close to her was about ten minutes from checking her into the Ha Ha Hilton as it was. Besides she couldn't afford to blow up at her ex, or Katy, or her publisher or her agent or a dozen other people she'd like to rip a new one because they held all the cards and she had nothing, zilch, *nada*.

She'd had to bite her tongue so much this past year she had permanent scarring.

There was an E-mail from one of her fans, Bertha from Pennsylvania. She always had such nice things to say about Tamara's work she was sure this would cheer her right up. But when she opened it, it was that damn chain letter again, the one with the two-year curse that she hated so much. She started to delete it and then she noticed the woman in the picture and stopped. She ran in the living room and grabbed a newspaper.

"What's up?" Katy asked.

"Same, same," Tamara droned idiotically and ran back into her hole with the paper. She flipped it open to the article about their new congresswoman and she held the picture up to the one on the screen. There was no doubt; there was a strong resemblance. She grabbed her glasses—the ones she only wore when all the words ran together on her monitor—and put them on. What language was that? What music was the lute playing? She had no idea and neither did all the idiots who just kept sending it out over and over again. If it had gotten to her three times already, how many times had it been around? How many people had just sent this right on without having any idea what it said, or if it said anything at all?

She blew up the letters on her computer, and when she did the words vanished like smoke. She took off her glasses and rubbed her eyes. She tried the process again and again the words turned to smoke.

Tamara tried to remember if she'd had anything to drink. She hadn't, so then she wondered if maybe she ought to go get something.

Then it all made perfect sense. Sure lots of total dumb asses wound up in congress spouting utter crap, but not poor, unknown dumb asses. This Selantra Dupree had done a spell.

Tamara herself was no stranger to spell craft. She'd played with magic as a teenager, and like so many dabblers had gotten out the first time she did something she couldn't explain away. As she got older and wiser she'd studied the craft again but mostly as a visitor, not as a practitioner. That didn't mean she didn't know magic when she saw it.

Or maybe everything that had happened to her in the last few years had just driven her completely mad and she was lashing out at something she hated because everything else seemed out of her grasp.

It wasn't hard to find Congresswoman Dupree's E-mail address. She forwarded the chain mail to her and typed, "Congratulations on your congressional seat," in the subject line, knowing that it was very hard for anyone not to open something that might be praise. Then she wrote with a fervor she hadn't felt in months.

It's a great idea, feeding off people's gullibility to build your power. Nothing quite as strong as people's belief is there? All those people, millions of them, believing they are going to have good luck or avoid bad luck by sending it on, each picking at least ten friends they don't mind risking to the "curse" to forward the message to. And every day it's more people and more power. And I know how to take it all away; it's almost too easy.

Tamara hit Send.

Selantra's inauguration party—held in the lavish Gold Hotel Ballroom—was just starting to wind down when the pains started. They went from her stomach to her brain and back again. She excused herself quickly and practically ran to her hotel room where she threw up for ten minutes. Feeling dizzy she rinsed her mouth, washed her face, and stumbled to her bed expecting the pains would stop and her strength would come back tenfold as it had the last two times. This time was different. She continued to feel weaker and weaker and the pains kept coming. Finally she forced herself up and crawled to her computer to see if she could figure out what was going on.

She used her magic to get past the mass of E-mails from well-wishers and find the letter from Tamara

Black. Her fingers trembled as she opened the E-mail. She had just finished reading Tamara's message when another wave of pain went through her body.

She quickly wrote back, "What the hell are you doing to me?"

Tamara's answer was quick. "I encoded your message so that no one could open it, and then I sent it to everyone on my list with the message to send it back to me. When they do, I delete it. Every time I delete a message I get stronger and you get weaker. I will keep doing it till there is nothing left of you but a greasy spot."

As another pain shot through her body Selantra asked, "What exactly will it take to get you to stop? What is it you want?"

Tamara sat signing book after book, smiling and talking to her fans. Her cell phone rang and when she saw who it was she sighed. "Wait a minute, I have to take this. It's the president . . . again." She snapped the phone open, stood and walked away from the signing table.

"What?" she demanded.

"We don't want global warming, right?"

"How can you be such a smart witch and know nothing about the environment or politics?" Tamara asked in a harsh whisper.

"I just want to be in control. I don't really care about anything else, remember?"

"Like most politicians," Tamara muttered.

"Global warming, yes or no?" Selantra hissed.

"No we don't want global warming. Sign the air purity bill."

"All right, thanks."

Tamara shut her phone and looked at the long line of adoring fans that snaked out the door of the bookstore and through the mall. She supposed she should have thwarted Selantra's plan to take over the world, but then she'd still be stuck in Katy's apartment waiting for Robert to sell the house.

Esther M. Friesner is the author of thirty-three novels and over one hundred fifty short stories and other works. She won the Nebula Award twice as well as the Skylark and the Romantic Times Award. Best known for creating and editing the wildly popular *Chicks In Chainmail* anthology series (Baen Books), recent publications include the Young Adult novels *Temping Fate*, *Nobody's Princess*, and *Nobody's Prize*. She lives in Connecticut with her husband, is the mother of two grown children, and harbors cats.

Twice a Year

Esther M. Friesner

It hadn't been the best of days. Come to think of it, as far as Lois' professional life was concerned there *were* no best of days. She knew that when she'd decided to go into the glamorous (*snicker*) and high-paying (*bwahahaha!*) field of dental hygiene, it was tantamount to telling the world, "Why yes, I *would* like to be the second-most-dreaded health professional on earth! And making small children cringe at no additional charge? Bonus!" No sane person ever *wanted* to visit the dentist, and the prospect of seeing the dental hygienist for the recommended twice-yearly check-up and cleaning was only slightly less appalling.

As if I were the one to blame for their oral hygiene problems! Lois thought as she finished tidying up her work station. *Is it my fault their teeth look like prairie dog towns? Never mind that the closest that most of our patients come to using a strand of dental floss is chomping on a licorice whip.* She channeled her frustration into scrubbing out the spit-sink until it had a blinding gleam.

She had just double-double checked the equipment and was about to go home when Bonnie the receptionist came in. She was a pretty, red-haired local girl whose present expression was the embodiment of Please Don't Shoot the Messenger.

"All right, Bonnie, what *don't* you want to tell me?" Lois kept her tone calm—Bonnie looked upset enough already—but she could feel her fingernails digging deep into her palms in anticipation of whatever stomach-churning information the receptionist was about to impart.

"Um, Lois, there was a complaint about you today. A big one."

"Who from? I had appointments with four screaming kids, but they're my regular screamers. Besides, I know their moms." *No big surprise in a town as small as Sea Meadows,* Lois thought. *We're a flyspeck on the Connecticut shoreline, and from the looks of this place, that fly needs to eat more fiber.*

"It wasn't any of them," Bonnie said. "It was—"

"Wait! Don't take all the fun out of it." Lois held up her hand. "Was it my three o'clock? Mr. Baxter the Nervous Talker? Yak, yak, yak, all the way through his cleaning! Was he mad that I didn't sufficiently appreciate his brilliant conversation because I was busy trying not to stab him in the tongue?"

Bonnie shook her head. "It was the man who came in to see you at noon, remember him? Another new patient, blue eyes, silver hair, about six-foot-eight. He looked like a cross between Pierce Brosnan and George Clooney."

"I think a match like that *might* still be illegal in Connecticut. Bonnie, dear, if you're going to drool like that, *don't* do it in the spit-sink; I just cleaned it."

The receptionist blushed and spoke on quickly: "His name's Dylan Shoreham and when he left the office, he told me to let you know he was going to send a letter of complaint about you to Dr. Petersen."

"Did he happen to mention what he's going to complain *about*?"

"He said that the whole time you were cleaning his teeth, you wouldn't stop trying to sell him a valentine." Bonnie managed to look both perplexed and apologetic as she added: "Even if he *does* send that letter, Dr. Petersen's just going to throw it out because he'd never believe it. I mean, he knows you better than *that*. You've been working here since . . . forever."

"That's right, *forever*," Lois echoed, taking the word for a drive down Irony Lane. "I still remember my first day on the job. I *told* those silly dinosaurs that if they didn't floss, they were going to be in big trouble, but would they listen?"

A fresh blush brought Bonnie's skin tone into close competition with her hair color. "I only meant that Dr. Petersen would never believe you'd do something so unprofessional. And on top of that, trying to sell someone a *valentine*? In *June*? That's crazy."

"It certainly is," Lois agreed. But she was not smiling. *I didn't have a noon appointment. I was out of the office for lunch today. So he's back again, with all of his stolen magic—my magic! Twice a year, like clockwork, and every time he finds a different, more obnoxious way to send me his challenge. He thinks he's so clever! But clever or not, he* is *serious. I'd better see to this at once.* With Bonnie at her heels, she went to the coat closet and put on the windbreaker she kept there in case of sudden downpours. The day was warm and sunny, but her action had nothing to do with weather. She needed pockets.

"Well, I just wanted you to know what was going on, so if Dr. Petersen mentions it, you won't be taken by surprise," Bonnie said. "But what's the worst that can happen? Dr. Petersen would never fire *you*."

"I should hope not," Lois replied with a smile. Casually she scooped a couple of toothbrushes and a spool of dental floss from the basket on the receptionist's desk and stuffed them into her left pocket. Then she picked up Bonnie's *While You Were Out* message pad and a pen. Fixing the girl with a hard stare, she spoke four words *sotto voce* and drew an emphatic line through the word *While*.

Bonnie's head dropped forward onto her chest, her breath the breath of deep sleepers. Lois grabbed her before she could hit the floor, taking the opportunity to whisper in the sleeper's ear, "There was *no* patient here today named Dylan Shoreham." She then dragged the girl's limp body back to her desk and made the necessary changes to the office records before shredding the altered *While You Were Out* slip.

"Huh?" Bonnie snapped awake, confused.

"You have a good day too, dear," Lois said sweetly. "See you tomorrow." She turned on her heel and was out of the office before Bonnie could reply.

Lois crossed the parking lot, making for her car at a pace that was only a half-step below a full-out sprint. She had just clicked her seatbelt closed and was reaching for the ignition with her key when all of her haste was brought to a screeching halt by a female voice shrilling her name.

"Lois, dear! Yoo-hoo!" A tall, pudgy woman in a

red sundress toddled up on a pair of wedgie sandals so high, they made her look like a candied apple on a stick.

"*Yoo-hoo*"? Lois thought as her unwelcome assailant hooked scarlet acrylic claws onto the driver's side rear view mirror. *Who says "yoo-hoo" any more? Are we living in a back issue of* Archie *comics?* Aloud she said, "Oh, hello, Emily, so nice to see you, I was just leaving."

"But you *can't!*" Emily protested in a voice that could have annoyed fingernails on a blackboard. "This is the *only* time I've got free to talk to you!"

Lois kept her face expressionless. It was useless to protest that her own free time did *not* coincide with Emily's. The whiny wench viewed other people as 24-hour convenience stores. Trying to make her see that you had a non-Emily-related life was like punching rice pudding: Messy, frustrating, and futile. You accomplished nothing and wound up with raisins between your knuckles.

"Yes, Emily, what can I do for you?" Lois asked wearily.

"You have *got* to show me those adorable valentines of yours again, right this very minute!" Emily chirped. "I think I've finally decide on which one I want to buy."

"I'd love to, but I don't have any with me."

"Oh, don't be silly, of *course* you do!" Emily giggled in a manner that would have been inappropriately kittenish even for an *anime* schoolgirl. "You *always* keep them in the trunk of your car. You *said* so."

Dammit, when did I ever tell her that? Lois wondered. *Not that it's untrue—I always keep* everything *in there.* "I'm sorry, but I took them out of the trunk last night. I wanted to rearrange the showcases."

"Then let's go to your house." Emily had the persistence of a famished leech.

"I'm not going home right now. How about tomorrow?"

"Tomorrow's *awful* for me!"

"The day after?"

"Nooooooo!" Emily whimpered. "Lois, please, please, *please*, you have got to let me see those valentines today! I absolutely, completely, *totally* have to buy one right this very instant! I swear to God, if you do this for me, I will buy *two* of them. Honest!"

Mentally, Lois counted to ten. She knew how this was going to go: She'd cave in to Emily's dogged pushiness and "discover" that she *did* have the valentines in the trunk. She'd show them to her avid customer, who would take a good fifteen minutes or more poring over the contents of the showcases before announcing that golly, no, she wasn't going to buy one—let alone two—after all.

Oh, heck, it's called the inevitable for a reason. Might as well get it over with.

"You know, Emily, on second thought, maybe I *did* put the cases back in the car after I rearranged the valentines. Let me check." Lois got out and popped the trunk.

And there they were. Of course they were. Whenever Lois wanted to lay hands on any one of her personal possessions, all she had to do was reach into her car trunk and *voilá*! Or in more modern parlance, *whoomp*, there it was, thanks to the portal spell Lois had placed on said car trunk back in the days when it was still the

bed of a horse-drawn wagon and Sea Meadows was a
huddle of marshland huts filled with religious fanatic
rejects from the Massachusetts settlements.

Inside the trunk was a stack of black velvet-lined
showcases of the sort used to show off fine jewelry.
Inside all was an assortment of small, glass-topped
octagonal wooden boxes and within these . . . a feast
of wonders. Each eight-sided box contained a marvel
of meticulous art to rival the jeweled splendor of a
butterfly's wings: an intricate pattern of breathtaking
complexity and astonishing beauty, picked out in a
delicate palette of seashells. Every one was a master-
piece. Lois couldn't help smiling when she looked at
them, even though she'd known each from the time
when it was nothing more than an empty container,
a mixed heap of shells laid out on her dining room
table, and a handy bottle of glue.

Valentines, she mused. *When most people hear that
word, they think of the holiday hype. I would happily lay a thousand year curse on the greeting card
industry for turning something as wonderful as love
into a joyless obligation.*

Lois' creations had nothing to do with the dire and
daunting Obligatory Displays of Mercantile Affection
crammed down the public's throat every February 14,
and yet they *were* valentines: *Sailors'* valentines. In the
nineteenth century, they'd been crafted by the natives
of Barbados and sold to English and American sailors
making port on their homeward voyages and seeking
gifts for their wives and sweethearts.

Lois remembered the first one she'd ever seen. It
was a gift of the heart from her husband, a laughing
young man named Tommy Meigs, who didn't care a

fig for all the gossip that called his darling a witch. *I wish you were a witch,* he'd said, lifting her off her feet and swinging her around light as a puff of apple blossom. *You could use your magic to keep me safe on every voyage, and to help me make my fortune!*

She tried to tell him that magic was no laughing matter. She tried proving that her own powers, though limited, were no joke. She was no grand sorceress in the style of Circe, no all-powerful enchantress who could rule storms and summon lightning or dead calms on a whim. She was, in fact, a very modest, domestic sort of witch, more likely to make a good cup of tea than a gruesome cauldron of potion. Her powers were circumscribed by and confined to the realm of a single Law of Spellcraft:

As Above, So Below.

Lois laid out her showcased stock of sailors' valentines in the otherwise empty trunk, took a step back, and waved one hand over them. "Well, Emily? See something you like?" She couldn't help feeling a surge of pride as the other woman studied her handiwork. (And the sailors' valentines *were* her handiwork, quite literally. She had not used any smidge of her power in their creation. Even a witch needed a hobby.)

"Ooooh," said Emily. She gazed at those gems, those delights, those bits of poetry captured in snail whorls, cats-paw scallops, mussels like purple wings, heart-shaped cockles, and took a deep breath. "So you'll give me a *good* discount if I buy two, right?" she chirped. She proceeded to make Lois an offer that would have been lowball for a chipped conch shell from a Key West discount bin.

"Emily, that's nowhere near the price I charge for

one. I told you, each of these is hand-made. It takes me a long time to put them together. The work is painstaking."

"My goodness, just listen to you, Lois! For someone who didn't want to take the time to show me these boxes, you certainly turn on the hard sell as soon as we start talking money. That's okay, I can play your game." She upped her opening bid by a dollar and declared, "Take it or leave it."

"Good idea," Lois replied. She began to lower the car trunk lid.

"What do you think you're doing?" Emily squealed, grabbing her wrist.

"Leaving it," Lois answered, shaking free.

"But you can't! I want to buy one! Where do you have to be that's so important you can't take the time to—?"

Lois closed her eyes. She knew Emily all too well from the eternally interwoven strands of suburban life in Sea Meadows. The woman could and *would* natter on, ad infinitum, until she wore down her chosen target to a nub of compliance. Or, if the target in question continued to resist her persistent whining, Emily would switch gears and turn the foolish upstart into fodder for some of the meanest, dirtiest, most artful character assassination imaginable. The thing about suburban gossip was that it did not need to be true to survive and spread; it only had to be entertaining. *Anything* to distract the listeners from the fact that they were living in a town where the biggest thrill on tap was betting on senior prom pregnancies.

Lois didn't mind what people said about her, but she did mind anything that got her noticed too much.

Sea Meadows was more than her home, it was *hers*, and she was here to stay. Centuries ago, the New World Witchly Council assigned each magical emigrant to America a generous patch of land to call her own. Witches could be more territorial than cats, except that when they felt threatened, they marked their turf by spraying it with destructive magic. *Nothing* got the smell out.

The Council's way of preventing such cataclysmic spats among its members was practical, but far from perfect. To keep things fair, the witches' designated areas were assigned by lot. If a witch didn't like where she was sent, she could ask for a change, but the Council was notoriously slow to review and act on appeals. Their motto was: *"Bloom Where You Are Planted. Or Don't. See If We Care."*

Being stuck in Sea Meadows for over three hundred years *and* the foreseeable future was hard enough. It was no picnic having to fake her own death periodically (and show up as her own heir afterwards) to maintain appearances. The effort of casting the spells to affect the minds and memories of an entire town—plus those of anyone of her acquaintance residing in the neighboring communities—always gave her raging migraines for two weeks. She did not need people paying *attention* to why her "distant cousin from Nebraska" looked exactly like her recently "deceased" incarnation.

She did not need Emily making trouble.

Lois reached into the darkest recess of the trunk and a large clamshell was in her hand. It was a perfect specimen, upper and lower halves of the deceased bivalve intact and still hinged together. She held it up, wide open, in Emily's startled face and muttered, "As above, so below." Then she shut it with a resounding *clack*!

Emily's jabbering mouth did not go *clack*! when it shut, but it did make a satisfying sound of teeth coming together so hard that someone wearing cheaper dental caps might've chipped a porcelain-clad incisor. While Emily remained stunned by what had just happened, Lois' hand dipped into the trunk yet again and retrieved an old-fashioned school slate. "As above, so below," she breathed over the dusty black surface as she drew a quick cartoon of Emily, complete with bubbly thought-balloon. The balloon held a very basic sketch of a sailor's valentine—just the eight-sided outline was enough for Lois' symbol-driven magic to work—but not for long. As soon as she drew it, Lois wet one fingertip and erased the small chalk octagon, leaving Emily's image with nothing on her mind at all.

As above, so below . . .

"Um . . . Was there something you wanted to ask me, Lois?" Emily said, tilting her head to one side. Her face wore the clueless expression of a five-week-old kitten, with none of the charm.

"Just if you'd made your next appointment with Dr. Petersen," Lois said smoothly as she tossed the slate and the clamshell back into the contained oblivion of her car trunk before closing the lid.

Free at last, she floored the gas pedal and tore through town, headed for one of Sea Meadows' many beach access roads. The path she chose was a narrow street with barely room for two cars to shoulder past one another. In the old days it had been the route by which Goodman Harney had taken his seven children into the marshes to hunt waterfowl. In those days,

Sea Meadows was more sea than meadow—poor for farming, worse for animal husbandry, useless as a trade port. The settlers would have upped stakes and moved if they'd had the wherewithal to go somewhere better. But no one did, and some were so cursed stubborn they wouldn't have left their original homesteads even if that were possible.

It took a powerful heap of duck and gooseflesh to keep the Harney brood fed, and Lois still recalled the heartbreak of seeing the little ones grow thinner and thinner in years when the flocks proved smarter than their father. She remembered thinking: *Children shouldn't have to bet their lives on just one flimsy source of food. If we could measure this town by acres instead of gallons, they'd thrive! We should open a route to the world's riches, for their sake.*

And soon enough, the afterthought: *I wonder if I could do that?* Shortly thereafter—once Lois got her hands on a big sponge and basin of sand and water—the residents of Sea Meadows woke up to find the marshes beaten back to a reasonable size, the waterfowl and other wildlife happy enough in their more compact quarters, and themselves the masters of a fine port and some of the best arable land in Connecticut.

The narrow street ended at a low stone wall over-run with beach roses. On the other side was a wide, clean stretch of pure white sand. Beyond that, the gentle waves of Long Island Sound had lapped the shoreline.

Except the sand was no longer white, no longer there. In its place, a shimmer of brackish water sloshed against the stone wall again and again, with the dull persistence of a trapped housefly banging its head against a closed window. The tame wavelets too had changed. In their place, slow, towering combers lifted their frothy heads high out of the sea and came crashing down on the now-nonexistent beach.

Lois popped the trunk and plucked something out of the depths, something small enough to fit comfortably in her closed hand. She knew this day would come—it came every six months, after all—and she was ready. She stowed the object in the right-hand pocket of her windbreaker, leaving the floss and toothbrushes in the left one. Then she climbed onto the wall and took the lay of the mostly vanished land.

A strand of luxurious houses ran all along the shore in either direction, high-priced seaside abodes for those rich enough to pay for the privilege of ocean views, either year-round or just for the summer. The swelling sea had already engulfed some of these well over foundation level, and it was creeping up the first story even as Lois watched. The people inside the houses seemed indifferent to the fact that their property was slowly being flooded, but even stranger was the sight of pedestrians and cars caught up in the inundation. They went on their way as if the chest-high waters didn't exist.

Which they don't, Lois reminded herself. *Right now, they're no more than illusions for my benefit;* him, *flinging the usual gauntlet in my face.* She pressed her lips together, well aware from past experience of how quickly illusion could become actuality, if she let it. *All it will take is for me to fail and the waters will be real.* She shook her head. *So I can't fail. Reality is not an option.*

As ill-omened as the drenched vistas to left and right were, she had to admit that the encroaching water was an impressive sight. But it wasn't a patch on the spectacle that was straight ahead, at a place in the heart of the rearing, tumbling waves, the very spot where, three hundred years ago, a young witch had cast her greatest spell on a huge stretch of sodden marshland.

On a throne of living harbor seals, a crown of starfish on his waterfall of silver hair, his right hand holding a narwhal's twisted tusk and his left resting on the head of an extremely cranky-looking walrus, the man who had caused Bonnie such erotic upheaval sat grinning.

"Mr. Shoreham, I presume?" Lois remarked coolly.

"Dylan Shoreham. I hope you appreciate the art behind the name?"

"Well, 'Shoreham's' painfully obvious, but Dylan— It means 'son of the sea,' doesn't it?"

He blinked those enchanting blue eyes in surprise. "How did you know?"

"I'm immortal unless someone kills me. That gives me a *little* extra time for reading." Her sarcasm was as pointed as the walrus' massive tusks. "I only regret I didn't use more of it to read your character. Or lack of any."

The being who named himself Dylan Shoreham laughed. "Still so bitter about my little dabblings in . . . self-improvement? I'd think you'd appreciate it. I only did it so that I could spend more time with you."

"Bullshit, Tommy Meigs!" Lois spat her former husband's true name back in his face with all the force she could muster. "You did it for yourself—first, last and always."

"Now how can you say that when you know I keep coming back to *you* time and again?" the metamorphosed mortal asked, his expression pleading and pathetic.

Pleading, pathetic, and *not* convincing to the woman who'd spent better than two hundred years dealing with the after-effects of her marriage. "It's not *me* you keep coming back for, Tommy," she said. "It's the land. The Council won't give you any territory of your own because you thieved your witchcraft from me. You couldn't fight the Council—none of us can—but you learned that though they control the land, they've no say over the sea! So you return here, time after time, to try using your stolen powers to help you steal even more. You want Sea Meadows to become your own private underwater kingdom, and to hell with the people who live here!"

"How can you doubt my devotion so cruelly, sweeting?" Tommy responded, but his mask of sincerity slipped just a mite. "It's what led me to wed you even when my friends warned me you were a witch."

"I wish they'd warned *me* about *you*," Lois countered. "I should never have left you alone in the house between your voyages. And if I did, I should've locked up my Craftbook. Children, dogs and husbands always get into things they're not supposed to."

Tommy leaped off his living throne and the seals scattered. He strode through the swelling breakers, naked except for a scanty draping of seaweed. The walrus galumphed along at his heels like an oversized bulldog. "At least *I* never lied when I swore I loved you!" he declared, brandishing the narwhal tusk. "But your love for me was only empty words. I'm living proof that your spellcraft had the power to let mortals cheat death, but if I hadn't taken that power for myself, you'd have let me age and die!"

"I would have let you live as you were meant to live," Lois answered. "As a man, not a monster. And don't you point that narwhal tusk at me!"

"Do I look so very monstrous? That red-haired wench didn't think so." A sly leer lifted the corners of his mouth. "Maybe I've been seeking my queen in the wrong places. Will it make you happy if I take that girl for my new bride? At least that way, one of your precious mortals will survive the deluge once I give all this land back to the sea."

Lois raised her closed hand. "You'll have to fight me for that first."

"As always." He made a low, antiquated bow such as he'd first learned in his mortal days when the War of 1812 was a recent memory and the Civil War was a nightmare yet to come. He held the narwhal tusk to his breast as he lowered his head, but with his other hand he made a short, imperious gesture.

The walrus charged.

Lois had expected as much. *He wouldn't have brought along a walrus if he didn't intend to use it.* Tommy never had been one for successfully playing his cards close to the vest. The only reason he'd gotten away with filching her sorcerous arts was because she'd been half-blinded by love and because the basic Law of Spellcraft she followed was so bloody simple to master, for anyone with the drive and ambition to pursue it.

As Above, So Below. It was the principle behind symbolic magic, the power that underlay the workings of such things as voodoo dolls. Its first manifestation was in cave paintings that showed a successful kill. Just as the images of spears and arrows were shown lodged deep in the quarry, so magic would compel the real weapons of the ancient huntsmen to find their targets.

Now as the enraged pinniped lumbered towards her, bellowing and slashing the air with its tusks, Lois jammed her left hand into the pocket of the windbreaker and pulled out two toothbrushes. Holding her ground atop the wall, she stuck them under her upper lip. "Av avov, vo bewhoa," she said as best she could, then whipped a length of dental floss from the spool, looped it around the first toothbrush, and *yanked*.

The walrus stopped dead in its tracks, a look of complete bafflement on its bristly face. Its right tusk was gone, as painlessly popped out of its mouth as the toothbrush had left Lois' upper lip. "*Baroo?*" the creature uttered, turning questioning eyes toward its master.

"Don't just stand there, you waste of blubber, *get* her!" Tommy boomed.

Obediently, the walrus renewed its charge, only to have Lois repeat her symbolic spellcraft on its other tusk. Bereft, the beast gave Tommy a look that as good as said *Dude! This is* so *not worth it!* and beat flippers into the sea.

"Damn it, woman, how did you *know* I'd be packing a walrus?" the would-be sea king demanded. "How did you *know* to bring the right weapons to overcome him?"

"I didn't," Lois replied. "I could have used those toothbrushes against anything you threw my way. They're remarkably versatile props for symbolic magic, and a good witch's best asset is her imagination. On the other hand—" She reached into her right pocket and drew out the object she'd taken from the car trunk. "—defeating *some* foes calls for special preparation."

It was one thing to create an elaborate seashell design in a box, but to do the same with the gutted husk of an antique pocket-watch was little short of a miracle. Yet there it was, in Lois' hand, the old watch framing the same baroque seashell work as in the larger, eight-sided boxes. But such tiny shells! Such intricate patterns, dainty as a spider's smallest web! It was a miniature works of genius, dazzling to the eye.

Tommy Meigs was intrigued. "And what might you have there?"

"Nothing worth much," Lois relied. "Only your heart. As above, so below!" She gave the altered pocket-watch a firm squeeze.

Tommy dropped the narwhal tusk and clapped both hands to his chest. The cry he uttered was more surprise than pain. Lois nodded with satisfaction. "You feel it, Tommy. You know the magic's strong. This watch holds the selfsame pattern as in the sailor's valentine you brought me from Barbados, when your own heart was still true to me. It's taken me months to duplicate, but now it's mine, to have and to hold—or to crush, if that's my will!"

"You wouldn't do that, would you, my angel?" Now Tommy's pathetic, pleading expression was the real item.

She dropped to the landward side of the stone wall

and ducked from sight for an instant. When she leaped back up again, she gave him a good view of the big rock she'd chosen. "It would be fair payback, crushing the heart that once broke mine." She raised the lump of stone for an instant, as if about to smash the bespelled watch case, then lowered her hands. "But I won't. I'll only use this to drive you back into the sea!"

"Well, to be honest, you always *do* wind up driving me back into the sea, one way or the other, every time I try to flood this stupid town. And you always trounce me so thoroughly that it takes half a year before I'm fit to face you again."

Lois rolled her eyes. Was there ever such a man as this? Afraid for his life one moment, forgetting his terror the next, just for the sake of arguing a point with her.

"Yes, and for how many years, now? I wish my patients were as diligent as you about showing up twice a year! I'm tired of your shenanigans, Tommy. Before I emptied this watch of its works, I set the hands ahead so many turns that it will be a *hundred* years before you can recoup your powers for a return match!"

Tommy's silver brows rose. "You wouldn't."

"After all it took out of me to lift this town out of the marshes? After what you did to betray my trust and steal my spellcraft? After your continual efforts to undo my work not once, but *twice* every year? After you sicced a *walrus* on me?" Lois demanded. "*You bet your sweet narwhal tusk I would!*"

With astonishing speed and with the same dexterity that let her craft such dainty things as sailors' valentines, Lois managed to draw a length of dental floss from the spool in her pocket without losing hold of the rock or the watch-case. Five quick loops, a hasty knot, and rock and watch-case were a single, well-weighted entity.

"As above—!" Lois shouted, flinging her new-made missile well past Tommy's phantom tide, all the way to where the real sea lay. "—so below!" she concluded as it splashed down.

She had a throwing arm that a pro outfielder might envy. Virtual immortality gave a woman plenty of opportunity to build up her biceps. With a dreadful cry, Tommy was yanked backwards, the force of Lois' spell jerking him away to follow his "heart" into the depths. She watched him vanish under the waves, and smiled to see how all of his watery illusions streamed away after him. The beach was back. The upscale seaside homes were unmolested.

She hopped off the wall onto the beach and strolled down to the water, whistling happily. Just one more loose end to tie up in a pretty bow and for the first time in centuries, she'd have a little closure with her ex-husband.

The day was almost done, the sunlight fading, but it didn't take her long to find—or rather *summon*—what she needed.

Dr. Petersen came back to the office that evening in a foul mood. He'd gone home early to celebrate his wedding anniversary, only to discover just before dinner that he'd left his wife's gift at work. He intended to get in, grab it, and get out. He was in such a hurry that he almost didn't notice the light on in one of the treatment rooms. And why would he? He was annoyed, distracted, and he wasn't expecting anyone else to be there.

"*What* the—?" he began, jaw dropping when he saw the unscheduled patient his hygienist had in the chair.

Lois was prepared for this. "As above, so below," she muttered, turning from her work to pop one of Dr. Petersen's business cards into the small beer cooler at her feet. She'd stocked it with enough ice to last for the duration of her admittedly short and off-the-books appointment, just in case. As soon as the card—bearing Dr. Petersen's smiling photograph—hit the plastic bags of frozen cubes, the dentist himself froze where he stood. Lois only paused long enough to draw his caricature on her memory-wiping slate for later. Then she returned her attention to the patient.

"Now stop fussing and flopping around, you big baby," she directed. "This isn't going to hurt a bit. Really. Dental hygienist's honor." So saying, she picked up a large potato from the equipment tray and stuck a pair of toothpicks into the end where she'd drawn a round, small-eyed, nobly whiskered face. "As above, so below!"

"Ba-ROOO?" exclaimed the patient as the witch's magic did its work of restoring what he'd lost in their brief battle.

"And spit."

Once more the possessor of as fine a pair of tusks as anyone might care to see, south of the Arctic Circle, the walrus spat.

David Vierling wanted to be either a mad scientist or a paperback writer if he grew up. But he's not quite there yet, so he's settling for having built a solar-power array on his home and writing in his spare time. Dave is married, has three children, and works for the IRS to pay the bills. "It's good to have a *friend* at the IRS," he reminds people . . . leaving it to them to decide if that's a veiled threat. For more information on David's writing, including how to design and build your own home solar power system, see www.davidvierling.com.

Neighborhood Witch

David Vierling

Tommy pounded on the door. A woman opened it, eyeing the red-bearded, bear-like man in the flannel shirt. "May I help you, sir?" she asked.

"Afternoon, ma'am," said Tommy. "Is your husband home?"

Before she had time to reply, a man's voice called from behind her, "Okay, then, can *I* help you?"

Tommy held his hand out past the woman and said, "I'm Tommy. I'm sort of an unofficial welcoming committee."

"I'm Ansel," said the man inside the house, shaking hands with Tommy.

Tommy said, "Seein' as you're new to the neighborhood, we wanted to invite you over for a barbeque this afternoon. Sort of a guys-only thing." He glanced briefly at the woman, "You understand."

She shrugged and headed toward the kitchen. Ansel glanced toward the kitchen and said, "I'm kind of busy this afternoon . . ."

"Aw, come on, grow a pair!" said Tommy. "You wouldn't want your new neighbors to think you're whipped, would ya?"

"I guess I could break free for a little while," said Ansel, looking at his shoes.

"There's the spirit!" said Tommy, slapping Ansel on the shoulder hard enough to make him wince. "Seven thirty-three Herne's Lane, around three o'clock. See you then!" He turned on his heel and Ansel watched him head back down the walkway. As Tommy reached the street he crossed paths with a tall brunette woman dressed all in black. She sneered at him as she passed, then she stalked along the slate walkway to the house like a cat sizing up a mouse.

"Yes?" said Ansel as the woman strode up to the porch.

"I will speak to the Lady of the House," said the woman imperiously. She dripped silver jewelry, Ansel noticed.

"Hey Retta!" he shouted in the direction of the kitchen. "There's someone here for you." Addressing the visitor, he asked, "Would you like to come in?"

Without a word, the woman crossed the threshold but came no further into the house. Retta emerged from the kitchen, drying her hands on a small towel, which she tossed over her shoulder. "Yes?"

The tall woman eyed Retta for a moment and then extended her be-ringed hand. "I am Jade." Her nostrils flared a little when she spoke.

"Retta," she shook Jade's outstretched hand, setting off a sympathetic chime from the woman's bangle-bracelets.

Jade spoke as if she hadn't heard her. "Many of the

Ladies of the neighborhood will gather this afternoon for Tea. They wish to meet you. Join us at three o'clock. Nine twenty-six Moonstone Place. Until then?" She held out her hand again.

"Um . . . okay," said Retta. *Jangle.* Jade stalked away.

Retta closed the door. "That was Jade," she explained.

"I noticed. High tea, huh?"

Retta shrugged. "Wouldn't want the new neighbors to think I'm whipped, would I?"

Shaking his head and laughing, Ansel said, "I've got a bad feeling about this neighborhood."

"You've said that every time we've moved. It's not like we're staying here forever."

"Yeah, that's what *you* always say."

A knock on the door interrupted them.

They opened the door to find a man and a woman standing on the porch. "Hi!" said the woman brightly. "You must be Mister and Missus Cutter!"

"We're the Cutters," said Ansel. "And you are . . . ?"

"I'm Vicki, and this is Dion," the woman said. "We're sort of the unofficial welcoming committee for the neighborhood. Would you be able to join us for an hour or so this afternoon, say . . ."

"Around," interrupted Retta.

"Three?" hazarded Ansel.

"We were going to suggest four," said Dion.

"Sure," the invitees chorused.

"Unity Court, Number Two," said Vicki. "See you then!"

Ansel shut the door. "Are you thinking what I'm thinking?"

"That having somewhere to go at four o'clock might not be a bad thing?"

"Right there with you."

Three o'clock: The door opened before Retta's knock could land. "You must be Retta!" enthused a skinny man with a head of wooly hair, wearing a black pull-over and black jeans. He reminded Retta of a hobbit with a gland condition. "I'm Jazz. Everyone's in the parlor." Jazz wrapped his well-manicured hand around her arm and guided her down the hall. "Everyone! Retta's here!"

In the parlor, Retta found herself surrounded by whispering women wearing Too Much Black; black Indian cotton, black gauze, black lace, black spandex on hips and legs which should not be seen in spandex. And all of it set off with silver and crystals: rings, bracelets, amulets, anklets, nose-rings, earrings, pendants. The place sounded like a wind-chime factory.

An estrogen tsunami engulfed Retta, who found herself fielding questions faster than she could answer: "So, you're a software programmer! Does that pay well?" "Are you sure your contract is only for two years? Such a shame, to meet a new friend like you and know you'll be moving on so soon!" "Would you like some chamomile tea?" (This last came from Jazz, who floated through the group touching and petting everyone and serving hors d'oeuvres.)

While Jazz was out of the room replenishing his serving tray, Retta asked quietly, "Is he a servant of some sort?"

"Jazz is a man who knows his place," said Jade, who had not spoken until now. The buzz of overlapping conversations ceased; even the bangle-bracelet jangle dropped by 20 decibels or so. "Men need to know their place, Retta. For too long, the Earth-mother has languished in the suffocating grip of *man*. I asked you here to discuss this with us . . ."

Also three o'clock: Ansel eyed the iron-bound oak door at seven thirty-three Herne's Lane, unsure if he could lift the enormous horned-stag knocker. It looked as if someone shot a deer, dipped its head in bronze, and stuck it to the door. He rapped with his knuckles instead.

The door opened; out rolled a haze of cigar smoke. "Hey Ansel," said Tommy. "Let me introduce you to some of the boys. The big guy is Randy, the bald guy is Vic, and the skinny guy is James . . ."

Waving from the doorway, Ansel said, "I'll apologize up front . . . I'm terrible with names." As his watering eyes adjusted to the stogie smog, he saw that the door opened into a great room, sort of a combined living room/rec room/Addams Family room—it was decorated mostly in dead animals. The heads and horned skulls of antelope and deer adorned the walls, stuffed black bears flanked the huge stone fireplace, above which hung the skull of a cape buffalo. About a dozen men sat or stood around the room.

"You hunt?" asked Randy, shoving a beer into Ansel's hand.

"Sort of," said Ansel. Several of the men looked at him with expectation, perhaps even a touch of excitement. "I'm a nature photographer, so my work involves most of the same skills and techniques as a hunter . . ."

"'Cept for all the important parts, like the killin', the skinnin', and the eatin'," said Randy.

"Now Randy, don't be putting down our new friend," said Tommy. "I remember when you moved here, you'd never even touched a gun or a bow. At least Ansel gets out in the woods sometimes, even if he doesn't know the real reason why!" Tommy draped a heavy arm across Ansel's shoulders. "See, buddy, that's the problem with today's world. Men aren't allowed to be MEN. The male of the species is designed to fight and hunt. We're genetically programmed for it! But in the modern world, women have taken over and forced us to bury those basic parts of being a man . . ."

Four o'clock: Ansel rang the bell at Number Two Unity Court. From the back yard came a shout, "Come 'round back! Your wife's already here!"

The gate in the high wooden fence stood open. He spotted Retta by the outdoor hot-tub and gave her a hug. "You stink," she said observationally.

"Yeah, I don't know if I'll ever be able to get the cigar-stench out of this sweater," he replied. "I think I'll just burn it."

"Shave your head, too," Retta added helpfully. "It's the only way to be sure."

They met 10 or 15 couples, but with the way their days had gone, all the names began to run together. Come to mention it, all the couples seemed to run together, too. There was a lot of hugging, handholding, and open-mouth kissing going on, and not just between pairs who had been introduced as husband and wife.

"You're name's Ansel? And you're a photographer? Like Ansel Adams?" asked a pert blonde, sandwiched between two men who weren't her husband, one arm around each man's waist.

"Yes, like Ansel Adams . . . only not as good."

"You're just not as famous, dear!" said Retta. "He's so modest. He's really very good. You should drop by and see some of his pictures."

"I'd love to!" enthused the blonde, making Retta immediately regret issuing the insincere invitation. "You bought that two-bedroom stucco cottage on Oak Street, right? The one with the candycane lamppost?"

"I hate that tacky lamppost," said Ansel. "I want to repaint it, but Retta likes it."

"We bought the house over the Internet based on a picture—*I* think it's charming!" said Retta, smacking Ansel lightly on the arm. "My company only gave me a few weeks' warning before sending me on this job, so we really lucked into the house. It was like magic!"

"Magic . . . fate . . . kismet . . . karma," said Dion, the man who had accompanied Vicki to their house. "Call it what you will, but this neighborhood is truly charmed. It's the center of ley lines from all over this part of the country, attracting people who are sensitive to such forces, focusing all sorts of cosmic energy . . ."

"And human energy," said Vicki, linking her arm through Dion's. "That's the secret to tapping into and channeling the full magical potential of this area. Taking control of that energy through the yin and yang, the sun and moon, the maiden and the man . . ."

Five o'clock: Ansel closed the door, locked it, and shoved a kitchen chair under the knob for good measure.

Laughing, Retta said, "Aren't you being a little melodramatic?"

"Not in the least. I'd hang garlic and wolfbane on the door if I had any."

"We have some minced garlic in the fridge," said Retta helpfully. "You could smear that on the door. It might help cover the stench of your sweater."

Ansel peeled off the sweater, opened a window, and tossed it outside. "I told you I've got a bad feeling about this neighborhood."

Robes clutched against the pre-dawn chill, the Cutters joined the stream of people jog-trotting down the street toward the flashing red lights. A passing ambulance did a Red Sea number on the crowd, then pulled up alongside the fire and police vehicles at Number Two Unity Court. Hoses ran from the hydrant to the back yard; a pall of steam and smoke hung over the cul-de-sac.

Retta spotted Jazz and asked, "What happened?"

"Someone piled brush around the hot tub and boiled Dion and Vicki," Jazz said. On his face he wore the same cross of smugness and subservience she had seen at Jade's house; on his feet he wore bunny slippers.

"Dion and Vicki?" said Ansel. "We just met them a couple days ago! They seemed like a nice couple. Who found them?"

"Vicki's husband," said Jazz. "The light from the fire woke him, but by then it was too late."

Vicki's Husband. The Cutters let that sink in for a minute. Then Retta asked, "Why didn't they get out of the tub?"

"From what the firemen said, it looked like somebody had tied them up before they lit the fire." He scuffed at a rock, bunny-slipper ears flapping. "I guess all that 'balanced energy' mumbo-jumbo doesn't help you much if someone clubs you in the head while you're going at it." Spotting Jade over the crowd, Jazz slunk off for a huddled conversation with her.

POUND. POUND. POUND. Ansel opened the door. "Tommy! Who'd of thought it was you!" he said, noting that the paint had flaked where Tommy had beaten on the door.

"Somebody killed Randy," said Tommy. "A power company guy found his body this morning, up where the high-tension lines cross through the park. The cop said it looks like he was bow-hunting and someone zapped him with a taser."

"A taser?" said Ansel. "Like a stun-gun taser? That shouldn't kill someone."

Tommy shook his head. "Not unless you drop a live high-tension wire on them while they're stunned. Fried him to a crisp."

Retta shuddered. "That's three murders in less than a week."

"Thanks for letting us know," said Ansel. "We'll be on the lookout for anyone acting suspicious." He reached for the door.

"Just a minute," said Tommy, reaching for something propped next to the door, out of the Cutters' line of sight. "With a killer loose, I thought you might want this." He held up a double-barrel shotgun, offering it to Ansel. "You said you don't own a gun."

Ansel said, "I wouldn't know how to use it . . ."

"We'll figure out how to use it," interrupted Retta, taking the gun from Tommy and shoving it into Ansel's hands. "Our house backs up onto that park."

Tommy dug into his coat pocket and handed over a box of shells. "Doesn't work so well without these."

"Thanks, Tommy," said Ansel, closing the door and propping the shotgun and the box of shells next to it. He faced Retta. "You know what I'm going to say."

"So don't say it."

Dropping her laptop case next to the door, Retta called, "I'm home!"

Ansel came out of the basement darkroom. "The police were just here. There was a murder last night. Your buddy Jazz."

"Last night?!" said Retta, her face going pale. "What happened to him?"

"Somebody slit his throat. Killed him in his bed."

Retta gasped. "Do the police have any leads?"

"I don't think so. They're going door to door notifying the neighborhood."

She hugged him. "Will we be next?"

Ansel hugged her back and smoothed her hair. "Given the cliques we've seen around here, I wonder if it was a revenge killing—someone from one clique dies; they suspect another group and kill one of theirs. Jazz didn't seem particularly sympathetic when Dion and Vicki were killed."

Retta nodded. "Borderline gleeful is the term I'd use. All right, it's time we did something to protect ourselves." She pulled out her laptop, hooked it to the printer, and turned them on.

✧   ✧   ✧

"I thought we'd get a bigger turnout," Retta whispered out of the corner of her mouth.

"It's like I said before; with all the cliques in this neighborhood, I don't think anybody trusts anybody else enough," Ansel answered, also *sotto voce*.

Maybe 20 people had shown up in response to the posters plastered on power poles by Retta:

TAKE BACK THE NIGHT!
DON'T BE THE NEXT VICTIM!
NEIGHBORHOOD WATCH
ORGANIZATIONAL MEETING
8 PM MONDAY
ASH STREET REC CENTER

Retta stood and cleared her throat. "I'd like to thank everyone for coming tonight. We have sign-up sheets for shifts patrolling the neighborhood, and I bought whistles for everyone to use in case you see something that looks fishy." She looked over the pitiful turnout. "Hopefully we'll get more people signing up later in the week."

As people queued up for shifts and whistles, Retta sought out Jade, who stood in the back near the cloak room. "I'm glad to see you came," Retta said, "After what happened to your friend Jazz, we need to take every precaution."

"*I* am taking every precaution against the violence brought by men," said Jade. "I only came here to see if *that*," she pointed a long-nailed finger at Tommy, "crawled out of its cave to be here." She widened her eyes and flared her nostrils (reminding Retta momentarily of a frilled lizard) as she leaned in close and whispered, "Do not trust that one alone with you or with any woman. Or with any man for that matter. I will warn the other women as well." With a toss of her long, dark hair, she glided away toward a small knot of women who had already signed up for shifts.

"And that was about . . . ?" asked Ansel, sliding up to Retta in imitation of Jade's haughty locomotion.

"Warning the women to stay clear of your hunting buddy Tommy," Retta replied. "She indicated he is bad juju."

"A lot of people say that about their ex-husbands," Ansel observed.

"Ex?"

"Uh-huh. His buddy Vic mentioned it."

"So many things are so much clearer now."

The Neighborhood Watch program had little effect. "Little effect" in the sense of "no *positive* effect." Four more people died in the next nine days: one smothered; one drowned in her bathtub (drowned with white wine, no less); two stabbed with barbeque skewers, from in front, through the heart. The last two were members of the Neighborhood Watch, on patrol, prompting the police to "insist on an immediate cessation of Neighborhood Watch activities."

Things stayed quiet for a few days. Then on Thursday Ansel came up from the basement darkroom and was startled to find Jade coming through the front door, a crystal-tipped wooden wand in her hand. "How did you get in?" he demanded. "That door was locked!"

"SILENCE, MAN!" Jade commanded, gesturing with the wand. Suddenly, Ansel's throat felt pinched, so parched he couldn't make a sound.

He tried to shove past her, reaching for the shotgun

which still sat propped beside the door, but Jade touched his chest with the wand and Ansel was slammed back onto the couch. When he tried to move, he felt as though his arms and legs were bound.

Jade smirked, enjoying the situation. "I know who you are—my Aunt in the old country heard about what is happening here and called to warn me about you two." The wand moved again. "You may speak if you wish."

"What's there to say?" said Ansel, eyeing the open door. "I should have known that locks would do no good against your kind."

"MY kind?! From you?!" Ansel was treated to the frilled-lizard thing with the eyes and nostrils, which looked even more impressive with Jade towering over him as he looked, helpless, straight up her nose. "I should expect such insolence from a cold-blooded killer."

"If you know who we are, you know we didn't start it."

"It does not matter to me how it got started; today, it ends." Jade put her hands on her hips, the wand still clasped in one be-ringed fist. "We will wait here until your wife gets home, and I'll have my revenge on you for killing Jazz . . ."

"Couple corrections, sweetheart. One, we didn't kill Jazz. I figure it was Tommy or one of his coven who did that. Worried the hell out of Retta when it happened—she thought we might be next. But I told her the competition would help keep suspicion off of us. Two, Retta's not my wife, although we have the same last name. And—I guess this makes three corrections—she's already home." The shotgun butt slammed into Jade's head. She went down like a raven smacking into a plate-glass window.

Retta kicked the wand away with her toe, then winked at Ansel. "See? I told you we'd figure out how to use this gun. But your buddy Tommy was wrong—it works just fine without shells."

Freed from the binding spell when Retta butted Jade's head, Ansel started rubbing life back into his arms and legs. "I told you I had a bad feeling about this neighborhood," he said.

"Yes, yes. So you said. Now help me take care of the body and let's get out of here."

The SWAT team from the county police listened to the briefing from the FBI Suit as the van rolled down the tree-lined lanes.

"The names on their passports are Greta and Ansel Cutter—she goes by 'Retta,'" said Special Agent Smallwood. "Guns aren't their MO, so that's a plus for our side. These two are serial killers, wanted in Albania, Germany, Poland, and the Czech Republic. Interpol tracked them to Canada about four years ago, but the trail went cold. They move into an area and people start turning up dead. They help cover their tracks by starting a neighborhood watch program—it makes them look like concerned citizens. That also gives them free run of the neighborhood, and ensures some of the victims will be out on the streets by themselves. Then they disappear before anyone figures out what they've done. Let's hope they haven't skipped town yet."

The heavily armed team started deploying before the SWAT van stopped moving. They surrounded the house, smashed in the front and back doors simultaneously, and swept the place from basement to attic but found no one.

Special Agent Smallwood came in after the SWAT members gave the all-clear. The leader of the SWAT team said, "They haven't been gone long—the oven's still warm." Savory smells of cooking filled the cottage. He shook his head. "Weirdest husband and wife team I ever heard of."

"They're not husband and wife," corrected Smallwood. "Ansel and Greta are brother and sister . . ."

Their eyes met for a moment, and then they turned toward the oven, stomachs sinking, already knowing what smelled so good.

K.D. Wentworth has sold more than seventy pieces of short fiction to such markets as *The Magazine of Fantasy & Science Fiction*, *Alfred Hitchcock's Mystery Magazine*, *Realms of Fantasy*, *Weird Tales*, and *Return to the Twilight Zone*. Three of her stories have been Finalists for the Nebula Award for Short Fiction. Currently, she has seven novels in print, the most recent being *The Course of Empire*, written with Eric Flint and published by Baen. She lives in Tulsa with her husband and a combined total of one hundred sixty pounds of dog (Akita + Siberian Husky) and is working on several new novels with Flint. Website: http://www.kdwentworth.com

Hex Education

K.D. Wentworth

Poppy's cell phone struck up the overwrought strains of the "William Tell Overture" as she was driving her son, Chase, to soccer practice. Obviously someone had been fooling with her settings again, and *The Lone Ranger* was Chase's favorite. Eyes narrowed, she glanced sideways at his eight-year-old snub-nosed face, but he remained focused on his hand-held Nintendo DS.

Annoyed, she flipped her cell phone open with one hand while scanning ahead for the turnoff to the practice field. "Hello?"

"Poppy, it's your mother," the phone said. "I have a bad feeling about your new neighborhood. Are you keeping your eyes open? You never did learn how to cast a decent circle."

A gust of chill autumn wind skittered red and gold leaf skeletons across the street. "Mom, you know I love you, but you've been dead now for three years," Poppy said, spotting her turn on the other side of the

Quik Trip just ahead. "At some point, you're going to have to quit calling so much."

"So you're too grown up to listen to your mother now," the phone said mournfully.

"No, of course not," Poppy said. "I just want you to enjoy your Afterlife, take it easy, meet some new people, catch up with old friends. There's bound to be someone interesting—"

"Oh, ho, your father's dating again, isn't he?"

"Mom, he doesn't like me to discuss his private life with you, now that you're, you know, *gone*," Poppy said.

"Well, *he* won't take my calls anymore."

"And whose fault is that?" Poppy said. "You jinxed his neighbor, Mrs. Hanson, when she took him a green bean casserole the week after you died. The poor old soul's TV didn't get the Shopping Channel for months. She almost expired from boredom."

"The vixen!" her mother said. "That red hair is straight out of a bottle. The old bat has been after him for years!"

Poppy slowed and signalled for a left-hand turn. "Mom, I have to go," she said. "Why don't you sign up for a celestial seaweed wrap and try to relax?"

"But—"

"Bye!" Poppy folded the phone and tucked it in her purse. Beside her, Chase was rocking back and forth, muttering at the excruciatingly cute animated forest creatures on his tiny screen. "Die, Thumper, die, die!"

The road was clear of on-coming traffic so Poppy swung the steering wheel left.

The SUV, though, turned *right*. She braked, then

parked on the side street, flustered. Someone had been mucking about with the Honda, even though she'd always been careful to not *Wake* it. "Chase," she said, "have you been practicing hexes in the car again?"

His thumbs flew over the control buttons. "Die, Bambi, die!"

She reached over and pulled out his earbuds. "Chase!"

"Jeeze, Mom, I almost made it to Level Fifty in *Enchanted Forest Terminator!*" His hazel eyes were resentful. "Now I'll have to start all over again."

"What have you been doing to this car?" she insisted.

"Nothing," he said and glanced at the dashboard clock. His eyes widened. "Hey, if I'm late, Coach Gibbs will make me run laps! He's already on my case all the time."

That was true. On his old soccer team, before they'd moved out to the suburbs, Chase had been a starter. These days he seemed to fumble every opportunity, warming the bench more and more each game. Sighing, she laid a hand on the dashboard, willing the Honda SUV to behave. "Okay, we're turning around. No funny stuff!" The car rattled once dramatically, then died.

Chase rolled his eyes. "Nothing we have ever works like other people's stuff!" he mumbled, not quite under his breath.

She punched the hazard lights on. "It's only half a mile," she told her son. "I'll walk you down, then call for a tow."

Scowling, he jerked his sports duffle from the back

seat and slid out of the car. He slammed the door, then trudged at her side, head down, as though being conscripted into a chain gang.

Behind them, the SUV's engine rumbled to life. The dark-green car executed a perfect three-point turn, sans driver, and then rolled along at their heels like a good-natured hound.

"Oh, don't try to make up now," Poppy said to the SUV over her shoulder. "I'm really quite vexed. You can just darn well park yourself and stay here until I get back."

The SUV revved its engine. The windshield wipers flicked back and forth in what might have been interpreted as an apologetic manner.

"I think it's sorry, Mom," Chase said. "Can't we *please* give it another chance so I won't be late?"

The two front doors flew open invitingly. "All right," Poppy said against her better judgement. Someone Gifted had definitely had a hand in this and unfortunately she had more than a passing suspicion that it had been her husband. Dominick had a history of ineptitude with mechanical matters, culminating with his recent misadventures with her new smoothie-maker. In the end, they'd just had to repaint the kitchen. Well, she'd have to find out what he'd done to the SUV and see if she could then quietly reverse it without ruffling his masculine pride any more than necessary.

They climbed back in and drove to the practice field without further incident until the Honda absolutely insisted upon parking next to a massive white Lincoln Navigator, even though there were better spots closer in.

"Flirt!" she said as she clicked the door shut. The locks promptly engaged themselves. They walked to the sidelines, then she held Chase's duffle while he stuffed his shin guards down into his socks. "Now, remember: Even if Albert trips you again, even if there's *blood*, no hexes. I don't care if anyone is looking or not!"

He nodded solemnly, then trotted off to run down the field with his nonGifted teammates just like any eight-year-old boy. She'd been worried last spring when Dominick got a promotion that required them to move out here from Queens so that he could run a local grocery store distribution center, but so far they were fitting into the nonGifted scene with only occasional misfires.

She still missed her old coven, though, where spells and hexes were the subjects of everyday conversation and they shared recipes for Conjuring Peace and Curing Discord, rather than the intricacies of Raspberry Supreme Jello Icebox Cake.

She perched on the rickety wooden bleachers next to Mary-Ann McGovern, who was so slim and perfectly turned out with her freshly pressed jeans and lacy cuffs that she made Poppy's teeth ache. Several other matrons made room for her and then she did her best to participate in a tediously earnest conversation that ranged from school bake sales to "unreported stains."

None of it captured her interest, though, and she found herself speculating on what exactly her husband had done to the car. It was showing signs of self-awareness, which was never good news in a machine. *Wakened* devices were unpredictable and had unsettling senses of humor.

"Do you have Chase on vitamins?" Mary-Ann asked

when Poppy's son lagged behind the other boys as they ran wind sprints. "The poor dear seems a bit peaked." Mary-Ann's son, Ethan, was bounding back and forth like a young gazelle without a bead of sweat, looking amazingly fit. On the surface, the woman's expression was concerned, but Poppy thought she detected a hint of smugness. Their sons played the same position: forward. Ethan was a starter, Chase, since moving here, second string.

"Why, yes," Poppy said, resisting the temptation to whisper a *Reveal* spell and make Mary-Ann confess her inner thoughts in front of all her friends. That wouldn't be *nice*, she told herself firmly, and everyone here in Windsor Heights Rancho Estates was *nice*—all the time—even if it killed them. "But maybe I should change brands."

Once practice was over, she discovered the dark-green Honda SUV was not parked next to the Navigator where she'd left it. "Gosh," Chase said, duffle in one hand, bottle of blue sports drink in the other. "Do you think someone stole it?"

"I wish!" she said under her breath as one by one the rest of the mothers loaded their sons into their cars and drove away in the fading light. Finally, she and Chase located the SUV at the far end of the parking lot where it had shamelessly crept off to cozy up to Mary-Ann McGovern's magnificent black Hummer.

"The car's acting funny," Chase said that night as the three of them sat down to roasted pork tenderloin.

His father, Dominick, looked up from his plate, then reached for the mustard sauce. "What's wrong with it?"

"Nothing, *really*," Poppy said, giving Chase her most deadly not-one-more-word look.

"It turns wherever it wants, not where Mom wants," Chase said, blithely oblivious. "What's for dessert?"

Dominick's brow furrowed. "But I just worked on it."

"Oh?" Poppy said, her suspicions confirmed. Her husband had little talent for mechanical matters, which wasn't his fault. Different Gifts ran in different family bloodlines. Everyone knew that. Her father-in-law, a male witch who was strongly Gifted himself, had warned her on her wedding day to keep Dominick away from automotive and do-it-yourself projects.

"He has a good heart, our Dominick, but not the slightest idea what all those little bits inside an engine are for," her father-in-law had said. "Once, when he was thirteen, he accidently spelled the lawn mower into thinking it was a vacuum cleaner. We had shredded blue carpet everywhere."

Poppy shuddered at the mental image that conjured.

"Yes," Dominick said, "the engine seemed a bit rough when I drove to Home Depot Wednesday night, so I smoothed it out with an old *Tuning* incantation, my dad's favorite, never fails."

"Chase is exaggerating," Poppy said desperately. She shot her son a withering look, then spooned broccoli onto his plate despite his attempt to wave her off. "I'm sure the car is fine."

"I'll just take a look at it after dinner," Dominick said.

They ate in blessed silence then, the only sound silverware clinking against the white pottery plates, but her mind whirled. The last thing that car needed was for him to take another go at it. Maybe she could head him off with a request to help Chase with his home-work. That was entirely plausible. School was another area where their son had done better before the move. These days, he struggled to bring home even C's.

"Grandma called again today," Chase said around an oversized bite of crescent roll. "When I told Brian at soccer practice, though, he didn't believe me. He said other kids' dead grandmas don't call *them*."

"I told you not to talk about that with outsiders!" Poppy said. Bats, rats, and snakes! She'd thought, or at least hoped, he was too preoccupied with his Nintendo to notice when Grandma had called. "Other people don't understand."

"Mom never lets me speak to her, though," Chase said thoughtfully, after swallowing a mouthful that would have choked a python. "How come?"

Dominick put down his fork and met Poppy's eyes. "Weren't you going to have a discussion about that with Grandma?"

"She's just having a little difficulty fitting in up there," Poppy said. The pork, painstakingly marinated for twenty-four hours, suddenly tasted like damp sawdust. "I'm sure any day now she'll join a celestial bowling league or take up angelic poetry slams and be having so much fun, she'll forget to call."

"When I get to the Afterlife, I'm going to be a NASCAR racer!" Chase said, ignoring his broccoli and reaching instead for a second helping of mashed potatoes.

Poppy excused herself and went to the kitchen to dish up the chocolate mousse. Just as she opened the refrig-erator, though, the phone rang. Seconds later, she heard Chase in the living room exclaiming, "Grandma!"

✦   ✦   ✦

She was almost finished loading the dishes into the dishwasher when Dominick came in. His dark hair was mussed and he had a manly smudge on one cheek from peering under the hood. "I drove the car around the block," he said. "It seems fine."

"Told you." She dried her hands. "Did Chase do his homework?"

Dominick leaned against the cabinet. "He talked to Grandma for twenty minutes, then claimed he didn't have any."

She sighed. Chase always said that. Asking about homework was the equivalent of starting a Third World haggling transaction. The "No Homework" statement was only an opening position. He didn't expect them to believe him.

Having fooled his father, no doubt the young rascal now intended to hex his teacher, Mrs. Gruber, into forgetting to collect homework tomorrow. The first time Chase had done that, soon after they'd moved to Windsor Heights Rancho Estates, the poor woman had forgotten where she lived and emigrated to Tibet. His class had suffered a substitute teacher for weeks until she and her memory had returned.

"I'd better double-check," she said. She found Chase on his knees, staring out the living room window. "About that nonexistent homework," she said.

"The car!" he said, turning to her. "It just sneaked out of the driveway."

"Right," she said, crossing her arms. "Like it could open the garage door on its own. Do you have Math or Language?"

His face was flushed. "No, really!"

She peeked out and saw red taillights as a car made a left-hand turn at the corner. It did look like their SUV.

"Should I get Daddy?" he said, standing up.

"No!" She tried to think. The Honda had seemed bent on socializing today, first the Lincoln Navigator, then—the Hummer. The McGoverns lived just three streets over. "I have to find it before anyone notices it's trundling around the neighborhood on its own. You stay here and do your homework."

"But—"

"No arguments!" She snatched up her purse from the coffee table, then ducked into their home office where Dominick was seated before the computer. "I'm going to run to the store."

He nodded, focused on the latest wrenchingly bad You Tube *American Idol* audition.

Back in the living room, she shrugged into her jacket, kissed the top of Chase's head as he sorrowfully thumbed through his Science book, then dashed out the front door. Outside, the night was crisply chill, the half-moon visible behind a few wispy clouds, shedding a pale silvery radiance once her eyes adjusted.

She hiked through the darkness to the McGoverns' faux Victorian, fuming. She loved her husband, but Dominick had only made the car worse. Calling him on it, though, was sure to bring on masculine sulking. She got enough of that with Chase.

The Honda SUV was parked in the McGoverns' driveway next to the gleaming black Hummer, playing its radio softly, tuned to a station that specialized in romantic ballads. She tried the car door, but it was locked, so she dug in her purse for the key.

"Having a spot of trouble there?" someone said from the dark recesses of the broad porch.

Her heart thumped. "Mary-Ann?"

"I heard the car pull up," Mary-Ann McGovern said, walking down the path. She held something snuggled in her arms.

Inexplicably, the Hummer rumbled to life and turned on its headlights. "I—" Poppy started, but could think of no plausible explanation for her presence in their driveway. "Um, Chase—"

"Yes, poor sweet Chase." Mary-Ann was wearing a dazzling white ski jacket against the chill. In the darkness, it seemed to float toward Poppy. "Ethan says he used to be a starter."

"Yes," she said slowly. Chase had played much better before, often the game's top scorer. Now his passing was sloppy and he seemed to lose focus almost immediately when the coach did allow him into the game, which was less and less.

"Maybe you should take him back to his old team," Mary-Ann said, "so that he can play more at his own level." Her voice dripped with fake solicitude. "He's out of his depth here."

Poppy realized the bundle in the woman's arms was an overweight pug. It sniffed at her, then growled. "There's more to life than soccer," she said, her groping fingers finally encountering the cool metal of her keys. "I'm sure he'll adapt."

"As for this little car," Mary-Ann said. "It's so—compact, so—well, cramped. I don't know how on earth you manage."

"It gets good gas mileage." Poppy clicked her remote, but the Honda's locks didn't disengage.

"And that's an important consideration, isn't it?" Mary-Ann stopped a few feet away, fingers stroking the obese dog. "It is expensive living out here. The life-style is not for everyone. It might be cheaper if you moved back to the city and commuted."

Poppy's cell phone launched into the *Lone Ranger* theme (she'd forgotten to reset it) and Mary-Ann stifled a laugh with her well manicured hand. Irritated, Poppy pulled the phone out of her purse, flipped it open and checked the number. "Withheld," of course. "Mother?"

"I told you to keep your eyes open!"

"Not now, Mom, please!"

"Yes, *now*," her mother said. "Chase—"

"Later!" Poppy snapped the phone shut, then inserted her key into the lock. It wouldn't turn.

Mary-Ann laid a hand on the Honda's hood. "I'm afraid our Hummer has become rather fond of this quaint little car." She smiled and her teeth glimmered in the moonlight. "This model is practically an antique, though. I'm surprised it's still running. Automotive love—inexplicable isn't it?"

What was going on? "Cars don't—" Poppy began, then broke off as the stupid pug winked at her.

"Go home," it said in a growlly little voice. "This is our territory."

It was a *familiar*. Poppy had never possessed one, but she recognized the breed. She looked at Mary-Ann, finally understanding the situation. "You!"

"As Precious said, this is our family's territory," Mary-Ann said. "My great-grandparents claimed it long ago when the area was just farms and fields, and we have defended it since against all intruders."

The woman's fingers formed a *Repel* sigil and Poppy could feel the sickening force of it driving her away. "The longer you stay here where you're not wanted, the worse things will get. I'm afraid you're hopelessly outclassed."

Mary-Ann was *Gifted*. Poppy felt so incredibly stupid. She should have seen it weeks ago. No wonder poor Chase fell over his own feet every time he took the field. He'd been hexed.

Her phone rang again. She flipped it open without taking her eyes off Mary-Ann's smug face.

"Poppy, you have to listen to me! Chase has been—"

"Yes, Mom, I just figured that out."

"I could tell when I talked to him earlier," her mother said. "What are you going to do about it?"

"Later, Mom!" She closed the phone and shoved it back into her purse. With a chill, Poppy had not the slightest doubt what was wrong with her car either. Dominick, with all his well intentioned bumbling, hadn't *Wakened* it. He didn't have the talent. Mary-Ann had done it just to make trouble. As for Chase, whatever her neighbor's feelings about a new Gifted family intruding into what she considered to be her "territory," no one had the right to take it out on her kid!

Her hands clenched so that the car keys bit into her fingers. "You hexed an eight-year-old boy!"

"Actually, it didn't take much," Mary-Ann said, nuzzling the pug's head. "The child is inherently clumsy. He must have gotten that from you, dear." She smiled poisonously. "I only heightened his innate tendency to fall on his face."

Poppy's cheeks flushed, the heat of her anger

rushing through her all the way down to her toes. "Take it off!"

"No." Mary-Ann's eyes were bright with satisfaction. "I won't—ever. You might as well crawl back to where you came from—Queens, wasn't it? Then you can do cute little *Cleansing* rituals with basil, bake *Love* crumpets out of coriander, and dance in broomstick skirts under the moon with all the other kitchen-witches. We do things with a little more class here."

A car turned and drove down the street, blinding her for a moment with its headlights. Poppy put her hand on the Honda and, summoning all her will, murmured, *"Open!"* The locks disengaged, the door opened. She glared at Mary-Ann. "This isn't finished!"

"On the contrary, little mouse," Mary-Ann said, stroking the pug. "I think you'll find that it never even got started."

Poppy climbed into the Honda and drove back to her garage, seething. There, she closed the door and disengaged the automatic opener to keep her wandering vehicle home.

Dominick was in the living room when she came in, still prickly with outrage. "Do you need me to carry stuff in from the car?" he said, eyes on the TV.

Belatedly, she remembered that she'd supposedly been "going to the store," but she didn't want to tell him about the McGovern woman. If he tried to intervene, he would likely only make matters worse. "They—were out," she said, dropping her purse.

"Of what?" He was watching *Dance Idol Countdown*, a competition with scantily costumed female dancers who twirled and arched their backs most fetchingly.

"Um, everything." She went to hang her jacket up.

"Oh," he said, leaning forward as a lithe young thing, clad in little more than a thong and a pair of bandanas, performed a magnificent handspring into the splits. "That's—odd."

She ran fingers through her wind-tossed hair and tried to think through her anger what she should do. "Where's Chase?"

"I sent him to brush his teeth and go to bed."

She found her son sitting in the middle of his bedroom rug, playing with his Nintendo again. His thumbs flew over the tiny buttons. "Die, Flower! Die, Faline! Die, Bambi! Die, die!"

"Put that up for now, please," she said, then settled cross-legged beside him as he reluctantly set it aside. Smoothing ash-blond hair back from his forehead, she said, "Did Ethan or his mother give you something?"

He shook his head, looking longingly at the Nintendo.

"Think hard," she insisted. "Anything at all, even something really small like a piece of gum. This is important."

"No, Mom," he said. "Ethan hates me." He knuckled his sleepy eyes. Can I finish my Nintendo level?"

"Tomorrow," she said. "It's time for bed."

"Coach said I can't play in the next game unless I do better in Friday's scrimmage," he said, slipping under the covers.

"It's all right," she said, kissing his forehead. "I can just about guarantee things are going to improve."

"I want to go home," he said. Tears welled in his hazel eyes. "Everything was easier, and I miss my friends. No one believes me here about anything. They all just think I'm weird."

"Well, you can't talk about Grandma's calls." She smiled. "Even I have trouble believing that!" She tickled him until he laughed with her. "Good night."

"'Night, Mom," he said and turned over.

She sighed and went to pick up discarded clothes scattered like fallen leaves across the carpet, then noticed that the Nintendo was still on. Tiny animated rabbits and fawns were dashing through the forest, fleeing a lumbering rifleman. Why had Dominick ever bought him such a violent game? She certainly wouldn't have.

She picked up the device to turn it off and a tingle ran through her fingers, up her arm, deep into her brain. She dropped the plastic case back to the carpet, suddenly *lost in a forest with looming, closely spaced trees, hearing footsteps and echoing gunshots.* "Chase," she said, staring at her prickling hand, "where did you get this game module?"

He rolled over sleepily. "*Enchanted Forest Terminator?* I swapped one of my old games with Lonny." He sat up. "I was tired of *Street Car Rally* and this one is really rad. Even when it's not on, I can see the forest and the rifleman and the animals in my head all the time. It's like I'm always playing."

Always playing—when he was at school, supposedly listening to his lessons, and at soccer practice, during games, and even at night when he was doing his homework. The poor kid probably even dreamed about it. No wonder A's were a thing of the past and he couldn't focus! "Who—is Lonny's best friend?"

"Ethan."

Right. She'd known that the second she'd asked. "Okay, go to sleep, kiddo. Like I said, tomorrow should be a much better day." She used his discarded T-shirt to scoop up the Nintendo without touching the case again, then turned off the light and shut the door.

Her heart thudded as she walked down the hall. This malevolence had breached their home on her watch. It was up to her to take care of it. She regarded the Nintendo balefully.

The phone rang. "I'll get it!" she called to Dominick who was still lost before the TV in the wispy-costumed wonders of *Dance Idol Countdown*. She snatched up the kitchen handset.

"Poppy, darling, I'm so sorry," her mother said.

"Can you tell me how to fix this?" Poppy said.

"Not allowed," her mother said. "They're very strict about such things Up Here. I could lose my phone privileges."

Poppy sank onto a chair at the kitchen's breakfast bar. "It's Chase's game," she said. "Mary-Ann McGovern hexed it."

"Think, Poppy," her mother said. "In your heart, you already know what to do."

Her fingers gripped the plastic handset so tightly, they were going numb. Mom had always taught her that bad magic could be reflected back on its originator, even sometimes magnified in the process, if one were skillful enough, but she didn't want to hurt Ethan. He was only a child.

Mary-Ann must have another weakness. Everyone did. "Mom, I can't talk right now," she said. "Call me back later." She hung up, then examined the Nintendo. It wasn't the device that was hexed. Chase had been fine until he traded game modules with Lonny. It had to be the game itself. Using the T-shirt, she pushed the button to eject the slim square.

This had come from Mary-Ann, she thought grimly, and it was only polite to return borrowed items. She swathed it in the T-shirt and then put on her jacket again.

They were just presenting the night's voting results for the dance contest. "I'm—going to a different store—where they're not out of, you know, stuff," she said to Dominick whose eyes only flickered sideways at her. "Back before bedtime."

"Mmmm," he said as the live studio audience burst into cheers for a practically nude red-haired favorite.

She slipped outside. The wind had come up since she'd been out earlier and chased the clouds away. Stars glittered down, hard and bright, but she could still see the ghostly overlay of the *game-forest* as she walked. And that was after only touching the module for a second. She thought of the hours Chase had devoted to that stupid game. It would be days, perhaps even weeks, before the effects dissipated.

The T-shirt bundled against her chest, she tramped the three blocks to the McGoverns' house. As she'd hoped, the black Hummer was still in the driveway. It really was a monster and she doubted that it fit in the two-car garage with their other vehicle.

She tried the passenger door, but it was of course locked. *"Open!"* she whispered, her hand on the freezing metal.

Instead, the horn beeped. Drat, it was probably warded against interference, as she should have done with her Honda.

The porch light winked on and the front door opened. Mary-Ann and the pug appeared on the threshold. The dog was wearing a silly black-and-orange Halloween coat. Poppy flattened to the driveway's cold pavement using the Hummer's bulk to hide.

"*Reveal!*" Mary-Ann called.

An electric tingle of power pushed at her to stand, but Poppy formed a *Conceal* sigil with shaking fingers. *It was only blowing leaves!* she thought desperately. All around her, the night hung cold and still with a pregnant edge as though something might precipitate out of sheer starlight. Poppy's gloveless fingers ached with the strain of holding the sigil. She couldn't breathe.

The pug-familiar shivered, then licked its mistress's face. "I'm cold!"

"Sorry, Precious," Mary-Ann said and closed the door.

Poppy waited five minutes, then started again, hunkering by the massive car, cheek pressed to the door. "*Open!*" she told it.

No response.

It had been *Wakened*, like her Honda, and had at least some will of its own. She'd seen that earlier when it turned on its headlights and engine. "Don't you get bored out here in the dark by yourself?" she said, fingers spread on the chill metal. "Wouldn't you like something to pass the time?"

The dome light flashed on, indicating, she hoped, interest. She unwrapped the hexed module and pressed it to the door, using the T-shirt like a potholder. "My son loves this game," she said, "but it belongs to your family. Just unlock your door and I'll leave it with you. That's fair, isn't it?"

The lock snapped up. She moved aside and the door

opened. She peered into the gleaming black leather interior. Cars didn't have Nintendo consoles, of course, but this operated by magic. Contact was the key element. She reached far back under the passenger seat to wedge the slim square beneath the floor mat.

"Welcome to the Enchanted Forest," she said to the Hummer. "Now you'll never be bored again." Then she eased the door shut, shoved her freezing hands in her pockets, and hurried home.

Chase came to her at breakfast the next day, Nintendo in hand. "Mom, where's *Enchanted Forest Terminator?*"

"I got rid of it," she said, setting a steaming plate of pancakes in front of him.

"But it's my favorite!" His lower lip protruded dangerously.

"I know," she said, "but I'll buy you a better one that won't be in your head all the time so that you can't concentrate in school or at soccer. Decide what you want and we'll go to the game shop at the mall after school."

That mollified him somewhat.

Two days later, Chase was still seeing the forest game sometimes, especially in his dreams, but seemed more able to focus. When he brought home a B on his Spelling test for the first time in weeks, she knew the hex was wearing off.

As for the Honda, she burned angelica in the garage, salted the Four Quarters, and sprinkled basil under the car mats. It was, if not back to being *Unwakened*, at least more cooperative, though still clearly fascinated by Lincoln Navigators.

At Friday's soccer scrimmage, Mary-Ann and Ethan McGovern arrived in the black Hummer, which was driving erratically, dodging nonexistent trees, stopping abruptly every few feet, and honking at invisible deer and rabbits to get out of its way.

"What happened to your car?" Chase asked Ethan as the boy clambered out. "It looked like it was doing the Cha-Cha."

Ethan just ducked his head and scowled. Then Coach blew his whistle so the team fell in for a quick warm-up. Smiling, Poppy settled on the bleachers and watched the boys go through their stretches. Mary-Ann shoved in beside her and gave Poppy a malevolent look. "I know you're responsible!"

Poppy put her sunglasses on. The day was very bright with a fine sharp wind. She watched as the boys finished their warm-up, then split into two teams. Coach waved and the scrimmage started with a flurry of passes. "For what?" she said finally.

"Hexing my car!"

"Me?" Poppy said. "A mere `kitchen-witch?' Don't be silly. It probably just needs a good tune-up." Her cell phone rang, still the *Lone Ranger* trumpets. Poppy sighed and flipped it open.

"Dear," her mother said, "do you remember Uncle Vernon?"

Vernon Melton had been a family friend, not really a relative at all, just a big bluff balding guy with a ready smile. He'd loved playing cards and boating, she recalled, but had passed away about—what was it—five years ago? "Sure," she said.

"We ran into each other at the Wings and Things Bingo Palace and now he's taking me sailing!" her mother said. "I may not be able to check on you so much. Will you be all right without me?"

Her throat tightened. "Mom, I'll never be without you."

Cheers erupted and she looked up just in time to see Chase score a goal.

Jan Stirling writes: "When I was thirty-eight they came out with a statistic that women my age were more likely to be killed by terrorists than married for the first time. Along came Steve, who proposed, rescuing me from those hypothetical terrorists. We married, I changed my name and moved to another country (Canada), thus beginning a whole new life. Within two years I tried writing for the very first time (I hear this happens to a lot of SF&F spousal units, must be something in the air) and two years later I made my first sale to *Chicks in Chainmail*."

S. M. Stirling was born in France in 1953, to Canadian parents—although his mother was born in England and grew up in Peru. After that he lived in Europe, Canada, Africa, and the US and visited several other continents. He graduated from law school in

Canada but had his dorsal fin surgically removed, and published his first novel (*Snowbrother*) in 1984, going full-time as a writer in 1988, the year of his marriage to Janet Moore of Milford, Massachusetts, who he met, wooed and proposed to at successive World Fantasy Conventions. In 1995 he suddenly realized that he could live anywhere and they decamped from Toronto, that large, cold, gray city on Lake Ontario, and moved to Santa Fe, New Mexico. He became an American citizen in 2004. His latest books are *In the Courts of the Crimson Kings*, from Tor, and *The Sunrise Lands* from ROC books. His hobbies mostly involve reading—history, anthropology, archaeology, and travel, besides fiction—but he also cooks and bakes for fun and food. For twenty years he also pursued the martial arts, until hyperextension injuries convinced him he was in danger of becoming the most deadly cripple in human history. Currently he lives with his wife Janet, also an author, and the compulsory authorial cats.

The Importance
of Communication

Jan and S.M. Stirling

Maggie set down her purse on the granite topped
island and took a deep breath of kitchen air redolent
of the aroma of baking and vanilla.

"You're doing a different kind of magic these days,
I see," she said.

I grinned and picked up a cupcake to frost. "Brady
needed sixty of these for class tomorrow."

"There are sixty kids in his class? And cupcakes? I
learned all about those before I even hit school."

"They're having a do," I said. "At least this time I
knew about it." I glanced at Maggie who was eyeing
a cupcake and frosted a lopsided one for her. "There
you go."

"Mmmph! Fangyou," Maggie said. "C'n I have
some sprinkles?"

When I'd opened the door to find my former partner on the doorstep I'd been delightfully surprised.

Now I was beginning to wonder if this was just a casual drop in. Back before I was married, I'd been a member of the Cabal, what we'd jokingly called our association of white witches who fought practitioners of black magic. Maggie had continued the fight and close as we'd been we seldom saw one another any more. So naturally I wondered.

"Can you stay for dinner?" I asked.

"You bet. I want to see the kids. They must be what . . . fifteen and eight now?"

"Your memory always amazes me. Brady is eight, but it's fifteen going on sixteen and 'when am I getting a car?' for Lisa."

Maggie laughed. "We were the same," she said. "Except I don't think we expected to have a car given to us. I seem to recall earning mine."

"These days it's the least you can do to show your unworthy love. We parents should get together more often so that we can show some solidarity. Then when someone gets crazy, the majority can stand firm instead of feeling like the isolated skinflint whose poor misunderstood kids are being laughed at by their peers for having to take the bus."

With a laugh Maggie nodded, then grew more serious. "So has Lisa shown any interest in the craft?" she asked, elaborately casual.

Aha! I thought. Raising an eyebrow I asked, "Is that why you're here?"

"Kinda." Maggie shrugged. "She's the right age for questions."

"You don't know teenagers if you think they ask questions about what you expect them to," I said. "I've never discussed it with her and no, she's never brought it up. As far as I can tell it's not even a cloud on her horizon."

"She could easily have the gift," Maggie pointed out. "It is or was very strong in you before you gave it up."

That was a sore point with my friend. Joe had told me that he couldn't bear to see me put myself in danger. It was as simple as that. He was prepared to walk away from what we had, but I just couldn't let him. Truth was I was more than a little burned out by then and didn't see it as a sacrifice. More as a rescue, really.

I shook my head. "She's never shown any sign of it." I frosted another cupcake.

"No odd occurrences around the house, for instance?"

I squeezed the cupcake until the top popped off. "You can have this one too if you'd like," I offered. Then looked at her. "What are you getting at?"

Maggie held her hands out in surrender. "Okay. What about the nose incident?"

The nose incident. There was only one way she could know about that. Diana must have told her.

"Yeah, that was weird," I agreed.

One morning Brady had been breathing through his mouth, when asked about it he said his nose was stuffed up. Something odd about the way he looked had prompted me to take a look only to find his nostrils thick with fur. Definitely a curse. I was way out of practice, so I called on my old group leader Diana who'd made it go away.

"Weird? C'mon, Ann, Diana said it looked like a mink had been stuffed up his nose."

"That doesn't necessarily have anything to do with Lisa."

"I'm not saying she'd do it deliberately. But who else would it be? And if it isn't looked into then next time Brady could wake up looking like Bobo the dog-faced boy. You were lucky this time."

I had to admit that was true. Maybe I was being an ostrich about this. But I'd promised Joe, my husband, that I was through with magic and I'd kept that promise. Still, it was possible that one or both of the kids had the gift. If it showed up it would have to be dealt with.

"Do you want her to be picking up her information on street corners?" Maggie prompted.

I laughed. "I doubt they discuss magic on street corners," I said. "Sex yes, as in olden times, but not magic."

"No, now they talk about it on the internet. Which is way worse," Maggie said, "because it's so private. Do you know how much dangerous information and misinformation is available to anybody with a computer? You don't even have to look that hard. And talk about predators. That's where I spend most of my time these days, on computer cases."

"Times have changed," I agreed, trying to stave off that "bad mother" feeling.

Brady came in from school then and saved me from a discussion I didn't want to have. It took him a minute but he remembered Maggie as a fun friend of Mom's and unselfconsciously monopolized her until his sister came in when they both fought for her attention.

I finished the cupcakes and started dinner, throwing in a comment every now and then to show I was paying attention. But all the while I worried at what Maggie had said. Had Lisa cursed her brother? Unintentionally I was sure. That is if she had. My kids got along very well and loved each other I knew. But there were spats and little brothers will get annoying at times. And she certainly had the genes for it. I stifled a sigh. No question about it, I was going to have to have a heart to heart talk with my daughter.

Dinner was marred slightly by the fact that Maggie and Joe can't stand each other. My husband is the most reasonable of men about most things, but magic and the Cabal are not among them.

We were having dinner in the dining room in honor of our guest. The table is round and I'd intended to have Maggie sit next to me where she'd be out of Joe's line of sight. But the kids insisted she sit between them, which placed her directly opposite him. He glowered at her the whole time. She glowered back. It was a full on glower-off.

The kids picked up on the hostility and watched their sniping with fascination. So much so that I dismissed them the minute dinner was over. I'd do the dishes myself tonight. Maggie could help. It was the least she could do.

When Lisa came in a little later to say that she was going over to Blair's to study Maggie piped up.

"Blair McCall?"

Lisa was taken by surprise, but then, so was I.

"Yeah," Lisa said. "You know her?"

"I've heard of her. She's a role player, I believe."

My daughter nodded, giving our guest the once over. Obviously wondering how an adult could know of such things.

"Be home by ten," I told her. I'd have given her a hug but my hands were wet. I hate using the dish washer, it sounds like a war is going on in that thing.

With husband and children elsewhere I turned to Maggie.

"So, how do you know Blair?" Whom I had yet to meet, hint though I would.

Maggie bit her lip as she dried a plate. "She's come up on our radar. Based on the sites she visits and the comments she makes she's someone we're watching. We're pretty sure she hasn't done anything yet, but she could be dangerous."

I looked at the door my beloved daughter had just exited, then back at my friend. "*Now* you tell me?"

With a shrug and a defensive tip of her head Maggie said, "Like I told you, she hasn't done anything yet. She may never act on any of the things she's said. You know how melodramatic girls that age can be. We're watching the situation." She bowed her head and looked up at me from under her eyelashes. "I was going to tell you."

Right. If there was one thing I knew it was that the people on the Cabal's radar were not being watched for their lack of potential. They posed a danger to themselves and others. Whether through malice or ignorance didn't matter, the results tended to be the same. Messy.

"What's going on?" I asked. There were a lot of other questions I wanted answered, and I intended to get those answers, but now was not the time.

"According to Blair's messages they're planning a ceremony tonight in the woods behind Johnson's farm. It could just be role playing," she said quickly. "Like I said it's something she does. Avidly."

I took off my apron and dropped it on the counter. "Then we'd better get in position."

Without another word I walked out in search of my husband who was in the den. "Honey," I said, "Maggie and I are going out for a drive. Remind Brady to go to bed at nine if I'm not back by then." Then I left him sitting there before he could think of anything to say. And he would have.

Maggie had her purse and a grim expression when I met up with her in the hallway.

"We'll take my car," she said. "I've got equipment."

That was good, because after all these years I didn't even have a wand. I was glad she wasn't arguing with me about how out of practice I was because I had no defense. Still, as I got in the car it felt like old times. It felt good. Or would have if it wasn't my daughter we were going to rescue.

"Tell me what you know," I said as I fastened my seat belt.

"They mean to call up Leonard," she said.

"Leonard!" I yelped. My blood ran cold. "Is she nuts?" Despite the innocuous sounding name, Leonard is a demon of the first order, chief of the minor demons and Inspector General of Black Magic. He was master of the sabbats and presided over these in the form of a giant black goat with the ears of a fox. No one knows why goat ears weren't good enough for him. Probably he wasn't content with being supernatural, he had to be unnatural, too. It's a demon thing.

"Are we there yet?" I asked in subtle encouragement.

The woods behind Johnson's farm barely deserve the name. You can walk through them in any direction in half an hour and come out on a road or neighboring farm. None of the trees is over thirty years old, so they're fairly slim and healthy and the undergrowth is extreme, brambles everywhere. But like the primeval forests in the Brothers Grimm it has a dandy clearing perfect for magical mischief making; or picnics, which is probably its daytime job.

Things were already underway by the time we got there. Thirteen kids all predictably robed and hooded in black, except Blair whose robes were trimmed in crimson. Lisa was wearing white and was bound spreadeagled on the makeshift altar. By makeshift I mean it looked like an old dining room table. It wobbled when Lisa shifted, earning her a glare from Blair. My daughter mouthed "Sorry," ignored by her friend.

The circle had been cast, candles were lit and the young acolytes were swaying and droning like extras in a horror movie. I looked at Maggie. Maybe they *were* just role playing.

She shook her head, eyes fixed on Blair. Just then the young high priestess began her invocation. In perfect Latin. It was the right one, too. Maggie hadn't been kidding about the kinds of things you can find on the net.

Within moments a thick, black cloud began to form over the table and the kids stopped their noise and froze in place. Blair picked up a knife that looked longer than her arm and Lisa finally began to look worried.

A goat's head began to form out of the cloud. It had three horns and, as advertised, a fox's ears. I don't know how it managed it with a goat's features, but the face leered and Lisa screamed. So did the other kids. I didn't blame them, there was a feeling of overwhelming evil rolling off the monster. To paraphrase Martha Stewart, it was *not* a good thing.

"Where is my sacrifice?" it asked in a voice like the grinding of rocks.

"Right here," Blair said in a voice that implied, *dumbass*.

The demon actually sighed. "The sacrifice requires a virgin," it said with exaggerated patience.

"You fink!" Blair snapped at Lisa.

The demon looked around. "Ah," it said. "That one will do."

Leonard and its cloud moved toward a runty acolyte who fell over backward, squealing in horror.

Frantically I looked at Maggie. She fired a flare into the cloud that burst with an array of demon banishing chemicals causing Leonard to join the general screaming going on and vanish, putting a firm period to little Blair's invocation.

I rushed forward over crackling leaves saying loudly, "This is what happens when you call on demons. Sometimes they show up!"

"Mom?" Lisa said, somehow sounding mortified in just the one word.

"I'll just borrow this if I may," I said to Blair, removing the knife from her limp fingers.

Then I began sawing at the clothesline that bound my daughter. The knife was very sharp and she was free in moments. Her friend looked like she was in shock. Though why I was still thinking of Blair as her friend when she'd obviously intended to kill Lisa is beyond me.

"Where are your clothes?" I asked my daughter.

"In the car," she said sullenly.

"Go get them," I commanded in the mommy voice that brooked no argument. "Meet me back here. Now!"

She hurried off holding up the hem of her virginal white costume. Virginal. Well at least that was one thing I didn't have to worry about tonight.

Blair made to slip away, but Maggie detained her with an authoritative hand on her slender shoulder.

"Oh, no, my dear. We need to talk," Maggie said.

The talk would determine several things, one of which was whether her abilities, which seemed substantial, would be permanently blocked and how susceptible she was to demonic influence. Which may have been the cause of this whole episode. Or, she could just be a rotten human being.

Lisa and I rode in the backseat. That's because I knew that the front passenger side seatbelt can be locked from the driver's side. I also figured Blair was eager to escape that little talk that Maggie had promised so the lock would be necessary.

Blair crossed her arms. "I can't believe you didn't tell me you weren't a virgin," she muttered.

"Yeah?" Lisa said. "Well I can't believe you were going to kill me. I thought you were my friend!"

Blair turned around as far as the seat belt would permit, looking shocked. "I wasn't going to kill you! What kind of lunatic do you think I am?"

"You had a knife," Lisa pointed out.

"Purely for ceremonial reasons," Blair shot back.

"So what was Leonard supposed to get for a party favor?" Maggie asked.

"Yeah," Lisa said. "What?"

Blair sat forward again. "Your soul," she muttered.

"My what?"

"You wouldn't even have missed it," Blair said impatiently.

"She would eventually," Maggie muttered.

"Bigtime!" Lisa agreed.

"That's one of the things we'll be discussing, Blair," Maggie said.

I wanted to do more than just discuss things with

the little rat, but I knew that was no longer my prerogative.

Sure enough when we got to my house Blair attempted to get out, saying, "Thanks for the ride, I'll just call my folks to come get me." When the seat belt wouldn't disengage she became frantic. "Let me out of here!" she shouted, yanking on the belt. "You have no right to keep me here!"

"Well, you have no right to sacrifice your friends to Satan. Let me tell you, girl that's one slippery slope you're on. I promised you a talk and a talk we shall have. You guys had better go," Maggie said over her shoulder.

"Let me know how this goes," I said.

"You got it," my friend assured me.

I got out, but my daughter hung back. "But . . . ," she started to say.

"Out!" I snapped.

Lisa's heart was in the right place, but her mind was in neutral to say the least. She popped out of the car like a Jack-in-the-box at my tone of voice, giving Blair a look at once angry and regretful.

At that point Blair began to scream. The sound was muffled by the specially made little Ford, but you could still hear her. I hoped she gave out quickly or my friend would be deaf in two shakes.

We waved them away from the end of the driveway and then I turned to my daughter, still clad in her sacrificial gear.

"What were you thinking?" I asked. I couldn't hold the question back any longer.

"I thought we were role playing," she whined.

"She had a knife," I pointed out. "You were tied up and she was planning to sacrifice you to a demon."

"Ma-awm! I'm not stoopid. If I thought she was going to kill me or something of course I wouldn't have let her tie me up. But we've role played before and nothing like this ever happened."

"She's tied you up before?" I visualized all sorts of kinky scenarios.

"No! But this was a new game. At least that's what she said."

"Have your other games involved magic?" I asked.

Lisa studied her feet. "Yeah, I guess."

I bit my lip. How to be subtle at this point? "Did anything you role played ever seem to come true in real life?"

She looked thoughtful. "Y'know, sometimes I think it kinda did. Like there was one time we wanted to avoid a test so we cast a spell to make the teacher not be able to give it? And Ms. Calabrini didn't make it in to school that day."

"What happened to her?" I asked. This could be serious.

"Oh, her car broke down. Nothing too bad either. At least I don't think it was, she's still driving that car." Now she gave me a *look*.

Despite my relief at Ms. Calabrini's fortuitous escape I dreaded what was coming next. Now she would accuse me of spying on her and invading her privacy. Never mind I'd just saved her soul. That small fact would be blithely forgotten in rampaging teenage paranoia.

"How come you were following me?" she demanded.

"Well, my dear," I said, brushing the hair from her forehead, "that's a story that starts before you were born. We need to have a talk too."

"Mom, my best friend just tried to sacrifice my soul

to a demon. Don't you think I've been punished enough for one night?"

She almost had a point, but I'd been a mother long enough to persevere.

"There's the small matter of your, ahem, virginity," I pointed out.

Even in the dark driveway I could see her blushing.

"That's private!" she snapped. "Did you tell grandma when you gave up yours?"

Now I blushed, because I sure hadn't. Oh, I had options, I could have said, "I'm not you," like a lot of parents would. But that was a cop out. I took a deep breath.

"Did you at least take precautions?"

"Of course we did," she muttered.

"There's no of course about it, my love. When two teenagers get together to have sex it's usually as well planned as a car crash."

"Well, we did." She kicked an imaginary pebble.

I smiled, because she was whole and safe and sound. And probably not pregnant.

"I'm glad we had this talk, sweetie, because I can't emphasize enough the importance of communication at this point in your life."

"Then how about telling me the story that starts before I was born?" Lisa asked.

Damn! She would ask. Well, sometimes, good parenting means coming through on your platitudes.

"Okay," I sighed. "But I need a stiff cuppa cocoa and a cupcake, how about you?"

"Mom, I've never needed a cupcake so bad in my life."

David D. Levine is a lifelong SF reader whose midlife crisis was to take a sabbatical from his high-tech job to attend Clarion West in 2000. It seems to have worked. He made his first professional sale in 2001, won the Writers of the Future Contest in 2002, was nominated for the John W. Campbell award in 2003, was nominated for the Hugo Award and the Campbell again in 2004, and won a Hugo in 2006 (Best Short Story, for "Tk'Tk'Tk"). His "Titanium Mike Saves the Day" was nominated for a Nebula Award in 2008, and a collection of his short stories, *Space Magic*, is available from Wheatland Press (http://www.wheatlandpress.com). He lives in Portland, Oregon with his wife, Kate Yule, with whom he edits the fanzine Bento, and their website is at http://www.BentoPress.com.

Midnight at the Center Court

David D. Levine

Julian's mother reached out and tucked a stray lock
of his black hair behind his ear, but as soon as she
turned away he shook it back down. He was thirteen,
not a little kid any more, and if he wanted to wear
his hair free and easy he would. "Of course it isn't
fair, honey," she said, taking down a bottle of henbane
from the kitchen shelf and whisking nonexistent dust
off of it with a bright pink feather duster.

"But it's just a simple little divination spell!" He'd
found Astarte's Pool in his grimoire that morning and
had already memorized the incantation. It looked like
a piece of cake, and he couldn't see any reason why
it should be forbidden to males.

Julian's mother's own brassy hair was never out of
place. That solid helmet of hair never even budged. She
frowned, resting the feather duster on one earthtone-
polyester-clad hip. "Now, honey, you know better than

that. The Twofold Deity has two aspects for a reason. Boys and girls each have their own parts to play."

She didn't seem to have noticed the hair hanging in his eyes. He was half relieved at missing the usual lecture about looking like a hippie, and half annoyed she couldn't even spare him that much attention. "But how come it's the girls who get all the really interesting spells?"

"I'll answer that if you tell me why a woman earns fifty-nine cents for the same work a man does for a dollar."

"Look, just let me *try* it. I swear I won't tell anyone in the coven. You know you can trust me—I've never told a soul at school about the Craft, not like that blabby Dan Corry."

She finished her dusting and hung the duster in the pantry. The Lakeshore Bank calendar on the pantry door read SEPTEMBER 1974, with a picture of bright abstract autumn leaves, and the word MABON was written on Sunday the 22nd. She tapped the date with one long pink-lacquered fingernail. "We can talk later. Right now I need you to practice your incantations. You have a very important support role to play in tonight's sabbat."

"Support," he muttered, turning away.

"I heard that," she snapped. A chill touch on his shoulder, and suddenly he was facing her again, across the immaculate sunset-and-harvest-gold expanse of the kitchen linoleum. Just another example of the kinds of spells reserved for women. But her anger was quickly replaced with a sympathetic expression. "Oh, honey, I know how you feel. But everyone has their job to do in balancing the universe between light and dark.

The God is *consort* to the Goddess, born of her at the new year, mating with her in the spring, and dying in the fall. Only the Goddess is eternal."

And then she smiled, and Julian knew what was coming next. "You'll understand when you're older."

Julian rolled his eyes.

"Now run along," Julian's mother said cheerily, and waggled her shiny pink fingernails. "No mistakes tonight!"

"Yeah, whatever."

This time she let him go.

After two hours of studying, sprawled across his Partridge Family comforter with his nose in a grimoire, Julian was able to convince his mother he had his little incantation down pat and she released him for the afternoon. He immediately hopped on his bike and headed for the mall.

Justin lived in Lakeshore, a pathetic little suburb so bogus that the nearest mall was in the adjacent suburb of Alewife Bay. The mall was usually outside his range, a good forty-five minutes away by bike, but after this morning's argument he really needed something sweet to drown his sorrows, and the frozen yogurt shop at Alewife Bay Mall fixed a mean banana split.

It really wasn't fair, Justin reflected as he pedaled, dry leaves crunching under the wheels of his five-speed Huffy. Outside of the Craft, the policemen and doctors and bankers were almost all men. But within it . . . oh, every coven was theoretically co-led by a priestess and a priest, representing both aspects of the divine, but it was the priestess who made all the decisions. And all the really cool spells, like levitation, invisibility, and divination, were Goddess spells. The God spells were all about healing, or providing energy for another spell, or just general feel-good mush. But whenever Julian asked to learn any of the spells that were actually *good* for anything . . . well, it was as bad as the time he'd asked for an Easy-Bake Oven for Yule.

He still didn't understand why that was such a big deal.

Julian's spirits lifted a little as he rolled up to the mall entrance, because he saw his friend Liz's bike lying next to the bike rack. There was no mistaking The Monster—it used to be pink, but she'd spray-painted it black and put a sticker of big pointy teeth on the handlebars. Julian's own bike was yellow, decorated with blue and white Crazy Daisy stickers.

Julian had first met Colleen Elizabeth O'Malley—she hated her first name—about five years ago, right here at the mall. She lived nearby, and on that day she'd been one of a group of kids from Alewife Bay Grade School who'd ambushed him outside the entrance and begun tickling him unmercifully.

Julian hated being tickled. When he was tickled, he started hiccupping, and then he couldn't breathe, and then he threw up. He'd been humiliated by tickling hundreds of times in his grade school and middle school career.

But unlike anyone else, when Julian gasped out "Stop that!" . . . Liz had stopped, and she'd made the other kids stop too. And she'd never tickled him again.

They'd become fast friends that day. It was a weird friendship; Liz was a twelve-year-old tomboy, a wiry freckled redhead whose cat's-eye glasses were always getting broken in some sporting event or other, while

Julian was a pale skinny wimp whose favorite sport was Skittle Golf. When they'd played together as kids, Julian was the one who got out the toy pots and pans while Liz wanted to play kickball. But they kept hanging out together, kindred spirits in some indefinable way.

Julian locked his bike to the rack next to The Monster, making sure the combination was properly scrambled, and went inside.

The mall had changed a lot since the last time he'd been there. It used to be a standard strip mall, one line of stores facing a parking lot, but in the last year they'd decided to enlarge and enclose it, building a second row of stores and putting a roof across the space between them. Some of the new stores were already open, huge expanses of glass reflecting the older stores opposite, old-fashioned display windows and storm doors braced for a winter that would never return. Other new stores were incomplete, with exposed metal beams and work lights hanging from yellow electrical cords.

He found Liz in the frozen yogurt shop, licking at a chocolate soft-serve yogurt cone. He said "Hey," then went up to the counter and ordered a large banana split with chopped walnuts, strawberry topping, and extra hot fudge.

"Why so glum, chum?" Liz said as he returned with his big styrofoam boat full of gooey goodness.

Julian sighed. One of the most stringent rules of the Craft was that its existence must never be revealed to lay people under any circumstances. There were very good reasons for this, but it made it kind of hard to talk with people about what was going on in his life.

"It's my mom. I've got a . . . a project I want to do, and she won't let me."

Liz winked, crunching on her flat-bottomed cake cone. "So do it, and don't tell her."

"She'd find out for sure." Magic—at least any magic worth doing—left an imprint on the universe, and to a priestess as powerful as Julian's mother that print was as blatant as a road sign. "And then I'd really catch hell."

"Huh." She opened her mouth wide and popped the last inch of cone into it, chomping it with gusto, then wiped her mouth with the back of her hand. "What is this big secret project, anyway?"

Julian shook his head. "It's personal." That was his first line of defense, and with Liz it was usually enough.

The yogurt shop was getting crowded, so they walked to the middle of the mall. A big old department store had been torn down here to make way for a new central court, a broad open corridor running east-west across the north-south line of the original strip mall. In the center a fountain was under construction, half-tiled in bronze and gold with a collection of lead pipes sticking up in the middle.

They talked for a while about the new Saturday morning shows, and whether *Land of the Lost* was a ripoff of *Valley of the Dinosaurs* or vice versa, while Julian scooped up his yogurt with a long white plastic spoon. But as he ate, looking up at the central court's broad expanse of exposed beams and fiberglass skylights, Julian began to become aware of a peculiar, cold feeling in his gut. And it wasn't the yogurt.

Julian didn't have the Sight, and all the spells for

divination were Goddess spells, but he knew the forces of darkness when he felt them.

Every coven's primary job was to help maintain the balance of light and dark in the world. Light was order, and required work—human beings, channeling the energies of the Goddess and the God, to align things that had gotten out of order and put problems right. Darkness was chaos, and the forces of darkness were always pushing things awry and out of kilter.

Darkness wasn't evil, as such. Order without chaos was stagnation; a certain amount of darkness was necessary in the world. But like a rising flood or a raging forest fire, the uncontrolled forces of darkness could be mindlessly destructive.

And they were threatening to burst out here.

"What's wrong?" Liz said.

"Nothing. I'm just not hungry any more."

Liz gave him a look. "Julian, you're a thirteen-year-old boy. If you're not hungry, something's wrong."

Julian dropped the uneaten half of his yogurt in a trash can. He wandered around the mall, all his perceptions fully extended, but he couldn't find a specific nexus for the disquieting feeling of darkness. Although it was strongest near the center court, the whole mall seemed saturated with it.

Liz stayed with him as he prowled around. "Are you looking for the draft?"

"Huh?"

"There's cold air coming from somewhere." She rubbed her shoulders, though the air didn't seem particularly cold to Julian.

"Uh, yeah."

Julian searched as hard as he could. If he could

find the cursed object or locus of summoning that was the source of the energy, it could be removed or disenchanted . . . but the energy was just everywhere.

"This is as hard as science class," Liz said, looking up at the ceiling. "If only we had some kind of draft-o-meter."

That gave Julian an idea. "Maybe we can make one."

"How?"

"I did a . . . a science project, in school. I just need a cup, and some water." Liz was terrible at science. She'd never know the difference between a science project and a magic spell.

They scrounged up a plastic cup from a trash can in the center court and filled it with water from the drinking fountain. Julian held it between his hands and muttered under his breath.

Astarte's Pool. He wasn't supposed to use it—it was a Goddess spell—but if he could figure out what was going on here maybe his mother would forgive him.

"What's that you're saying?"

"I'm . . . I'm trying to remember the scientific formula."

"Better you than me."

As Julian murmured the words of the spell, the surface of the water began to shimmer. His heart raced; it was working!

And then a recorded trumpet call blared through the mall, shattering Julian's concentration and destroying the spell. Infuriated, Julian looked around for the source of the sound.

It was a giant wrapped package mounted above

the door at the far end of the center court. As Julian watched, the ten-foot box's sides and lid swung back, revealing a toy European village populated by dozens of painted wooden people and animals. They danced and bobbed about to a recorded tune, something upbeat and music-boxy, which ended with a little wooden boy in lederhosen coming out on a platform with a mallet and striking a large gong six times. The little wooden mallet didn't actually touch the gong, but each near-strike was accompanied by a loud recorded *bong*.

As the box closed itself up, the wooden people and buildings folding themselves back inside, Julian realized it was a clock, and it had just struck six. Six o'clock, and he had to be back home in time for dinner before the Mabon sabbat, which would begin promptly at sunset—6:50 PM. And home was forty-five minutes away.

"Oh, man," he said. "Sorry, I gotta run."

Julian's parents were already in their long black sabbat robes when he arrived at 6:40. He'd dropped his bike unceremoniously on the porch, too tired even to work the garage door opener after his frantic race home.

"There you are," his father said, fingering his gray-flecked black goatee as he often did when he was nervous or upset. He was proud of that goatee, although even Julian's mother said privately that it looked like the wrong end of the goat. "We were very concerned."

But Julian's mother wasn't concerned . . . she was furious. She held him by the shoulders at arms' length, and he felt the cold searching pressure of the Sight.

"This isn't right," she said, tilting her head, eyes narrowed. "Astarte's Pool . . . with an unconsecrated vessel . . . in front of a *layman*?" Her fingers tightened painfully on his shoulders.

"Mom, I had to . . ."

She let go of his shoulders and turned away, pacing the creamy shag carpet of the living room. "After all we've taught you . . ."

"But Mom, listen, there's, there's some kind of big dark-energy *thing* at the mall . . ."

She turned back to him, the spark of anger snapping in her eyes. "Don't try to lie your way out of this one, mister!"

Julian turned to his father for support, but his face was equally hard. "I am very, very disappointed in you."

"You are *so* grounded, young man," his mother said. "No sabbat tonight for you!"

No sabbat? On top of everything else, this was too much. Julian felt the hot sting of tears in the corners of his eyes, but he refused to cry. "But what about my part of the ceremony? All those incantations I had to memorize? I thought you said it was important."

Julian's mother shook her head. "We'll get Dan Corry to do it."

"But Corry stutters!"

His father was impassive. "If you keep your nose clean, we *might* consider letting you assist at Samhain. Not before."

"And until then," his mother continued, "no television, and come straight home after school."

Six weeks of house arrest. But Julian knew that any protest at this point would only make it worse. "Yes, ma'am," he said, hanging his head. All he wanted to do now was go to his room and fall over.

His mother stared, blinking, her expression a mixture of anger and sadness. Then she shook herself and gathered up her coat and purse. "Your dinner's on the stove. Don't forget to clean up."

"Take this opportunity to study the Principle of Consequences and think on what you've done," his father said. "We'll see you in the morning." Then he closed the door—gently, but with finality. They'd be back some time after midnight.

Julian reheated his Hamburger Helper Cheesy Enchilada and took it to the TV room to eat while he watched the second half of *The Million Dollar Duck* on Disney. Part 1 had been last week, and he'd been disappointed that he would have to miss part 2 on account of the sabbat, so at least some good would come of this. But as he reached for the switch, he remembered that he was grounded, with no television.

"Damn," he said to the silent house.

He ate his dinner without tasting it—which was probably a good thing—washed the pan, and put his dishes in the dishwasher.

His father had said to study the Principle of Consequences. He already knew that basic principle by heart, but he went to his locked bookshelf and took down the grimoire anyway. Not like he had anything better to do. But as he read over the familiar words, the old black-letter script and musty paper as comforting in their arcane way as Dick and Jane, his mind drifted.

What was it, exactly, that he'd felt at the mall? Why should such a powerful dark force be hanging out at such an ordinary place? It made as much sense as The Fonz suddenly appearing on *Little House on the Prairie*.

He flipped through the grimoire in search of answers, and soon found a section about places that concentrated energy, both dark and light. That seemed promising, but it was all rivers and mineral deposits and other natural features . . . nothing that could explain why a shopping mall should suddenly become a focus of magical energy.

And then he turned a page, and saw an entire two-page spread of symbols of power. There was the pentacle, of course, and the ankh, and the eight-pointed Maltese cross . . . and the gammadia, or voided cross. A cross with the centers taken out, like four letter L's back-to-back.

Exactly the new layout of the mall: four L-shapes of stores, converging on the central court.

He read further, cross-referencing. A gammadia could be used to capture and concentrate energy of any kind. But this one, having been constructed by lay people without any specific magical purpose in mind, attracted chaotic dark energy by default. Being so large, the amount of energy involved would be enormous.

And tonight was Mabon, the autumnal equinox, one of the eight days of the year on which the membrane between this world and the other was at its thinnest . . .

Julian's hands had gone all cold. He rubbed them under his arms, trembling.

Tonight at midnight, an unknown but vast amount of unfocused dark energy would be released into the world at Alewife Bay Mall. The consequences could be devastating, in the physical world as well as the spiritual.

And Julian was the only person who knew about it.

His first impulse was to tell his parents. But there were no phones in Rockwood Park, where the sabbat was being held. All the other members of the coven would be there as well. He could bike there . . . but the magical circle would be closed by now. Even if he could attract the attention of someone inside, they would be extremely unwilling to open it, since that would mean starting the whole ritual over from the beginning. And what if he was wrong? He'd be grounded for the rest of his life.

Julian rocked back and forth on the couch in front of the TV's dark eye. There was only one thing to do.

He would have to seal the gammadia himself.

He knew the exact incantation to use. Dispelling energy wasn't that hard, especially energy with no specific purpose to it. It was so easy, even a male could do it. All he needed was candles, some salt, a little garlic, and some . . .

Wine.

Damn.

He went to the closet anyway. But, of course, his parents had taken the equipment trunk with them to the sabbat. And apart from ritual purposes, they were teetotalers . . . there wasn't another bottle of wine in the house.

Where could a thirteen-year-old boy get a bottle of wine at nine thirty on a Sunday night?

He sat, drumming his fingers on the couch arm, thinking hard. And then he remembered something Liz had said . . .

It took him three tries to dial her number correctly. "Hello?"

The receiver's hard plastic creaked in his grip. "Hello, Mrs. O'Malley, my name's Julian Greene . . ."

"Oh, of course, Julian, I remember you. Would you like to speak with Colleen?"

Colleen? Oh, right. "Uh, yes, please."

A long moment later, Liz came on the line. "Hey, Liz, it's Julian."

"Heya. Whazzup?"

He wanted to lean in close, cup his hand around the phone, and whisper. But he reminded himself he was alone in the house. "Listen . . . remember I told you about that project I wanted to work on?"

"Yeah . . ."

"I need a favor. A really, really big favor. It's . . . it's going to be really difficult for you to do, and you can't tell *anyone* about it. Especially your parents. Understand?"

"Ohh-kay . . ."

"Okay. Here's what I need you to do. This is going to sound really strange, but you know you can trust me, right?"

"Right."

"I need a bottle of wine."

"Julian!" Her tone was astonished.

"Not to drink!" He covered the receiver with his hand for a moment, thinking fast. "It's for a science project. Extra credit. Due Monday. But my parents wouldn't approve. They don't drink." That last part was true, anyway. "You told me once that your brother has some wine hidden in his old treehouse. Can you get me one bottle? Tonight?"

"I think so."

"Meet me at Alewife Bay Mall. By the south entrance. At . . ." He glanced at the clock. "Ten thirty?"

"Okay!" He could practically hear her grin. Liz was always up for anything weird or risky.

"You're a great friend. See you there."

Despite the cool of the late September evening, Julian was sweating heavily when he pedaled up to the mall entrance. Exhaustion from the many miles he'd traveled today, concern about the ritual he was about to do, worry that maybe Liz hadn't been able to get the wine or get out of the house so late at night, and fear from the traffic he'd faced with no headlight all combined into a cold, angular lump in his stomach.

"Psst!"

Julian started, then spotted the source of the sound. It was Liz, lurking in the bushes behind the bike rack. He hustled over there, stashed his bike next to The Monster.

"You're late."

"Sorry," he whispered. It had taken a lot longer than he'd figured. He was still worn out from this afternoon's frantic ride. "Did you get the wine?"

"Yep." She pulled a bottle of Boone's Farm Strawberry Hill from her backpack. It wasn't exactly sacramental, but it would do.

"Thanks. I owe you one."

He stood there, holding the bottle, waiting for her to leave. Maybe he shouldn't have had her meet him right here at the mall.

She wasn't leaving.

"Well, I guess I'll be heading home now," he said. He'd have to double back after she'd left.

"I'll ride with you as far as Clear Spring Boulevard."

He couldn't ride that far, double back, and still finish the ritual by midnight. "No, that's okay. I'll be fine."

"Look, what's with you? And what kind of middle school science project needs a bottle of Boone's Farm?"

"It's . . . it's personal."

She just gave him a look.

He glanced at his watch. Already past eleven. Maybe he could scare her off with a form of the truth. "Okay. Look, I didn't want to tell you this, but . . . but . . . dark, evil forces are gathering in there. *Very* dark. *Very* evil. I have to go in and perform a ritual. To contain them. By midnight. Or else all hell's going to break loose."

"Really? Cool!" In the cold mercury vapor of the parking lot lights, her eyes shone with enthusiasm.

This was *so* not going the way he'd hoped.

He looked at his watch again. "Oh, hell. Come with me."

Locks were simple, unintelligent things. "Wow," Liz said. "How'd you do that?"

"I'll explain later." He had no such intention, of course. "Now keep quiet . . . there might be a night watchman."

The mall seemed huge in the darkness, with the pale light of a waxing crescent moon shining through the skylights and a few lamps here and there casting strange, hard-edged shadows. They crept past orange

plastic cones and silent, dusty-smelling concrete mix-
ers to the half-finished fountain at the center of the
central court. They met nobody, but the chill of
seething, chaotic dark forces was much stronger than
it had been that afternoon.

Quickly, but as carefully as he could, Julian traced
out a circle for the ritual, dabbing each of the four
cardinal points with wine. Liz watched, fascinated,
as he invoked the God in each direction. "It's very
important that you not leave the circle now," he whispered, "until I say it's okay. Understand?"

Liz nodded, but said nothing.

He took out a mortar—a small, heavy brass bowl—
from his backpack and splashed some more wine in
it. The cheap strawberry stuff smelled like fermented
candy. He added salt, then used the matching brass
pestle to crush in a couple cloves of garlic. The
resulting paste smelled vile, but it was just the thing
for grounding and dispelling the forces of chaos. He
dabbed a little on his eyelids, ears, nose, and—yuck—
lips, then did the same to Liz. "For your protection,"
he told her.

She giggled. "Like that paper strip on the toilet?"

"I mean it. Stay in the center of the circle and don't
move."

Now came the tricky part. Chanting quietly, he lit
five candles and set them at the corners of a pentagram
within the circle. Next, he began tracing out the lines
of the pentagram with the wine-and-garlic paste. The
spacing had to be precise, and the lines straight. His
tongue poked out of the corner of his mouth as he crept
about on hands and knees, laying down tiny dabs of the
stinky stuff with the tip of a sharp knife.

And then a recorded trumpet blared. Julian's entire body jerked, and he barely kept from spilling the mortar's contents all over himself.

He looked up at the source of the noise, and saw that the giant package at the far end of the center court was opening.

Did the stupid thing run twenty-four hours a day?

No, wait, even worse. He looked at his watch, and confirmed what the mall's clock was telling him with its cheesy music-box fanfare: it was just two minutes to midnight. And he still had almost two full sides of the pentagram to trace out.

"Liz, I need your help." Wooden villagers and animals danced around as the feeling of dark energy grew stronger and stronger. "Take this knife and lay down a line of this stuff from here to there. Hurry. But be as precise as you can." He scooped out half the remaining glop into his left palm, then started tracing out the other line with his fingernail.

On and on the mechanical performance went, the cheery music blaring and echoing through the empty space. The little wooden boy in lederhosen moved toward the gong. Julian's gut clenched, and not just from fear—the chaos was building. "Hurry!" he whispered, but Liz was making better progress with the knife than he was with his fingers. He concentrated on his half of the work.

Three feet to go when the first *bong* sounded. He was nearly out of the paste. He spread it thinner. *Bong. Bong. Bong.* Two feet to go, dab after dab after dab. Couldn't put too much space between dabs. *Bong. Bong. Bong.* Was that six *bongs*, or seven?

"Done!" said Liz. *Bong.*

"Great!" *Bong*.

"But I'm out of stuff." *Bong*.

Bong.

"Me too."

Six inches of dry floor lay beyond the end of his line.

Bong.

The darkness came flooding through the gap in the pentagram like water from a fire hose, chilling Julian and driving the breath from his lungs. He was forced physically back, toward the center of the charmed circle, watching helplessly as potted palms swayed and stretched their spindly limbs toward the moonlight and exposed rebar twisted itself into strange shapes. The little wooden boy tugged at his own feet, trying to free them from the platform to which they were attached.

Darkness was taking over the mall.

"I'm sorry," Julian said.

And then he felt Liz's hand on his own. She was pushing it forward.

He looked back at her, wondering what she was doing.

She seemed deep in shadow, though there was nothing to throw such a shadow. It was as though a large dark man were crouching protectively above her, a man with a strange huge angular head.

She pushed again against his hand. The left one. The one that still had garlic-and-wine paste worked into its creases.

At last he understood. He threw all his strength into crawling forward, shoving his left hand into the gap. He could never have done it alone, but the addition of Liz's strength made it possible.

He smeared his palm across the gap in the pentagram.

And it all stopped.

As the last *bong* echoed away and the box began to fold itself up, the chill feeling of darkness and chaos drained out of the mall like water from a tub. The wooden boy grew still, the swaying palms sank back into their pots, and the rebar stopped moving. It was still twisted, but not-moving was a definite improvement.

Julian lay gasping on the hard tile of the half-finished fountain.

After a while, he sat up. Liz was sitting on the fountain's edge, just watching him.

"How . . ." he began, but had to swallow several times to clear the dryness from his throat. "How did you know to do that?"

"There was a . . . guy." She seemed kind of stunned. "With these . . ." she gestured vaguely above her head. "Whatchamacallums. Antlers. He told me what to do."

"You saw the *Horned God?* He *spoke* to you?"

"Um, I think you're the one who should be answering that."

Julian stood up. His legs could, perhaps, hold him. Riding home was another question, but he'd face that in a little bit. "Have I ever introduced you to my parents?"

"No . . ."

"I think I'm going to have to correct that right away."

They limped together toward the mall entrance and their bicycles, supporting each other as they went.

Robin Wayne Bailey is the Nebula award-nominated author of numerous novels, including the *Dragonkin* Series, *Shadowdance*, And the *Frost* saga. His novel, *Swords Against The Shadowland*, inspired by Fritz Leiber's famed Fafhrd and the Gray Mouser stories, will be reprinted later this year. Robin's science fiction stories were recently collected in *Turn Left to Tomorrow*, and his work has appeared in many anthologies and magazines. He lives in Kansas City, Missouri. Visit him at his website, www.robinwaynebailey.net

The Price of Beauty

Robin Wayne Bailey

In every way it was a wretched morning. Lightning carved jagged slices from the gray sky and shook the roiling clouds with volleys of thunder. Rain pelted the windshield, blew across the roads in blinding sheets that made a nightmare of the mid-morning traffic. The elms and maples that lined the avenue bent double as the howling wind stripped away their leaves.

Hunched behind her steering wheel, Jane snarled and cursed the weather as she stomped on her gas pedal and cut across the front bumper of another commuter. The angry honking that followed didn't deter her. She sped across two more lanes, yanked hard on the steering wheel and darted into the sprawling parking lot of Birnam Woods Mall.

There seemed to be no empty parking spaces near the entrance, and that meant she'd get drenched making her dash inside. She cursed again at the thought of ruining her expensive blue business suit. Then, by luck, with little hope left, she spied a convenient space and wedged her Mercedes SLK between two other vehicles with barely room to spare. She stomped on the brake at the last minute, nearly standing her car on its nose to avoid hitting the car already parked directly in front of her, a move that wasn't entirely successful. Bumpers kissed, but she didn't care.

Jane flung her car door open, dinging the paint job of the car parked next to her. She didn't care about that, either. In a panic, she slammed her car door shut again and ran for the mall entrance.

Her spiked high heels made little splashes on the wet pavement, and her red-varnished toenails flashed as she crossed the parking lot. The neatly coiffed bun on the back of her head came undone as she ran, so that damp wisps and locks of bottle-blond hair trailed over her collar in a totally unacceptable state of disarray.

It was early—barely nine o'clock—but Jane had very little time. Strengthened by urgency, she shoved open the doors, breaking two manicured, press-on nails in her carelessness. A giant-sized advertising poster for Maybelline cosmetics hung on the wall just inside the door. It shook under the impact. Jane hesitated, clutching her purse to her side for the briefest moment, fearing that the poster would fall. Then she began to study the advertisement and the incredibly beautiful, dark-haired woman portrayed in it. Beauty Jane could only wish for!

With an exasperated gasp, Jane rushed on. A hair stylist just opening her shop paused in her doorway and stared gape-jawed as Jane passed. Jane pretended not to notice, but she gave an inward whimper. Another shopper already about her morning errands stopped in her tracks as Jane approached. A shoe store clerk dropped the stack of boxes he was carrying. "What are you looking at?" Jane snapped as she picked up her pace and hurried on.

Despite her headlong rush through the mall, the store windows caught her eye. Everywhere she looked she saw advertisements for beauty products—Max Factor, Clairol, Neutrogena, Ponds. The pretty, smiling faces in those advertisements mocked her, and her head swam with an inundation of messages: manicures here, pedicures there, facials by appointment, cures for dry skin, cures for oily skin. This for shimmering skin; that for a more youthful appearance. Wrinkle creams, anti-aging creams, blemish creams, eye creams.

Jane wanted to scream.

Finally, deep in the heart of the mall, she reached her destination. The shop was unlocked, and the soft lights within glittered promisingly on the quaintly Victorian shelves of brightly packaged goods. Pausing to catch her breath, Jane looked up and read the store's name: Crab, Tree, and Eva Lynn.

And just below that in pink neon letters: *Natural Beauty Supernaturally.*

But there wasn't time to waste. Remembering her schedule, Jane dashed inside. None of the shop's three proprietors were in sight, but she knew them like dear friends and called out in a desperate voice.

At the sound of her name, Miss Crab rose up from behind a rack of perfumed soaps with a look of surprise and a quick smile. Behind the cash register on the other side of the shop, Miss Tree also rose from where she'd been crouching at some task. She, too, smiled as she adjusted a pair of horn-rimmed eyeglasses on her nose.

At the rear of the store, a pair of black curtains whisked open, and Eva Lynn emerged with a glare of annoyance on her face. Of the three shop owners, she was the only one who never smiled, which always startled Jane, who firmly believed that the law required shop personnel to greet every customer with a smile.

All three ladies, well into middle age, but prim in business-cut black dresses with nary a gray hair out of place, advanced on Jane. Their complexions were still radiant, their hair shimmery, and their teeth dazzling. Except for Eva Lynn's. It was hard to tell with Eva Lynn.

"Through this fog and filthy air, who comes?" said Miss Crab. Her voice was high-pitched, and she had a way of singing her words. "Why it's Jane Paddock come to see us!"

"Such thunder, lightning and rain!" said Miss Tree as she clucked over Jane. "You look a frightful mess, my dear!"

Eva Lynn looked mildly disgusted. "What the hell's all this hurly-burly?" she demanded. "We haven't been open five minutes!"

"I'm sorry, Evil Lynn, but I'm desperate!" Jane blurted. Then she clapped one hand to her mouth.

Eva Lynn's gray eyes narrowed to slits. "It's *Eva Lynn*." She repeated it, stressing the proper pronunciation. There was an edge of strange menace in her voice, and the lights in the shop seemed momentarily to dim and the corners to fill with shadows.

Jane licked her red Estee Lauder lips and glanced at her watch. There wasn't much time! "Look at me!" she shrieked. "I'm ugly again! Your spells are wearing

off too quickly, and I've got a presentation in less
than an hour!"

Miss Tree patted Jane's shoulder sympathetically while
Miss Crab took Jane's hand and noted the two broken
nails. "Now calm down, dear! You are not ugly!"

Miss Tree ran a hand through Jane's hair and pushed
a damp lock back into place as they guided her to
the rear of the store. "Indeed, you are not! You just
get such a silly idea out of your head. We don't even
use that word in this store!"

Eva Lynn hovered as they pushed Jane into a styling chair before a large mirror and an array of tools
and products. With a flourish, she flung a smock over
Jane and secured it behind her neck. "Too much
lightning in the air," she muttered, "steals the magic
from your hair. Yet, we three can make you fair, then
off to work with time to spare!"

Jane stared into the mirror and screamed at her
own hideous reflection. In tears, she clapped her hands
to her face and knocked one of her false eyelashes
askew. Through her fingers, she dared to look into the
mirror again. Hair like Medusa! Cheeks the color of
tombstones! Cracks and wrinkles! The horrible creature
she saw was her! It was really her!

"If my bosses ever see the real me . . . !"

Miss Crab snatched up a jar of cream, which bore
the shop's name and logo. With a twist, she cast away
the lid and began smearing a green goop on Jane's
face. It reeked of month-old cucumber. "Eye of toad
and blood of hare; give yourself into our care. Nothing
wrong we can't repair with little effort or fanfare!"

Miss Tree tipped Jane's chair back with a sharp
motion and poured a bottle of yellowish syrup into

her hair. A potent floral odor crawled into Jane's nose. "Men will see you, stop and stare!" she chanted. "Lesser females will despair!"

Eva Lynn opened a decorative powder box and shook the puff over Jane, making her sneeze. "This special glamour will hit them like a hammer!"

Her chair began to spin. Faster and faster it went until the shop became a blur. Jane's legs flew up in the air, and she flung out her arms. The smock fluttered over her head, blinding her, and her senses churned. "My face! My face!" she cried.

A cool tingling spread from her chin to her brows, and a euphony of bells pealed in her ears. From the darkness of the encasing smock, a dozen different perfumes wafted into her nostrils. Suddenly, unbidden, words bubbled from her lips. "Round and round and round we swirl! L'Oreal and Cover Girl! Make me shimmer like a pearl—but stop this chair before I hurl!"

The chair slowed to a stop.

"Unseal her!" Miss Crab sang. "Reveal her!"

"A butterfly," chanted Miss Tree, "to every eye!"

Eva Lynn's voice cut in like a saw blade. "Oh, just unwrap the silly sap!"

The smock slipped away from Jane's face. To her surprise, she found that she'd been squeezing her eyes shut tightly. Now she peeled the left one open and braved a glance into the mirror. She gave a little gasp of pleasure, and her right eye snapped open.

"I'm beautiful again!" She ran her fingertips over smooth, unblemished cheeks, over a flawless button nose and along rose-colored lips. Her hair looked freshly colored and restyled. "Just a few more touches," she breathed, "and I'll be perfect!"

Snapping open her purse, she drew out a tube of *Magic-Lips* lip-gloss and applied the red cream liberally. She followed that with a quick brush-up of rouge, a brand called *Superstition*, then with two quick strokes added blue shadow to her eyelids. She smiled at the product's name as she put it away—*Devilicious*. "Pardon me," she said. Nudging Miss Crab back a pace, she leaned closer to the mirror and affixed a fresh pair of curly false eyelashes. "Almost done!" she announced, snapping the purse closed again. Taking final stock of her new self, she rubbed a finger briskly over her front teeth to brighten them, then flashed a big smile. "It's like magic!" she proclaimed as she studied her perfected reflection. "You're miracle-workers!"

"Not exactly." Eva Lynn rolled her eyes and folded her arms over her breasts

"You give us too much credit," Miss Crab responded.

"Just remember that beauty is only sin-deep," Miss Tree added. Then she chuckled behind her hand. "I mean, skin-deep."

Jane glanced at her watch. She still had a few minutes for shopping, and she just had to have some more of the wonderful products these ladies produced. She'd been coming here for months now. The anti-wrinkle creams, the skin-tightening lotions, the bath soaps that really softened the skin, the potions that really did kill toenail fungus—it all really worked!

But only temporarily. This morning had been a bitter reminder of that when she woke and looked into her bathroom mirror. Toothbrush in hand, with a mouthful of paste, she'd watched her beauty dissolve before her very eyes to reveal the true, wretched ugliness that she tried so desperately to hide from the world.

With a hopeful sigh, she dumped her purchases on the sales counter and waited while Miss Tree rang them up. "How long will it last this time?" she asked in a weak voice. She'd been coming every week for fresh beauty treatments, but lately, she seemed to require them more and more often. "My job depends upon my looks, you know. It isn't easy for a woman in business."

Miss Tree nodded sympathetically as she bagged Jane's items. "You have to believe in the magic," she answered.

Miss Crab stepped behind the counter to stand beside Miss Tree. "And you have to believe in yourself," she added.

Eva Lynn held the shop door open for Jane, but it hadn't quite closed when she turned to the other ladies. "Modern women," she said in a disdainful voice. "Underneath all that *stuff*, do you ever wonder if there's anything real?"

Jane stopped in her tracks, surprised and a little bit hurt by the overheard comment. But the door closed, and after a moment, she wondered if she'd actually heard correctly. She didn't give the matter much more thought, because a poster for Dior in another store window caught her eye, and the beautiful woman in the advertisement looked just like Jane! So did the woman in the Prada poster and the Givenchy advertisement! Jane smiled to herself as she strolled through the mall, turning little pirouettes and swinging her packages as she made her way to the exit.

An hour later, poised and confident, lightly drenched in a special perfume called *Enchantment*, Jane Paddock stood at the head of the board room table as the agency's leading advertising executives and corporate lawyers filed in for her eleven o'clock presentation. The company president, himself, led the client into the room and seated him near Jane's right hand.

All eyes were on her, and she touched her throat. Having loosened the two topmost buttons of her blouse, the coy gesture served to draw attention to the gentle swell of her cleavage. She drew a delicate breath and flashed a smile around the room. This was her dream job, and she was standing exactly where she'd dreamed of standing, making her first presentation to a high-powered client!

Jane moved a little to one side while the president introduced her. She barely listened to his brief speech, and she doubted if any of the others really heard it, either. Instead, she basked in the admiring glances of her all-male audience. When the introduction was over, she waited for her boss to resume his seat. Then, she moved to the front of the room once more and struck a pose beside an easel upon which rested a stack of poster-sized cards.

The rest of the room seemed to vanish as she focused all her attention on the client. This was the moment she'd been waiting for—her moment. "Sir," she said with firm politeness. "You're in the business of selling beauty products. And we're in the business of selling . . ." she paused for effect. "You. We're all in the same business. We're all selling the same product. But that product is not beauty."

Jane removed the top card on the stack, which was a blank white. The next card contained a single word in large, stylized letters. "The product is sex." Someone gasped. Jane barely heard. She exposed the next card, a portrait of a flame-haired woman in a passionate embrace. "Wear the right lipstick," she continued, "and you'll get sex." She exposed the next card on the easel, a portrait of a muscular man in all his broad-chested, post-shower glory, his face richly lathered, and a woman's hands on his bare, rippling abdominals. "Use the right shave cream . . ."

Someone else in the room finished her sentence. "And you'll get sex."

Jane's boss cleared his throat before he interrupted. "Don't we prefer the word *romance*?"

She'd anticipated her boss's reaction. Jane put on a patient smile and drew another breath as she touched her throat again. All eyes followed her hand. "We might pretend so," she admitted, "but let's be honest. That's not the bottom line for girls or guys." She pulled one card after another off the easel, each more lurid than the previous one. "Wear the right scent, use the right blush . . ."

Someone interrupted, "And you'll get sex."

She pulled down another card. "Apply the right foundation, splash on the right aftershave. . . ."

Still another board member chimed in. "And you'll get sex."

Jane smiled secretly to herself. It was working like a charm. Get them into the rhythm, and they responded like church-boys at catechism.

A nod went around the conference table, but her boss frowned. "It seems a bit cynical to me."

The client stood up. "I like it," he announced. "In fact, I think it's the finest presentation I've ever seen." His gaze fastened on Jane's cleavage as he reached to shake her hand.

Jane beamed, but her triumph was short-lived. As she reached out to return the client's handshake, her left eyelash fell off, and a strand of blond hair fell upon the dark pinstriped sleeve of her business suit. The client's eyes widened as Jane felt her heart lurch. A horrible sensation crept through her. She could feel her face cracking, the make-up peeling. The magic was failing too soon!

Hiding her face behind her hands, she fled from the boardroom.

Sobbing and half blinded by tears, Jane raced back to Birnam Woods Mall and shot into the nearest parking space. The rain had ceased for the moment, but thunder boomed like cannon fire, and lightning danced crazy jigs across the clouds. The wind surged around her, destroying her coiffure as she got out of the Mercedes. She gave a cry of dismay as she slammed the car door and ran across the wet pavement to the mall entrance.

Just as she reached the glass doors, a young couple burdened with packages emerged. At the sight of her, they stopped as if frozen in their tracks and stared with jaws agape. "Don't look at me!" Jane snarled. Then she hit the doors with her palms, shoving them open with enough force to cause long cracks in the thick glass panes.

She didn't care about the damage or about the couple. Raising her hands again to conceal her appearance from the other shoppers, she hurried past the stores and kiosks. Everybody stared at her! The nearest ones shrank in horror from the monster in their midst. Others pointed and mocked her! Under so many gazes and glares she could feel her face degenerating, as if somehow *they* were responsible! That was it! They were leeching her beauty!

Yet they weren't alone! The posters and advertisements in the windows and along the walls, they also seemed to mock her just as the shoppers did! The photographs with all those beautiful women with perfect skin and deep eyes and bright lipsticks, the young voluptuous models urging you to buy, buy, buy! They were changing before her very eyes to mirror her own crone-like ugliness!

Her tears gave way to a red rage by the time she reached the shop. Once again, she paused and read the name above the door: Crab, Tree, and Eva Lynn—Natural Beauty Supernaturally!

Miss Tree rose from behind the counter as if she'd been crouched there all day. "Why, Miss Paddock!" She put on a big smile of greeting. "How nice to see you so soon!"

Jane flung her hands up into the air and screamed. "Your magic sucks!"

Miss Crab appeared from behind a shelf of ointments on the other side of the shop. "Why, Miss Paddock!" she sang in her strangely happy little voice. "Our very favorite customer!"

Jane growled. Seizing a bar of lavender-scented soap from a display table, she threw it at Miss Crab, who caught it neatly and set it aside.

"Fakes! Charlatans! Cheats!" Jane shouted as she grabbed another bar of soap and flung it after the first. Then, she was throwing everything she could get her hands on—soaps, herbal balms, perfumed oils, lotions, miracle creams, chap sticks with high spf factors. Unscrewing the lids for the fullest splattery effect, she let fly, taking aim at nothing and everything while Miss Crab and Miss Tree flew about the room like a pair of shrieking Halloween witches, ducking and dodging.

Her rage, however, was interrupted without warning as an icy chill swept through the shop. In defiance of all laws of motion, every missile and flying jar of face cream froze in mid-flight and hung suspended in the air. At the back of the store, the black curtains parted. Eva Lynn emerged, her face dark with menace, and as she advanced toward Jane she batted aside each suspended projectile that blocked her path.

Undaunted, Jane picked up an orange pomander and wound up for the pitch, but Eva Lynn pointed one warning finger. "Hair of dog and witch's tit—put it down, you silly twit!"

Cowered behind a spinning rack of sachet packets, Miss Crab clutched her breasts protectively. "Witch's tit?" she protested. "I resent that!"

"Resent this!" Jane muttered, drawing back with her sweet-smelling missile. But the pomander exploded in a shower of fine powder before it left her hand. Startled, her anger momentarily subsided, and she looked as if she would cry. "Well, great!" She glared with moist eyes at Eva Lynn as she brushed her sleeve and lapels. "Now you've ruined my best suit, too! Is this your idea of customer service?" She shot a look around for something else to throw, and her gaze fell on a stack of mail and a letter opener by the cash register.

She was already a monster. Did it matter if she was a murderess, too? She looked at the three sisters and made her decision—Evil Lynn would be the first to go. "*Evil Lynn. Evil Lynn. Evil Lynn!*" she chanted, knowing how irksome her foe found that name. Her fingers curled around the letter opener's hilt. With a little laugh, she observed that all her carefully manicured nails were chipped and broken.

Eva Lynn snapped her fingers as Jane came closer. With a thump and clatter, every floating object fell to the floor. "Put that down," she ordered, fixing Jane with eyes that were black, limpid pools of age and time. "Trust me. You don't want the blood on your dainty little hands."

Hugging Miss Crab, Miss Tree nodded with a serious expression. "You'll never get the spots out."

Miss Crab forced a nervous smile. "She's right, you know. Been there—done that!"

Jane stared at the three women, then around the shop at the mess and damage she'd caused. The letter opener slipped from her grip as her rage finally evaporated. For a moment, she felt drained and numb. Then she choked up and cried out from a deep well of pain and despair. "All the magic soaps and lotions! I bought them all!" Jane sank down to her knees. "You promised me I'd be beautiful!"

Miss Tree came closer and placed a hand on Jane's shoulder. "The poor dear still doesn't understand."

"It's you that doesn't understand!" Jane wailed, knocking the hand away. "Look at me! I'm ugly!" Trembling, she looked up at Eva Lynn, who loomed over her. "Don't you see?" she appealed. "You can't get anywhere in this world unless you're picture-perfect beautiful! Nobody looks at you! Nobody listens to you! Nobody—nobody wants you!"

"Stuff and nonsense!" Eva Lynn snapped.

But Miss Crab knelt down and took Jane's hand. "Be patient, Sister," she said to Eva Lynn in a calmer voice.

Jane hung her head and stared at the floor. *Ugly forever*, she thought tearfully. *There is no magic! There is no magic!* Clenching her fists and lifting her head, she cried out, "O, Caliban!"

Miss Tree clucked her tongue. "Wrong play."

Eva Lynn dropped down to her knees before Jane and, reaching out, brushed the younger woman's chin. "Of course, there's magic," she said in a softer voice. To prove her point, she raised a finger and the white powder staining Jane's suit blew upward in a little swirl and reassembled into an orange pomander. Eva Lynn caught it and set it aside, then pressed a fingertip to the center of Jane's forehead. "But there's another kind of magic. Sometimes it's good magic, and sometimes it's bad magic, but it's the strongest magic of all."

Miss Tree knelt down on Jane's right side. "Sometimes it's cruel, and sometimes it's blind," she whispered.

Miss Crab knelt on Jane's left side and softly sang. "Sometimes it's sweet, and sometimes it's kind!"

"It's in your spirit," Eva Lynn continued as she took both of Jane's hands in her own. "And it's in your mind." Without warning, she clapped her hands together under Jane's nose. Jane looked up sharply and blinked. "And boy, this time it's all in your mind!"

Jane's head swam. Confused, she met Eva Lynn's gaze and wondered if the other woman was trying to put another spell on her. "What are you talking about?"

Miss Crab smiled. "You *are* beautiful, my dear! We've been trying to convince you!"

Jane recoiled. "You're nuts! I'm uglier than a pig in mud! People stare at me because I'm so ugly!"

"They stare because you're . . ." Miss Tree paused

and rubbed her chin. "What's the modern expression? Because you're drop-dead gorgeous? A hot fox?" She chuckled and blushed. "Why, if it wasn't for our patient-client relationship, I could go for you, myself."

Jane bit her lip. "No thanks." She looked around for a mirror.

"You didn't believe in yourself." As if she'd read Jane's mind, Eva Lynn produced a gold-framed, hand-held mirror from the pocket of her black dress. "Now see what others really see when you pass by. See why they really stare."

Jane wiped her eyes and looked into the glass. "I know this part," she said. "Mirror, mirror, on the . . ."

Eva Lynn snapped her fingers under Jane's nose. "Just shut up and look."

A cloudy smoke filled the mirror. It shifted and crawled upon the glass, then began to clear. Jane leaned closer to see her reflection. Her hair stuck up like Medusa's snakes, and her eyes were garishly discolored. Her face looked like an old pick-up truck with a bad touch-up paint job. She tried to believe—but she couldn't shake that twinge of doubt.

Eva Lynn produced a handkerchief from her dress pocket and made a single pass at Jane's face. "But first, take off all of this ridiculous goop. Even with our products there can be too much of a good thing."

The reflection in the mirror flickered and settled down again. Everything that was horrid about her appearance faded away. Everything that was repulsive transformed, became lovely and natural. "Is this really me?" Jane asked.

"You only have to believe," Miss Tree said.

Jane pressed her hands to her face with rising

excitement. "But this is marvelous! Wonderful!" She gazed into the mirror again, delighted with what she saw. If the glass could be believed, she really was a head-turner! "What do I owe you? How can I pay?"

Miss Crab rose to her feet. "You have already paid, are paying, and will pay," she warned.

Miss Tree also rose up. "The price of beauty . . ." she said.

Eva Lynn got to her feet, as well, and interrupted. ". . . is always the fear of losing it."

Jane Paddock thought about that for a moment. She didn't understand what these crazy old women were talking about, and she decided that she didn't really care. She got to her feet, too, and brushed her skirt, certain that, by kneeling down among all the clutter on the floor she'd ruined her favorite suit beyond all hope of salvage. "Thank you! Thank you!" she said, shaking their hands joyfully and giving each of them little hugs. "You've taught me a valuable lesson, and one I'm sure that I'll always remember." She glanced at her watch. "Now I really need to get back to work. I'm well-stocked on soaps and lotions and ointments right now—but I'll be back soon!"

With her goodbyes and thank-yous said, Jane made a quick exit. If she'd caused a mess in the shop, she was desperately afraid that she'd left a bigger one back at the ad agency.

Yet as she left, she caught snatches of a curious conversation.

"She still doesn't get it, does she?" said Miss Crab.

"Dumber than a toad in stump water," Miss Tree answered.

"Things were simpler when I really was Evil Lynn."

Miss Crab chuckled. "When shall we three meet again?"

Miss Tree sighed and sounded suddenly bored. "In thunder, lightning, or in the goddamned, never-ending rain?"

Eva Lynn only shrugged. "Personally, I'm for Sheboygan."

Brenda W. Clough has been a finalist for the Hugo and the Nebula awards. She lives with four cats and a great many balls of yarn in a cottage at the edge of a forest. She is the author of seven novels and many short stories, and makes her living with reviews of books about death, grief and misery. Her latest SF novel, *Revise the World*, is appearing serially at bookviewcafe.com.

Making Love

Brenda W. Clough

The policewoman behind the reception desk lifted the flaps of the cardboard box, and squealed. "Ooooh, aren't they *cute!*"

Milly said, "The blankies are at the bottom."

The policewoman pulled out a pullover vest the size of her palm. It was blue with a small red intarsia heart knitted over the tummy. "Kitty wants to try one on right away!" She took a toy beanbag cat from its perch on the security monitor.

"A black kitty would look better in this," Milly suggested. She dug a tiny pink sweater out of the box.

"Too right!" The policewoman crammed the toy's head through the tiny turtleneck and pulled the limp front paws into the pink thumb-sized sleeves. Milly had ribbed the neck and sleeve cuffs out of some leftover white mohair, so the toy cat now took on an ineffably ZsaZsa Gabor air. The policewoman held the clothed toy to her cheek. "It's soooooo cute!"

A passing cop peered into the box. "You got any bear sweaters?"

Milly gave him an Aran cabled cardigan five inches across. The policewoman laughed at him. "Now Jim, what're you gonna do with a bear on drug busts?"

"You'd be surprised," the cop said. "Last bear we had, we gave it to a crackhead. Traded it for his automatic—he was all set to blow his brains out. It was like a magic trick."

"My goodness!" Milly peered mildly over her bifocals at him, to see if he was joking.

"Well, he wasn't what you'd call rational at the time," the cop conceded. "We'll put your donation to good use, ma'am." He held the security door open for her.

"I'm sure of it, officer." Milly crossed the parking lot and got into her old Chrysler, musing on the many uses of a sweater-clad toy. She had thought she was knitting clothes for toys to soothe frightened children after auto accidents or some such. But a crackhead? Amazing.

There was just enough time to swing by the yarn store. The owner greeted her with respect. The bag of donated yarns was ready for her behind the counter. "Sorry about the colors," Aylin said.

Milly peeked inside and winced at the acid greens and unsaleable harsh pinks. "Snugglies, for the animal shelter," she said.

"Good idea—dogs are color-blind. All they'll feel is the love you put into it. Oh, and while you're here, have a look at this new yarn."

"Mmmm." Milly sank both hands up to the wrist into a hank of buttery soft merino worsted. "And the color—so peaceful and soothing!"

"Like rain clouds over the ocean," Aylin agreed. "And machine washable!" Obviously it was impossible not to buy just one skein to try out. Milly jammed it into the top of her bag, and hurried back to work.

The information desk at the mall was never busy. Except for the occaional shopper looking for Sears or in need of directions to the restroom, Milly had plenty of time to knit. That afternoon she made a child-sized pair of mittens in red with white snowflakes, two square pet snugglies out of the ugly green yarn, and added another four inches to the back of a raglan pullover in red wool sprinkled with colored flecks. She only hoped that Ryan her grandson wouldn't have outgrown the pullover before he got it for Christmas. She knitted back and forth, thinking about Ryan's bad grades and how much Louisa worried about his progress through second grade. Perhaps Louisa could use a nice fluffy hat for Christmas? Milly couldn't remember when she last knitted her daughter-in-law a hat. Maybe it was time.

Her shift was over at four. Traffic back through Oakton was terrible. The light at the corner was so long she had plenty of time to ponder the mysterious text up on the Methodist church's signboard. Today it was, "All hail the power of Jesus' Name." How odd, she mused. Names were only words, without power. Power was woven out of fragility, linked, cunningly purled and stranded and cabled into a steel-strong fabric. Words had nothing to do with it.

When she got home she found that Frank had put the casserole into the oven. "We're out of soda," he greeted her from his barcalounger in the living room. "And how come we never have any parkerhouse rolls?"

"I'll put it on the grocery list, dear," Milly said.

With his diabetic disabilities, her poor husband had of course made no other dinner preparations. She hung her coat up and bent to plug his wheelchair battery into the wall outlet—it would take all night to recharge. "How was your day?"

"The leg's worse," Frank said gloomily. "Those copper bracelets are no more use than a headache, let me tell you. Damn if I'm not going to be bedridden by the new year."

"Oh now, it's not so bad as that," Milly said, hiding her dismay.

"Or maybe I'll die," Frank went on, set on wringing the worst out of the situation. "Quit being a burden to you."

"Now, dear." They had been married for 37 years now, and Milly could not imagine life without Frank. She would never say so, however, and Frank would have been stunned if she did. Instead she said, "A nice tunafish casserole, that's what you need."

After dinner they watched TV, as they always did. Frank held the remote and sat in the barcalounger with his bad leg propped high. Milly's armchair was surrounded by baskets, bags, and boxes of yarn. If she kept at it she could finish this beanie sweater before bedtime.

Frank always had a standard complaint for each TV show, and he didn't miss today. "Lookit that Dick Van Dyke," he groused. "His legs are good, and he's older'n me!"

"He's an actor," Milly said, placatingly. "Now you hush, so you don't miss any of *Diagnosis Murder*."

"I miss Laura Petrie," Frank said, another perennial comment.

But the leg was evidently giving Frank no peace. He

adjusted the angle of the recliner, shifted his bulk, all without relief. "I could take that bracelet off," Milly offered. "Maybe it's cutting off your circulation."

"That Joel, I don't know why I listen to him." Frank hitched up his pants cuff for her. "Him and his wacky ideas."

"Now, that's what I always say." Milly unclasped the heavy copper chain-link bracelet from around Frank's puffy pale ankle. "Your toes are so cold—do you think a nice pair of socks would help? No? Well, an afghan then." Milly took the big crocheted afghan off the end of the sofa, dislodging the two cats, and draped it over Frank's legs and feet. She sat down and stared intently at Dick Van Dyke on the screen. If Frank would get interested in the crime Dr. Sloan was solving, and let the afghan do its job . . .

But as soon as the commercial came on, Frank restlessly kicked the afghan away. "Too many holes in this damn thing," he grumped. "No warmth in it. You think it's time for my pills?"

Frustrated, Milly went on her lunch hour the next day to another local yarn store. "I just don't understand it," she told the owner. "You would think that Frank wasn't half so boneheaded as a crack addict."

"We always put all we love into everything we make," Mrs. Fitzsimmons said. "Maybe you just haven't hit on the right thing for Frank. Do you think he'd wear some nice felted slippers?"

Milly bought the pattern, but no yarn. "I have some nice grayish blue worsted that he'd put up with," she said.

"Well, take this instead, for the baby blankies." She passed over a bag of odd balls of yarn.

Milly went back to work and began knitting the slippers with the gray yarn she had bought yesterday. Only then did she notice the label—this was a machine-washable yarn, which meant it wouldn't felt. She had to unravel it all. Disgusted, she cast on for a bear sweater with it instead.

Then she had a phone call from Frank. He hardly ever phoned her at the mall. "What's wrong?" she demanded.

"Nothing's wrong," he said. "I'm having coffee with the guys." In the background she could hear the bustle and noise of McDonald's, the old guys' favorite afternoon hangout. Frank rode there every day in his motorized wheelchair. "Joel told me about this new thing. He saw it on TV, on the Home Shopping Network. It's sure to help the leg."

Milly was wary. "What?"

"Buckwheat," he said in triumph. "A buckwheat pillow. You microwave it, and it gives off this moist heat, you know what I mean?"

He sounded so excited and hopeful, Milly hated to pour cold water on the idea. "Well, I guess I could go over to Penney's and see if they have one."

"Bring it home tonight and I'll try it out."

He hung up. Milly sighed and took up her knitting again. If only, she thought sadly, he'd give-up on these nostrums and stupid quack cures, and wear a nice knitted legwarmer or sock on the bad leg! Still, when it was time for her break she went over to one of the mall stores and bought a long sausage-shaped buckwheat pillow for him.

Once again the homeward traffic was dreadful. She was never going to be able to make her left turn.

The Methodist church had changed their signboard again, to read, "Because of their unbelief He could do no great works." How come the Methodists never put up a plain sentence? The light turned green but the cars ahead didn't move, so Milly had time to puzzle over it.

Unbelief could prevent great works . . . Of course Frank didn't believe in the power of knitting and crochet, but then Milly had never tried to explain. There was no point. To Frank these were all women things, uninteresting by definition. But the dogs and cats in the animal shelter didn't believe either, and neither did the children who received sweater-clad toys. Yet these innocents could access the benefits Milly offered. What was Frank not doing or believing, that he couldn't?

The light turned red. Somebody back in traffic began to honk their horn. Obviously nobody was going anywhere for awhile. Milly reached for her knitting bag and began to knit on the gray merino tube that would become a bear sweater. She didn't have to look at her fingers while she worked, so she'd be ready if traffic began to move.

The old fool, how can he be so gullible about that Joel and his ideas? A different cure every week . . . Well now, there was a thought. Whatever else you could say about Frank, he really did believe in Joel's suggestions. Suppose she gave up on combating those notions? Would it be possible to sort of piggyback her work onto some of this quackery?

The light turned green and the cars began to move. Milly gunned the Chrysler's engine and zipped through her left turn before the oncoming traffic could cut her off. How big was this silly buckwheat pillow anyway? She had a tape measure at home.

After dinner when they settled down in front of the TV she was ready. Frank had read every word on the label of the buckwheat pillow, and supervised her jealously while she ran the thing through the microwave for two minutes on high. He leaned back in his Barcalounger and she laid the limp crunchy pillow over his ankle and lower leg. "Does it feel okay?"

"Kind of precarious, you know? But nice 'n' warm."

"It might be better to have something to lay over it, and keep the heat in," she suggested. "Maybe even something like a rubber band or tube, to hold it snug to your leg."

"Could be." He clicked the remote.

She pretended to watch the commercial for a moment. "I have part of a bear sweater here—it's about the right width. Suppose you try if that feels okay."

He made no objection, so she slid the tube of knitting over his ankle and up over pillow and leg together. Every stitch of this soft gray-blue merino had been lovingly set with Frank in mind. If this failed, it was hopeless. Their favorite doctor drama was just beginning, so she sat down, waiting for his standard comment.

To her surprise, however, after five minutes he said, "You know, that Joel, I think he's hit it on the head this time?"

"Does it really feel better?"

"It feels great!" He grinned at her, quite in the old way.

"Well, that's so nice!" She dropped the latest knitting,

a snugglie, into the nearest workbasket so she could hold hands with Frank. To give Joel all the credit for the improvement bothered her not at all. As long as her knitting could slide in under the radar of a buckwheat pillow, Frank would continue to get better. The success quite made her heart pound. She'd finally gotten a handle on this, the most intractible difficulty of her life. There was nothing beyond her now!

Luckily, Frank brought her down to earth with his standard complaint about the show. "Chicago Hope's gone down the drain since Mandy Patinkin left," he said, as he always did.

"Yes, I really miss that Dr. Geiger," Milly agreed.

A lifetime denizen of suburbia, **Ellie Tupper** is—in order of longevity—a writer, wife, science book editor, cerevisiologist (yes, *that* Ellie Tupper), and mom. Her daughter can use "litotes" in a sentence and mean it. Ellie is grateful to Critters, SFReader, and countless workshoppees for showing her how it's done. No brie was harmed in the making of this story.

Yo Moms a Dragon

Ellie Tupper

I pulled open the door of Frontiers Bookstore, and reeled back from a blast of perky. The sound system was trilling, "*Now* I *know* my *Ay*-Bee-*Cees!!*" and a salesgirl with a blonde ponytail bounced up and squeaked, "Welcome! to the Frontiers ABCs of Life™ celebration!!"

Beside me, my normally unimpressable eleven-year-old, Greta, was staring at another associate wearing a fluffy Afro with a pink hairband. "The ABCs of Life Sisterhood™ are here today!" this one gushed. "Launching their newest ABCs of Life Guide™, *The ABCs of Parenting: Getting the Perfect Kid!* Forty percent off, today only!!" In their voices, you could almost hear the ™ reverberate with infinite multimedia tie-in possibilities. An adorable Asian tried to hand me a number for the waiting line.

"Thanks, no thanks." Greta and I waded through the enthusiasm towards the KIDS section. I knew about the ABCs—three local self-help mavens who'd hogged the bestseller list for three or four years now. Frontiers threw a party every time they published another book. Today the whole sales staff was dressed up in pink with blonde, black, or frizzy wigs—even the guys. Lines of customers snaked through the whole store as the inescapable music tootled, "Ay-bee-*cee*-dee-*EE-yeff-GEE* . . . *!*"

Greta sized up the bookshelves with her eyes alight, and I grinned. Books were her life. Our annual birthday trip to Frontiers was unbreakable tradition. "Go wild, kid," I advised, and she plunged in.

This would take a while. I wandered over to watch the crowd. I couldn't see the authors, just a huge pink banner with the ABCs logo. Harried employees toted stacks of shiny pink books into the mass as happy customers wandered out, admiring their copies. Some had three or four. The *ka-ching* of success was almost as loud as the stupid song.

A man in the crowd caught my eye. It wasn't his looks—though he was Denzel-stunning, tall and suave—but some grabbing sense of familiarity. Then he turned and I saw him clearly.

I swore, and a nearby copy of *A-merry-can Chix*™: *Hetty's Hissy Fit* burst into flames. Damn, I'd thought I had gotten past these little accidents. I'd have to buy the stupid book now. I slapped the fire out, then stalked over. "What're you doing here, Flavian?" was my gracious salute. "You following me?"

"Well, Kat. —Sorry: *Doctor Feuer*," the man sneered. "How's it going, the being-human thing? A few little dragon habits hard to shake?" He eyed the scorched book in my hand with all-too-familiar disdain.

I stuck the book under my arm and gave him a glare that would have fried an army back home. "That's not your problem any more. If you didn't come all the way from Meliniseth to check up on me, what are you doing?"

"In point of fact, the reason I'm here has nothing to do with you. Take a look." Gazing out over the scrimmage complacently, he gave a little gesture, and the crowd drifted apart. Under the pink banner sat three women, smiling at their adoring fans and scribbling in book after book.

"Meet Anmaree, Brytni, and Cynthia," Flavian smirked, "the ABCs of Life Sisterhood™," and the ™ jangled like a Raihezi banker's moneybags.

"Yeah, I know," I sniffed. "Self-improvement advice from strangers is for morons. So?"

"I'm their agent."

My jaw dropped. "What? You came to Earth to *work?*"

Flavian looked smug. "Eight best-sellers in four years, and this one's heading for the top. And it's all because of me. Look at the books, Kat."

"They're pink," I said. But they did look odd. I switched to othersight, and gasped. On each cover the ABCs logo blazed like a firedrake's crucible. "What have you done to those books?"

"It's a glamour. It makes people crave the book. Then when they read it, they see only the words they want to see." He preened. "This new book's press run is half a million copies, and I personally placed that glamour on every one of them."

That was impressive, even for a mage of his caliber. He'd been the King's High Wizard back home in Meliniseth when I left for Earth with baby Greta ten years ago.

When, to be precise, he'd had me banished.

I'd made a decent life for us, though there was still the occasional slipup like poor charred *Hetty* here. But this was *my* world now, and I didn't appreciate His Sniffiness barging in. "Why here?" I demanded.

"They called me."

"They *what*?"

"They're witches. They asked for my help." His expression added an unspoken, *And aren't they cute?* "I've taught them everything they know."

I rolled my eyes and started to turn away. But a soft voice interrupted, "Flavian! There you are," and the ABCs Sisterhood™ joined us.

I resent pretty women. As a dragon in Meliniseth, my size and gleaming ebony scales had boosted my status in the Dragonrick; being lanky and black in suburban Virginia got me only "You play basketball?" I was ready to hate the ABCs.

But they were *nice*. Anmaree gave a tidy little geisha-type bow, Brytni flabbergasted me with a miniature Black Power fist salute. Cynthia shook hands, and I liked her instantly. "We're pleased to meet any friend of Flavian's."

"We owe him so much," Anmaree murmured.

"He's the man," Brytni added.

"He's taught us everything we know." Cynthia smiled, slipping her arm through his. Flavian looked like a cat in a dairy.

"So I hear," I said. My conflict with Flavian was private, so I was polite, but I was glad to excuse myself and head back to Greta.

As we checked out with her stack of books and drove home, however, my mind was far off in Meliniseth.

I'd known Flavian for centuries, and never liked him. Then, twelve years ago, he advised King Haruil to try recovering the Isles of Minrec from Emperor Tizhem. Bad idea. Tizhem's sorcerer was tough, and a third of the Dragonrick were lost in the typhoon he raised. Drowning is a hideous death for a firedrake, and my comrades' cries will echo in my mind to the day my fires go out.

After the Dragonrick's finest were slaughtered—and Minrec stayed firmly Tizhem's—I rose quickly in rank. We dragons hold grudges well, and I never hid my opinion of Flavian. Then came my tour of duty at Billow Harbor, and the handsome sea-dragon Yskaraaz who taught me the terror and exhilaration of flying underwater . . . and Greta was egged. The prohibition on cross-mating between species should have been suspended after the Minrec fiasco, but nobody got around to it. And now Flavian had his most vocal opponent right where he wanted her.

At least the Court gave me my option of dimensions and body forms. I chose Earth and human, because humans were the most varied and curious creatures I'd heard of. If Greta had to grow up not in her own form, at least let her be something with choices and the imagination to make them. But it still wasn't home.

So to see Flavian moving in, using his magic to get still more money and power when he'd had all he wanted already—the unfairness made my ears smoke. It took a Thai curry and a bedtime reading to Greta from *Dragonflight* to calm me down.

But now that I knew about Flavian's link to the ABCs books, they seemed to crop up everywhere.

Pink covers gleamed on the bus and peeked out of tote bags. My barista barely glanced up from *The ABCs of Beauty: Getting Your Dream Look* to serve a businessman clutching *The ABCs of Power: Getting What You Want, NOW*. A woman on the Metro had wrapped her copy in another jacket, but my other-sight saw clearly the title, *The ABCs of Love: Getting Happy Ever After*.

I didn't get worried till I saw the mother wheeling her kid into the doctor's office—the bright scarf wrapping the little bald head—with determination in her face and *The ABCs of Medicine: Getting Well YOUR Way* in her bag.

This was too much. I didn't care if Flavian made millions—well, not much—but what he was doing to these soft-headed humans was downright wicked. I went straight back to Frontiers to see what those books were really all about. The 40% sale was over, that's how seriously I was taking it.

I sat down in the kitchen with a pan of brownies in the oven, Greta due home from her violin lesson in a couple of hours, and *The ABCs of Parenting* on the table—

—and woke up to a tugging on my arm. I blinked. The kitchen was full of smoke, and Greta was pulling at my sleeve in that unstoppable way she has. Only then did I hear the smoke alarm.

"Fewmets!" I yanked the smoldering pan out of the oven without bothering with a potholder, zapped the smoke alarm with a glare, and sat back down. Greta stood watching me with those big sea-green eyes. Strange visions rattled around my mind as I looked back at her sweet brown face. I could make her be anything I wanted. The book said so. Phi Beta Kappa, Nobel . . . Olympic gold, Carnegie Hall, CEO . . . Dame Greta, Honorable Greta, Saint Greta . . . All I had to do was, was, was—

"*Sulfurated* fewmets." I grabbed the phone book. I had to talk to the ABCs, and Frontiers would know how to find them. But first I paused for a reality check. "Sweetie, if Mom could do one thing to help you be everything you want, what would it be? What should I do?"

Greta thought, and said, "Brownies."

I pulled her into an extra-long hug, laughed, sniffled, slammed both books, and reached for the chocolate.

The human pediatricians never found anything wrong. She wasn't autistic or disabled; on paper, she tested "gifted." But the only time Greta ever spoke was to me, and often days would go by without a word. The smartest of the doctors guessed at trauma at a sensitive point in her development. Ha! Close. Being snatched from her warm, stony nest when she was barely hatched, shunted into a flimsy body nothing like her own, and planted in a different dimension would mess anyone up. I made up some mumble about a divorce and stopped going to doctors.

The scholarship to Almacari School had been a godsend. Stuffed with learning specialists, Almacari was perfect for Greta, though I hated the "learning disabled" label as much as the "minority" one. She was valued and encouraged; somehow, without even talking, she was able to make good friends. She was doing fine.

But whatever happened, I would never forgive Flavian for depriving my daughter of a normal childhood— human or dragonet. The ABCs were such sweeties, they couldn't possibly realize how that greedy charlatan was using them. It was time I put a little kink in his plans.

"I appreciate your time, Ms. Huntingdon."

"Cynthia, please! Come in!" Beaming, the blonde third of the ABCs Sisterhood™ shook my hand, then led the way through her house. Mansion, rather: elegant and enormous, in the outer Virginia-burbs. It's hard to intimidate a dragon, but I had to remind myself that, in true form, I could torch the place with a burp.

We finally reached a glassed-in conservatory overlooking the Potomac River. Here the decor was Southwestern, with adobe and ruddy tile that glowed in the early February sunset. Priceless Navajo weavings draped over cow-hide armchairs, and a multicolored lizard snoozed in a terrarium.

The other two ABCs greeted me, Anmaree with her little geisha bow and Brytni with a yo-sista fist knock. Cynthia Huntingdon was already offering tea. It was perfect too, of course, smoky and delicious. "Dr. Feuer—"

"Kat," I had to say.

"Kat, it's so nice of you to come out all this way. It would've been too complicated to talk at the reception tonight. I understand your daughter goes to Almacari School? You know we're Alma girls too?"

"Yes, I saw that in the lecture announcement." You have to do the small-talk thing with humans. Greta's private school, Almacari, had invited their famous alumnae for a lecture that night. The beginners' string quartet Greta was in was performing at the reception afterward, so we'd have met there anyway. But what I had to say called for privacy.

Finally I managed to get to business. "So, Cynthia—how much do you know about Flavian Fortescue?"

"We owe him so much," Anmaree whispered.

"He's the man," Brytni declared.

"He's a wizard," Cynthia smiled. ". . . But not as great as he thinks he is."

I choked on my tea, and all three women smiled wider.

"Did he tell you we called him and he came to help us?" Anmaree.

"And he taught us everything we know?" Brytni.

I was nodding, stunned, and Cynthia laughed. "Kat, he came because I made him. I stole his Life."

"You *what*?"

Wizards in our part of the universe always hide their Lives, in case of magical accident. They bottle up their essence—their soul, if you think those arrogant cretins have one—and tuck it away someplace secret. But Flavian's should have been impossible—

"He's so traditional. It was in a vial of adamant, sealed with fifty spells, in the heart of a volcano. However," Cynthia twinkled, "the volcano was in Maui, right under everyone's nose."

"But how—"

Cynthia waved a hand. "It doesn't matter how I got his Life out of there. What matters, Dragonrick Subcommander Kaatrzekh'na—" and by the gods, she had the aspirates perfect, for a human— "is, I *read* it."

Somehow I managed to shut my jaw. Cynthia glanced at Anmaree and Brytni, still perched smiling on the couch. "Businessmen say you can talk to their associates as if you were talking to themselves," she said. "Here, it's literally true." She lifted one trim eyebrow, and the two women simply *dissolved*. Their forms faded till I could see the Navajo stripes behind them, then slurred into a pastel streak that entered Cynthia's body just beneath her string of perfectly matched pink pearls.

Cynthia turned eyes on me that saw down to the insides of my scales, and said sweetly, "And you were going to warn me about Flavian?"

Great flames, this woman had *power*. Now I saw she'd even enchanted me—me!—with that handshake back in the bookstore. I should have guessed from the glamours: pink is not Flavian's color.

"I guess I've got nothing to tell you," I said feebly.

"Well, no," Cynthia said. "However, there are a few things you should know. *Sit*." My knees buckled, and I plopped back into my chair. Something was wrong. —*The tea!*

Cynthia leaned forward, a small object in her hand. "Here, look." It was a gleaming silver box, no bigger than her palm. Sunlight flashed off it, making me blink, and then the bottom dropped out of the world.

I awoke warm and comfortable. I lay on a sandy slope, just like home—but not quite. The forelegs under my nose were a charming emerald green, the toes curling up at the ends. Baffled, I could only think, Wait, I'm not supposed to be a dragon any more.

Then Cynthia's quiet chuckle woke me completely. "Isn't it nice to have a tail again?"

I craned to see where the voice was coming from. A hot, reddish light blazed overhead. Beside me, a tall leafy plant overhung a pool of water.

Beyond the water lay a similar scene: leaves, sand, a small green lizard. I was looking at a reflection—my own reflection—in a monstrous sheet of glass. Only the glass wasn't monstrous, I was tiny.

She'd turned me into a *gecko*.

Cynthia's voice continued. "Quite a useful spell, my silver box. Absorbs power like a sponge. You're an interesting case: there wasn't much of you that wasn't magic."

I turned around so fast I almost knotted my tail, but I couldn't see her anywhere. Then I heard a rustle and spun back.

At the crest of the slope above me loomed a gigantic Gila monster.

It opened its jaws, and Cynthia Huntingdon's voice came out. "Generations of Huntingdon women have used this box to gather magic, even from ordinary humans. It's remarkable how much some of those losers contain. There's a piece of this spell in every ABCs book."

I backed away slowly, appalled. How could this human control so much power?

"It's not easy," the lizard continued, as if in answer to my thoughts. "You've no idea how difficult it is to do magic in a world where it's *not supposed to work.*"

It gaped mockingly, its beady eyes gleaming. "Binding Flavian was brilliant, I think," it purred. "And then to find you and your daughter in his Life—well, I've heard marvelous things about dragon's blood . . ."

Dragon's blood! I'd been just as stupid as Flavian. I never considered I could be in danger from her *myself*.

"I located you years ago," Cynthia continued. "I arranged that scholarship to Almacari to keep you nearby. Then I waited till your brat was big enough to be useful. Now's my chance. When you hear this

message, I'll be at Almacari School making friends
with Greta. Soon I'll have *two* little lizards to play
with. I figure I can tap lots of blood out of you both
before you die.

"So make yourself comfy. Nostradamus here will
keep an eye on you. No problem if he eats you—I'll
still have Greta. B'bye!" The Gila monster's head
drooped as Cynthia's speech-spell released it.

My toes curled in fury. Greta was at a friend's
house this afternoon; her mother was driving both
girls to school for their performance at this evening's
reception. When I didn't turn up, Cynthia could easily enchant the school authorities into allowing her to
give Greta "a ride home."

Forget Flavian. Cynthia was harming innocent
people. She intended to drain my daughter and me
to a husk. Even Anmaree and Brytni, discarded as
soon as she didn't want them— They were only a
gimmick, but nobody gets to evaporate sistas even if
they aren't real.

I was taking this witch *down*.

I'd realized finally where I was: the lizard tank in
Cynthia's conservatory. I could climb the glass walls
if I could only reach them. But on three sides the
water pool stretched to the wall, and in the other
direction Nostradamus stood guard.

If I could just get past the Gila monster while it
was still groggy from Cynthia's spell . . . But even as I
thought of it, the beast lifted its head and hissed, back
to normal. The next instant, Nostradamus charged.

I bolted, but not fast enough, and his fangs sank
into my tail. I scrabbled in the sand in agony and
panic. *Greta!*

Suddenly, miraculously, I was free. I raced for the plant and up onto a leaf overhanging the water, then looked back. Nostradamus stood munching thoughtfully, my tail sticking out of the corner of his mouth. Now I remembered, some lizards' tails could break away if attacked. It had saved me, but damn, it *hurt*.

I couldn't outrun the critter. That left me only one way out of here. Against every instinct I owned.

The Minrec typhoon still haunts my nightmares. But Yskaraaz—sleek, sea-green, the very color of Greta's eyes—had guided me past my fears. In his deep blue oceans, I'd discovered a soaring freedom uncannily like that of my native skies.

I was the only firedrake in Meliniseth who wasn't afraid of water.

I held my breath, let go the leaf, and plunged in. No wings to paddle with, but my gecko toes clung to the bottom. I walked underwater to the wall of the tank, and then climbed. When I emerged, Nostradamus was crouched in the sand, hissing. I flicked my tongue at him, then scooted up the glass and down the other side.

I was out! But not home free. Cynthia had my magic in her spell-box. I was a gecko, not even a whole one. My child was thirty miles away, and commercials notwithstanding, geckos can't drive.

But there on the wall was an electric socket.

Flavian, and thus Cynthia, didn't know everything about Yskaraaz, or she'd have put a lid on that tank. And she'd made one more wrong assumption. In this world, I was *all* magic. So the fact that I still even existed, after the silver box's spell, meant I had some left—enough, I hoped, to convert raw energy into power I could use.

I'd been forbidden to transform on Earth, on pain of being sent somewhere worse. But for Greta, I'd live in the Gnashlug Swamp. I zipped up the wall and stuck my toes in the socket.

If anyone was watching that evening, instead of swearing as their fancy plasma HDTV fritzed out, they would've seen darkness spreading across Fairfax County like a pool of ink as one after another electric web was drained to blackness. A few minutes later, I smashed up through the glass roof of Cynthia's conservatory, spread great wings the color of night, and beat away across the Potomac and into the chill winter sky.

As I glided shadow-like down to the school, the line of cars leaving the parking lot made my heart sink. Was I too late? I landed in the soccer field, trying to keep the skirt and sweater clutched in my talons out of the mud. Transforming hastily, I threw on my clothes and ran in the school's kitchen entrance.

The catering staff were washing dishes and carrying in decimated trays of nosh. The reception was almost over. In panic I raced out to the lunchroom, where a couple dozen school parents were still chatting. Cynthia's creepy pink aura shone around them—more souls for her silver box. She hadn't left yet, thank the gods.

But Greta was nowhere to be seen.

I spotted Helen Albright, Greta's friend's mom who was supposed to have brought the two girls here. I barged through the crowd to her and demanded, "Helen, where are the kids?"

"HollyMadison was wonderful," Helen creaked. She

has a voice like claws on granite. "One of the girls broke a violin string, so HollyMadison gave her one of hers . . ." HollyMadison was Greta's best friend, and how a sweet kid like that had sprung from Helen I never understood. "HollyMadison is so good in emergencies," she blathered. "Just like me. I was the only person with a safety pin when the Ambassador of— Do you have moths?" She was eyeing the talon holes in my sweater.

Hers was cashmere, of course. But I'd had enough of suburban one-upmanship, and just demanded, "Where are they?"

"HollyMadison's getting her coat," said Helen. "We have to leave, HollyMadison has glockenspiel practice and her Azerbaijani lesson tomorrow. You know her teacher won the—"

"*Where's Greta?*" I snarled.

Oops. Too much dragon. Helen's eyebrows didn't burn only because they were mostly pencil. But strangely, she didn't notice that her bangs were smoking. She gazed at the crowd by the exit, her eyes glowing as if she'd met the entire Royal Family. "Cynthia's wonderful. She said we're probably related. You know, my grandmother's name was Huckerson . . ."

Way too late, I refocused my othersight. Cynthia's enchantment coated Helen like a bucket of pink slime. Helen was still yammering, "So of *course*—"

I spun and opened my jaws. Below human hearing, my bellow shifted the crowd like an earthquake. Cynthia stood near the door, facing me—I was sure she'd felt it when I broke her gecko spell. Beside her was Flavian, looking bewildered. A smile chilled Cynthia's face, and her hand rested on Greta's shoulder.

With a blink, I filled the doorway behind her with a sheet of flame.

Cynthia's smile widened. Ignoring the blaze, she raised her free hand and fired a magical blast at me.

Good. I needed it. She still had most of my magic in her spell-box, I could feel it. Amazing the thing wasn't setting her purse afire. I had almost nothing to stop her. I was charged full of Dominion Power's finest kilowatts, but she'd stolen so much of my magic I barely had enough left to control them. And I had to aim well—she had Greta for a shield. I spread my arms to absorb Cynthia's blast and shot a flare back.

The witch was fast and smart. She recognized instantly that raw magic only strengthened me. As a firedrake, I'm really only vulnerable to water or organic stuff. She deflected my flare into the crowd of parents—melting three lawyers' toupees—and reassembled a cantaloupe from the fruit tray beside her. I dodged too late, and the hurtling melon smacked me backward over a table.

I hate fruit.

Straight force wouldn't work against Cynthia either. I needed weapons of my own. Wheezing, I struggled up and met a pair of blue eyes. "HollyMadison! What are you— Duck!" I cried as spring rolls zoomed overhead, releasing hordes of reanimated and snapping shrimp. Cabbages attacked my ankles.

"She never touched the hummus!" HollyMadison yelled. "Try that!"

No time to wonder how she knew to suggest it. I sprang to my feet and aimed the bread bowl full of spicy goop, re-forming the original ingredients in midflight. Chickpeas battered Cynthia like bullets. A hot pepper got her in the eye and she let go of Greta. My daughter vanished among the panicking guests.

Cynthia yelled in anger, and every tablecloth in the room flew up to entangle me. I scorched them to ashes easily, but Cynthia had both hands free now and a fleet of murderously spinning pita breads dive-bombed the room. One disk sliced through the "WELCOME ABCs™" banner, draping it over a tangle of Capitol Hill wonks. I fired a tray of satay skewers, but Cynthia snagged them with a wheel of brie.

A tug at my sleeve. "*Greta!*" She'd sneaked behind overturned tables and hysterical parents to find me. I held her tight, but she wriggled free. "Punch!" she said.

"What?"

HollyMadison popped up. "She's a *witch*, Dr. Feuer. Get her wet!"

"I can't!" It takes a lot of magic for a firedrake to control liquids, more than I had right then. I could barely wield the firelike elements: heat, spices . . .

"Greta can do it," HollyMadison urged.

A barrage of giant fruit tarts hurtled past. I heard a shriek and glanced back. Helen Albright stood there, nothing visible between frizzled bangs and fancy sweater but a slab of meringue. HollyMadison said, "Oops."

"Brownies," Greta persisted. "Cheese?"

Yes. The jalapeño cheese dip. And as for chocolate . . .

I swatted the ex-fajita chicken that was trying to peck my eyes, and focused. Hot cheese flooded over Cynthia's pointy-toed shoes, gluing her feet to the floor. She staggered, swearing, and I knocked her flat with a giant chocolate fist. Greta waved her hand, and a tsunami of orange punch surged up from the huge glass bowl beside her. Water magic––by the gods, I'd forgotten my daughter was half seadrake!

The neon-colored wave swept over Cynthia, drenching her from head to foot. I never want to hear a scream like that again. Even HollyMadison stopped bouncing and looked awed. Greta just watched Cynthia shrivel away into evil-smelling fumes, then said, "Lime seltzer. Mango sherbet. Gotta hurt."

The fight was over. I hugged Greta as if I couldn't let her go, while HollyMadison cheered.

Then a chilly "Ahem" interrupted our glee. Flavian stood there, glaring and spattered with tahini. "If you don't mind," he said, "that *hag* has something of mine."

Mine too, I remembered.

Cynthia's things still lay in the congealing pool of cheese. I fished out the spell-box cautiously, but with Cynthia dead, the box's magic too had died. I opened the lid, and staggered as my magic swept back.

"Hrmph," said Flavian. He'd cleaned himself up, but still looked peevish. "And my Life?"

"Right there." Even if I hadn't seen Anmaree and Brytni vanish into it, I would have known that Cynthia's pearl neckace—that icon of upscale suburban femininity—was the center of her power. Flavian snatched it up and concentrated.

Nothing happened.

Frowning, he laid the necklace on a table and gestured widely, muttering words of power that hazed the air. Zero.

I tried a shot of my own reclaimed magic, and the rebound nearly knocked me over. Nothing was going to break into those pearls.

"Mom?"

Flavian and I both looked at Greta. Flavian sneered—but I'd just seen my daughter work her first spell, one I could never have managed. I handed them over. "Sure, sweetie. Give it a try."

Greta and HollyMadison bent their heads, curly black and curly red, over the pearls. Then they looked at each other and burst into giggles. Greta put the necklace back on the table, waved her hand limply at it, and said, "Eh. Whatever."

The necklace exploded. Pearls shot all over the room, a speck of Flavian's Life blazing from each one. Flavian yelled and ran after them, while I gaped at the girls. "What was *that?*"

"My therapist calls it passive aggression," said HollyMadison. "It's kind of the universal force around here. My grandmother's almost as good at it as that witch was."

"And how do you know so much about magic anyway?" I demanded of her.

"*Mo*-om," said Greta. "*Books.*"

Flavian came back, as pompous and self-satisfied as ever. "*Good*-bye," he said, and raised his hands in a transport spell.

"Not so fast," I said. "I got your Life back, you ingrate. And look at this mess." The parents were picking themselves up, swearing and planning lawsuits. "This is your fault."

Flavian barely gave them a glance. One wave of his hand and tables righted themselves, ashes formed back into linens, food retreated to platters. The smoking doorway regenerated.

Helen appeared, staring at Flavian like the second coming of Elvis. "Mister Fortescue! May I call you

Flavian? That was wonderful! You know, my cousin works with David Copperfield . . ."

"*And* the memories," I said.

Flavian snarled, but raised a hand. Greta quickly pulled my arm, and indicated HollyMadison. "Hold it, Flavian," I said. "Hol, are you sure you want to remember all this?" This girl had seen her own mother enchanted into obeying a murderous witch—and then, even worse, thoroughly pie'd.

HollyMadison shrugged and grinned. "She's my mom. I still love her. And who would I ever tell?"

"Good point. Okay, Flavian. Everybody but Holly-Madison."

Flavian glared. He knew HollyMadison's memory would include him. He gestured once more, turning the scared and angry faces of the crowd back to their normal blandness, then vanished.

"Wait!" I yelped, but too late: he was gone. I gritted my teeth. Not a word of thanks, and not a chance of getting home. Ungrateful bastard.

But Greta gave my sleeve one more tug. When I looked down, she smiled and held up a tiny gleaming object. "Try this?"

HollyMadison comes with us sometimes to Melinis-eth. She loves it when Greta gives her a ride, soaring through the clear hot skies.

And Greta's as graceful underwater as she is in the air. She and her father dive together for pearls, and they've amassed a gorgeous assortment, one for every visit, all colors and shapes.

But the prize of her collection is a single, perfect pearl that glows with just a hint of pink.

For nearly 30 years Berry Kercheval has been herding computers in the Bay Area for LLNL, Xerox PARC, and numerous startups and has published two technical books. Having recently discovered that when writing fiction you can MAKE IT ALL UP he has started selling short stories and is working on a novel.

Witch's Brew

Berry Kercheval

Mo flicked her black bangs from her eyes as she glanced up from her notebook to check on the mall coffee shop. All the patrons were happily slurping their cappuccinos and lattes and decaf soy-milk mochas. OK, duty done, back to work.

It was bad enough that she had to go to regular school, which sucked big-time. Witch School on top, two afternoons a week, totally cut into her social life, and to have to have a *job* besides was beyond tedious. At least her boss at the Coffee Spot didn't mind if she studied when it was slow, and while studying was boring, it kept Mater Ruth off her back. And it wasn't like there was a whole lot to do in the shop in the middle of the afternoon. As long as no one actually read her spell notebook over her shoulder it was safe.

The bell on the door jangled as Justin walked in, just the hottest boy in the class. He was with Heather. Mo grimaced. The cute ones always went for the cheerleader types.

Justin came up to the counter. "Hi, can I have two large mochas, please?"

Mo stared at him. Her stomach tingled, then she blinked and remembered her job.

"Sure, Justin, two large caffé mochas coming up, Justin." *Ohmigod, I said his name twice!* She turned to the espresso machine to hide the blush that rose from the collar of her black t-shirt. The routine of tamping the ground coffee, pulling the shots and steaming the milk calmed her. She assembled the drinks and put them on the counter.

"That's six dollars. Thanks!"

Justin took the drinks and sat at the table Heather had found for them. Mo sighed and went back to her notebook behind the counter. She turned the page and read about the summoning spell they were working on this week. The incantation was written next to the diagram.

"By my will and by thy true name . . ." she muttered under her breath to set the words in her mind. *Mater insists everyone memorize the spells, can you believe it?* she thought. *It's like, hello, we have PDAs and computers now, that's what they're for.* She felt the hairs on the back of her neck tingle with the magic. Since she had deliberately not set out the herbs and stuff, the spell wouldn't fully activate with just the diagram and incantation, so no wards were needed. The first level wards she could do were a pain in the ass anyway. It would be easy to explain the candles to her boss as part of the cross-promotion with Kandle-Kwik across the mall, but the salt circle? No way. She could hardly wait for the advanced wards, which were harder to set but needed less *junk* scattered around.

"Excuse me, I just need the cinnamon." Justin had come back and set his mocha on the counter. Mo handed him the cinnamon shaker without looking up from her notebook. Why fool herself? There was no chance with him.

She restarted her incantation. As Justin reached for the cinnamon shaker his elbow knocked over the drink. The hot milk, coffee, and chocolate spilled onto the counter top, off the back edge and dripped onto the book.

"Whoops!" said Justin, reaching for the spilled drink and knocking over the cinnamon as well. "Sorry . . ."

"—I summon thee! Oh shit!" cried Mo as the spell diagram on the drenched page began to glow. Clouds of yellowish smoke gathered over the book and a twisting maelstrom of chaos grew in the middle of the page. A taloned hand poked through the portal. A scaly arm followed it and a small, plump imp crawled through. It looked just like a standard demon: smell of rotten eggs, check; razor-sharp talons to flay the skin from your flesh, check; barbed tail to whip your back into bloody shreds, horns to disembowel you, check and check. The only unusual feature was, it was eighteen inches tall and cute as, well, the devil.

"Khresk smaz fthagn!" it shouted. While everyone in the coffee shop turned and stared, it jumped down from the counter, wove through the legs of the crowd and scooted out into the mall before anyone could even realize it was time to scream.

"Whoa!" said Justin. "That was, like, *cool*! Do another!"

Mo burst into tears.

"All right, Maureen Imogen Sanderson, tell me what happened here." Mater Ruth had no patience with pretensions and always used Mo's real name. She had apparated into the back room and swept out into the shop seconds after the imp disappeared. "Your safety amulet signaled an unwarded spell. From the page open in your notebook it appears to have been the lesser summoning we've been studying. Did something escape?"

"I didn't mean to, it just—Justin spilled the—and then—" Mo was just starting to get her tears under control.

"You were reading aloud again, weren't you? And without wards! Didn't I warn you about that?"

"But none of the physical items were present, just the diagram." Mo was near whining.

"Hey? Like, what the heck? I mean . . ." Justin was trying to get Mater Ruth's attention.

"Pish," said Ruth. She took a pinch of powder from her purse and blew it into the air. "Congenium frigident!"

The folks in the coffee shop ceased all motion, except Mo, Mater Ruth . . . and Justin.

"Achoo! What was that?" he asked.

Mater frowned at him. "You're immune to the spell. Do you have the Talent?"

"Spell, you mean like witches and wizards and stuff? Cool! Where's the camera? What show is this?"

"Oh dear. Well, stand over there and remain silent, there's a good lad."

Justin rested his elbows on the counter, watching in fascination.

"Now, let's close this rift and see if we can clean up the mess." She extracted a wand from her purse and passed it over the roiling vortex still churning in Mo's notebook. A tentacle protruded from the portal and started feeling around on the counter. She poked it sharply with the wand. It jerked back as if stung before retreating.

"Got it," Mater said. "Now, my dear, kindly close it off."

"Me?" Mo wailed. "Why me?"

"Your spell, young lady, you clean it up." Her voice took on the tone of an exasperated but patient teacher. "How do we shut down spells?"

"Um, normally we brush the salt out of the spell diagram but there's no salt here, just . . . uh . . ."

Mater tapped her wand on the other hand, waiting. Mo looked at the portal, swirling mist embedded in a page of her notebook. "We need to, um, disrupt the geometry another way, so, maybe this will work."

She reached out and took a corner in both hands and tore sharply across the page. The vortex closed with a greasy plop that left a strong smell of raisin-nut cookies in the air. Mater sniffed. "That would be the cinnamon. Nicely done, young lady, but you're still in a lot of trouble, you know that?"

"Well, I thought it would be OK . . ." Mo started.

"And now you've learned better. Again. Time to clean up this mess, Maureen, dear. Better get started."

"Get started? Where? How?"

"Come now, my dear, I've taught you all you need to deal with this. Think it through logically."

Mo pondered. "Well, I guess I . . . I need to, like . . . find the imp, bring it back here, and return it to . . . wherever."

"Excellent!" said Mater. "Go ahead."

"Well, track the imp . . . the spell of finding seems obvious. We need something related to the imp."

Justin had been watching raptly as this interchange went on. His elbow slipped in something wet and slimy. "Eeeeuw!" he said.

"Imp slime! Perfect!" said Mo. "Now a focus, preferably organic." She plucked a wooden coffee stirrer from a container on the counter.

"I'll do the wards," said Mater Ruth. A quick mutter, a sprinkle of salt for protection, a few gestures, and a sparkle settled on the walls of the shop.

Mo rummaged in her schoolbag, took out a few items and set to work. She quickly tied a length of string to the stick, rubbed it in the slime, sprinkled some powdered herb—cowslip for finding—and paused.

"Go on, dear, you've done this before."

Mo squared her shoulders and repeated the familiar incantation. Another sparkle condensed on the stick.

"Hey, that was a neat effect. I thought you added those later with CGI? Or is this just glitter and a laser pointer?" said Justin.

Mater was surprised. "You can see that? Very interesting, very interesting indeed." Mo could almost see the facts dropping onto Mater's mental notebook, adding to a neat "To-Do list."

Mo held the string up, and the stick dangled below, spun, and swung toward the doorway.

"It went thataway!" cried Justin. "Let's go, pardner."

Unsure whether Justin was being ironic or just goofy, Mo looked at Mater. "Go on, dear, it's just a minor imp and should be no problem for you to handle. I'll—what is the phrase?—hold down the fort and keep the powder dry."

As the two teens left the shop, the stick pulled to the left. They followed it briskly out into the mall.

They set off down the corridor, passing the Pottery Hut. They saw the imp perched on top of a cell phone kiosk, bouncing up and down. The phones started ringing. The imp had set them all to use "The Macarena" as their ringtone. Forty tinny versions, all slightly out of step, blared from the display.

"Oh, shoot me now!" said Mo, "One Macarena is bad enough."

The imp jumped down and scampered along the corridor. Justin and Mo followed close behind, leaving the kiosk attendant trying to shut down all the phones.

They passed a Beach, Bar and Bed store and emerged into the open atrium where the mall corridors crossed. There they saw the imp climbing onto the gazebo in the Tot Shot children's photography stand in the middle of the atrium. During the holidays this was where Santa or the Easter Bunny posed with the kids, but the rest of the year it was where doting parents took their kids for pictures to send to Grandma.

As the imp capered on the top of the kiosk, Justin asked "How come no one's screaming?"

Mo looked from the parents and photographer behind the camera to the young boy sitting on a chair under the gazebo. "I guess the imp can control his visibility. I can see him all the time because I'm a witch."

"So if I can see him, what does that make me?" asked Justin.

"Good question, but we can ask Mater about it later."

The imp screwed up its face as if it were making a great effort and leaned over the edge of the gazebo. The young boy looked up and screamed just as the flash went off.

Justin laughed. "Oh, what a great shot!"

Mo punched him in the arm. "Come on, this is serious." Then she giggled too. "But it will be a great shot." They approached the gazebo and the imp spotted them, jumped down and ran off down a service corridor.

Following him into the passage, they could see the tiny imp at the end, leaping frantically, trying to reach the doorknob.

"There he is!" Justin shouted.

They stepped into the passage blocking the imp's exit. "Come on, little fellow," crooned Mo. "Come to mama . . ."

The imp turned, looked around and scooted up the side of the passage toward them. "Don't let it get past you!" shouted Mo.

"How?" cried Justin.

"I don't know, just do something!"

Justin took out a pencil, pointed it at the imp with a flick of his wrist and shouted "*Stupefy!*"

"You idiot!" Mo said, "That only works in *Harry Potter*."

Justin pointed. The imp, frozen in a running position, slowly toppled over and fell onto its nose. "Ooooh, that's gotta hurt."

"How did you do that?"

"I dunno. It just seemed like the right thing. And it worked when Hermione did it to what's-is-name," said Justin.

"But . . . but . . . but we can work that out later. Let's get this little guy back to the Coffee Spot so Mater Ruth can deal with him." She pulled a Pottery Hut shopping bag from a trash bin and scooped up the imp.

Mo dumped the still-frozen imp onto a table in the Coffee Spot. "There! Now you can send him back. Send it. Whatever."

Ruth laughed. "Oh no, this is your mess, dear. Think of it as a learning experience." Mo rolled her eyes; she'd gone through some of Mater Ruth's "learning experiences" before.

"But let's see what you've got here." She held her hands over the rigid imp and concentrated. "Interesting. Did you use Gellman's Petrifaction? I didn't think we'd worked with spells that advanced."

Mo blushed. "Um . . ."

Justin spoke up. "I did it. I think. Probably."

"Did you?" said Mater Ruth, raising one eyebrow. "What a talented young man you're turning out to be. Now, Maureen, send this little fellow back to where he came from. May I suggest that a standard 'dispel evil' should do the trick?"

Justin looked at Mo. "Maureen?"

Mo blushed deeper. "It's the name my parents gave me. Mater Ruth insists on using it."

"I kinda like it."

Ruth tapped her fingers on the table and inclined her head toward the diminutive imp, which was starting to twitch. Mo said "Oh, right. Let's see." She took some chalk from her schoolbag and quickly drew a pentagram around the imp, saying a containment spell as she did so. Sparkling motes condensed from the air and swirled around it. Then she pulled out a small sack and removed a pinch of sweet-smelling cloves and sprinkled it on the imp, saying "By my will and with thy name, I conjure thee, uh, I conjure thee—Shoot, I don't know its name!" The sparkle faded out.

"Name?" asked Justin. "Why do you need its name?"

Mater Ruth stepped in. "Magic works best if you know a thing's true name. The easiest way to get rid of this imp is to use its true name to compel it to return home."

"But I don't *know* its name!" wailed Mo.

The imp twitched again and started to move its arms.

"How did you get it here?" asked Ruth.

"Justin spilled his coffee when I was practicing."

"Hey," said Justin, "if you need its true name to send it back, don't you need it to get it here too? What exactly did you say in the incantation?"

Mo sniffed. "Well, I was going to use a place holder. You know, 'I summon thee, insert name here', but then you spilled the coffee and ruined *everything*!"

"Calm down. Remember what you actually said," said Justin.

"Insert name here?"

"No, what you actually said was 'I summon thee— Oh shit!' so try that. What could it hurt?"

"Talented *and* clever," Ruth said. "Give it a try, Maureen, dear. After all, now that he's properly contained the worst that could happen is the little fellow will laugh at us."

"Well, OK," Mo said. The imp moved its arm and rolled over onto its back. She got out another pinch of cloves and sprinkled it onto the imp. It sneezed, and she started again. "By my will and by thy true name, Oh Shit, I conjure thee—"

The imp sat up suddenly and stared directly at Mo.

"—take thyself back to the place whence thou came, and return not an ye not be summoned." Mo raised her arms and shouted, "BEGONE!"

"Bye-eep!" The little imp grinned, waved and vanished in a puff of greasy black smoke.

Mo sat down in a chair abruptly.

"Wow!" said Justin. "Maureen, that was cool! Can you teach me?"

"No," said Ruth, "but I can. Tuesday and Thursday afternoons after school, don't be late, and bring a blank notebook."

"What?"

"Well, you have the talent, that's clear. You need training if for no other reason than to enable you to control it. Come by and we'll make sure you get that. You can escort Maureen; she'll show you the way. Now let me release these poor folks. Luckily that spell has a ten minute amnesia built in."

Ruth snapped her fingers and the patrons of the shop resumed their activities, oblivious to the near disaster that had unfolded under their noses. She swept out of the shop before Justin could frame a reply.

"Justin?" Heather called from her table, "What's going on?"

"Later!" Justin said without looking away from Mo.

"Justin!" Heather stood and actually stamped her foot. "I said, *later*."

Offended, Heather picked up her bag and stormed out of the shop.

"Your girlfriend left."

"Oh, she's not my girlfriend, really. But what about this spell class? Do I have to come? Don't I get a choice? And what's with the 'Mater' stuff."

"No, you don't really get a choice," Mo said. "Mater's just like that. It means 'mother' in Latin, which is what we call the leader of a group of witches. She's a bit sharp and bossy, but she's a really good teacher and mostly patient as long as you're trying."

"Yeah, I can see that. Like how she let you figure out how to do this without yelling. I wish Mr. Farnsworth was like that in Algebra."

"Um, well, you know, I could help you with the Algebra. I mean, if you like."

"That would be nice." Justin looked at Mo. "Hey, you know what? I thought you were just a weird nerd, like everyone says at school. Well, you *are* weird, but it's cool-weird!"

Mo laughed. "Cool-weird, huh? I can live with that. Here, let me get you a fresh coffee."

Daniel M. Hoyt grew up in the wild suburbs of Ohio, attending school, dutifully doing his homework on time, mowing patterns in the lawn in the summer, and flipping through pocket books he found at the grocery store, notably one on the subject of white witchcraft. A career in mathematics, software architecture and rocket science later, those carefree days in Ohio were all but forgotten—until witches moved into his present neighborhood, resulting in the strange but true story presented here. Since his first sale to *Analog*, in which he discovered with a shock that it's possible to get paid to lie (without getting arrested), Dan has sold several stories to other magazines and anthologies, including Baen's *Transhuman* anthology, and even crossed over to the dark side of anthology editing with *Fate Fantastic* (DAW) and the recent *Better Off Undead* (DAW). Catch up with him at http://www.danielmhoyt.com

The FairWitch Project

Daniel M. Hoyt

"Why is it," my mother asked from my bedroom doorway, "that we have the only dead lawn in Cauldron Acres?" Even without seeing her, the sound of her flats tap-tap-tapping the hardwood floor in the hallway made it clear she was annoyed.

I shrugged from my prone position in bed, swabbing my face across a line of drool on my sweat-soaked pillow. Resisting the urge to wipe, I lay still, not bothering to open my eyes. It was my duty as a teenager to feign indifference.

"How is it even *possible*, young man? Isn't the mower bewitched to cut the lawn to precisely two inches every Thursday? Aren't the sprinklers bewitched to weed-and-feed every Tuesday evening? How, how, *how* can we *possibly* have such a crappy lawn?"

Shrugging again, I opened one eye and lazily glanced her way. "Maybe they're broken," I mumbled. That was the truth. I'd removed the spark plugs from the mower the previous fall, and cut the power to the sprinkler system months ago. Funny thing about bewitching machines from the mortal world: most witches expected the machines to be in working order to begin with, and only spelled the additional functions—like simple scheduling. If the machine didn't actually *work*, the additional spell wouldn't work, either.

Mom harrumphed and slammed my door shut. A minute later, I could hear her arguing with Dad in the living room. I figured I had maybe ten minutes until he'd come in for The Talk. Time to get up.

Grabbing my cell phone on the way to the shower across the hall from my bedroom, I thumbed the speed dial button for my best friend and fellow mortalo, Steve Lickens. "Slick? What you got going on today over in Spell Woods?"

"Not much," he said. "Painted a big pentagram in purple on the garage door last night. Half the neighbors are over trying to de-spell it."

I chuckled. Witches could be so dense sometimes, always looking for the spell or charm, with the obvious mortal answer staring them in the face. I think that's what attracted me most to the mortalos—not the "return to simple mortal times and values" that everyone thought, but the entertainment value of seeing clueless witches running around with their metaphorical pointy hats up their—

"You planning on living in that bathroom, *Junior*?" my dad's voice boomed outside the door, accompanied by barbaric pounding that rattled the hinges.

"Headcase," I mumbled into the cell. "Later, Slick." I snapped the cover closed, twisted the shower faucet on, clenched my teeth and called out, "In a minute."

Showering as slowly as I dared, I made sure to

lather up extra hard with my mom's flower-bouquet soap and baby shampoo. When I opened my bedroom door forty-five minutes later, baby blue towel wrapped around my hair and wearing a fluffy pink, floor-length bathrobe, I found Dad sitting on my bed, fuming. I shuffled in, wrapped in a cloud of violets and hyacinth.

Rolling his eyes and wrinkling his nose, he said, "*Must* you smell so much like a girl, Marvin?"

Ah, the official start of The Talk. First Topic: *My Name*.

I turned my back on him to open my closet door and smiled. Mortalo 1, Dad 0. "I prefer Headcase, Dad." I grabbed some boxers and slipped them on under my robe.

"Not that Headcase doesn't suit you, but I distinctly remember naming you Marvin Denworth Case, Jr."

I pulled on cream-colored jeans and slipped off the robe, letting it heap on the floor. "I'm sure you did. But I still prefer Headcase."

"Is this another one of those mortalo things?" Mom said from the open doorway, sighed, and stepped in to retrieve my robe. "This silly name? Is it a mortalo name? *What* you see in mortal ways, I just don't understand. Witchcraft has made our lives so much *easier*!"

Pulling the towel off my head, I handed it to Mom so she could retreat to the safety of the doorway. The towel had already served its purpose, which was to confound Dad. My short blond hair would be dry by now, anyway. I selected a bright red polo and slipped it on.

"Maybe it's *too* easy, Jenny," said my dad, no doubt

leaning on my nightstand as he struggled up from my bed. "Maybe we've done him a disservice by giving him so much." He stomped to the doorway.

Topic Number Two of The Talk: *What Went Wrong?*

"Hey, look," I said, turning to face my parents in the doorway. "I know we still haven't covered Topics Three and Four of The Talk—*What Do You Want From Us?* and *Grounded for Life!*—no, wait, that's Topic Five; Four is *Why Aren't You More Like Your Brother?* Anyway, the point is, I've got stuff to do. Later."

I pushed between them, ignoring their startled, open-mouthed stares, and headed for the front door.

"Yo, Headcase," String Cheese called out to me from one of the swings at the elementary school playground. "Heard you got a sick lawn this year." Behind him, Slick laughed and launched himself face-down into an open swing, Superman style.

"In all senses of the word, yeah," I yelled back, took a deep breath of asphalt fumes and jogged over to them.

Most of the playground was empty, but there were a few other mortalos hanging out, two guys on the monkey bars and six or seven girls sitting in the grass over by the soccer field. Ironically, mortalos hated the malls because there were too many mortals there. Here, we could talk freely, without worrying about dropping the wrong words to the wrong people.

Mortals didn't know about witches. We lived in our own communities—like Cauldron Acres and Spell Woods—that had glamours cast over them in case any mortals wandered in. Costwold Acres and Fell Woods, for instance, both butted up to the same private golf course in the Fairway development, along with a half-dozen other neighborhoods, all of them mortal. Costwold and Fell looked just like Pennington Green to the mortals—smiling residents mowing and watering their perfect green lawns mid-morning on their assigned days. Without the glamour, though, they'd see that no witches pushed the mowers in Cauldron Acres and Spell Woods, only magic.

Grabbing the third swing, I plopped onto the rubberized slat-seat. "Took out the spark plugs last year. Can't schedule a rock very well."

"Nice," said Cheese. "Wish I'd thought of that."

"I set the height low," said Slick. "Practically scrapes the dirt on half the lawn, leaving big patches of bare earth. Got the old man buying a new mower every month, trying to figure it out."

Cheese snickered. "You two are *dangerous*, you know that?"

"I put the plugs back in before I came over," I said, casually. "Keeps 'em guessing if it works for a week every now and then. I'll break it again next Thursday."

Slick said, "You guys help me paint the garage tonight? I figure it'll drive 'em nuts trying to figure out which counter-spell worked, and why it took all night."

String Cheese perked up. "I'm in." He turned to me expectantly.

"Sure." I shrugged. "Why not?" Maybe by then I'd gather enough courage to broach the subject I'd been meaning to discuss for a while.

"Don't you think these pranks are getting a little old?" I asked between paint strokes on Slick's garage

that night. We were about two minutes from finish-
ing. "I mean, we've been mortalos for a couple years,
right? But what have we actually *done*? What's the
point?" I swathed on more paint.

Slick stopped dead and stared at me. "Are you serious? These things are *classic*. You should have seen
my pop's face when he saw the pentagram!"

"That's not what I mean. I know we've done stuff,
but I mean . . . what have we done that's, you know,
not just a stupid—"

Slick looked as though I'd just removed his kidney
and offered it to him as a snack.

"Forget it," I said. "I was just thinking."

Cheese brushed his final stroke and tossed the
paint brush into the trash bag we'd brought along to
cart away evidence. He stepped back, folded his arms
and nodded. "I think I see what Headcase means.
We need to step up. Do something they'll *remember*.
Something *big*."

That was definitely *not* what I meant.

Slick grinned and finished up his section of the door.
"Yeah. Something big. And I've got just the thing."
He tossed his brush in the trash bag. "Grab the paint,
Cheese. Head, get the trash bag. Let's do it!"

My stomach twisted a couple times and I froze.

"C'mon, Headcase, we've got to get moving if we
want to do this tonight." Slick hoisted the trash bag
and turned to go.

"Do *what*, Slick?"

Cheese snickered. "Who cares? Slick knows what
to do. Let's just do it."

I grimaced. "No. I want to know. What are you
planning?"

Slick put down the trash bag and turned around to face me. "You know how the glamour on the sign at the entrance to neighborhood makes it look like *Fell Woods* to the mortals?"

I nodded. "But you can't un-glamour it. And painting it won't be visible on the outside. It's just witches who'll see it, not mortals."

Slick smiled and jerked a thumb at the garage. "Yeah, like the pentagram. I know. Mortals couldn't see it."

"Then why the paint?" Cheese asked.

"Because," Slick said, "we're going to paint the *other* entrance signs—the ones that aren't glamoured."

"The ones to the mortal neighborhoods?" Cheese asked.

Slick nodded, grinning.

"Pentagram Green?" I asked, hopefully. "Charm Clubhouse, Batwing Hazard—that sort of thing?"

"No glamours on those," Cheese said, nodding vigorously, "so mortals'll see the paint. I like it!"

I had to admit, this had all the makings of a mortalo prank to be remembered. Maybe String Cheese was right; maybe my unrest was really rooted in the fact that we hadn't yet done anything *distinguishing*.

"I'm game," I said after a moment's pause. "Let's do it."

"We made the papers, Head." Cheese's voice boomed tinnily from my cell phone's micro-speaker before I got it to my ear. "Your pentagrams on the grass in front of the signs were a nice touch. Got the mortals all in a panic now, wondering if some kind of Satanic cult has moved in here. They're calling it the FairWitch Project."

"Hold on, I got another call." I flashed to Slick on call waiting, and switched to a three-way conference with String Cheese.

"I told you guys it'd be big, didn't I?" said Slick proudly. "The whole town's talking about it! We're gonna be famous!"

"Yeah!" said Cheese. "Famous!"

"Hold on," I said. "Nobody knows it was us. You want to *confess* to this? Just to get the credit?"

"Well, yeah," said Slick. "Not right now, of course, but after it blows over. Couple of weeks, probably, just to make sure none of the other mortalos lets it slip. Once the press is hooked on some other scandal, nobody'll care about who did this. We'll be safe then."

"Sounds great," Cheese said, a little too enthusiastically for my tastes. "Just say the word, and I'm there with you."

"Yeah," I said, secretly hoping that day would never come.

My bedroom door burst open. My father, panting, said, "They've caught . . . the FairWitch vandals . . . they're Unipagan Church members . . . damned wannabe witches . . . want to be a recognized religion." He closed the door.

"This just in," said the pretty blonde anchorwoman on News 6 at 7. "Houghton County school officials have just revealed incontrovertible proof that witchcraft does indeed exist. You may recall, the FairWitch Project vandals, as they call themselves, brought this issue to the public eye just two days ago when they relabeled most of the neighborhood entrance signs in the Fairway development northeast of town with . . . *witchy* names. All but two of them, Costwold Acres and Fell Woods, now sport names like Pentagram Green and Toadstool Drive."

"And pentagrams, Stephanie," her co-anchor added, off-screen.

"And pentagrams," Stephanie the news anchor repeated, chuckling. "Thank you, David. The Fair-Witch Project, they said, was a crucial part in raising the awareness of our government's refusal to grant them official church status. The Unipagan Church has been operating in the red for several years now, and in an exclusive interview obtained by this reporter yesterday, one of the high ranking church officials there—who asked to remain anonymous for fear of retaliation from rival church members outraged at the vandalism—admitted that the only thing keeping them from operating in the black is the church's tax bill. This official speculated that some church members privy to this information simply may have gotten tired of waiting and decided to take action on their own. The official stressed that this was *not* an authorized operation."

"So, it was just some kids goofing around, then, Stephanie?" David asked, off-camera again.

"That's what you'd think, David," said Stephanie. "But, no, that doesn't seem to be the case. School officials at Fairway High brought in a team of spectral analysts from a company called Ghost Hunters yesterday. Tom Shadow-Walker, from Ghost Hunters, is here with us to explain. Tom?"

"Thank you, Stephanie." The camera panned over to a gray-haired man in a crisp black business suit, white shirt and black tie. "Ghost Hunters has been in the area for about seven years now, investigating haunted hotels and houses. We've developed some state of the art equipment specifically geared for measuring spectral wavelengths commonly used by spirits that have crossed over. We've had great success with this equipment in recent years."

"And it was this new technique that proved the haunting at the Sanford Hotel last year, isn't that right?"

"Yes, it was, Stephanie. We're the first operation of this kind to be certified by a major industry. Even the science community is taking notice."

David muffled an off-screen chuckle, and Tom glanced at him briefly just before his cheeks flushed slightly. He kept smiling and said nothing.

Stephanie didn't miss a beat. "And you found something interesting at the school yesterday, correct?"

"Yes," Tom said, straightening his tie. "We were in the area on another job, and noticed an incredible amount of spectral waves in a certain range emanating from somewhere close by. We identified the source as the newly remodeled high school and contacted school officials. We went into the property and located a wall at the end of a corridor that was just bursting with spectral wave activity in the frequency used by crossed-over spirits. There's just a fenced-in empty field on the other side. Nobody uses it; the maintenance staff didn't even remember keeping it up, although it was clearly maintained."

"And that's when you found proof of witchcraft, right? Folks, we've got some truly amazing video footage here to show you. Tom, tell us what's happening here."

A split-screen view appeared, outside Fairway High on the right, a blank wall on the left. Both views had running digital clocks in their lower right corners, with identical times.

"Hey, I know those places!" David said off-camera.

"Yes," said Stephanie coolly, "so do I."

"We keep a video record," said Tom, "of all our operations with a high-speed camera, usually for later review. Sometimes the spectral phenomenon only lasts for a fraction of a second, so we want to capture as much detail as possible. You can see on the left side where one of our investigators, Candy, is trying to locate the source of the interesting spectral waves. She's locked onto what she thinks is the source, she's leaving the room now to remotely bombard it with a short burst of xenon radiation—it can burn or blind her if she's still in the room. The xenon reacts with this particular spectral frequency to move normally invisible waves into the visible spectrum so our cameras can capture it more easily. But here, watch what happens."

On-screen, the wall in the left view disappeared, revealing an extended hallway with about a dozen doors identical to the classroom doors in the foreground. Simultaneously, a two-story building appeared in the right view, attached to the school. There was no break in the video, and both view clocks continued ticking away identical times.

"Holy smoke!" barked David off-camera. "Did you see that?"

"As near as we can tell, there was a glamour in place, and we broke it," Tom said triumphantly.

"A glamour?" Stephanie asked calmly.

"It's something witches do to make us see something other than what's there. They can cast one of these glamours on pretty much anything, and make us see whatever they want."

"So that's it, folks," said Stephanie. "Proof that witchcraft exists. The question remains: Should it be allowed?"

"They caught the *real* FairWitch vandals this time," Dad said from my doorway. "It's the Society for Everyday Witchcraft. They say the Unipagans are just trying to capitalize on the press the FairWitch Project's been getting over the last week. The SEW produced documents dated a month ago showing their official plan for FairWitch-like vandalism in communities all over the country. They say this was just supposed to be the first, but they don't need to do any more, now that they've got national coverage for their cause." He closed the door.

I flipped open my cell, punched in Slick first, then conferenced in String Cheese. "This is not good," I said. "That chick on News 6 pointed out that our two neighborhoods weren't vandalized, and a couple days ago that stupid Ghost Hunter guy sent a crew over here. They xenoned the glamour and then drove down the block with cameras going! They stopped in front of our house and zoomed in on the dead lawn. I'm so screwed."

"My pop's hiding in the house," Slick said. "People at work know where he lives. He told them he's not a witch, but they hassled him so much his boss told him to take some time off. Mom's talking about moving. She thinks it's not safe any more."

"Where would you go?" Cheese said, with startling clarity. "Glamours have been cracking all over the world. There's nowhere to hide. My folks have been working with some of the others to come up with a xenon-proof glamour. They say it's the best they can do."

"Mortals will forget," I said. "They always do."

"Yeah," said Slick, "but not until they've burned a few of us at the stake."

"Maybe. But, still, what are we going to *do*? We started this mess; we need to do *something* about it."

"It's spun out of control, Head, gone nationwide. What can we do now? Tell everyone it's just a prank?"

"Cop to it *now*?" yelled Slick. "I don't think so! They'll crucify us!"

"I need a walk," I said. "Can't think straight. Playground, ten minutes."

On the way, I passed by a guy—he looked familiar, but when he glanced up and recognized me, he looked down quickly and changed course slightly away from me. I could tell he was using an invisible glamour. I moved to intercept. About three feet away from him, he noticed me and looked up, startled. "Get away from me," he said sharply and continued on. "It's not safe for us to be seen together."

I headed back to the playground and found Slick and Cheese by the swings, like normal. The rest of the playground was deserted.

"That guy, Jason, was over by the monkey bars," Cheese said. "Saw us coming and took off. You see him?"

Looking back, I realized where I'd seen the guy terrified to be seen with me. "I think so. Didn't want to be seen with me. Had an invisibility glamour."

Slick shook his head grimly. "Figures. Weekend mortalo, that one. First sign of trouble and he's wearing a glamour."

"You gotta admit," Cheese said, "it's still effective for moving targets. They can't xenon bomb us if they don't know where we are. Too dangerous to scatter shoot xenon *everywhere*."

"True," I said, and an idea struck me. "But maybe we can use the glamour to help us. We're going to need some help."

"Look around, Head," Slick said. "The other mortalos are gone, hiding. I've heard it's like this everywhere. Who's going to help us?"

"I was thinking of asking our parents," I said and grinned.

"The Salem Revolution is behind it all," Dad said when the three of us walked in. "They said the SEW faked those documents. They aired a *video* of one of their council meetings from last *year*, talking about their Witch Emanicipation Plan."

I sighed. "It's not a revolution, Dad."

"Phase One was a major media event to start the revolution—what became the FairWitch Project—they even claim they suggested the name to the media."

"It was us, Dad."

"Phase Two was the disclosure of withcraft. Turns out one of their members is one of the founders of Ghost Hunters, and she admit— What?"

"It was us. We did it. *We* painted the signs. I did the pentagrams myself."

Dad stared. "What? What about the Lickens' garage door? Bob said there were some suspicious characters lurking around that night, and then the purple pentagram appeared."

Slick rolled his eyes. "I painted the pentagram the *previous* night. *We* painted over it that night, that's all. There was never any spell."

Dad narrowed his eyes. "Is this one of those mortalo things again?"

"No," I said. "And you don't have to worry about that any more. I don't think anybody's going to want to go mortalo for a while."

"They were just pranks, Mr. Case," Cheese said. "Like the dead lawn. We were just having fun."

"The lawn?" Dad said, clearly confused.

"I broke the mower and the sprinkler. The spells you put on them can't work on broken machines."

"You broke the machines?" Dad's voice rose. "On purpose? Why? Why would you do something like that?"

Mom ran in when she heard the yelling. "Marv? What's going on?"

By this time, Dad was hyperventilating. "Junior . . . *sabotaged* . . . the mower and sprinkler!"

Mom glared at me. "Is this true, Marvin?"

I glanced at my friends. I never told them my real name. Slick choked on his giggling; Cheese mouthed, "Marvin," and pantomimed gagging himself on his finger.

"Headcase," I mumbled. To my mother, I said, loudly, "Could we postpone the *Grounded for Life* part of The Talk until later, please? We need your help to fix this."

"I'm listening, young man," Mom said. "What did you have in mind?"

✧   ✧   ✧

"We have some special guests tonight, folks," Stephanie the news anchor said. "We have three local boys and their parents here, and *they* claim to be the brains behind the FairWitch Project. Isn't that right, boys?"

"Yes, ma'am," I said. "It was all Sli— Steve's idea."

"Why don't you introduce yourselves," Stephanie prompted.

We did, and Slick gave her the short version: what mortalos were, how we'd been pranking our parents, and how we wanted to do something we'd be remembered for.

Stephanie the news anchor laughed. So did David the sidekick. "Really, boys. Do you really expect us to believe you? The Salem Revolution's evidence is *very* convincing, and you're just three teenagers."

Cheese smiled. "Gosh, Miss Stephanie," he said innocently, "I didn't know *you* could lose your cool. I thought Mr. David was the buffoon." Cheese could be amazingly insightful when he wanted to be.

David the co-anchor stopped laughing immediately.

Stephanie's smile dropped momentarily, then returned at the forefront of a forced chuckle. "How sweet."

"I think what my friend Ross meant," I said quickly, "was that while we certainly realize it sounds less glamorous—if you'll excuse my pun—that this whole thing was just a teenage prank gone awry, it's the truth."

"Yeah," said Slick, "how hard do you think it is to manufacture a few memos and a video and claim credit?"

Stephanie raised an eyebrow. "And what's your evidence?"

"Now see here, Miss," Dad said sharply and pointed at her accusingly. "Are you doubting my son?"

"It's all right, Dad," I said and pushed his arm down. "We don't have any evidence, ma'am."

"Which is why you should believe us," Cheese said.

Everyone turned to stare at him.

Cheese leaned forward. "If we *had* evidence, would you doubt its veracity?"

"Of course," Stephanie said. "We've already had three groups claim responsibility with manufactured evidence."

"Exactly," Cheese said triumphantly, and sat back in his chair.

There was about ten seconds of silence. Even Stephanie didn't know what to say.

Cheese rolled his eyes. "Why would three teenagers with no evidence claim responsibility if it weren't true?"

"For the fame?" Stephanie said slowly. "Just like the others?" She looked at Slick. "Didn't you say you wanted to do a prank big enough for recognition?"

"Yes we did, ma'am," Slick said. "And I think we managed that, don't you?"

Stephanie looked unconvinced, but Slick's pop chimed in before she could respond. "Miss? It really doesn't matter if they're telling the truth or not. The point is that the situation has gotten completely out of control, and we've got a proposition to solve it."

Stephanie blinked, then turned to the front camera. "There you have it, folks. A way to fix the mess that is the FairWitch Project. We'll see what that is when we come back."

The director, standing by the camera, silently counted off three fingers, then said aloud, "Clear. You've got three minutes."

Stephanie the nice news anchor rounded on Slick's pop, eyes flaring. "What the hell is this? You never said anything about any proposition, just confessions."

"Would you have had us on if we had told you?" Mrs. String Cheese's Mom asked.

David chuckled. "Of course not. It's not good news copy."

Mom folded her arms. "*This* is. Trust me."

"Do you seriously think," Stephanie said with an air of strained patience, "that I'm going to put you back on without knowing what you plan to say? Not likely!"

"Look, lady," Dad said in a low voice through clenched teeth, leaning over so that his face was inches from hers. "Witches are *real*, and we're not going away. We've hidden our power for centuries, so you mortals wouldn't be scared and try to pull another Salem, but now that you know about us, we need to change the rules. You can fear us because we're different, or you can embrace those differences and let us help you improve your quality of life—it's your choice. All we want is to live our lives without fear of persecution, and you can help us do that. We just want peace, and we think we know how to make it happen. Make no mistake about this: we'll turn you into a frog on live TV, if necessary, but we *will* have our say, whether you like it or not."

Stephanie blanched.

Dad leaned back and straightened his tie.

"Thirty seconds and we're live," the director called out.

"Security!" Stephanie yelled. "Get them out of here *now*!"

The next few seconds never made it on the air at News 6, but they made quite an impression on the rest of the world once the footage leaked. The short version was: two beefy security guys run in with guns drawn, two guns clatter to the ground in front of the news desk, two frogs jump across Stephanie's desk, Stephanie the news anchor screams and falls backward in her chair, David the sidekick jumps up and bolts off-camera, two security guys materialize where frogs were in mid-jump, headed for the floor, general pandemonium ensues, director yells, "Roll commercial!"

"You're witches, right?" the slim redheaded kid said without preamble, walking up to us at the swings on the playground.

Slick nodded. Cheese and I said, "Yeah," in unison.

"I thought so. We're over in Turnstile Drive, and we got a mower spell from some guys going door-to-door, but it didn't work. We need it fixed. Everyone says go to the guys at the swings."

"Yeah," Cheese said. "Witch Plus, That's Us."

"Sounds like you went with one of the fly-by-nights," Slick said, shaking his head. "Poor sap. They weren't Better Witchcraft Bureau certified, right?"

The redhead shook his head and looked down. "But they were really cheap!"

I put my arm around the kid's skinny shoulder. "We hear it all the time. You went cheap; now you want quality. Let me tell you about us. We're the real deal. BWB certified and everything. But we're not just ordinary witches. Any decent BWB witch can do a spell for you. Auto-wash your car, auto-mow your lawn, that sort of thing. We're gonna do that for you, sure, but for just a little more than our competition, we're gonna make your machines work, too, so that the spells work. That's our commitment to you, and that's why everyone says come to us, even though we cost a little more. We'll take care of you."

I took the kid's information and set up an appointment, then text-messaged it to my dad so he could get a crew out there pronto.

Dad had been right about changing the rules, and led the way personally. After helping form the BWB, Witch Plus was the very first BWB-certified company *anywhere*, and now that we're franchising out, our operations are appearing in neighborhoods all over the world like popcorn. Slick's mom and pop quit their jobs and Dad gave them a franchise at no charge. Cheese's folks, too, since we were all there from the start.

It's funny—despite Dad's complaints just a couple months ago, he's the *primo* mortalo of witching now.

And our lawn is *always* nice and green.

Julia S. Mandala is a reformed lawyer who does penance by writing fantasy and science fiction. Her works appear in *The Four Redheads of the Apocalypse*, *Dracula's Lawyer*, *International House of Bubbas*, *Houston, We've Got Bubbas*, and *Flush Fiction*, available from Yard Dog Press, in *The Four Redheads: Apocalypse Now!* and *House of Doors*, coming soon from YDP, and in *Best of the Bubbas* from BenBella Books. Her other stories have appeared in *The Mammoth Book of Comic Fantasy II*, *MZB's Fantasy Magazine* and *Adventures of Sword & Sorcery*. She is a scuba diver, underwater photographer and belly dancer.

Valley Witch

Julia S. Mandala

Drake opened the door to the high school counselor's office. His mother flounced past him in a miniskirt and camisole. The Dread Witch Tiffany Owens of Beverly Hills currently possessed the body of a fifteen-year-old girl—magic only witches could do, and then only for themselves. Drake wished Tiffany hadn't chosen someone his age for her disguise. Seeing his mother in a nubile, scantily clad body made him distinctly uncomfortable.

The counselor, a round-cheeked woman with spectacles, looked up from the papers on her desk. "Hello, Carmen. And this young man must be Nigel Churchill, the new exchange student."

"Huh?" Drake said, then grunted as Tiffany slammed her elbow into his ribs. "Uh, yes."

"I'm Mrs. Jones," the woman said.

"What a rare and beautiful name," Drake said.

Mrs. Jones smiled slyly. "Aren't you the charming one!"

Tiffany blinked in surprise, then surveyed her son critically. "Charming? I'm, like, so sure. *Not!*" Tiffany lowered her voice. "'Nigel,' can't you slouch even a little? It looks like that stick up your butt goes clear into your skull."

Over the past three days on the run, a revelation had struck Drake. While his mother might or might not love him, she most definitely didn't *like* him.

"My parents," Drake said, giving Tiffany a resentful glare, "paid thousands of ducats to send me to a school where slovenly behavior was punished by beating with a thumb-thick rod."

"That's child abuse!" Mrs. Jones exclaimed. "You should report that school to the authorities."

"As if," Drake muttered, using one of Tiffany's favorite phrases.

Tiffany rolled her eyes. "Don't *even* go there. You just sound like even more of a total dork."

Mrs. Jones wrinkled her forehead. "You said 'ducats.' Don't they use pounds in England?"

Drake winced even before Tiffany cast him a scornful look. In less than five sentences, he had already made a foolish error that could ruin their disguise.

Tiffany looked at the large wall clock, then raised her hands to her cheeks. "Ohmygawd! If we don't, like, hurry, we'll totally be late for first period."

Late periods were bad. Not being from this dimension, Drake wasn't sure why, but he'd overheard Tiffany saying that to her handmaiden once.

"Let's print your schedule, Nigel," Mrs. Jones said, her fingers dancing over a board covered with letters and numbers.

Tiffany had used her magic to conjure faked

transcripts and to assure that "Nigel" was in the same classes as "Carmen."

Mrs. Jones hmmed. "Nigel Churchill. Any relation to . . ." She trailed off as though Drake should know the last word.

"No way," Tiffany said, then whispered to Drake, "I like, you know, never thought people would still remember that dude. He's been dead for*ever*."

"What dude?" Drake asked, but his mother ignored him.

"Is it retro '80s day, Carmen?" Mrs. Jones asked. At Tiffany's puzzled look, the secretary said, "I just assumed, since you're talking like a valley girl."

"Bitch," Tiffany said under her breath, then louder, "It's just, like, you know, a phase that's gotten into me."

His mother had been going through that "phase" all of Drake's life. The Dread Witch Tiffany was the most powerful witch in Drake's home dimension of Zirconia, and she felt no pressure to conform.

"Everything is in order—Oh, wait." Mrs. Jones chuckled. "Someone put Nigel in girl's gymnastics. That won't do."

Drake didn't really care what courses the school assigned him. He had no desire to attend Olathe High. It had no magic courses of any sort. Every day Drake spent away from Evil Academy, he fell farther behind in his sorcerous studies.

His mother had dragged Drake away from boarding school after Scolon the Scabrous sent henchmen to kidnap Drake. The evil sorcerer's plot came within a hair of succeeding, before the dean, a demon of significant powers, blasted Scolon's henchmen to cinders. Tiffany had thought it best to take Drake into hiding until Drake's father and older brothers dealt with the rival sorcerer. Spells made with the body parts of relatives rendered the victims particularly vulnerable, and Drake's parents were taking no chances. Having no desire to be chopped into spell components, Drake had only put up a token fuss. After a series of portal hops to throw off any pursuit, Tiffany and Drake had materialized in her home dimension, where she knew they could blend in and disappear until it was safe.

Drake wasn't so sure.

"Can you just, like, put Nigel in some gym class for dudes, like dodge ball?" Tiffany asked.

"Well, Carmen, I'm so pleased to see you taking an interest in helping someone else," Mrs. Jones said. "You're really growing into a mature young woman."

"Mature! Gag me with a spoon!" Tiffany's face screwed into a grimace. "That is like, the meanest thing anyone's ever said to me."

Mrs. Jones's smile stiffened. "You should learn to take a compliment gracefully."

"What*ever*," Tiffany said with a dismissive wave. "So what classes are open during the period I have gymnastics?"

"Botany, political science, auto shop, remedial sex education—"

"No way!" Tiffany exclaimed.

"Way," Mrs. Jones said gamely. "It's for pregnant girls, jocks and anyone who admits to contracting V.D."

"I've never taken a remedial class for anything," Drake said, seizing on the one concept he understood. The flood of strange terms left him dazed. It *sounded* like the same language he spoke, yet he only understood half of it—the half that was participles and pronouns.

"Have you ever had sex-ed, Nigel?" Mrs. Jones asked.

Drake's face went hot.

"The British totally don't teach that stuff in school," Tiffany said.

"Then, we'll put Nigel in remedial sexual education," Mrs. Jones said. "I think he'll find it beneficial."

After Drake and Tiffany left the office, she looked over Drake's printed class schedule. "Trig, physics, *glee* club? This is the worst . . . schedule . . . *ever*!" Tiffany looked over the body she occupied. "You'd think someone with such a bitchin' bod would take classes that matter, like cheerleading and drama. Good acting will get you out of a lot of sketchy situations."

Drake fidgeted in the unfamiliar fitted clothing— jeans, a T-shirt and a striped shirt which for some reason he wasn't allowed to button or tuck. The sneakers, at least, were far more comfortable than the slippers that boys of noble birth wore.

"You're quite certain *this* is what young men wear in this dimension?" Drake asked.

"I'm like *totally* certain no one in Olathe, Kansas says 'quite certain,'" Tiffany said. "Anyway, that's what the rad dudes are wearing on the boob tube."

She must have been right, because the glances Drake received from several passing girls held speculative interest rather than scorn. *Every* young man that passed ogled his mother's half-clothed body. Drake resisted the urge to smack the lust off their faces, since he and his mother were trying to be inconspicuous. He suspected Carmen didn't usually wear such skimpy clothing. After looking in Carmen's wardrobe, Tiffany had bewitched Carmen's mother into giving her a "platinum card," which in this world was treated more like gold.

"Okay, first period is trig," Tiffany said, ignoring the goggle-eyed boys. Then again, she was used to that kind of attention. "Trig is, like, a bogus kind of math."

Drake's stomach twisted into a knot. "I don't know 'trig.'"

"Don't have a cow," Tiffany said. "Teachers always cut the new kids some slack. If anyone looks at you funny, just tell them you're British. That should totally explain why you seem like an airhead."

Drake's worries eased when the trig teacher didn't so much as address a question to him, merely gave him a textbook and the next assignment. When the same thing happened in physics class, Drake felt secure in leaving Tiffany to go to remedial sex education.

She pointed to double doors marked "Gymnasium." "If, like, *anything* sketchy happens, you bug out to the gym and find me. Don't try to take on Scolon's men yourself."

Drake rolled his eyes.

"I'm majorly serious, young man. For real. If you think you can take on grown sorcerers with years of spell-casting experience, you're trippin', dude."

"I think I can manage to keep my feet," Drake said drily.

"Dork," Tiffany muttered, then headed into the gym.

Drake gritted his teeth. She treated him like a child. He doubted his mother knew he had the best grades in his year and was in advanced studies. But

Drake didn't push himself in hopes of receiving his parents' approval—to attain that, his parents would have to notice Drake's existence other than during holidays and crises. He pushed himself so that one day he could subjugate a land of his own and have hordes of evil minions doing his bidding.

Drake found the classroom right as the bell rang. Six pregnant girls, twenty burly young men, and eight other bored-looking teens were already seated. Drake took a desk at the back and slouched down. This class might be the only one that wasn't a waste of his time. He knew what sex was, but judging from the girl's disappointed expression the one time he'd stolen a kiss, he could use some additional knowledge. Actually, her disappointment hadn't bothered him nearly as much as her pity.

A man in beige pants and a knit shirt strode in. "All right, everyone, settle down." His gaze locked on Drake. "I see we have a new inmate."

"I'm Nigel Churchill, from England," Drake said.

"Any relation to . . ."

"No way," Drake said, parroting his mother's answer for lack of a better one.

"I'm Coach Smith," the teacher said.

"Coach. What an unusual name."

The class laughed as though Drake had made a clever jest.

"Well, Nigel," Coach Smith said cheerily. "Let's see what you know."

"What?" A heated flush crept up Drake's neck to his cheeks. The only things Drake had heard about sex came from the highly suspect bragging of upperclassmen at Evil Academy.

"Okay, Nigel, you're on a date," Coach Smith said. "The girl is smokin' hot and willing. You don't have a condom. What do you do?" He gave Drake a meaningful stare. "What do you *do*?"

The disoriented feeling swept across Drake again. "Throw a wet blanket over her to douse the fire?"

The class laughed again, and not in a nice way. "What a dumbass," one burly boy whispered to another.

"Now, now," Coach Smith said, clapping his hands for silence. "While Nigel may be clowning around, at least his answer showed concern for the young lady."

Several of the pregnant girls smiled at Drake, and a few boys shifted in their seats.

"Okay, how about this, Nigel?" Coach Smith said. "Your girlfriend has herpes, but she's not currently having an outbreak. Is it safe to have sex with her?"

A girl smirked and raised her hand.

"Yes, Hannah?"

"Does he have a condom?" she asked, then giggled.

"No, but assume she's on the Pill," Coach Smith said. "So, Nigel, is it safe sex?"

"No?" Drake ventured.

"Are you guessing, Nigel?"

"Yes, sir." Drake bowed his head and braced himself. Getting caught guessing at Evil Academy carried painful consequences. The consequences for lying about guessing were even more severe. The school motto was, "Nothing encourages learning like a good whack on the head."

"At least you erred on the side of caution, which is what you should always do in a sexual situation," Coach Smith said. "And, as it happens, you guessed correctly. It is *not* safe. You get a prize." He pulled a small square package from his desk drawer and threw it to Drake. Printed on the crinkly plastic wrapping was the word "Trojan." Drake felt a flexible, raised circle inside.

His classmates snickered. "Jeez, he really is a dumbass," another boy said, loud enough for Drake to hear.

"Thank you, sir," Drake said, hastily stuffing the Trojan in his backpack, beside his new books, his wand and the bottle of animation potion he had brewed at prep school.

After remedial sex education, Drake was actually relieved to find his mother outside the classroom.

"How'd it go?" she asked, giving him a teasing grin. "Learn anything?"

"I won a prize." Drake dug out the Trojan.

"Ohmygawd! Like, high school has totally changed." Looking around in mortification, Tiffany snatched the Trojan and stuffed it into his backpack again. "Don't be waving that around. I mean, barf me out!"

Drake shrugged off his mother's histrionics. He had to admit—at times, he didn't like her much either. "The schedule says we have lunch now."

"Don't get all excited," Tiffany said. "High school cafeterias have the worst . . . food . . . *ever.*"

Drake snorted. "You don't have to tell *me* that. I'm used to eating three meals a day at a prep school dining hall."

The array of foreign foods in the cafeteria left Drake as mystified as the rest of the day had. At Evil Academy, one ate what the troll chef cooked. It didn't pay to insult a troll, especially one adept at using large knives.

Tiffany pushed Drake in the back. "Just pick something, you spaz."

"What do you think I'd like?" Drake asked.

"It all sucks," Tiffany said, earning a glare from a cafeteria worker sporting plastic gloves.

Drake nodded glumly. "The food must be bad if it isn't even safe to touch."

"Hey, we only have thirty minutes for lunch, asshole," someone shouted.

"He'll have pizza," Tiffany said. At Drake's quizzical look, she said, "It's flatbread and cheese. They can't screw that up too bad."

The dried-out square slapped onto his shiny metal tray belied his mother's claim. Herding him along, Tiffany added a carton labeled 'milk' to Drake's tray.

"It, like, builds strong bones and teeth," Tiffany said.

Drake smirked. "I'm stunned that you care."

"You think I want a toothless hunchback for a son? Puh-*leez*!"

As they headed toward long tables and plastic chairs, two girls waved.

"Carmen!" one shouted. "Come sit with us! And bring your cute friend."

Tiffany looked askance at Drake. "Is everyone here, like, totally lacking in standards?"

"Maybe to girls *under* the age of thirty, I'm handsome," Drake said.

Tiffany cast him a scorching glare. "What-*ever*!" She stomped toward the two girls who had waved.

Drake started to follow, but stopped when a strange man appeared in the nearest cafeteria doorway. Between his black robes, the evil smirk and the wand aimed at Tiffany's back, Drake surmised the man was one of

Scolon's sorcerers. The robed man spoke an incantation for casting a magic bolt. Drake lunged and thrust out the metal tray, sending his pizza and milk flying. The bolt deflected off the metal surface, hitting the ceiling and sending down a shower of dust. A shock jolted through Drake. He fell, twitching, onto his pizza, which had landed cheese-side up. *Idiot,* he berated himself. Metal didn't just reflect magic; it conducted it. He had received enough of the deadly bolt's energy to leave him helpless.

Tiffany whirled and whipped a wand from her purse. "Clean the tables," she incanted. Witches knew lots of housekeeping spells. Food, trays, cups, and plasticware rose into the air. Tiffany flicked her wrist and everything went flying at the sorcerer. He threw himself to the floor, but two more sorcerers rounded the corner in time to be pelted with half-eaten food, soda cans, milk cartons, sporks and metal trays. Tiffany levitated a chair and sent it flying. It knocked one food-blinded sorcerer across the hall and through a plate-glass window.

Tiffany pumped her fist. "Suh-WEET!"

Students screamed and stumbled over chairs and each other toward the cafeteria's other exit. Drake's muscles still twitched from the magic shock. He could only flounder and hope no one stepped on him. A sneaker quickly crushed that hope—and Drake's toes.

"All right, you douche bags," Tiffany said, advancing on the two remaining sorcerers. "I'm *so* going postal on your asses."

The sorcerer on the floor gripped an amulet around his neck and muttered an incantation. A protective shield glowed to life around him. He stood, a

chuckle rumbling in his throat. Drake felt a stab of
envy. Such a laugh would earn perfect marks in Evil
Mannerisms class.

The Dread Witch Tiffany glared at the sorcerer.
"Don't think that protection spell will save you, Scolon. No way some barf bag threatens my little dude
and walks. So, like, what did Drake do that gave us
away?"

Drake wanted to protest, but managed only a feeble
growl.

"It wasn't him, my dear," Scolon said, giving Tiffany
a smug smile. "It was you."

"*Me?*" Tiffany huffed. "As if."

"I created a spell that homed in on your outmoded
speech patterns," Scolon said. "After we scared the
wits out of a middle-aged waitress in San Fernando
Valley, it led us straight to you."

Tiffany's eyes narrowed. She turned her wand on
a table. "Move it!"

The table scuttled forward like a flat-topped cock-
roach. It bounced off Scolon's protective shield, swung
into the remaining food-covered sorcerer, then squashed
him against the cinder block wall.

Scolon the Scabrous pulled a different amulet from
his robe pocket. Drake tried to shout a warning, but
his thick tongue defeated him.

A determined scowl on her borrowed face, Tiffany drew back her wand. Before she could speak an
incantation, Scolon said, "Ice queen."

"Douche—" Tiffany didn't get to finish her epithet
as the amulet's pre-made spell kicked in. Ice spread
across her skin and frosted her hair and clothes,
freezing her like a statue.

"By the Darkness," Drake swore, then realized his voice had returned. His hands still trembled and his brain was too muddled to use his wand. When Scolon used the second amulet it canceled the protection amulet's spell, a weakness of amulets, but Drake couldn't take advantage—

The animation potion! Drake groped in his backpack, pushing aside the fat physics book. His fingers wrapped around the stoppered potion bottle.

Scolon paused to admire his frozen handiwork, then broke off a chunk of Tiffany/Carmen's frozen hair. At least someone was having a good time.

Drake felt the crinkle of plastic. He clamped the Trojan against the potion bottle with his fingers, then extracted both from the backpack. He set down the potion and tore open the Trojan's plastic wrapper. A rolled rubber tube dropped into his palm.

Scolon started toward Drake, his eyes gleaming with amusement. "What sort of evil sorcerer throws himself in the path of a lightning bolt meant for another? I never thought I'd see the Dread Witch Tiffany's son acting like an idiot hero."

Scolon had a point. Pushing aside shame, Drake unstoppered the bottle and poured potion on the rubber tube. *"Virat!"* he intoned.

The rubber tube unrolled on its own, then air rushed in. The tube grew longer and fatter. For some reason, Drake felt suddenly stronger and more manly.

Scolon stared at the burgeoning tube. "You must be joking." He raised his wand. "Now I will stun you, take you back to my lair and cut you into spell components—"

The Trojan bent in the middle, then whipped

forward, striking Scolon's hand. His wand clattered
to the floor.

From under a lunchroom table, a boy yelled, "Wow,
Trojans really *are* strong!"

The ice around Tiffany was melting, but not fast
enough.

Drake willed the rubber tube to wind around Scolon's
right wrist. When Scolon reached to pull it free, the rest
of it whipped around his left wrist. The ends stretched
and wrapped around the sorcerer's waist, binding his
hands to his body.

Scolon smiled at Drake. "Fairly impressive for one
of your tender years."

"You talk too much." Drake's instructors always
harped on how that was a common weakness among
villains.

"Perhaps so, my dear boy, but *you* have missed
one important fact," Scolon said, casting an assessing
glance at the water dripping off Tiffany.

"What fact is that?" Drake asked, his fingers curling loosely around his wand, though he wasn't sure
whether his wits had recovered enough to use it.

"The condom you used was lubricated." Scolon
shimmied his wrists free.

"Why in the Nine Hells would anyone lubricate a
rubber tube?" Drake demanded in frustration.

"Why, for *her* pleasure, of course." Scolon laughed
until he grabbed his sides. "Delightful. What a pity
I can't keep you alive for my amusement, but you're
far more useful in pieces."

Tiffany's little finger wiggled. Drake had to stall.

"Of all four sons, why did you choose me?" he
asked.

"You're the most powerful, and not as well-trained as your older brothers—and you're much taller than your younger brother, so you'll provide a greater quantity of components." Scolon readied his wand like a conductor's baton. "Now, dear boy, say farewell to your dear, frozen mother—"

Shattering ice flew in all directions. "Smallify!" Tiffany shouted. Red light shot from her wand.

Scolon turned in surprise. The light engulfed him, and he shrank to the size of a thumb.

As Scolon started a reversal incantation, Drake pulled out his physics book. It was so heavy in his weakened fingers that it dropped onto Scolon of its own accord. Not that Drake hadn't *intended* to squash the smug bastard. After second period, Drake now knew the book had fallen because a sorcerer named Newton invented a spell called gravity . . . or something like that.

Tiffany brushed dripping water and ice chips from her arms, then set her toe on the book and ground down with her full weight. *"That's* for breaking my hair, barf bag!"

Drake pulled himself into a chair, the effort leaving him gasping.

Tiffany gave her son a rare hug. "Hey, you were, like, awesome."

"Thanks—I think."

"Since we're on Earth, you want to, like, go hang at the mall or catch a flick?" Tiffany asked.

Drake wasn't sure what either option entailed, but he'd had enough excitement for one day. "I think I'd just like to get back to the academy."

Tiffany grinned and mussed Drake's hair. "Dork."

Jody Lynn Nye lists her main career activity as "spoiling cats." She lives northwest of Chicago with two of the above and her husband, author and packager Bill Fawcett. She has published more than thirty-five books, including six contemporary fantasies, four SF novels, four novels in collaboration with Anne McCaffrey, including *The Ship Who Won*; edited a humorous anthology about mothers, *Don't Forget Your Spacesuit, Dear!*; and written over a hundred short stories. Her latest books are *An Unexpected Apprentice* (TOR Books), and *Myth-Chief*, co-written with Robert Asprin (Wildside Press). And, yes, she does believe in magic.

There's No "I" in "Coven"

Jody Lynn Nye

The whining from the rear seat of the station wagon was enough to make any mother lose her equilibrium. Ceridwen Locke Shapiro leveled one baleful eye on her two children by way of the rearview mirror.

"If I have to pull this vehicle over, you two will lose privileges for a week!" she exclaimed.

"Mom, he's leaning over onto my side!" wailed Angelica, a stony-faced nine-year-old who was looking as unlike her name as possible at that moment.

"Mom, her homunculus is trying to eat my homework!" shouted Heimdall, trying to remain on his twelve-year-old dignity.

"He keeps poking at Albiades's cage. He broke the rune seal *himself*."

Heimdall looked indignant and guilty at the same time. "I did not!"

Angelica was adamant. "If I can't turn him in today for Conjuration, I'm going to get an F, and it will be all *his fault!*"

Ceri groaned and pulled the wheel hard right, bringing the Dodge Runemaster into the nearest open parking space on the main road of Mystic, Massachusetts. There was a snort from under the hood as the wyrm that ran the gears braked hard. Any moment it would unwind itself from the mechanism and go off to socialize with others of its kind in nearby vehicles or seek out a feeding station, leaving the family vehicle stranded. Her husband had warned her it needed fresh bespelling at the dealership. Between the kids' school, lessons, team sports, play dates, shopping and everything, she had had little time to take care of anything else. She turned around in the front seat and frowned at her children.

Both children had hazel eyes, dark brown hair, freckles and matching pouts and firmly folded arms. The one unmatching piece in the back seat was the homunculus, a foot tall demon-lite with red skin, a gargoyle's face, pointed tail and cloven feet. It was on Heimdall's side of the seat.

"Make her lock it up, Mom!" he said.

"Come on, honey, put him back in his cage."

Angelica frowned and pointed at the manikin. "Tie the imp, bind him fast, hold him while the spell do last!"

The homunculus stuck out its tongue at her and danced up the inside of the car door until it was standing upside down on the ceiling.

"If you can't order around a miserable little hobgoblin, how are you supposed to play defense in Pentackle?" Heimdall fleered.

"Mom!"

Ceri sighed. She clenched her hand to gather up power and threw it toward the little creature.

"Imis incarceratus bos ipso," she said.

"No!" squeaked the homunculus as a tiny whirlwind formed in the opening of the cage. The mouth of the funnel cloud reached out like a vacuum cleaner hose. The sprite ran all over the car, scrambling over their heads and under the seats to get away from it. The spell was relentless, though. A loud *pop!* sounded behind the rear seat, and a lump traveled down the writhing gray tube. It spat the homunculus into the cage. Angelica clapped it shut and put her thumb on the wax seal of the lock. The miniature demon danced his fury.

"There," Angelica said. "Now, hurry up, Mom, or we'll be late!"

Ceri paused for a moment to glance at her son. "You know that spell. You could have helped her."

Heimdall grimaced. She knew he was trying to find a way to justify letting Angelica squirm. "I know. Sorry. But she has to learn to do it herself!"

"Yes, and until she can, it would be nice if you'd remember that karma cuts both ways." She turned back and nudged the accelerator. The wyrm started its eternal lemniscate again around the mechanism, and the car rolled.

He knew what she was talking about. In an ordinary family, arguably a minority in Mystic, karma meant that an action rebounded upon the one who did it. Rob someone, and you will lose something of value. Behave in a selfish manner, and you'd come to need help. For witching families, karma had a threefold return. Wrong someone, and three times the wrong would strike back. See wrong being done and do nothing, and you'd find yourself in a bad situation three times worse. Heimdall ought to have remembered that. Children with talent had to learn the lesson early. To their credit and their parents', most of them did. There was less bullying in Mystic than in many places that Ceri had visited, especially while playing in Pentackle tournaments as a youth and a teen player.

While soccer, baseball, swimming and countless other sports appealed to athletic children, Pentackle was her favorite. She came from a long line of famous players. She could have gone pro, but decided in favor of a career and a family instead. Ceri had cherished secret hopes that her own offspring would share in the talent of their ancestors, and was openly delighted when Heimdall started to play in the Amulet League (ages 6–7), and Angie had followed as soon as she could cast a spell.

Ceri recognized that many of the coaches thought that her children would have greater ability at Pentackle than other children without such an illustrious history. It was tough on them having to live up to her reputation. She knew that added extra pressure to a very complicated game. So far, they had done her credit. Heimdall was already a star player. Ceri had concerns about Angie and her tendency to panic on the field.

She pulled into the semicircular drive at the front of Oculus Elementary, where hosts of other children were milling around waiting for the doors to open. The kids were almost bouncing up and down in their seats in impatience.

"All right, give me a kiss!" she ordered. Angelica, homunculus cage in hand, slid over to peck her hastily on the cheek. Heimie took a look around to make sure none of his friends were watching. "I'll be at the game later on. Do you both have your grounding shoes?" They nodded. "Don't forget: keep back your best group-spell for the clinch. Keep your eyes on your teammates and your energy up. Defend each other. Remember, there's no 'I' in 'coven.' You're all working together for a harmonious win."

"Mooo-oom!" the children protested in chorus. Ceri smiled. She knew they were thinking that Mom was an unrepentant jock. They were right. She didn't mind.

"Go on! Have a good day!"

"Bye, Mom," Heimie said, finally seeing an opening to give his mother a quick kiss. He bounded out of the car, yelling, toward his friends. Angelica got out more carefully, and carried the cage up to the school doors, where her friends were waiting with their homework assignments. The brother and sister did love each other, but they would never let that show to anyone, least of all their mother.

Ceri started to pull out, then realized the kids' lunch boxes were still on the front seat beside her. She opened the window and sent the containers floating out after them. She didn't mind a little forgetfulness, as long as it didn't interfere with their studies—or Pentackle.

"Students, parents, teachers and guests!" the principal, Omar Geraldius, bellowed, his voice amplified by a triton's seashell. "Welcome to today's match! Today the Oculus Genies face off against the Sempster Dragons!"

On her bleacher seat in the brilliant sunshine of a late April day, Ceri cheered loudly. Most of the parents around her were old friends she had known since before Heimie had started school. She and her husband Jim, when he could get away from his demanding job at the state's Weather Station, joined them in tailgate parties and after-game celebrations, whether the Genies won or lost. On rainy or snowy days they collaborated on anti-weather spells that protected the whole bleachers. Nothing stopped them coming to enjoy their children's game—ever!

Before the cabal hut on each side of the field, the mascots for each team paced back and forth. Most genies that Ceri had seen in the past were sullen and resentful. The Oculus genie was a huge sports fan. He loved everything about Pentackle, and had not missed a game since 1765. He knew statistics about every famous player, both professional and amateur, since the game began. The coach often asked him for advice. His huge muscular torso floated on a trail of smoke emanating from his bottle, green and gold like the Oculus banner, and the silk of his turban matched the children's uniforms. He waved to the audience. Ceri and her friends cheered him, too. He couldn't have been a better mascot. Once a year he generously granted one wish to the Oculus Player of the Year. Heimie was doing so well that he might be up for the honor that season. Ceri was keeping her fingers crossed for him.

The Sempster dragon lunged out to the length of its chain, snorting hot steam from its nostrils. The single eye in the middle of its forehead, bright gold like an owl's, glared at the opposing team. The cheerleaders, dressed in abbreviated silver outfits simulating suits of armor with blue jupons, bounded athletically just out of reach of the dragon's jaws.

"A game in the treasure chest for Sempster! One

point, two points, three points, four! Five points victory! Score, team, score!"

In response, a trio of witches in Ceri's section started a chant in three-part harmony.

"Oculus, oculus, oculus! Third eye bright! Genie, grant our wish, to win tonight!"

One of the visiting parents, a man in a gaudy Hawaiian shirt with a dragon pattern, shouted out a jeering chant.

"Oculus, octopus, ignoramus! Third eye blind! Think you're gonna win? Well, you're out of your mind!" Other visitors picked it up, and repeated it, grinning.

Ceri didn't get upset about a little trash talk. She laughed at them.

"Third eye blind?" she snorted. "Oh, sparks! Can't you lizards think of anything more original than that?"

The man in the dragon shirt sneered at her. "Genies are losers! Genies are losers! How about that? Is that original enough for you?"

Ceri shrugged. It might have stung if the Genies lost frequently, but they didn't. The coach was so confident that he could maintain the winning average that he put in players who were marginal or actually blew scores, in the fervent belief (often justified), that they would become more confident later, and win games instead of losing them. They have to play to learn, he had pointed out. Ceri figured his attitude was grounds for some seriously good karma, if she had anything to say about it. It was certainly good news for Angie, who had a way to go before she would be the first picked for any side, even in the junior league.

The referees gathered at the sidelines on their

magic carpets, small and streamlined so they could get into the midst of the action from any angle. The seven officials would confer if any conflict arose, and their decision was final.

Practicing at home had brought out the problems each child had in the game. Heimie was a very serious player, and could be a little stiff at the start of the round. Angie had not yet shown the same amazing talent, but she had more personality, and was better liked by their teammates, if Ceri had to admit such a thing. Angie had just the one good spell—she'd get the hang of more later on—but as such, Sticky-Foot could be vital in a close game. Still, she had the younger-sister habit of taking out her shortcomings on her brother. More than once at home she had deliberately bollixed up one of Heimie's spells. Ceri reproved her, but she didn't always stop her: Heimie could expect such a play from an opponent. Better that he was prepared for anything.

School teams, like the professionals, were made up of both boys and girls. Pentackle was not entirely reliant upon upper body strength or superior speed, so it didn't put girls at a disadvantage. Team captains were also more likely to choose a witch with great magical chops over a boy who could maneuver through the opposing team's defenses.

The coaches brought their teams out onto the five-sided field to choose the lineup for the opening play. The parents began to murmur among themselves. Ceri crossed fingers on both hands, hoping that Angie and Heimie would be picked. Parents were strictly forbidden, on pain of ejection and exclusion from future games, from using magic to make sure their child was included. Each coach threw seven feathers into the air. Ceri held her breath, aware that every parent around her was doing the same thing. Each of the narrow slips of color swirled around and landed in the hand of a child, who held it up in triumph. Heimie had one—and, yes, Angie did, too!

"Yay!" Ceri shouted, then hastily fumbled for her handbag. Her husband, Jim, couldn't miss a game that both of their children were playing in! She drew out a rectangular mirror and hurried to chant the requisite spell. She frowned as her reflection grew hazy and disappeared in a swirl.

"Hurry, darn it!" she admonished it. The picture cleared at last. Around her, other parents were casting spells to record the game, using mirrors, rolls of parchment or blank books, even a camera or two (not every magical child had two witch parents). It was one of the few permitted enchantments they could use. Burke Deesey and Barbara Wencel released faceted floating crystals. The glittering globes took off and zipped along to the sidelines. Ceri envied them. They got wonderful shots of the child they were assigned to follow. Her mirror only picked up the big picture.

The first referee sailed out onto the center of the field and blew his whistle. The players who had not been chosen ran back to the cabal hut, in case they were needed as substitutes. The cheerleaders gave them a rousing hurrah! The day's teams lined up and faced each other. Ceri felt the familiar rush of energy rising in her. She longed to be out there, ready to duel for the glory of the school.

The rules, handed down since the sixth century, were simple. Each team had to get at least one player into each of the five bases set around the perimeter of the field, known as the points, Head, Right Hand, Left Hand, Right Foot and Left Foot. Players used spells to drive back their opponents and defend against the other team's magic. Strict guidelines prevented any spell from killing or directly injuring another player, but pretty much anything else went. Illusions, particularly intimidating ones, were popular, as were minor cantrips that caused a player to trip, stumble or run in the wrong direction. Group-effect spells, such as bindings, could tie up a number of players at the same time. Once a player stood on a point, he or she could no longer cast spells to help his or her side. In teams that were closely matched, the endgame consisted of two players setting spells against one another in a magical duel. At other times, a lone player might have to face all his opponents. The first team that cleared all its players off the field with all five points filled was the winner.

The captains, or Elders, traditionally the oldest player, shook hands. Ceri knew the girl who was the Oculus Elder, Mavis Shenanadoah. The ninth grader was very slim, with dark hair and bright blue eyes. She was nearly as tall as her opposite number. The Dragons' captain was a big, dark-skinned boy with a mat of tightly curled hair and black eyes. He winked at Mavis as they bowed and stepped away from one another.

A strand of gleaming blue light stretched out between the captains' hands. Mavis and the other captain snapped their hands back. The strand broke and recoiled. The largest ball of light was in Mavis's hand. The Genies would start. The referee threw three Casting Orbs to each Elder. Only players holding the orbs could throw spells. Once you cast an enchantment, you had to pass the orb off to another player. Spells only lasted as long as you were holding an orb. Each team had three in the first third of the game, two in the second, and only one in the third, which meant timing was all-important. Mavis leaped up to catch them, tossed two to her teammates, and flew off across the field toward the Head Point with Angie tearing along the ground at her heels. The Dragons dashed after them. The spectators exclaimed to one another. The gambit had caught the visiting captain off guard. He was probably expecting an offensive spell of some kind. Was Mavis going to take the Head Point first thing, and leave the younger, possibly weaker players on their own?

Ceri cast a professional eye on the Genie team. Heimie, of course, as one of the two designated Mages, was a primary defender. The other Mage, a girl named Gloria Wasson, who had transferred to Oculus only that year from the Pacific Northwest, was a good player but far too nervous about her skills. Ceri had watched her several times. She was very competitive. If she could only get outside her own head and just *play*, she'd be wonderful. The three Journeymen—and all efforts to find a non-gender specific translation of the name had failed heretofore—acted as offense. They would drive in among the opposite team and cast spells intended to disrupt its defense. The last player, Angie, was the Apprentice. Her job was to shadow the Elder and defend her back. In return, the Elder would see her safely into a point before entering one herself.

The Dragon Mages, a couple of lanky boys, one with long red hair and one with a black buzz cut, put on a burst of magically-enhanced speed to catch up with Mavis. Angie, with admirable instincts, spun on her heel as they approached. She threw out her arms and screwed up her face in concentration. Ceri held her breath and crossed both sets of fingers. Would Angie's spell work?

From the girl's fingertips, loops of yellow energy spread out underneath the Mages' feet. The redhead actually laughed. He and his partner eluded the snares with no trouble at all. Angie screeched in frustration.

"Mavis, look out!" Elmo Wasson shouted at his daughter's back. The Mages had almost reached her, but she had almost made it to the Head Point.

Ceri should have trusted Mavis. The girl flitted neatly to the side, and the Mages went hurtling past her and out of bounds. Two referees on flying carpets blew on their conch shells. Play halted briefly as the Mages returned sheepishly to the pitch and penalty points were assigned.

The dragon on the sidelines roared, and the coach called his team together for a conference.

"Look!" Mimi Sanremo leaned close to Ceri to show her the book in which her son's play was being recorded by a quill dancing over the page. "It can hear what the other coach is saying!"

"Hey, you can't do that!" the man with black hair shouted. "Hey, ref! They're eavesdropping over here!"

A referee on a carpet whisked up to hover over the two women.

"Mrs. Sanremo, turn it off."

"But Lucia is playing!"

"Then, change the spell. Now, please. The timeout is almost over. Ten seconds. Nine. . . ."

"Arrgh!" Mimi groaned. She flipped to the back of the book and scanned through the index.

The whistle blew again. Ceri looked up. The Oculus Mages, Heimie and Gloria, tossed one Casting Orb between them, daring the Dragon Journeymen to guess which one of them was going to throw the next spell. Enchantments flew between the players holding orbs. Boxing gloves pummeled Heimie, while his lightning spell made another Dragon player dance to avoid the little bolts.

A bright golden flash and a wild yell distracted her attention to the other side of the field. The Dragon Elder had blinded the Oculus Journeyman holding the third orb, and his Apprentice, a skinny boy with brown skin and sleek black hair, darted in to take it. The Apprentice spun on his heel and flared out his fingertips. Ropes of power hurtled toward the Journeyman and tied up her feet.

"Good job, Miguel," muttered the man on the bench with Ceri and her friends. "Now, pitch it back to Siggy and get out of the way." His voice seemed to echo, and he glanced around guiltily. The boy flipped the orb to the Elder and ran around behind one of the Mages for safety.

"You're coaching him!" Ceri declared. "I saw it. He just did what you told him to. You can't do that! You know what kind of bad karma you're invoking?"

"Mind your own business!" the man snarled.

"I am minding my own business," Ceri insisted. "You must not come to a lot of games. The power that builds up inside the wards on the field is like a big balloon. Anything can set it off. When it goes POP! it won't just be your kid caught in the backwash. We've had everything from confetti to a crater the size of a house. Now, please stop it."

With bad grace, the man flicked his fingers. Ceri watched as he put a little silver shell in his pocket. He crossed his arms and pointedly ignored the two women. Ceri didn't care as long as she didn't have to disenchant the kids on the way home.

She felt a little guilty when she noticed Miguel looking confused, but he had to learn to play the game without having his father hovering over him the whole time.

Speaking of hovering, that couldn't be Jacob Olmstetter again! Talk about your helicopter parents. He always started out on the bleachers with everybody else, then gradually sneaked closer and closer with his box camera until he was on the sidelines. The referees ignored him unless he got in the way. His daughter Beth, playing Journeyman position, found him absolutely embarrassing—true, everything parents did was embarrassing, but even Ceri found Jacob over the top, this time literally. He came in closer and closer, then crept out into the airspace above the playing field. He was too low. Ceri could see it. She and Mimi stood up.

"Look out!"

Everyone shouted as the big Dragon Elder came hurtling down the field, hands out to catch an orb pitched by one of his Mages. Beth Olmstetter dashed after him in pursuit, and stopped, mouth open in horror, as the Elder crashed into her father. The camera flew up. A referee on his flying carpet caught it in midair. He blew his conch shell.

"Parental interference! Substitute! Three game suspension for Olmstetter."

Beth was stricken. The Dragon Elder extricated himself from the tangle of arms and legs on the field and helped Jacob Olmstetter to his feet.

Jacob shook himself free of the big youth's grasp and glared at the official. "Three games? How dare you?"

The referee was patient. "You know the rules of karma, Mr. Olmstetter. Threefold shall be the penalty for any voluntary infringement."

"It's just a game!"

"Exactly," the Genie intoned in his deep voice, coming to float beside the referee. "As is life. I mind me when I used to chat with Confucius about life, that celestial sage had many observations upon games . . ."

"Not now, please, Genie," the lead referee said, very politely. The Genie's stories tended to go on long into the night if unchecked. "Substitute, please!" Lancelot Cabot jumped off the bench and trotted onto the field.

Ceri felt sorry for Beth Olmstetter, but her attention came right back to the game.

Heimie was blocking well. Every time he got hold of an orb he threw distracting spells that set the Dragons running around in circles. Ceri wanted to cheer at the clarity of his illusions. Twice the opposing players fell into a mud puddle he had created because they couldn't tell the difference between the real ones and the mirages.

"That's my boy!" she shouted. "Keep 'em guessing!" He was a natural.

Gloria, a few yards away, didn't look happy. Ceri knew she was desperate to make her mark on the team. She wanted to be Player of the Year, but it looked as though Heimie really might make the title this time. Gloria looked upset. She heaved an orb back toward him. He just caught it with the tips of his fingers. That fumble centered the attention of the Dragon Journeymen on him. Heimie flung a handful of energy at the three which became a saw horse. The first Journeyman, heading for the Left Hand point, tripped over it. Their center player countered with a barrage of wet gumdrops at Heimie. He withstood the rain of sticky treats, but he couldn't return fire, since the globe had to go over to Gloria. He dashed downfield, hoping to draw them with him. They weren't fooled by the ploy; instead, they concentrated on the Oculus Mage. Gloria concentrated hard on the globe in her palm.

To Ceri's admiration, the Dragons began to slow down. One of the Journeymen threw a tripwire spell, but the magical line appeared too far away to catch the feet of any of the Genies. Smokescreen cantrips blossomed over the heads of Oculus players instead of around them. The Dragons' spells seemed ineffective, not what Ceri would have expected from such a highly rated team. They all looked as confused as little Miguel had when Ceri shamed his father into stopping the long-distance coaching. Their hesitation gave the third Oculus Journeyman an unobstructed run for the Left Foot point. Safe! Good for Gloria. That was world-class Pentackle!

But Gloria was still hanging onto the orb. She hadn't cast the befuddlement enchantment. Ceri shook her head. Whose spell was it?

Out of the corner of her eye, Ceri caught a glimpse

of Gloria's mother, Anitra, muttering to herself. She couldn't be interfering with a whole *team* . . . but Ceri could just see her lips form the word 'confundus' and knew she was doing it.

Ceri was upset. What was Anitra thinking? The kids could get hurt! She couldn't want Gloria to win the Genie's wish that badly.

The referees were downfield, hovering over a battle going on between the two Elders, with the Apprentices and Mages running around. Little Miguel threw a spider-web spell at Angelica. With a globe in hand, she had no trouble turning it back toward him. Whether from inexperience or confusion he didn't jump out of the way, and ended up flat on his back. The bigger children weren't paying attention to him. He was going to get trampled.

Ceri stood up and waved both hands at the Genie. His attention was fixed on the melee. She had to do something!

"What's the matter?" Mimi asked.

Confundus spells fanned out in a cone shape from the caster. Almost without thinking, Ceri dashed toward Anitra along the bounding boards of the bleachers. She launched herself into the path of the enchantment, at the same time throwing her own counterspell to undo the charm so it would stop working.

It had been at least fifteen years since her last championship game when she had done a dive-and-dispell to help win the national league title for the Massachusetts Coveners. So close to the source, she felt the full wave of bewilderment and apprehension hit her. Her muscles, receiving no clear orders from her brain, went unexpectedly slack. Ceri got just one glimpse of Anitra's horrified face before she went tumbling head over heels off the end of the bleachers. The ground bodyslammed her, and she rolled over onto her back, groaning. The sky was a dot of blue, surrounded by a ring of red pain.

In moments, the air was full of uniformed referees and the irate coaches from both teams.

"Mrs. Shapiro, what's the matter with you?" the lead referee demanded. "Are you all right?"

"I'm a little sore," Ceri tried to say, but she couldn't exactly remember how her mouth worked. What came out was "Mwah mvba."

The league nurse shoved her way in between the hovering carpets. "Move!" she ordered. The referees retreated a foot or two, letting in some light. The nurse opened her bag and took out a gleaming lens. She ran it up and down Ceri's body. "Nothing broken, but it hurts a handful. Here." She took her wand out of the case and touched it to the middle of Ceri's forehead. Thankfully, the pain receded.

"She just jumped at that woman and threw some kind of spell on her!" the dark-haired man announced.

"That's right," Mrs. Wasson said, arms crossed indignantly over her chest.

Ceri groaned. She couldn't understand everything said, but she did comprehend that the visiting dad had just ratted on her and Anitra Wasson was pretending not to be involved. She was outraged, or thought she might be. She just wasn't sure. But when she could talk again she was going to have a lot to say to both of them.

"I think it's pretty obvious what happened," said the coach of the Dragons. "Mrs. Shapiro here confoozled my kids. You saw them out there, knocking into each other like bumper cars. Then she ensorcelled this other lady, probably to keep her from telling anyone about it."

The lead referee was a fair man. He studied Mrs. Wasson. "She looks all right. But there it is, Mrs. Shapiro. You were seen to commit an act of aggressive magic that interfered with a game in progress."

"Omf munv!" Ceri protested, struggling to stand up.

"No one saw that," Mimi said, putting an arm around her shoulders. "We saw her jump over Anitra, that's all."

"That's bad, too," the referee said. "Parents using magic on each other on the sidelines is also forbidden. Your children will be out for three games. Each."

The shock brought Ceri's faculties back to her with a rush. She understood. For the good of the team as a whole, she had to accept the punishment. The game had to be played fairly. She couldn't let the other mother make it happen.

Heimie and Angie appeared at her side.

"Mother, how could you?" Angie demanded. "I was going great! And now I will be out for the rest of the month! It's the end of my life!"

Heimie said nothing, but Ceri could read the despair on his face.

"Time out," said Mimi, holding up her hands in a T-shape. "Am I the only one who thinks this doesn't make any sense? Nobody sticks closer to the rules than Ceri does. She never does anything without a reason. You of all people . . . er, beings, ought to know that," she added, appealing to the Genie.

"Indeed I do," the turbaned spirit said, crossing his arms. "I remember you well, Miss Locke. Your playing stats were most impressive. I enjoyed watching you play. What happened?"

"Well," Ceri began. Anitra Wasson gave her a panicky look. Ceri didn't want to tattle on her. The damage was done, and undone. "Everyone saw it. I don't want to belabor it. Let's just get on with the game."

"Moooo-oom!" Heimie moaned. His perfect record would be ruined. Ceri touched his shoulder apologetically. He shifted away. Ceri felt her heart sink. One day he might understand.

The Genie shook his great, bearded head. "I do not believe it. Let us look at the record."

He reached into the air and removed from it an enormous scroll. A quill pen was busy writing on it. Annals of the great game of Pentackle had been recorded in this fashion for sixteen hundred years. Ceri treasured a copy of the illumination of her making a great save in her varsity year against the Rhode Island Wayfarers.

The Genie unfurled the upper roll of parchment and held it out for the judges to see. "Ah, very interesting." He pointed past the field of play illuminated in the center of the page to the line drawings of the parents in the bleachers. "Do you see? There is mystical energy around the head of not Miss Locke, but Mrs. Wasson. She is the one who interfered. She confounded the entire visiting team. Miss Locke undid it. Though she did bespell another parent, I do not believe she should also be punished. She prevented a default of the entire game."

The Genie's word was always final. The lead referee turned to Anitra. "Your daughter is out for three games. I know it's hard to watch your kid struggle, but you have to let her do it herself. Your job is to watch and cheer. Substitute!"

Head high, Anitra Wasson cocked a finger at her picnic basket, her crystal ball, and her daughter's gym bag. The objects lifted themselves up and floated toward the parking lot. Without looking back, she marched to the family's vehicle. Gloria gave Heimie an apologetic glance and ran to catch up with her. Ceri felt sorry for her.

A second substitute went in. Heimie slapped hands with the new Mage, Dana Ingleworth, an old friend of his.

"Thanks," Ceri said to Mimi. It was inadequate for the gratitude she felt for her friend for defending her, but Mimi made a self-deprecating face.

"I just told the truth," Mimi said. She nudged Ceri in the side. "Come on, it's starting again."

Play in the last third of the game moved so fast that even Ceri was amazed. Each team was down to only one orb each. One by one the other players made it into points, until only Heimie, Dana and Angie were left defending against five of the Dragons. The Dragon Elder wound his hands in a complicated pattern, creating a web of blue and scarlet lines of force. His Journeymen moved to surround the two Mages. Ceri could tell he was prepared to make a grand play, possibly taking out all of them at once. Dana was in position to get into the Left Foot point if there was a distraction. Heimie saw the opening, too, and grinned. Without hesitation he threw the orb right across the field between the legs of the Elder and straight into Angie's hands.

The big youth jumped. He spun, undecided now

as to where to throw his spell. He ended up facing Angie.

Angie's eyes went wide. She hesitated for a moment as the five big players turned and charged at her.

"Bind them!" Heimie yelled. "Come on, Ange! You can do it!"

Bind them? Ceri saw her mouth move. She clenched her fists and hoped. Would Angie remember?

"Imis incarceratus bos ipso!" Angie shrieked out. Blue fire welled out of the globe in the Elder's hand. He tried to shake it off, but the ribbons of light grew outward until they grasped all five of the Dragon players. With a loud POP! they all vanished. The orb dropped to the ground. Ceri screamed herself hoarse. She was so proud of Angie doing something so far beyond the simple spell she had trouble with that morning.

"Good move!" Dana cheered, and made a dash for the Left Foot point.

Looking stunned but pleased, Angie threw the orb back toward Heimie. The second the crystal left her hand, the five Dragon players exploded out of the globe, falling in a heap. The Elder recovered his wits first. Dana was hit by a barrage of cream pies that blinded her, but she stumbled into the empty haven on her hands and knees.

That left only Angie and Heimie. With the globe, Heimie caused a pit of mud to appear one step ahead of the pursuing Dragons. The Journeymen without orbs stumbled into it, giving Heimie a few more yards on them. The little Apprentice dashed around behind him, and gave him a spaghetti shampoo. Heimie had to stop to dash the noodles out of his eyes. He ringed

Miguel with an inner tube, then tossed his orb back to Angie. The Dragon Apprentice struggled, but did not get out of the way of the point. It was against the rules for Heimie to push or lift him physically. He ran for an opening around the field. He could dive in if he could get past the defenders, but that would leave Angie alone on the field. She could use only one spell, then she would have to abandon the orb. The Dragons could win. Ceri refused to allow herself to think it could happen.

The Elder signed to his people to spread out, blocking Heimie from getting into the points. Angie stood with the orb in her palm. Ceri knew how she would solve the conundrum herself. But would a junior-league Pentackle witch figure it out? Her two children would have to work together, something they were not good at yet.

Angie stood in the middle of the field. Ceri could tell her dander was up by the mulish look on her face. She tossed the orb up and down in her hand. Halfway between the Left Foot and Right Foot, Heimie signaled for it. The other players already in the points shouted encouragement. Angie shook her head at Heimie.

"Come on!" he yelled. "Don't be a pig."

"I'm not a pig!" she yelled back.

Ceri almost stood up and told them not to bicker. Not in the middle of a game!

But it was a ruse. As soon as Heimie had dashed past the Right Foot point, Angie pivoted on one foot and tossed the little globe directly at him without casting a spell of her own.

The Dragons, taken by surprise, rushed away from

the points they were guarding to intercept Heimie. One of the Journeymen had the single enemy orb. Heimie was ready for them. With a wave of his hand he filled the air with purple smoke. The Elder retreated, gagging. Ceri caught a whiff of the smoke before it dissipated, and choked, her eyes watering. Skunk!

Angie was far enough away from the action to see Heimie's actions but not get caught in the stink. The orb came hurtling out of the air and smacked into her palms. She didn't even look down at it. Before the Dragons could draw a breath, she threw her best spell, the Sticky-Foot.

This time it worked. The Dragons hadn't enough time to turn around before they tripped on their own feet. Heimie jumped over the body of the nearest Journeyman and hurtled into the Right Hand point.

Angie was alone on the field. Ceri leaped to her feet, screaming encouragement. The Journeyman crawled toward her. She ran like a rabbit toward the nearest point, the Head. The Journeyman hit her solidly in the back with a dodgeball. Angie fell down. Ceri gasped. Angie rose to knees, then feet, and stolidly made a dash for the Left Hand point. The players inside it reached out to her. She made it just as the stream from a magical fire hose appeared at the entrance. It washed the grass sideways. Angie jumped up and down, cheering. The referee blew his conch shell. The game was over. Oculus won!

The Genie floated over to hover beside Ceri. "Some very fine playing by your children," he said pleasantly.

Ceri smiled at him proudly. "Yes, indeed," she said. "And maybe two most valuable players in one season?"

The Genie chuckled, well, genially. "We shall see," he said. "They play excellently well as a team. It must be the Locke genes."

"Maybe," Ceri said, with a rueful grin. She rubbed her ribs, though they were no longer sore. "I prefer to think that it's karma. They've seen what happens if they don't pay attention to it."

The Best of
JIM BAEN'S
UNIVERSE

Edited by Eric Flint

Top-selling writers and brilliant newcomers appear regularly in the online magazine *Jim Baen's Universe*, edited by Eric Flint. Now, Flint and his staff select a generous serving of the best science fiction and fantasy stories that have appeared so far in the magazine. Contributors include: Mike Resnick, David Drake, Gene Wolfe, Gregory Benford, Esther Friesner and many more.

FREE CD-ROM INCLUDED
IN THE FIRST HARDCOVER PRINTING
CONTAINING THE ENTIRE CONTENTS
OF THE MAGAZINE'S FIRST YEAR,
ILLUSTRATIONS FROM THE MAGAZINE,
OVER 20 NOVELS BY ERIC FLINT
AND MUCH MORE!

1-4165-2136-4 ★ $25.00